This Man

This Man

JODI ELLEN MALPAS

First published in Great Britain in 2012
by Jodi Ellen Malpas
This edition first published in 2013
by Orion Books
an imprint of The Orion Publishing Group Ltd
Orion House, 5 Upper Saint Martin's Lane
London WC2H 9EA
An Hachette UK Company

15 17 19 20 18 16 14

A CIP catalogue record for this book is
available from the British Library.

ISBN (Mass Market Paperback) 978 1 4091 5148 7
ISBN (Ebook) 978 1 4091 5149 4

Typeset by Input Data Services Ltd, Bridgwater, Somerset

Printed in Great Britain by Clays Ltd, St Ives plc

The Orion Publishing Group's policy is to use papers that
are natural, renewable and recyclable products and made
from wood grown in sustainable forests. The logging and
manufacturing processes are expected to conform to the
environmental regulations of the country of origin.

www.orionbooks.co.uk

For Big Pat and Bubbles

Acknowledgements

When I first self-published *This Man*, I had just a few people to thank, namely my family and the few friends who I eventually told about what I'd been up to. My appreciation is still huge and always will be, but my list of people to thank has extended considerably since October 2012.

The first person on that list is my attorney, Matthew Savare. Matt, I'd have been lost in New York without you, quite literally. You were the first one on board and have enjoyed this crazy ride with me. You also kept me sane when I thought I might lose my mind! I'll never be able to thank you enough, but I'll always try.

My agents, Andrea Barzvi and Kristyn Keene of ICM Partners, who just get me, knickers and all! When I arrived at your office for the first time, you hugged me and that was just what I needed amid the madness. The hugs followed by the passion with which you spoke about me and *This Man* sealed the deal for me. I've never looked back.

Beth de Guzman of Grand Central Publishing – you took a chance on an unknown author and her debut novel. My gratitude is immeasurable.

And Selina, my editor. I'll always say 'Bloody hell!' and I'll smile every time I hear you say it too.

I had a story to tell, and I'm so glad I told it. This little British girl is on Central Jesse Cloud Nine.

Join me.

This Man

Chapter One

I riffle through the piles and piles of paraphernalia sprawled all over my bedroom floor. I'm going to be late. 'Kate!' I yell frantically. Where the hell are they? I run out onto the landing and throw myself over the banister. 'Kate!'

I hear the familiar sound of a wooden spoon bashing the edges of a ceramic bowl as Kate appears at the bottom of the stairs, her red hair piled high in a mass of curls. She looks up at me with a tired expression. It's an expression that I've become used to recently.

'Keys! Have you seen my car keys?' I puff at her.

'They're on the table under the mirror where you left them last night.' She rolls her eyes, taking herself and her cake mixture back to her workshop.

I dart across the landing in a complete fluster and find my car keys under a pile of weekly glossies. 'Hiding again,' I mutter to myself, grabbing my belt, heels and laptop. I make my way downstairs from the flat above Kate's workshop, finding her spooning cake mixture into various tins.

'You need to tidy your room, Ava. It's a fucking mess,' she complains.

Yes, my personal organisation skills are pretty shocking, especially since I'm an interior designer for Rococo Union and spend all day coordinating and organising. I scoop my phone up from the chunky table and dunk my finger in Kate's cake mixture. 'I can't be brilliant at everything.'

'Get out!' She bats my hand away with her spoon. 'Why do

you need your car, anyway?' she asks, leaning down to smooth the mixture over, her tongue resting on her bottom lip in concentration.

'I have a first consultation in the Surrey Hills – some country mansion.' I feed my belt through the belt loops of my navy pencil dress, slip my feet into my heels, and present myself to the wall mirror.

'I thought you stuck to the city,' she says from behind me.

I ruffle my long, dark hair for a few seconds, flicking it from one side to the other but give up, piling it up with a few grips instead. My dark brown eyes look tired and lack their usual sparkle – a result, no doubt, of burning the candle at both ends. I only moved in with Kate a month ago after splitting with Matt. We're behaving like a couple of university students. My liver is screaming for a rest.

'I do. The country sector is Patrick's domain. I don't know how I got stuck with this.' I sweep the wand of my gloss across my lips, smack them together, and give Kate a kiss on the cheek. 'It's going to be painful, I know it. Luv ya!'

'Ditto. See you later,' Kate laughs, without lifting her face from her workstation.

Despite my lateness, I drive my little Mini with my usual care to my office on Bruton Street, and I'm reminded why I Tube it every day when I spend ten minutes driving around looking for a parking space.

I burst into the office and glance at the clock. Eight-forty. Okay, I'm ten minutes late, not as bad as I thought. I pass Tom's and Victoria's empty desks on the way to my own, spying Patrick in his office as I land in my chair. Unpacking my laptop, I notice a package has been left for me.

'Morning, flower.' Patrick's low boom greets me as he perches on the edge of my desk, followed by the customary creak under his weight. 'What have you got there?'

'Morning. It's the new fabric range from Miller's. You like?' I stroke some of the luxurious material.

'Wonderful,' he feigns interest. 'Don't let Irene clap her eyes on it. I've just liquidated most of my assets to fund the new soft furnishings at home.'

'Oh.' I give him a sympathetic face. 'Where is everyone?'

'Victoria has the day off and Tom's having a nightmare with Mr and Mrs Baines. It's just you, me, and Sal today, flower.' He takes his comb out of his inside pocket and runs it through his silver mop.

'I've got a midday appointment at The Manor,' I remind him. He can't have forgotten. 'Are you sure I'm the person you want on this, Patrick?'

I've worked for Rococo Union for four years, and it was made clear that I was employed to expand the business into the modern sector. With luxury apartments flying up all over London, Patrick and Tom, with their specialty of traditional design, were missing out. When it took off and the workload got too much for me, he employed Victoria.

'They asked for you, flower.' He pushes himself to his feet and my desk creaks in protest again. Patrick ignores it, but I wince. He has to lose some weight or stop sitting on my desk. It won't take the strain for much longer.

So, they asked for me? Why? My portfolio holds nothing that will reflect traditional design – nothing at all. I can't help but think that this is a complete waste of my time. Patrick or Tom should be going.

'Oh, Lusso launch.' Patrick tucks his comb away. 'The developer is really pushing the boat out with this party in the penthouse. You've done an amazing job, Ava.' Patrick's eyebrows nod with his head.

I blush. 'Thank you.' I'm dead proud of myself and my work at Lusso, my greatest achievement in my short career. Based on St Katharine Docks and with prices ranging from three million for a basic apartment to ten million for the penthouse, we're in the *super rich* realm. The design specification is as the name suggests: Italian luxury. I sourced all materials, furniture and art from Italy, and enjoyed a week there organising the shipping schedule. Next Friday is the launch party, but I know they've already sold the penthouse and six other apartments, so it's more of a showing off party.

'I've cleared my diary so I can do the final checks once the cleaners are out.' I flick the pages of my diary to next Friday and scribble across the page again.

'Good girl. I've told Victoria to be there at five. It's her first launch so you need to give her a heads up. I'll be there at seven with Tom.'

'Sure.'

Patrick returns to his office and I open my e-mail, sifting through to delete or respond where necessary.

At eleven o'clock I pack up my laptop and poke my head around Patrick's office door. He's engrossed with something on his computer.

'I'm off now,' I say, but he just waves his hand in the air in acknowledgment. I walk through the office and see Sally fighting with the photocopier. 'See you later, Sal.'

''Bye, Ava,' she replies, but she's too busy removing the paper jam to acknowledge me with her face. The girl's a calamity.

I walk out into the sunshine and head for my car. Friday mid-morning traffic is a nightmare, but once I'm out of the city, the drive onward is pretty straightforward. The roof is down, and Adele is keeping me company. A little drive in the countryside is a lovely way to finish my work week.

I pull off the main road and onto a little lane, where I find myself in front of the biggest pair of gates that I've ever seen. A gold plaque on a pillar states The Manor.

Bloody hell! I take my sunglasses off, looking past the gates and down the tree-lined gravel road that seems to go for miles, images of a stuffy, cigar-smoking Lord of The Manor springing to mind immediately. I get out of my car and walk up to the gates, looking for an intercom.

'It's behind you.' I nearly jump out of my skin when the low rumble of a voice comes from nowhere, stabbing at the silent country air.

I look around. 'Hello?'

'Over here.'

I turn and see the intercom farther down the lane. I drove straight past it. I run over, pressing the button to announce myself. 'Ava O'Shea, Rococo Union.'

'I know.'

I look around and spot a camera installed on the gate. 'Well are you going to let me in?' I ask, just as the shift of metal breaks the countryside peace around me. The gates start opening. 'Give me a chance,' I mutter as I run back to my car. I jump in my Mini and creep forward as the gates swing open, all the time wondering how I'll remove the glass of port and cigar that are, quite clearly, wedged up that miserable sod's arse. I'm looking less forward to this appointment by the minute. Posh country folk and their posh country mansions are not in my area of expertise.

Once the gates are fully opened, I drive through, and after a mile or so I pull into a perfectly round courtyard. I take my sunglasses off and gape at the huge, looming house. It's superb.

The black doors – adorned with highly polished gold trim – are flanked by four giant bay windows, with pillars of carved stone guarding them. Giant limestone blocks make up the structure of the mansion, with lush bay trees lining the face, and topping off the site is a fountain in the centre of the courtyard, spraying out jets of illuminated water. It's all very imposing.

I cut the engine and fumble with the door release to get out of my car. Standing and holding on to the top of my car door, I look up at the magnificent building and immediately think that this has to be a mistake. The place is in amazing condition.

The lawns are greener than green, the house looks like it receives daily scrub downs, and even the gravel looks like it receives a daily hoover. If the exterior is anything to go by, then I can't imagine the inside needing any work. I look up at the dozens of sash bay windows, seeing plush curtains hanging at them all. I'm tempted to call Patrick to check that I've got the right address, but it did say The Manor on the gates, and that miserable sod on the other end of the intercom is obviously expecting me.

While I'm pondering my next move, the doors open, revealing the biggest man I've ever seen. He saunters out to the top of the steps, and I physically flinch at the sight of him, stepping back slightly. He has on a black suit– specially made for sure because that's no regular size – a black shirt and a black tie. His skin is the colour of rich ebony, his shaved head looks like it's been buffed to a shine, and wraparound sunglasses conceal his eyes. If I could build a mental image of who I would have expected to walk out of those doors, he, most definitely, would not be it. The man is a mountain, and everything about his presence screams bodyguard. I'm suddenly slightly concerned that I've turned up at some mafia control centre, and I search my brain trying to remember if I transferred my panic alarm to my new handbag.

'Miss O'Shea?' he drawls.

I wilt under his massive presence, putting my hand up in a nervous wave gesture. 'Hi,' I whisper.

'This way,' he rumbles deeply, giving a sharp nod of his head and turning to walk back into the mansion.

I consider cutting and running, but the daring and dangerous side of me is curious about what lies beyond those doors. Grabbing my bag, I shut my car door and climb the steps, crossing the threshold into a huge entrance hall. I gaze around the vast area, and I'm immediately impressed by the grand curved staircase that leads up to the first floor.

The décor is opulent, lush, and *very* intimidating. Deep blues, taupes with hints of gold, and original woodwork, along with the rich mahogany parquet floor, make the place striking and massively extravagant. It's exactly how I would have expected it to be and nowhere near my design style. But then again, looking around, why any interior designer would be here is becoming more and more confusing. Patrick said they requested me personally, so I would be inclined to think that they want to modernise, but that would've been before I got a glimpse of the place. The décor suits the period building. It's in perfect condition. Why the hell am I here?

Big Guy heads off to the right, leaving me to scuttle after him, my tan heels clicking on the parquet floor as he leads me toward the back of the mansion.

I hear the hum of conversation and glance to my right, noticing many people seated at various tables; eating, drinking, and chatting. Waiters are serving food and drinks, and the distinct voices of The Rat Pack are purring in the background. I frown, but then I understand. It's a hotel – a posh country hotel.

This is all beginning to make sense to me. I want to say something to the mountain of a man leading me God only knows where, but he hasn't looked back once to check that I'm following. Although the click of my heels must tell him I am. He doesn't say much, and I suspect he wouldn't answer me if I did speak.

We continue past two more closed doors before he leads me into a summer room – a massive, light, stunningly lavish space that's sectioned off into individual seating areas with sofas, big arm chairs and tables. Floor-to-ceiling bi-fold doors span the room, leading to a Yorkstone patio and a vast lawn area. It's really quite awe-inspiring, and I inwardly gasp when I spot a glass building housing a swimming pool. It's incredible, and I shudder to think how much the nightly rate is. It has to be five stars – probably more.

Once we've passed through the summer room, I'm led down a corridor until Big Guy stops outside a wood-paneled door. 'Mr. Ward's office,' he rumbles, knocking on the door, surprisingly gently given his mammoth size.

'The manager?' I ask.

'The owner,' he replies, opening the door and striding through. 'Come in.'

I hesitate on the threshold, watching as the big guy strides into the room ahead of me. I eventually force my feet into action, moving into the room, while gazing around at the equally luxurious surroundings of Mr Ward's office.

Chapter Two

'Jesse, Miss O'Shea, Rococo Union,' Big Guy announces.

'Perfect. Thanks, John.'

I'm dragged from my awed state straight into high alert, and my back straightens.

I can't see him; he's obscured by the big guy's massive frame, but that raspy, smooth voice has me frozen on the spot, and it certainly doesn't sound like it's coming from a cigar-smoking, overweight, wax jacket-wearing Lord of the Manor.

Big Guy, or John as I now know him, moves to the side, giving me my first glimpse of Mr Jesse Ward.

Oh good God. My heart crashes against my breastbone and my nervous breathing rockets to dangerous levels. I suddenly feel light-headed, and my mouth is ignoring my brain's instruction to say *something*. I just stand there staring at this man, while he stares back at me. His husky voice halted me in my tracks, but the sight of him ... the sight of him has just turned me into a non-responsive, quivering wreck.

He rises from his chair and my gaze travels up with him. He's very tall. His white shirt is casually rolled at the sleeves, but he still wears a black tie, loosely knotted and hanging down the front of a broad chest.

He makes his way around his massive desk and slowly walks toward me. It's then that I take in the full impact of him. I gulp. This man is so perfect I'm almost in pain. His dirty blond hair looks like he's half attempted to get it into some semblance of a style but given up. His eyes are sludgy green, but bright and way too intense, and the stubble covering his square jaw does nothing to conceal the handsome features beneath it. He's lightly tanned and just ... Oh God, he's devastating. Lord of the Manor?

'Miss O'Shea.' His hand comes toward me, but I can't persuade my arm to raise and clasp his outstretched offering. He's beautiful.

When I don't offer my hand, he reaches forward and clasps both of my shoulders, then slowly leans in to kiss me, his lips brushing lightly over my burning cheek. I tense all over. I can hear my pulse throbbing in my ears, and even though it's completely inappropriate for a business meeting, I do nothing to stop him. I'm all over the place.

'It's a pleasure,' he whispers in my ear, which only serves to make me moan slightly. He must feel my tension – it's not difficult; I'm rigid – because his grip eases up and he lowers his face to my level, looking me directly in the eyes. 'Are you okay?' he asks, one side of his mouth lifting into a semblance of a smile. I notice a single frown line across his forehead.

I snap myself out of my ridiculous inertia, suddenly aware that I've still not said anything. Has he noticed my reaction to him? What about Big Guy? I glance over, seeing the big guy standing motionless, glasses still in place, but I know his eyes are on me. I mentally shake myself and step back, away from Ward and his potent grasp. His hands fall to his sides.

'Hi.' I cough to clear my throat. 'Ava. My name is Ava.' I offer him my hand, but he's unhurried in accepting it, like he's unsure whether it's safe to, but he does ... eventually.

His hand is clammy and slightly shaky as he squeezes mine firmly, and sparks fizz, a curious look flitting across his stunning face as we both retract our hands in shock.

'Ava.' He's trying my name on his lips, and it takes all of my strength not to moan again. He should stop talking – immediately.

'Yes. Ava,' I confirm. He's the one who seems to be off in his own little nirvana now, while I'm becoming increasingly aware of my rising temperature.

He suddenly seems to come to his senses, shoving his hands in his trouser pockets as he shakes his head slightly, retreating a few steps. 'Thanks, John,' he nods to the big guy, who smiles slightly, softening his hard features, then leaves.

I'm alone with this man, who has rendered me speechless, motionless, and pretty much useless.

He nods toward two brown leather couches, positioned opposite each other in front of the bay window, with a large coffee table sitting between them. 'Please, take a seat. Can I get you a drink?' He drags his gaze from mine, walking toward a cabinet with various bottles of liquor lined up on top. He surely doesn't mean alcohol? It's midday. Even by my standards it's too early. I watch as he hovers at the cabinet for a few moments before turning to face me again, looking at me expectantly.

'No, thank you.' I shake my head as I speak, just in case the words don't come out.

'Water?' he asks, that smile playing at the corners of his mouth.

Oh God, don't look at me. 'Please.' I smile a nervous smile. My mouth is parched.

He collects two bottles of water from the integrated fridge and turns back toward me, and it's then that I persuade my shaky legs to carry me across the room to the sofa.

'Ava?' His voice rolls across me, causing me to falter en route. I turn to face him. It's probably a bad idea. 'Yes?'

He holds up a highball. 'Glass?'

'Yes, please.' I smile. He must think I'm so unprofessional. I settle myself on the leather couch, retrieve my folder and phone from my bag and place them on the table in front of me. I notice my hands are shaking.

Christ, woman. Get a grip! I feign making notes as he strolls back over, placing my water and a glass on the table before he sits on the sofa opposite me and crosses one leg over the other, his ankle resting on his thigh. He stretches back. He's really making himself comfortable, and the silence that falls between us is screaming as I write anything and everything to avoid looking up at him. I know I've got to look at the man and say something at some point, but all standard enquiry questions have run, screaming and shouting, from my brain.

'So, where do we start?' he asks, forcing me look up and acknowledge his question. He smiles. I swoon.

He's watching me over the rim of his bottle as he raises it to those lovely lips. I break the eye contact, reaching forward to pour some water into my glass. I'm struggling to rein in my nerves, and I can still feel his eyes on me. This is truly awkward. I've never been so affected by a man.

'I guess you should tell me why I'm here.' *I speak!* I look back up at him as I take my glass from the table.

'Oh?' he says quietly. There's that frown line again. Even with that, he's still beautiful.

'You requested me by name?' I press.

'Yes.' he replies simply. He smiles again. I have to look away.

I take a sip of my water to moisten my dry mouth, and clear my throat before returning my gaze to his potent stare. 'So, may I ask why?'

'You may.' He uncrosses his leg, leaning forward to place his bottle on the table, resting his forearms on his knees, but he says no more. Is he not going to elabourate on that?

'Okay.' I struggle to maintain eye contact. 'Why?'

'I've heard great things about you.'

I feel my face burning up. 'Thank you. So why am I here?'

'Well, to design.' He laughs, and I feel stupid but slightly irritated as well. Is he making fun of me?

'Design what, exactly?' I ask. 'From what I've seen, everything is pretty perfect.' He surely doesn't want to modernise this lovely place. Country estates may not be my forte, but I know class when I see it.

'Thank you,' he says softly. 'Do you have your portfolio with you?'

'Of course,' I reply, reaching into my bag. Why he wants to look at it is beyond me. It won't reflect anything like this place.

I place it on the table in front of him and expect him to drag it over to his side, but to my horror, he stands in one fluid movement and walks around toward me, lowering his lovely lean body onto the sofa next to me. Oh, Jesus. He smells divine – all fresh water and minty. I hold my breath.

Leaning forward, he opens the folder. 'You're very young to be such an accomplished designer,' he muses, slowly turning the pages of my portfolio.

He's right, I am, but it's only thanks to Patrick for giving me free rein on the expansion of his business. In four years, I've left college, picked up a job in an established design company – that had financial stability but lacked new freshness in modern ideas – and made a name for myself on the back of it. I've been lucky, and I appreciate Patrick's faith in my capabilities. That, coupled with my contract at Lusso, is the only reason I'm where I am at the age of twenty-six.

I look down at his lovely hand, his wrist adorned with a beautiful gold and graphite Rolex. 'How old are you?' I blurt. Oh, good God. My brain is like scrambled egg, and I know I've just blushed a sharp shade of red. I should just keep my mouth shut. Where the hell did that come from?

He looks at me intently, his green eyes burning into mine. 'Twenty-one,' he answers, completely poker-faced.

I scoff mildly, and his eyebrows jump up questioningly. 'Sorry,' I mutter, turning back to the table. I'm feeling flustered. I hear him exhale heavily as his lovely right hand reaches back down to my portfolio to start turning the pages again, his left hand resting on the edge of the table.

I notice no ring. He's not married? How can that be?

'This, I like a lot.' He points to the photographs of Lusso.

'I'm not sure my work on Lusso would fit in here,' I say quietly. It's way too modern – luxurious, yes, but too modern.

He looks up at me. 'You're right; I'm just saying … I really like it.'

'Thank you.' I feel my colour deepen as he studies me thoughtfully before returning to my portfolio.

I make a grab for my water, resisting the temptation to chuck it down my front to cool me off, but very nearly do when his trouser-clad thigh brushes against my bare knee. I shift quickly to break the contact, glancing out of the corner of my eye to see a small smirk breaking at the edge of his mouth. He's doing this on purpose. It's too much.

'Do you have a toilet?' I ask as I place my glass back on the table and stand. I need to go and compose myself. I'm a ruffled mess.

He rises from the couch swiftly, moving back to let me pass. 'Through the summer room and on your left,' he says with a smile. He knows he's affecting me. The way he's smiling at me, knowingly – I bet he has this sort of reaction from women all the time.

'Thank you.' I edge out of the small gap between the table and the sofa, my task hampered as he makes no attempt to give me more space. I have to virtually brush past him, and that has me holding my breath until I'm clear of his body.

I walk toward the door, feeling his eyes on me, burning a hole through my dress, so I roll my neck to try and rid myself of the goose bumps jumping onto my nape.

Stumbling out of his office, I head down the corridor before wandering through the summer room and staggering into the ridiculously posh lavatories. I brace myself over the sink and look in the mirror. 'Jesus, Ava. Pull it together!' I scorn my reflection.

'Met the Lord, have we?'

I swing around and find a very attractive business lady, faffing with her hair at the other end of the room. I have no idea what to say, but she's just confirmed what I already suspected – he does have this effect on all women. When my brain fails to deliver on anything suitable to say, I just smile.

She returns my smile, amused and knowing the reason for my flustered state, before disappearing from the toilets. If I wasn't feeling so hot and nervous, I might be embarrassed at my obvious condition. But I am hot, and I'm very nervous, so I brush off my humiliation, take some steady breaths and wash my clammy hands with the Noble Isle hand wash. I should have brought my bag. I could do with some Vaseline on my lips. My mouth is still dry and my lips are suffering as a consequence.

Okay, I need to get back out there, get the details on the job, and be gone. My heart is pleading for some relief. I'm completely ashamed of myself. I re-pin my hair and exit the toilets, making my way back to Mr Ward's office. I don't know if I'm going to be able to work for this man; I'm just way too affected by him.

I knock before I enter, finding him sitting on the couch looking over my portfolio. He looks up and smiles, and I know now, I really have to leave. I can't possibly work with this man. Every molecule of intelligence and brain power I possess has been zapped from my body by his presence. And worst of all, he knows it.

I give myself a mental pep talk, making my way over to the table, ignoring the fact that he's following my every move. He leans back on the sofa in a gesture for me to squeeze past but I don't. I take a seat on the opposite sofa, perching on the edge.

He flicks me a questioning look. 'Are you okay?'

'Yes, I'm fine,' I answer shortly. He knows. 'Would you like to show me where your intended project is so we can start discussing your requirements?' I force the confidence into my voice.

I'm just following protocol now. I've absolutely no intention of taking this contract on, but I can't just walk out – as tempting as that is.

He raises his eyebrows, clearly surprised by my change of approach. 'Sure.' He gets up from the sofa and strides over to his desk to collect his mobile while I gather my things, stuff them into my bag, and then follow his gesture to lead the way.

He quickly overtakes me, opening the door and performing an exaggerated gentlemanly bow as he holds it open. I smile politely – even though I know he's playing with me – and exit into the corridor, heading toward the summer room. I stiffen on a gasp when he places a hand at the small of my back to guide me.

What's he playing at? I'm trying my hardest to ignore it, but you would have to be dead not to notice the effect this man's having on me. And I know he knows it. My skin's burning all over – almost certainly warming his palm through my dress – I can't get my breathing under control, and walking is taking every bit of coordination and effort I possess. I'm pathetic, and it's bloody obvious he's enjoying the reactions he's drawing from me. I must be quite amusing.

Annoyed with myself, I pick up my pace to break the contact, stopping when I reach the point of two possible routes.

He reaches me, pointing out across the lawns to the tennis courts. 'Do you play?'

I actually laugh, but it's a comfortable laugh. 'No, I don't.' I can run, but that's about it. Give me a bat, racket, or ball, then you're asking for trouble. The corners of his mouth twitch into a grin at my reaction, bolstering the green of his eyes and lengthening his generous lashes. I smile, shaking my head in wonder at this glorious man. 'You?' I ask.

He continues through to the entrance hall, me following. 'I don't mind the odd game, but I'm more of an extreme sports kinda guy.' He stops, and I halt with him.

He looks ridiculously fit and toned. 'What sort of extreme sports?'

'Snowboarding, mainly, but I've tried my hand at white-water rafting, bungee-jumping, and skydiving. I'm a bit of an adrenaline junky. I like to feel the blood pumping.' He watches me as he speaks, making me feel scrutinized. You would have to anaesthetise me before you got me doing any of his blood-pumping pastimes. I'll stick to a run every so often.

'Extreme,' I say, studying this magnificent man of an age I don't know.

'Very extreme,' he confirms quietly. My breath catches again, and I close my eyes, mentally yelling at myself for being such a loser. 'Shall we continue?' he asks. I can hear humor in his voice.

I open my eyes to be met by his penetrating green stare. 'Yes, please.' I wish he would stop looking at me like that. He half smiles again and walks into the bar, greeting two men by clapping them on the shoulders. The men are very attractive, young – probably late twenties – and drinking bottles of beer.

'Guys, this is Ava. Ava, this is Sam Kelt and Drew Davies.'

'Good afternoon,' Drew drawls. He's handsome in a rugged kind of way, his black hair perfectly styled, his suit pristine and his eyes shrewd. He's likely a smart, confident business type.

'Hi.' I smile politely.

'Welcome to the pleasure dome,' Sam laughs, raising his bottle. 'Can I buy you a drink?'

I notice Ward shake his head lightly on an eye roll, and Sam grins. He's the polar opposite of Drew – all casual and laid back, in old jeans, a Superdry t-shirt, and Converse. He has a cheeky face, complimented by one dimple on his left cheek. His blue eyes twinkle, adding to his boyishness, and his mousey brown, shoulder-length hair is all over the place.

'No, I'm fine, thanks,' I answer.

He nods at Ward. 'Jesse?'

'No, I'm good. I'm just giving Ava a tour of the extension.

She'll be working on the interiors,' he says, smiling at me.

I quietly scoff to myself. Not if I have anything to do with it. And anyway, he's jumping the gun a bit, isn't he? We've not discussed rates, briefs, or anything, for that matter.

'About time. There are never any rooms available,' Drew grumbles into his bottle.

'How was the boarding in Cortina, my man?' Sam asks.

Ward perches on another stool. 'Amazing. The Italian way of skiing follows pretty closely to their laid back lifestyle.' He smiles broadly, the first proper full-beam smile since I've laid eyes on him – all straight, white, and lush. This man is a God. 'I got up late, found a great mountain, ran the slopes until my legs buckled, had a siesta, ate late and started all over again the next day.' He's addressing us all but staring at me.

I can't help but return his beam. 'You're good?' I ask, because it's the only thing that comes to mind. I imagine he's good at everything.

'Very,' he confirms quietly. I nod my approval and, for a few seconds, our eyes are locked, but I'm the first to break it. 'Shall we?' he asks, pushing himself up from the stool and gesturing toward the exit.

'Yes.' I smile. I'm supposedly here to work, after all. All I've achieved so far is a hot flush and an establishment of extreme sports. I feel like I'm in a trance.

I turn to the two guys at the bar, smiling my good-bye, prompting them to raise their bottles before they continue with their conversation. Walking toward the door that leads back to the entrance hall, I feel him close behind me. He's too close; I can smell him. I close my eyes, sending a small prayer to God to get me through this quickly, with at least *a bit* of dignity intact. Jesse Ward is way too intense and it's throwing my senses in a million different directions.

'So, now for the main feature.' He begins to climb the wide staircase and I follow him up to a huge gallery landing. 'These are the private rooms,' he says, pointing to various doors off the landing.

I follow, admiring his lovely backside, thinking he possibly has the sexiest walk I've ever had the privilege of seeing. When I drag my eyes from his tidy rear, I see that there are at least twenty doors, evenly spaced and leading into rooms beyond. He leads me until we reach another grand staircase that stretches to another floor, and at the foot of the stairs there's a beautiful stained-glass window and an archway leading to another wing.

'This is the extension.' He guides me through to a new section of the mansion. 'This is where I need your help,' he adds, halting at the mouth of a corridor that leads to another ten rooms.

'This is all new?' I ask.

'Yes, they're all shells at the moment, but I'm sure you'll remedy that. Let me show you.'

I'm way past shocked when he takes my hand, tugging me down the corridor to the very last door. *Inappropriate!* His hand is still clammy, and I'm sure mine is trembling in his grip. The arched brow on a slight grin he flashes me tells me I'm right. There's some sort of super-charged current flowing through us – it's making me shudder.

He opens the door and directs me into a freshly plastered room. It's vast, and the new windows are a perfect match to those of the original property. Whoever built this did an excellent job.

'Are they all this big?' I ask, flexing my fingers until he releases my hand. Does he behave like this with all women?

'Yes.'

I walk into the centre of the room, looking around. It's a good size. I notice another door. 'En-suite?' I ask as I wander over and enter.

'Yes.'

The rooms are huge, especially by hotel standards. A lot

could be done with them. I would be excited if I wasn't so concerned with what's expected of me. This is no Lusso. I exit the bathroom, finding Ward leaning against the wall, his hands in his trouser pockets, his eyes all hooded and dark as he watches me. My God, the man is sex on legs. I'm almost disappointed that traditional doesn't feature in my design history. It's of no interest to me at all.

'I'm not sure that I'm the right person for this job.' I sound regretful, which is okay because I am. I'm regretful that I can't pull myself together.

He looks at me, those sludgy eyes stabbing at my defences, making me shift on my heels. 'I think you have what I want,' he says quietly.

'I've always dealt in modern luxury,' I look around the room again, slowly dropping my eyes back to him. 'I'm sure you would be happier working with Patrick or Tom. They deal with our period projects.'

He considers me for a second, does that head shake thing and pushes himself away from the wall by his shoulder blades. 'But I want you.'

'Why?'

'You look like you'll be very good.'

An involuntary rush of breath escapes my lips at his words. I'm not sure what to make of that statement. Does he mean for my design skills or something else, because the way he's looking at me tells me it's the latter. He's a bit bloody confident.

'What's your brief?' I ask, because all other words fail me. My colour is rising again.

A smile tickles the corners of his mouth. 'Sensual, intimate, luxurious, stimulating, invigorating …' He pauses to gauge my reaction.

I frown. It's not the usual brief. Relaxing, functional or practical were not mentioned at all. 'Okay, anything in particular

I should allow for?' I ask. Why am I bothering with these questions?

'A big bed and lots of wall hangings,' he states on a husk.

'What kind of wall hangings?'

'Big wooden ones. Oh, and the lighting needs to suit.'

'Suit what?' I can't help the confusion in my tone.

He smiles, and I dissolve on the spot into a hot pool of hormones. 'Well, the brief, of course.'

Oh God, he must think I'm something else. 'Yes, of course.' I look up, seeing chunky beams spanning the ceiling. The building is new, but they are not faux beams. 'Do all of the rooms have those?' I return my eyes to his.

'Yes, they're essential.' His voice is low and seductive. I'm not sure how much more I can take.

I grab my client briefing pad to start making notes. 'Are there any particular colours I should work to or against?'

'No, knock yourself out.'

I flick my head up to look at him. 'Excuse me?'

He smiles. 'Go for it.'

Oh, well, I won't be knocking myself out on anything because he won't be seeing me here again, but I should get as much information as possible so I can pass it to Patrick or Tom, with at least a bit of willingness.

'You mentioned a big bed. Any particular type?' I ask, trying to remain professional.

'No, just very big.'

I falter mid-note, slowly looking up to find him watching me. It's making me stupidly nervous. 'What about soft furnishings?'

'Yes, lots.' He starts walking toward me. 'I like your dress,' he whispers.

Holy shit, I'm out of here! 'Thanks,' I squeak, making for the door. 'I have everything I need.' I don't, but I can't stay here any longer. This man is like a sensory drain on me. 'I'll get some designs together.' I exit into the corridor, heading straight for the gallery landing.

Bloody hell, when I woke up this morning this was the last thing I expected. Posh country mansion – with a painfully handsome owner to round the package off – is not part of my regular daily routine.

I find my way to the top of the stairs, bolting down at a stupid rate, considering the tan stilettos I have on, and hit the parquet floor, wondering how the hell I got here. I'm a mess.

'I look forward to hearing from you, Ava.' His husky voice rolls over my flesh as he joins me at the bottom of the stairs, putting his hand out. I take it in mine for fear that if I don't, he may well clench me and place his lips on me again.

'You have a lovely hotel,' I say genuinely, wishing that my handbag contents consisted of spare knickers, a blindfold, earplugs and some armour. I might have been more prepared.

His eyebrows shoot up as he keeps hold of my hand and slowly shakes it, the buzz travelling through our joined hands making me tense all over. 'I have a lovely hotel,' he repeats thoughtfully. The buzz transforms to a full-on jolt of electricity, and I retract my hand under reflex. He looks at me questioningly. 'It really was nice to meet you, Ava.' He emphasizes the *really*.

'You, too,' I practically whisper.

I watch as his eyes dart briefly and he starts chewing his bottom lip. His shifting body eventually moves over to the centre table of the entrance hall, and he pulls out a single calla lily from the huge spray that's dominating the piece of furniture. He studies it for a few moments before he holds it out to me. 'Understated elegance,' he says softly.

I don't know why I do – maybe because my brain is mush – but I take it. 'Thank you.'

He puts his abandoned hand in his pocket, watching me

closely. 'You're more than welcome.' His gaze travels from my eyes to my lips. I take a few steps back.

'There you are!' A woman walks out of the bar and toward Ward. She's attractive – all blond, mid-length, layered hair and red, pouty lips. She kisses his cheek. 'Are you ready?'

Okay, I'm assuming this must be the wife. But there was no ring, so maybe it's the girlfriend? Either or, I'm completely stunned when he doesn't take his eyes off me, making no attempt to answer her question. She turns to see what's stealing his attention and eyes me suspiciously. I don't like her instantly, and it has nothing to do with the man she's draped all over.

'And you are?' she purrs.

I shift uncomfortably, feeling like I've been captured doing something naughty. Well, I have. I've been having extreme unwelcome reactions to her boyfriend. An unreasonable pang of jealousy stabs at me. How ridiculous!

I smile sweetly. 'Just leaving. Good-bye.' I turn, practically running to the door and scuttling down the steps. I jump into my car, letting out an almighty breath, and when my lungs have thanked me for the welcome air, I flop back in my seat and commence breathing-regulating exercises.

I'm going to have to pass this to Tom. But then I laugh at my stupid idea. Tom's gay. He'll be just as affected by Ward as I am. Even knowing he's taken, I still couldn't work with him. I shake my head in disbelief and start my car.

As I drive down the gravel driveway, I look in my rearview mirror at the imposing manor getting smaller and smaller behind me, and there, standing at the top of the steps watching me leave, is Jesse Ward.

'There you are. I was just going to call you,' Kate exclaims, without looking up from placing a figurine on the wedding cake she's decorating. Her tongue's hanging out, resting on her bottom lip. It makes me smile. 'Do you fancy going out?' She still doesn't look up.

This is good. I'm sure my face will give away any attempt to feign coolness. I'm still slightly flustered after my lunchtime meeting with a certain Lord of the Manor. I don't have the energy to get ready and go out.

'Shall we save ourselves for tomorrow?' I try. I know this will mean a bottle of wine on the sofa, but at least I can put my PJs on and chill out. After the day I've had, winding down my racing mind is paramount. I've got a headache, and I've lacked the ability to concentrate all day.

'Absolutely. Let me finish this cake, then I'm all yours.' She swivels the fruit cake on the stand, dabbing edible glue onto the icing. 'How was your day in the countryside?'

I laugh. What do I say? I expected a pompous country bumpkin, but I got a devastatingly handsome, suited God. He requested me by name, his touch turned me to molten lava, I couldn't look in his eyes for fear of passing out, and he liked my dress. Instead I say, 'Interesting.'

She looks up. 'Do tell,' she prompts, her eyes sparkling as she bends back down, her tongue popping out again.

'It wasn't what I expected.' I flick a piece of imaginary lint off my navy dress in an attempt to appear casual.

'Leave out what you expected and tell me what you got.' She's stopped trying to fix husband and wife to the top of the cake, and her eyes are narrowed on me. She has icing on the end of her nose, but I ignore it.

'The owner.' I shrug, fiddling with my tan belt.

'The owner?' she asks, her lips twitching.

'Yes. Jesse Ward, the owner.' I flick more imaginary lint from my dress.

'Jesse Ward, the owner,' she mimics me, pointing to one of the flowery tub chairs in her workshop. 'Sit, now! Why are you trying to sound cool? You're failing miserably, by the way. Your cheeks are the colour of that icing.' She points to a fire engine cake on the metal shelf stand. 'Why was the owner, Jesse Ward, not what you expected?'

I flop into the chair with my bag on my lap, while Kate stands tapping her palm with the handle of her spatula. She finally walks over, sitting in the chair opposite me.

'Tell me,' she presses.

I shrug. 'The man's attractive and he knows it.' I see her eyes light up as the spatula taps become faster on her hand. She wants more drama. She loves it. When Matt and I split up, she was the first on the scene to soak up the spectacle as a supporting friend. She needn't have bothered. It was mutual, very amicable and really rather boring. No plates were flying and no neighbours called the police.

'How old?' she asks keenly.

I shrug. 'He said twenty-one, but he's at least ten years past that.'

'You asked him?' Kate's jaw hits her lap.

'Yes, in a moment of pure brain-to-mouth filter malfunction, the question did slip. I'm not proud,' I mutter. 'I made such a fool of myself, Kate. A man's never done that to me before. But this one … Well, you would have been ashamed of me.'

A sharp shot of laughter flies from her mouth. 'Ava, I need to teach you some social skills!' She falls back in her chair, starting to lick the icing from her spatula.

'Please do,' I grumble, putting my hand out to her. She passes me the spatula, and I start licking at the edges. I've lived with Kate for a month and existed on wine, icing sugar and cake mixture. A loss of appetite after a breakup, I don't have. 'He was very self-assured,' I say between licks.

'As in?'

'Oh, this man knew he was sparking a reaction in me. I must have been painful to watch. I was pathetic.'

'That good?'

I shake my head in dismay. 'Ridiculously.'

'He's probably shit in bed,' Kate muses. 'All the hot ones are. What's your brief?'

'Ten new bedrooms in the extension. I thought I was going to a country mansion, but it's a mega-plush hotel-come-spa – The Manor; have you heard of it?'

Kate's face screws up into a clueless expression. 'Nope,' she replies, getting up to turn the oven off. 'Can I come next time?'

'No, I'm not going back. I could never look him in the eye again, not after my performance.' I push myself up from the chair, throwing the spatula into the empty mixing bowl. 'I've passed it over to Patrick. Wine?'

'In the fridge.'

We make our way up to the flat and change into our PJs. I dump my bag on my bed and it flops open, the calla lily Ward gave me making an appearance. Understated elegance. I pick it up and twirl it in my fingers for a few moments, then dump it in my wastepaper basket.

I load the DVD player with the latest offering from the local rental shop, jump on the couch with Kate and try to concentrate on the movie, but it's impossible. My mind's eye is trampled by a tall, lean, dark blond, green-eyed male of a certain age, with a dribble-worthy gait and bag-loads of sex appeal. I doze off with the words 'But I want you' pinballing around my head.

Chapter Three

After two progress meetings with clients and a stop at Mr Muller's new townhouse in Holland Park to drop off some samples, I'm back in the office listening to Patrick moan about Irene. It's a normal Monday morning affair after he's endured a whole weekend away from the office with his wife.

Tom breezes in with the widest grin on his face, and I know immediately that he must have hooked up over the weekend.

'Darling, I've missed you!' He air kisses me and turns to Patrick, who holds his hands up in a don't-even-think-about-it gesture. Tom rolls his eyes, completely unoffended, and waltzes to his desk.

'Morning, Tom,' I greet brightly.

'I've had the most stressful morning. Mr and Mrs Baines have changed their bloody minds for the thousandth time. I've had to cancel all the orders and rearrange a dozen workmen.' He waves his arms in the air in frustration. 'I got a sodding parking ticket for not displaying a permit in a residents' zone and, to top it off, I snagged my new jumper on those hideous railings outside Starbucks.' He starts picking the stray wool from the hem of his hot pink, V-neck jumper. 'Goddamn it, look! It's a good job I got laid last night or I'd be in the depths of despair.' He grins at me.

I knew it.

Patrick walks away, shaking his head. His attempts to tone Tom down to levels more appropriate for an office have proven ineffective. He's now given up.

'Good night?' I ask.

'Wonderful. I met the most divine man. He's taking me to the Natural History Museum at the weekend. He's a scientist. We're soul mates, for sure.'

'What happened to the personal trainer?' That was last week's soul mate.

'Don't; it was a disaster. He turned up at my apartment on Friday night with the *Dirty Dancing* DVD and Indian takeout for two. Can you believe that?'

'I'm shocked,' I tease.

'I bloody was. Needless to say, I won't be seeing him again. What's happening with you, darling? How's that gorgeous ex-boyfriend of yours?' He winks. Tom doesn't hide his attraction to Matt, which makes me laugh but makes Matt extremely uncomfortable.

'He's okay. He's still the ex and still straight.'

'Damn shame. Let me know when he comes to his senses.' Tom saunters off, tweaking his perfectly positioned blond quiff.

'Sally,' I call, 'I'm e-mailing you a design consultation fee for Mr Ward. Can you make sure you send it today?'

'I will, Ava. Seven-day payment terms?'

'Yes, thank you.' I turn back to my desk and resume colour matching, reaching over to grab my phone when it starts dancing around my desk. Glancing at my screen, I nearly fall off my chair when I see the name *Jesse* flashing up. What the hell?

I never stored his number – Patrick never got round to passing it to me and after handing the project over to him on Friday, I no longer needed it. I wouldn't be going back, and I meant it. And even so, I wouldn't have saved his number under his first name. I hold my phone in my hand, scanning the office to see if the continuous ringing has drawn any attention from my colleagues. It hasn't, so I let it ring off. What does he want?

I make for Patrick's office to ask if he's notified Mr Ward of the change in arrangements, but then it rings again, halting me in my tracks. I take a steady breath and answer.

'Hello?' I say, stamping my foot a little for sounding apprehensive in my greeting. I was aiming for sure and confident.

'Ava?' His husky voice has the same impact on my weak senses as it did on Friday. But at least over the phone he can't see me physically trembling.

'Who's speaking?' There. That sounded better – professional, businesslike, and steady.

He laughs lightly, and it throws me completely off guard. 'Now, I know you already know the answer to that question because my name came up on your phone.' I cringe on the spot. 'Trying to play it cool?'

How does he know that? But then realisation dawns on me. 'You added yourself to my contacts list?' I gasp. When did he do that? I mentally sprint through our meeting, settling on my visit to the toilet when I left my portfolio and phone on the table. I can't believe he went through my phone!

'I need to be able to get hold of you.'

Oh no. Patrick obviously hasn't told him. Nevertheless, you don't go around snooping through strangers' phones.

'Patrick should have contacted you,' I coolly inform him. 'I'm afraid I'm unable to assist you, but Patrick will be more than happy to help.'

'Yes, Patrick has been in contact,' he replies. I sag in relief but then frown. Why is he calling me then? 'I'm sure he will be happy to help, but I'm less than happy to accept it.'

My mouth gapes. Who does he think he is? He's called to tell me that he's not happy? I close my gaping mouth. 'I'm sorry to hear that.' I sound less than sorry; I sound irritated.

'Are you?'

No, I'm not sorry, but I'm not about to tell him that. 'Yes, I am.' I want to add that I could never work with an arrogant, good-looking swine like him, but I refrain. That wouldn't be very professional.

I hear him sigh. 'I don't think you are, Ava.' My name sounds like velvet rolling from his lips, causing a familiar shudder to course through me. 'I think you're avoiding me.' I'm clenching my jaw so tightly I'm going to dislocate it at this rate. He's right, of course. He sparks some very unwelcome feelings in me.

But again, I won't let him know he's right. 'Why would I do that?' I ask cockily.

'Well, because you're attracted to me.'

'Excuse me?' I splutter. His self-assuredness knows no bounds. Has he no shame? The fact that he's bang on the money is way beside the point. You would have to be blind, deaf and numb not to be attracted to this man. He's the epitome of male perfection and, quite clearly, he knows it.

He sighs. 'I said ...'

'Yes, I heard you,' I interrupt him. 'I just can't believe you said it.'

I'm completely stunned. The man has a significant other and he's flirting with me? I need to turn this conversation back around to business and get off the phone quickly.

'I apologise for not being available to assist with your work.' I blurt out and hang up, staring down at my phone.

That was really quite rude and extremely unprofessional, but I'm completely staggered by his forwardness. Passing the contract over to Patrick is looking more and more sensible by the minute. My phone dings as a text arrives.

I notice you didn't deny it. You should know the feeling's mutual. Jx

Fucking hell! I slap my hand over my lips to stop my mental explicit language from escaping my mouth. No, I didn't deny it. And *he's* attracted to *me*? I'm a bit young for him, or is he too old for me? What a cocky arse! I don't reply – I have no idea what to say to that.

Instead, I throw my phone in my bag and go meet Kate for lunch.

'Holy Moses!' Kate exclaims, staring down at my phone. Her red hair is swinging from side to side in its ponytail as she shakes her head. 'Did you reply?'

'No!' I laugh.

'And he's got a girlfriend?'

'Yes.' I nod, raising my eyebrows.

She places my phone back on the table. 'That's a shame.'

Is it? It actually makes things a lot easier. It totally trumps the looks and reactions he spikes in me. Kate's far more daring than me. She would have replied with something shocking and suggestive, and probably made *his* jaw drop. Confident, strong-minded and determined, she mostly scares men off on the first date – only the strongest survive.

'Not really,' I muse, picking up my cheeky lunchtime wine and taking a sip. 'Anyway, it's only been four weeks since Matt and I split up. I don't want any men in my life, not in any capacity.' I like the fact that I sound resolute. 'I'm enjoying being single and carefree for the first time ever.' I add. And it really does feel like the first time ever. I was with Matt for four years and prior to that, I was in a three-year relationship with Adam.

'Have you seen the prick?' Kate face distorts into one of disgust at the mention of my ex's name.

She can't stand Matt and was delighted when I split up with him. Kate catching him at it with a work colleague in a taxi only confirmed what I already knew. I don't know why I ignored it for so long. When I confronted him calmly, he fell apart with apologies and nearly fell over when I told him that I wasn't bothered. I really wasn't, much to my own surprise. The relationship had run its course, and Matt was of the same opinion.

'No,' I confirm.

'We are having fun, aren't we?' She grins as the waitress approaches with our lunch.

'I'm just going to the loo.' I get up, leaving Kate dowsing her chips in mayonnaise.

After using the toilet, I stand in the mirror re-applying my lip gloss and fluffing my hair. It's behaving today, so it's down and tumbling all over my shoulders. I brush down my black capri pants and pick a few hairs off my cream blouse, then make my way back to the bar. My phone rings, and I drag it from my bag, rolling my eyes when I see it's him again. He's probably wondering where my reply to his inappropriate text message is. I'm not playing games with him.

'Reject.' I huff at my phone, stabbing at the red button and stuffing it in my bag as I continue down the corridor. 'Oh God, I'm sorry!' I splutter, slamming straight into a chest.

This chest is a very firm chest, and the intoxicating fresh water scent that washes over me is way too familiar. My legs refuse to move, and I know what I'm going to see if I look up. His arm is already wrapped around my waist to steady me, my eyes are level with the top of his chest, and I can see his heart beating through his shirt.

'Reject?' he says softly. 'I'm wounded.'

I push myself away from his grasp, attempting to regain my composure. He looks stunning, wearing a charcoal suit and crisp white shirt. I laugh at myself and my inability to get my eyes past his upper body for fear of being hypnotised by the potency of this man's green gaze.

'Is something funny?' he asks. I suspect he's frowning at my random outburst, but because I refuse to look at him, I can't confirm that.

'I'm sorry. I wasn't looking where I was going.' I sidestep him, but he grabs my elbow, halting my escape.

'Just tell me one thing before you leave, Ava.' His voice prickles at my senses, and I find my eyes travelling up the leanness of his body until our stares meet. His face is serious, but still stunning. 'How loud do you think you'll scream when I fuck you?'

WHAT? 'Excuse me?' I manage to splutter around the lead that is my tongue.

He half smiles at my shock, placing his index finger under my chin and pushing my gaping mouth shut. 'I'll leave that one with you.' He releases my elbow.

I flash him a displeased scowl before I walk back to the table as steadily as my boneless legs will allow. I slide myself onto the chair, immediately glugging down my wine to try and moisten my parched mouth.

When I look up at Kate, she's openmouthed, exposing half-chewed chips and bread. It's not attractive. 'Who the fuck is that?' she mumbles around her food.

'Who?' I look around, pretending to be unaware.

'Him.' Kate points with her fork. 'Look!'

'I saw, and I don't know,' I grate.

'He's coming over. You sure you don't know him? Fuck, he's hot!' She looks at me, and I shrug noncommittally, picking up a stray piece of lettuce from my BLT and nibbling at the edges. I'm tense all over, and I know he's getting closer because Kate's gaze is lifting upward to accommodate his height. I wish she would shut her bloody gaping mouth!

'Ladies.' His low, throaty voice prickles at my skin, doing nothing to relax me.

'Hi,' Kate says, chewing rapidly to rid her mouth of the obstruction to speech.

'Ava?' he prompts, and I wave my piece of lettuce at him to acknowledge his presence but without having to look at him. He laughs lightly, and out the corner of my eye, I see his body slowly lowering until he's squatting at the table next to me, but I still refuse to look at him. He rests one arm on the table, and I hear Kate cough and splutter on the remnants of her food. 'That's better,' he says. I can feel his breath on my cheek.

Reluctantly, I look up through my lashes and find Kate gawking at me – all wide-eyed and yes-he's-still-there-*talk*-you-idiot! I can think of nothing to say. Once again, this man has rendered me useless.

I hear him sigh. 'I'm Jesse Ward, pleased to meet you.' I see his hand reach across the table, and Kate takes it eagerly.

'Jesse?' she splutters. 'Oh! *Jesse.*' I can feel her glaring at me accusingly. 'I'm Kate. Ava mentioned you have a posh hotel.'

I scowl across the table.

'Oh, she mentioned me?' he asks softly. I don't have to look at him to know he's displaying a smug, satisfied face at this news. 'I wonder what else she's mentioned.'

'Oh, this and that,' Kate flips casually.

'This and that,' he counters softly.

'Yes, this and that,' Kate affirms.

Fed up with the pointless little exchange they both seem to be enjoying, I take the situation into my own hands, turning my eyes to him. 'It was nice to see you. Good-bye.'

Our gazes latch immediately, and I'm ruined by his green eyes, all hooded, dark and demanding. I can feel his breath waver and it draws my eyes to his mouth. His lips are moist, slightly parted, and his tongue slowly creeps out of his mouth, running a leisurely path across his bottom lip. I can't take my eyes off him, and without any encouragement at all, my own tongue responds with a happy little adventure across my bottom lip. It totally betrays my effort to appear unaffected.

This is crazy. This … whatever this is … it's just crazy. He's over confident and arrogant, but probably has the right to be. I desperately do *not* want to be affected by this man.

'Nice?' He leans forward, grasping my thigh, causing hot liquid lava to flood my groin. I shift my legs, squeezing my thighs together to restrict the pulsation that threatens to break out into a full, hard throb. 'I could think of lots of words, Ava. *Nice* isn't one of them. I'll leave you to consider my question.'

Oh, good Lord! I gulp as he leans into me at half height, pressing his damp lips against my cheek, holding his kiss forever. I clench my teeth in an effort not to turn into him.

'Soon,' he whispers. It's a promise. He releases my tense thigh and rises. 'It was nice to meet you, Kate.'

'Hmmm, you, too,' she responds thoughtfully.

He strides off toward the back of the bar. Good God, he walks with purpose and it's sexy as hell. I close my eyes to mentally gather my wits, which are currently dispersed all over the bar floor. It's completely hopeless. I turn back to Kate, finding accusing bright blues gawking at me like I've just sprouted fangs.

Her eyebrows hit her hairline. 'Fuck me, that was intense!' she spits across the table.

'Was it?' I start pushing my sandwich around my plate.

'You better stop with the blah-fucking-zay shit now, or I'll shove this fork so far up your arse you'll be chewing metal. What question are you considering?' Her tone is fierce.

'I don't know.' I brush her off. 'He's attractive, arrogant and has a girlfriend.' I try for vague.

Kate lets out a long, over-amplified whistle. 'I've never experienced that before. I've heard of it but never witnessed it.'

'What are you on about?' I snap.

She leans across the table, all serious. 'Ava, the sexual tension batting between you and that man was so fucking supercharged, even I was horny!' She laughs. 'He wants you bad. He couldn't have made it any clearer if he'd spread you on that pool table.' She points, and I actually look.

'You're imagining things.' I snort.

'I've seen the text, and now I've seen the man in the flesh. He's hot ... for an older guy.' She shrugs.

'I'm not interested.'

'Ha! You keep telling yourself that.'

*

I return to the office and spend the rest of the day achieving absolutely nothing. I twiddle my pen, visit the toilet a dozen times, and pretend to listen to Tom harp on about Gay Pride and all things camp. My phone has rung four times – all Jesse Ward – and I've rejected each and every call. I'm staggered by this man's persistence and confidence.

I'm happy and enjoying my newfound freedom, and I have no intention of derailing my plans to be single and carefree. I'm not getting caught up with a handsome stranger, no matter how mind-meltingly delicious he is. Anyway, he's way too old for me and, more importantly, he's obviously taken. And that only reinforces the fact that he's an ultimate player. This is not the sort of man I need to be attracted to, especially after Matt and his infidelities. I need a man, eventually, who'll be faithful, protective, and look after me – preferably a bit nearer my age, too.

My phone declares a text, snapping me from my wandering thoughts and making me jump. I already know who it is before I look.

Being rejected isn't very nice. Why won't you answer my calls? Jx

I laugh to myself, drawing the attention of Victoria, who's rummaging through the filing cabinet near my desk. Her perfectly plucked eyebrow arches. I don't suppose he is familiar with rejection. 'Kate,' I offer, by way of an explanation. It seems to work, as she returns to sifting through the cabinet.

It should be obvious why I'm not answering my bloody phone. I don't want to talk to him and, quite frankly, I don't trust my body around him. It seems to respond to his presence with no prompt from my brain, and that could be very dangerous indeed.

My phone rings again and I quickly reject it. I'm never going to get rid of him. I need to be brutal.

If you need to discuss your requirements, you should be calling Patrick, not me.

There. He should get the message. I put my phone down, all set on getting something done, but it chimes again, and I pick it straight back up, grabbing my coffee with my spare hand as I do.

My requirement is to make you scream. I don't think Patrick can help me there. I'm gagging just thinking about it. That's a thought ... Will I need to gag you? Jx

I spray coffee all over my desk as I cough. The cheeky sod! How brazen and unashamed can a man be? I switch my phone to silent, chucking it down on my desk in disgust. I'm not even dignifying that with a response. Replying will only encourage him. There's a fine line between confidence and arrogance, and Jesse Ward triple jumps that. I feel sorry for old pouty lips. Is she aware of her man pursuing young women?

I watch as my screen lights up again and snatch it up, silencing it before it draws attention. I open my top drawer, drop it in, and slam it shut on a huff.

I make a meagre attempt to carry on with some work, but I'm far too distracted. Strange words – all having no place in work-related correspondence – are appearing in my e-mails as I absentmindedly tap away at my keyboard. When the office phone rings, I glance up, seeing Sally away from her desk.

So I answer. 'Good afternoon, Rococo Union.'

'Don't hang up!' he blurts down the phone, making me sit up straight in my chair. Even his urgent voice prickles my skin. 'Ava, I'm really very sorry.'

'You are?' I can't hide the surprise in my voice. Jesse Ward doesn't look like the kind of man to offer apologies willy-nilly.

'Yes, really I am. I've made you feel uncomfortable. I've over-stepped the mark by a long shot.' He sounds sincere enough. 'I've distressed you. Please accept my apology.'

I wouldn't say I was distressed by his bold behaviour and comments. Shocked would be more apt. Some people might even admire his confidence, I suppose. 'Okay,' I say hesitantly. 'So you don't want to make me scream or gag me?'

'Ava, you sound disappointed.'

'Not at all,' I blurt.

There's a brief silence before he speaks again. 'Can we start again? I'll keep it professional, of course.'

Oh no. He might be sorry, but that doesn't extinguish the effect he has on me. And it doesn't escape my thoughts that this is just a ploy to get me back on-side so he can recommence pursuing me.

'Mr. Ward, I'm really not the right person for this job.' I swivel in my chair to check if Patrick's in his office. He is. 'Can I transfer you to Patrick?' I push, mentally pleading for him to take the hint.

'It's Jesse. You make me feel old when you call me Mr Ward,' he grumbles.

I slam my mouth shut when my lips part and that question nearly falls out. I'm still intrigued on that subject, but I'm not going to ask again.

'Ava, if it makes you feel better, you can deal with John. What would be the next stage?'

John? Would that make me feel better? Big Guy has in-timidation in equal measure to Ward's boldness. I'm not sure I would feel any more comfortable with him, but the fact that he's prepared to step out of the equation tells me he really does want me to do the designs, and that, I suppose, is a compliment. The Manor will be a great addition to my portfolio.

'I would need to measure the rooms and draw up some schemes.' I spit the words out impulsively.

'Perfect.' He sounds relieved. 'I can get John to take you around the rooms. He can hold your tape measure. Tomorrow?'

Tomorrow? He's keen. 'I can't do tomorrow or Wednesday. I'm sorry.'

'Oh,' he says quietly. 'Do you do evenings?'

I don't like doing evenings, but many clients work nine-to-five jobs and are unavailable during the working day. I prefer evenings to weekends, though. I never get dragged into week-end appointments.

'I can do tomorrow evening,' I blurt, turning the page in my diary to tomorrow. My last appointment is at five with Mrs Kent. 'Seven-ish?' I ask, already pencilling him in.

'Perfect. I would say that I'll look forward to it, but I can't look forward to it because I won't be seeing you.' I can't see him, but I know he's probably grinning. I can hear it in his tone. He just can't help himself. 'I'll let John know to expect you at seven.'

'-ish,' I add. I don't know how long it'll take me to get out of the city at that time of day.

'-ish,' he confirms. 'Thank you, Ava.'

'You're welcome, Mr Ward. Good-bye.' I hang up and commence tapping my fingernail on my front tooth.

'Ava?' Patrick calls from his office.

'Yes?' I swing my chair to face him.

'The Manor, they want you, flower.' He shrugs, returning to his computer screen.

No, *he* wants me.

Chapter Four

I fly through Tuesday's appointments, leaving Mrs Kent's lovely new town house at just past six.

Mrs. Kent is the extremely high maintenance wife of Mr Kent – managing director of Kent Yacht Builders – and this Kensington house is their third home in four years. I've redesigned the interior on all of them. As soon as the work is completed, Mrs Kent decides she can't envision growing old there – she's seventy, if a day – so the house is on the market, sold and I'm starting from scratch on their new abode.

I jump in my car and set off for the Surrey Hills. I didn't divulge to Kate the reason why I'm going to be home late. Telling her would only fuel her curiosity as to why I'm returning to The Manor. I would, of course, lie and feed her the same crap that I've fed myself – that The Manor's project would benefit my portfolio. The magnet of lean loveliness has zero influence on my decision – none at all.

I stop at the intercom, but as I press to release my window, the gates start opening. I look up to the camera and figure John must be waiting. I drive up the gravel road to the courtyard and find the big guy standing on the steps, filling the double doorway, sunglasses firmly in place.

'Good evening, John,' I greet, grabbing my folder and bag. Will he speak today?

No; he nods and turns, walking back into The Manor, leaving me to follow him into the bar. It's busier than when I was last here.

'Mario?' he rumbles.

A little man pops up from behind the bar. 'Yes?'

'Get Miss O'Shea a drink, please.' John turns his concealed eyes back to me. 'I'll be back. Jesse wants a quick word.'

'With me?' I blurt, blushing slightly at my abruptness.

'No, with me.'

'Is he staying in his office?' I ask nervously. I'm asking too many questions about something so trivial, but he assured me he would leave me and John to it. Even the thought of the man reduces me to a nervous wreck.

John's lips twitch, clearly trying to fight a smile. I inwardly groan. He knows.

''S'all good, girl.' He turns, giving Mario a funny look, which the little barman acknowledges with a flick of his cloth, before he leaves me with him at the bar.

I gaze around, noticing a woman laughing with a middle-aged man at a table nearby. It's the woman I saw in the toilets when I was here last Friday. She's wearing a black trouser suit and looks extremely professional. She must be staying a while – business, maybe? The man accompanying her rises from the table, putting his hand out politely, and she accepts it with a smile as she stands, letting him tuck her hand under his arm and lead her out of the bar as they chat and giggle.

I perch on a barstool to wait for John, taking my phone out to check for messages and missed calls.

'You would like wine?'

I look up, finding the little barman smiling at me. He speaks with an accent, and I conclude that he's Italian. He's very short and rather sweet, with his mustache and receding black hair. 'I could do with one, but I'm driving.'

'Ah!' he exclaims. 'Just a small one.' He holds a small wine glass up, drawing a line across the middle with his finger.

Oh, sod it! I shouldn't drink on the job, but my nerves are

shot to bits. He's in this building somewhere and that's unsettling enough. I nod on a smile. 'Thank you.'

He holds up a bottle of Zinfandel, and I nod again. 'Your dress is very, urhh … how you say … striking?' He pours a little more than half a glass. In fact, it's full.

I look down at my black, figure-hugging dress. Yes, I suppose 'striking' would be a word you could use for my if-all-else-fails dress. I always feel nice in it. It shows every curve I have, and considering I'm a size ten, there are not many. But if I live with Kate for much longer, that may change. I ignore the little voice in my head asking me if I wore it in the hopes of seeing Ward. 'Thank you.' I smile.

'Pleasure, Miss O'Shea. I leave you in peace.' He picks up his cloth and starts wiping the granite counter.

I sip my wine as I wait for John. It goes down too well and before I know it, I've drank the lot.

'Hello.'

I swivel on my stool, coming face to face with the woman who was draped all over Ward on Friday. She smiles at me, but it's the most insincere smile I've ever had the pleasure of receiving. 'Hi,' I say politely.

Mario rushes over with a panic-stricken face, waving his cloth in the air. 'Miss Sarah! No, please. No talk.'

What?

'Oh, shut up, Mario! I'm not stupid,' she spits.

Poor Mario flinches before returning to wiping the bar, keeping his eyes on Sarah. I want to jump to his defence, but just as I'm contemplating doing exactly that, she puts out her hand.

'I'm Sarah. You are … ?'

Oh yes, the last time she asked me that I didn't answer and left rather hastily. I accept her hand, shaking it lightly as she eyes me suspiciously. I can tell she doesn't like me. She sees me as a threat.

'Ava O'Shea,' I offer, releasing my hold of her hand swiftly.

'And you're here because … ?'

I laugh lightly. I'm sure she knows exactly why I'm here, which only serves to confirm that she's feeling threatened and going out of her way to make me feel uncomfortable. *Sheathe the claws, lady.*

'I'm an interior designer. I'm here to measure up the new bedrooms.'

She arches an eyebrow, flicking her hand in the air to get Mario's attention. This woman is something else, with aloofness in equal measure to Ward's boldness. Her blond, layered hair is flicking here and there, her lips the same pouty red as they were on Friday, and she's wearing a fitted gray trouser suit. I'm being unkind when I put her at forty. She's probably mid-thirties – far closer to Ward in age than I am. I quickly rein in my wandering thoughts, mentally slapping my own desperate arse.

'Sloe gin and tonic, Mario,' she demands. No please and no smile. She really is quite rude. 'You're a bit young to be an interior designer, aren't you?' Her tone is unfriendly, and she doesn't look at me when she speaks.

I bristle. I really don't like this woman. What does Ward see in her, apart from over-inflated, pouty lips and obvious breast implants? 'I am,' I agree. She feels threatened by my youth as well. Good.

I'm beyond relieved when John appears in the doorway, pulling his glasses down and giving Sarah a peculiar look before nodding at me. What's with all these looks being thrown around? I don't dwell on it, though. John's nod is the cue I need to escape this woman. I place my empty glass on the bar more forcefully than I intend to, and Mario's head snaps up. I smile an apology, lowering myself from the stool.

'Nice meeting you, Sarah,' I say pleasantly. It's a lie. I don't like her, and I know the feeling's mutual.

She doesn't look at me. She accepts the drink that Mario hands her without so much as a thank you, and walks off to chat with a male business type at the other end of the bar.

When I reach John, he leads me up the grand staircase to the gallery landing and through to the new extension.

'I'll be fine on my own, John. I don't want to keep you.'

''S'all good, girl,' he rumbles, opening the door into the farthest room.

We get to work, measuring and working our way back through the rooms. John dutifully holds the tape measure for me, nodding every so often when I give direction. The phrase 'a man of few words' was invented with John in mind, I'm sure. He talks with his nods, and even though his eyes are covered with his sunglasses, I can identify when he's looking at me. I make all of the notes I need in my folder, ideas thrashing around in my head already.

An hour later, I have all the measurements I need and we're done. I follow John's huge body back onto the gallery landing as I search for my phone within my bag. I soon realise that in my desperation to get shot of Sarah, I left it on the bar.

'I've left my phone in the bar,' I mutter to John's back.

'I'll make sure Mario's picked it up. Jesse wanted me to show you one of the other rooms before you go,' he informs me evenly.

'Why?'

'So you get an idea of your brief.' He puts a keycard in the slot, opens the door and ushers me in.

Oh, okay. It can't hurt, and I am interested.

Wow! I walk into the middle of the room. Well, mini-suite would better describe it. The floor space is probably bigger than Kate's flat. Hearing the door close behind me, I turn to see John has left me to take it in on my own, so I stand silently, absorbing the opulent splendor of the décor.

These rooms are more lavish than the ones downstairs, if that's possible. A giant bed dominates the room, dressed in rich satin linen in deep purples and gold, and the wall behind the bed is papered in an embossed, intense swirling of dull gold. Heavy curtains pool at the thick, bouncy carpet, and the lighting is dim and soft. One of Ward's key requirements was sensuality, and whoever designed this room has achieved it in abundance. Why doesn't he just re-employ this designer?

I wander over to the huge sash window and look out over the rear grounds. The land The Manor stands on is vast, the views tremendous, and the lush greenness of the Surrey countryside rolls for miles and miles. It really is quite special. I walk over and run my palm across a lovely dark wooden chest of drawers and place my folder and bag on the top before lowering myself onto the chaise lounge in the window.

I sit and take in my surroundings. It's incredible and would undoubtedly rival many of the most famous hotels spread across the world's biggest cities. A huge wall hanging grabs my attention. It's quite odd but beautifully made, and I conclude that it must be an antique. Half attached to the wall and drifting up onto the ceiling where the huge beams span, it's grid-like in appearance, but there's no material or lighting adorning it. I tilt my head on a frown, but then fly up when I hear noise coming from the bathroom.

Oh shit. He's put me in an occupied room ... or has he? I can't hear anything now. I keep myself still and quiet, trying to listen for movement, but there's nothing, so I relax a little, but soon snap my head back up when I hear the door handle on the bathroom shift. Oh, heck.

I should be running to escape before some poor sod comes out of their bathroom, possibly naked, and finds a strange woman standing like a complete plum in the middle of their posh suite. I pelt toward the chest of drawers to retrieve my bag and swing around toward the exit. But I gasp, dropping my bag to the floor, when I'm confronted with the most magnificent sight.

I'm frozen on the spot and staring at Jesse Ward, who's standing in the doorway of the bathroom, wearing nothing but a pair of loose-fitting jeans.

'Is this some kind of joke?' I half laugh. I'm waiting for an explanation, but it's not forthcoming.

I try to ignore the mass of glorious man and frantically search my brain for guidance or instruction. It's useless. I'm not blind. I'll happily volunteer that I've imagined his chest, more than once, and it exceeds even my highest expectations. This man is way past perfect. What should I do? He's just standing there, with his head slightly lowered, staring up at me through his long lashes. His eyes are piercing me, his mouth slack, and I can see the rise and fall of his incredible chest. There's some serious definition; not too bulky, just clean ... cut ... perfection. If he's devastating fully clothed, then he's seizure-worthy now. I take a deep breath.

Oh God, he has the V, and his heavy breathing is causing his muscles to roll and ripple. What's he doing there like that in only a pair of jeans, looking all freshly shaven, revealing even more beauty? I mentally slap myself. It's obvious what he's playing at. I knew I shouldn't have trusted him. He's unreal and so bloody forward – it's almost unattractive ... almost.

I laugh lightly to myself. It's not unattractive – not at all. I'm a pooling mass of want.

His arms drape by his sides, but his stance is confident and determined. He's staring at me with complete intent, his look telling me I'm about to melt with pleasure. I should leave, but as much as I think I need to, as much as I'm battling with my sensible side to run, I don't. Instead, I run my eyes down to his denim-clad thighs, noticing the bulge at his groin. He's absolutely turned on, and judging by the coiled pang of desire that has just sprung into my stomach, so am I.

I part my lips to draw some steadying breaths, and then flex my neck.

'Relax, Ava,' he soothes me quietly. 'You know you want this.'
I almost laugh. Who wouldn't? Look at him!

I stand motionless. The only visible movement is my heart hammering out of my chest, and it increases tenfold when he slowly begins to walk toward me, his eyes fixed on mine.

When he's a few feet away, his fresh, minty scent engulfs me, making my body involuntarily rigid. I don't know how I manage it, but I keep my eyes on his, lifting them to maintain contact as he nears, until he's standing before me, as close as he can be without physically touching me.

'Turn around,' he orders gently.

I obey without even a thought or hesitation, slowly turning away from him as I puff my cheeks out and clench my eyes shut. What am I doing? I didn't falter in the slightest. My shoulders are tensing, anticipating his touch, and no amount of mental encouragement to relax is paying off. The only sound in the room is the heavy breathing coming from both of us. I stand for a few moments, then go to turn and face him again, but I'm stopped in my tracks when two firm, warm, slightly shaky hands rest on my shoulders, keeping me from following through on my intent. His touch makes me flinch, and he releases one hand slowly, as if to ensure I'll stay still, before he gathers my loose hair and releases it down my front. In my own private darkness, I can hear my head demanding I run away, but my body has a whole other agenda.

His hand returns to my shoulder and slowly massages my tense muscles. The feeling is divine, and my head rolls in appreciation as a small sigh escapes my lips. The pressure increases, and I soak up the delicious movements of his talented hands as I feel his hot, minty breath getting closer to my ear. I shudder, moving my face toward the source. I know this is inviting, but right at this moment, I've lost all sense. I want more.

'Don't stop this,' he whispers, the vibrations of his voice

propelling shockwaves throughout my body. I'm physically shaking. It's way beyond my control.

My breath catches at the back of my throat. 'I don't want to.' My voice is unrecognisable. I can't believe he's captured me like this; I can't believe I'm accepting this.

He presses his entire front against my back, his mouth dropping to my ear. 'I'm going to take your dress off now.'

My nod of agreement is almost nonexistent, but he catches it and answers by nipping my earlobe, which only assists in raising the relentless pressure in my already throbbing core.

'You're too fucking beautiful, Ava,' he purrs, skimming his lips across my ear.

'Oh god,' I lean back into him, his erection throbbing through his jeans, pulsing into my lower back.

'Do you feel that?' He circles his hips, and I moan. 'I'm going to have you, lady.' His words are spoken with absolute conviction.

I'm a complete slave to them. I know he's bound to have had practice in this area; he must have the gift of seduction down to a fine art. I'm not in denial. Women must be falling at his feet on a daily basis. He's a well-trained master, taking what he wants, but it doesn't bother me in the slightest. Right now, I'm here for the taking, with no conscience and no indecisiveness. Caution has been wholly and absolutely thrown to the wind.

I feel his index finger start at the base of my back, trailing a slow, definite stroke up the centre of my spine, causing my head to roll freely. I plead with my hands to remain at my sides, when all I want to do is turn and devour him, but he's already stopped me from turning to face him once. He clearly likes to be in control.

As he reaches the very top of my dress, he grasps the zip and places his hand on my hip. I jerk. It's my ultimate tickle spot and any friction on my hipbone, or the hollow above it, sends me through the roof. Squeezing my eyes shut, I use every ounce of willpower I possess to disregard the contact. It's hard, but the sheer size of his hand splayed across my hip grounds me, keeping me immobile.

The zipper of my dress slowly lowers and I hear him gasp at the exposure of my bare skin. He removes his hand from my hip, and I'm stunned when I miss the heat immediately. But then I feel both hands slide under the material of my dress and rest on my bare shoulders, and his fingers flex as he pushes my dress away from my front before slowly dragging it down my body, letting it fall to the floor.

His breath catches, and I thank everything holy that I put on decent underwear. I'm standing in my bra, knickers and heels, at the complete mercy of the Adonis looming behind me.

'Hmmm, lace,' he whispers. My waist is gripped and I'm lifted out of the pooling dress before being turned to face him. In these heels, my eyes are level with his chin and with a little flick upward, I'm focused on his full, beautiful lips and wishing he would lay them on mine. I'm swiftly losing my self-control and my conscience has long left the building. I'm wanton, and with this man, easy.

He lifts a hand to my breast and circles my nipple through my bra with his thumb, his gaze focused on his movements. My nipples tingle at the contact, lengthening behind the material of my bra, and a small smile plays at the corners of his lips. He knows the effect he's having on me. Introducing his index finger, he tweaks the stiff nub, causing my breasts to throb, becoming heavy, aching mounds on my chest. I'm completely rapt by this man studying me so closely, working me up into a shaking, desperate mess. I still can't believe I'm doing this, but damn, can I stop it?

I watch as he brings his other hand up to palm my other breast, and I can no longer keep my hands off him. My arms lift and my palms settle on his chest, the warmth and firmness hitching my breath. I start to trail my finger down the void between his pecs, smiling to myself when I feel him flinch under my touch and groan low in his throat, but before I can make the most of the access to his body, he turns me back around. I want to cry inside.

'I want to see you,' I breathe.

'Shhhh,' he hushes me, unclasping my bra and running his hands under the straps.

He lowers them down my arms, letting it drop to the floor, before his hands find my breasts and knead deliberately as he continues to breathe hot, heavy breaths in my ear.

'You. And. Me,' he growls and spins me around, crashing his lips against mine, robbing me of breath.

I'm back to where I want to be. His tongue skims my bottom lip, seeking entry, and I don't deny him. I accept him into my mouth, our tongues dueling, his mouth hot, his tongue lax but severe. I fling my arms over his shoulders to pull him closer as he presses his groin into my lower stomach, his erection hard as steel and bidding for escape from the confines of the denim encasing it. Every part of him feels perfect. He's everything I imagined.

A low moan escapes his mouth as both of his hands drift up my back to cup my head, his fingers splayed around the back, the heels of his palms resting on my cheek bones. He breaks the kiss and I whimper at the loss. His shoulders are rising and falling with the deep breaths he's struggling to get into his lungs, and he rests his forehead against mine with his eyes clenched shut. He looks in pain.

'I'm going to get lost in you,' he breathes, his hand travelling back down the curve of my spine to the rear of my thigh. With one gentle tug, he pulls my leg up to rest against his hip, cupping my bum with his other. He searches my eyes desperately. 'There's something here,' he whispers. 'I'm not imagining it.'

No, he's not. I think back to Friday, when I first laid my eyes on him. I felt like I'd been electrocuted, all sorts of strange reactions firing off in my mind and body. That wasn't normal, and I'm so relieved that I wasn't the only one to feel it. 'There's something,' I confirm quietly, watching as the look in his eyes changes from uncertainty to complete satisfaction.

I'm perched on one leg, semi-draped around his waist, ready to jump the gun and wrap my other leg around him. I need to feel all of him. I need his lips on mine, and as if reading my mind, he tilts his head and lowers his mouth, but this time he's calmer as he gently brushes his lips over mine at the most dreamy pace. He tilts his pelvis into me, and I instantly recognise the start of a huge build-up of pressure in my groin. I'm powerless to control it; I don't want to control it.

Grinding his hips against me, he continues to take my mouth slowly, the combined sensation having me tinkering on the edge. One touch and I'm likely to explode.

His kiss hardens, the grinding of his hips increasing. 'Oh, Jesus,' he mumbles against my lips. 'Don't ruin this.'

Don't ruin this? Why is he pleading with me, or is he pleading with himself? But then it all becomes clear when I hear someone calling Jesse's name. I recognise the cold, unfriendly voice as Sarah's, and just like that, my building pleasure dies, retreating faster than it came.

Fuck off, fuck off, fuck off! I'm screaming it repeatedly in my head. My languid, worked-up body suddenly stiffens, my fingers digging into Jesse's shoulders. What am I doing? His girlfriend is prowling around outside, and I'm shacked up in here with her boyfriend's hands all over me. I'm hideous!

He deepens the kiss, pushing onto my lips to the point of pain, his tongue invading my mouth with urgency. I know he's trying to keep me in the game. He releases my thigh and brings his hands to my hips to keep me still. He thinks I'm going to run. I *am* going to run, and when he releases my lips, my head drops automatically.

'The door's locked,' he assures me quietly.

I can't carry on with this now! I may not like the woman, but I'm no home wrecker. I've done some damage, but I can stop this from progressing to the point of no return.

He brings one hand up to seize my jaw, tilting my head up and holding it firm as he focuses his green pools straight on me. His frown line is clear as he searches my eyes for something – hope, I think.

'Please,' he mouths.

I shake my head slightly in his grasp, my gaze plummeting to his chest, my eyes squeezing shut. His hand tightens on my hip as he shakes my jaw slightly in a desperate attempt to drag me out of the shell I've crawled into.

'Don't run.' He almost grinds the words out, making it sound more like an order.

'I can't do this,' I whisper, feeling his hands drop away from me on a frustrated growl.

'Jesse?' I hear Sarah's voice again, but closer this time.

In a complete daze, I scoop my dress up from the floor before running into the bathroom, slamming the door behind me and flipping the lock. I lean against the wood, virtually naked, trying to control my erratic breathing, and look up to the ceiling in an attempt to prevent the tears from falling.

I think I hear the sound of muffled voices coming from the bedroom, and I try to stabilise my breathing so I can listen to what's going on. But there's nothing. No noise, no talking … nothing. Damn me for being half-naked so I can't escape. Instead, I've resorted to fleeing into the bathroom, hiding like the desperate tart that I am. I'm truly ashamed of myself. I've been cheated on plenty of times. Over many a bottle of wine, I've condemned those 'other women', bad-mouthed them and wished them some truly merciless reprisals. Now I'm one of them. I groan, smacking the heel of my hand on my forehead.

Tart!

When I hear a door shut, I stiffen and listen carefully. Is

that him leaving, or is he coming back? Either way, I need to get dressed, so I search for my bra within the bunching material of my dress that's gathered in my hands – no bra. Shaking my dress out frantically, I pray for its appearance but still ... nothing. I sigh and step into my dress, pulling it up my body and reaching around to fasten the zip. I'll have to do without because I'm certainly not attempting to retrieve it from the bedroom.

I walk over to the mirror to inspect myself, and it's as I suspected; I look dreadful. My eyes are swimming with unshed tears, my lips swollen and red, and my cheeks are flushed. I look harassed; I *am* harassed. I try in vain to straighten myself out, so I can at least exit with a *bit* of dignity intact, but there's no escaping the distraught look I'm displaying. This will be the ultimate walk of shame.

I flinch when there's a knock on the door.

'Ava?'

I keep quiet. Oh God, he sounds almost angry. I pull my fingers through my hair and dab my eyes with tissue to soak up the tears. I look no better, but I know I'll feel better when I'm out of here, so gearing myself up to face the music, I gingerly unlock the door. It flies open, nearly knocking me off my feet, and Jesse fills the doorway. He *is* angry. And he's blocking my path.

I look past him into the bedroom, finding we're alone. He must be a bloody convincing liar because he's still shirtless, and there's no Sarah trying to rip my hair out. As if he has the right to look at me all disapproving and make me feel like a letdown. I push past him.

'Where the hell are you going?' he shouts after me.

I don't respond. I keep my pace up, grabbing my bag and stalking out onto the gallery landing, hearing Jesse curse as I make my escape.

'Ava!'

I take the stairs fast, glancing up as I go, spotting Jesse flying out of the suite, fighting to get his t-shirt on. Detouring into the bar to collect my phone, I find Mario serving some gentlemen, but my good manners prevent me from demanding it immediately, so I stand patiently and wait, fidgeting and flustering the whole time.

'Did you get what you came for?' Sarah's cold voice stabs at my flesh. Oh God, does she know? Is there a double meaning there?

I turn, plastering on a false smile. 'Measurements? Yes.'

She looks me over, her elbow resting on her hip, with her sloe gin and tonic suspended in front of her face. She knows.

Jesse races into the bar, skidding to a stop in front of us. I look at him in horror. Could he be any more obvious? I glance at Sarah to gauge her reaction to this little scene, finding her looking thoughtfully at us both. She definitely knows. I need to leave.

I turn back toward the bar. Thank God, Mario spots me. 'Miss O'Shea, here; you must try.' He hands me a shot of some sort.

'Do you have my phone, Mario?'

'You try,' he demands.

In my desperation to get out of here, I knock the whole thing back in one foul gulp and wince when it burns the back of my throat.

My mouth forms an O as I squeeze my eyes shut. 'Wow!'

'It is good?'

I blow out a long, hot breath, handing the glass back to him. 'Yes. It's very good.' He takes the glass, winks and hands me my phone.

Smoothing my dress and taking a deep breath, I turn to face the two people I never want to see again.

'You left this upstairs.' Ward hands me my folder but doesn't release it when I tug gently.

'Thank you.' I frown at him as he stares at me, his brow completely furrowed as he chews his bottom lip. He finally lets it go, and I tuck it in my bag. 'Good-bye.' I leave them both in the bar, making my way to my car. He can't pursue me with Sarah there to bear witness, and that is a major relief.

I get in and start my car, ignoring the voice in my head screaming *You're probably over the limit!* This is so irresponsible of me, but desperation leaves me with no alternative. I reverse out of the space and see Jesse come bounding out of the doors. He can't be serious!

I frantically shift into first gear, pulling off sharply and leaving a cloud of dust in my wake. As the fog of dust clears behind me, I see Jesse in the rearview mirror, throwing his arms around in the air like some raving lunatic.

I speed down the tree-covered driveway, my head spinning – a mixture of drink and distress – trying to concentrate on the road ahead. Glancing down at the dashboard, I note I'm driving stupidly fast and without the headlights or my seatbelt on. My head is all over the place.

The gates come into view, and I release the accelerator. 'Open, please, open,' I plead as I pull to a standstill. 'Open!' I thump the steering wheel in frustration and the horn screams, sending me on a startled jump in my seat. The sound of a car approaching drags my eyes to the rearview mirror.

'Oh, fucking hell!' I curse as the headlights get closer.

It skids to a stop behind me, the door flies open and Jesse gets out. He strides forward at a leisurely rate, but I'm not trying to kid myself that he doesn't look fuming. Just because he didn't get his rocks off? I dramatically slump my arms and head onto the steering wheel, feeling completely flattened. My aim to escape, no questions asked or explanations given, has been well and truly dashed – not that I owe him any explanations.

The driver door is yanked open and he grabs my arm, gently pulling me from the car and taking my keys from the ignition.

'Ava.' He looks at me all disapproving. I want to yell at him, but he gets in first, 'You're half pissed! I swear to God, if you'd have hurt yourself ...'

I wince at his words, mentally scolding myself for being so reckless. I stand in front of him, soaking up his displeasure, feeling humiliated and pathetic. He grasps my jaw in his hand to look down at me. He's moving in for a kiss; I can see it in his eyes. Oh, please. I really don't need this. I pull my face from his grip.

'Are you okay?' he asks softly, reaching for me again.

I brush him off. 'Funnily enough, no, I'm not. Why did you do that?'

'Isn't it obvious?'

'You want me.'

'More than anything.'

'I've never met anyone so full of themselves. Did you plan this? When you rang me yesterday, was this your intention all along?'

'Yes.' There's absolutely no apology in his tone. 'I want you.'

I have no idea how to deal with this. He wants me, so he took me. 'Can you open the gates, please?' I start walking toward them, but they're still unmoving when I reach them. I swing around in the most threatening manner I can muster. 'Open the damn gates!'

'You honestly think I'm going to let you go wandering aimlessly out there when you're miles from home?'

'I'll call a cab.'

'Absolutely not. I'll take you.'

I look at his car. It's an Aston Martin – all black, shiny and beautiful. It figures.

'Just open the fucking gates!' I scream at him.

'Watch your fucking mouth!'

Watch my fucking mouth? I want to thump him, fall to my knees and cry in frustration. I feel such a fool – humiliated and ashamed. 'I'm not prepared to be a notch on your busy bedpost,' I spit. I have a little more self-respect than that ... kind of.

'You actually believe that?'

Our confrontation is interrupted when his mobile starts ringing. It's swiftly removed from his pocket. 'John?' He turns and starts pacing. 'Yeah ... okay.' The call is ended quickly. 'I'll take you home.' He holds his hand out.

'No! Please, just open the gates.' I'm pleading, and it wasn't the tone I was aiming for.

'No, I'm not letting you out there on your own, Ava. End of. You're coming with me.'

I snap my head up when a car pulls off the main road.

'Fuck!' Jesse roars, yanking his phone back out of his pocket, at the same time trying to make a grab for me.

The gates start to open, and I run to grab my bag from my car.

'John, don't open the fucking gates,' he yells into his phone, then pauses. 'Well, tell Sarah not to!'

As soon as the opening is big enough to allow, I squeeze through, just as they start closing again. I see Jesse run to his car, bashing something on the dashboard, and the gates start opening again. I get my phone out and dial a cab number as I start walking down the lane. The call connects and I go to speak, but the wind is knocked clean out of me when I'm grabbed around my waist.

I scream as I'm hoisted from my feet, spun around and tossed over his shoulder.

'You're not wandering around on your fucking own, lady.' His tone is full of authority, making me feel younger, or him older – I'm not sure which.

'What's it got to do with you?' I spit. I'm boiling mad and bobbing up and down as he strides back to his car.

'Apparently, nothing, but I do have a conscience. You're not leaving here unless it's in my car. Do you understand me?' He places me on my feet and guides me into his car before slamming the door and getting into my Mini to move it to the side of the driveway.

I smirk as I watch him slide the seat back as far as it will go, but even at its farthest away from the wheel, he still struggles to cram his tall, lean body in. He looks pretty stupid.

He huffs his way back and throws himself in his car, giving me a ferocious scowl before he starts the car and roars off.

The journey home is painfully silent and frighteningly fast. The man is a menace on the roads, and I wish he would at least put the radio on to rid the car of the awkward silence.

I begrudgingly admire the interior of his DBS. I'm cradled in the seat, with acres of black leather surrounding me, as I stare out of the window the whole way home. I feel his eyes fixed on me every so often, but I ignore it, concentrating on the guttural roar of the engine as it eats up the road ahead. What has just happened?

He pulls up outside Kate's after I direct him with short, sharp instructions, and I let myself out.

'Ava?' I hear him call me, but I shut the car door and race up the path to the house, cursing out loud when I realise he's got my car keys. I turn to make my way back down the path, but I hear the roar of his engine burning off down the road.

I screw my face up in my own private disgust. He's done that on purpose so I have to call him and ask nicely for them back. He'll be waiting a long time. I would rather go without my car. I traipse back up the path and bash on the door.

'Where are your keys?' Kate asks when she answers.

I think quickly. 'My car's having some new brakes. I forgot to remove my house key.'

She accepts my excuse with no further questions. 'There's a spare key in the pot by the kitchen window.' She runs back up the stairs and I follow, immediately opening a bottle of wine before rummaging through the fridge for something to eat. Nothing takes my fancy. Wine will do.

'Yes, please.' Kate comes breezing into the kitchen. She's already jimmy-jammed up, and I can't wait to join her. I pour her a glass while trying to morph my face into anything other than the shocked expression that I know is still visible.

'Good day?' I ask.

She collapses into one of the mismatching chairs around the chunky pine table. 'I spent most of the day collecting cake stands. You would think people would be kind enough to return them.' She takes a sip of her wine, sighing in appreciation.

I join her at the table. 'You need to start asking for a deposit.'

'I know. Hey, I have a date tomorrow night.'

'With who?' I ask, wondering if this one will make it past the first.

'A very yummy client. He stopped by to collect a cake for his niece's first birthday – a Jungle Junction cake. How sweet is that?'

'Very sweet,' I agree. 'How did that come about?'

'I asked him.' She shrugs.

I laugh. Her confidence is charming. She must hold the world record for first dates. The only long-term relationship she's ever had was with my brother, but we don't talk about that. Since they split and Dan moved to Australia, Kate has been on endless dates, none of them progressing past the first.

'I'm going to get changed and give my mum a call.' I get up, taking my wine with me. 'I'll meet you on the sofa soon.'

'Cool.'

I really need to speak to my mum. Kate's my best friend, but you can't beat your mother when you just want comfort. Not that I can tell her why I need comforting. She would be horrified.

*

Once I'm changed into my baggy pants and a vest top, I flop onto my bed and dial my mum. It rings once before she answers.

'Ava?' Her voice is shrill, but still soothing.

'Hi, Mum.'

'Ava? Ava? Joseph, I can't hear her. Am I doing it right? Ava?'

'I'm here, Mum. Can you hear me?'

'Ava? Joseph, it's broken. I can't hear anything. Ava!'

I hear my dad's mumbled moans in the background before he comes on the line. 'Hello?'

'Hi, Dad,' I yell.

'You don't have to bloody shout!'

'She couldn't hear me.'

'That's because she had the bloody thing upside down, stupid woman.'

I hear my mum laugh in the background, followed by a slapping sound that is, without doubt, her walloping my dad's shoulder. 'Is she there? Can you hear her? Give me it here.' There's a little scuffle before she's back on the line. 'Ava? Are you there?'

'Yes!' Why didn't I just ring the landline? She's insisted I ring her new mobile so she can get the hang of it, but good God, she's hard work. She's only forty-seven, but a complete technophobe.

'Ah. That's better, I can hear you now. How are you?'

'Good. I'm good, Mum. You?'

'Yes, everything's fine. Guess what? We have exciting news.' She doesn't give me a chance to guess. 'Your brother's coming home to visit!'

I sit up in excitement. Dan's coming home? I've not seen my brother for six months. He's living the dream on the Gold Coast as a surf instructor. Kate's going to freak out over this news, and not in a good way.

'When?' I demand.

'Next Sunday. Isn't it exciting?'

'Do you know what his plans are?' I press.

'He's flying into Heathrow, coming straight down to Cornwall for the week to see me and Dad, and then he's making his way back up to London. Will you come with him? You've not visited in weeks.'

I suddenly feel rotten. I've not seen my parents for nearly eight weeks. 'I've been so busy at work, Mum. I've got the Lusso launch. It's hectic. I'll try my best, okay?'

'I know, darling. How's Kate?' she asks. Mum still loves Kate. She was as devastated as me when Kate and Dan called it quits.

'She's great.'

'Good. Have you heard from Matt?' she asks tentatively. I know she's hoping it's a big resounding *NO*. She wasn't devastated at all when Matt and I split up. He wasn't Mum's favourite person. Come to think of it, Matt wasn't many people's favourite person.

'No, I'm just getting on with things,' I inform her, hearing her sigh in relief. I won't volunteer exactly what I have been getting on with.

'Okay. Joseph, get the door, will you? Ava, I've got to go. Sue's here to pick me up for yoga.'

'Okay, Mum. I'll ring next week.'

'Okay. Good luck for your launch and have some fun!' she orders.

''Bye, Mum.' I hang up. Dan's coming home. That's cheered me up a little, and I always feel better when I've spoken to my mum. They're miles away and I miss them like crazy, but I'm comforted by the fact that they've escaped the rat race of London, taking early retirement in Newquay after Dad's heart attack.

My phone starts ringing and I look at the screen, expecting to see my mother's number – she's probably forgot to lock the keypad and sat on it – but it's not. It's Jesse Ward.

Ughhhhhhhhh! 'Reject,' I huff as I throw my phone on my bed and leave my bedroom to go and join Kate on the sofa, hearing it ring again as I walk down the hall.

Chapter Five

'Morning,' I sing to Tom as I sashay past his desk on Thursday.

He looks up at me over his thick-framed spectacles – a blatant fashion statement and Tom's effort to be taken more seriously. I should tell him to lose the canary yellow dress shirt and grey trousers that are verging on leggings. That would do the trick.

'Did someone get laid?' He smirks. 'Join the club, I'm exhausted!'

'Tom, you're such a tart.' I feign a disgusted look as I throw my bag down by my desk. 'Anything to report?' I ask to divert the conversation from Tom's sexcapades.

'Nope, I'm just going over to Mrs Baines to give her a cuddle. You know, she rang me at eleven last night to ask if she could expect the electricians in this morning. Interrupted me right in the middle of ...'

'Enough!' I hold my hands up. 'I don't want to know.' I sit down, swinging my chair around to face him.

'Apologies, darling. It was really good, though!' He winks and springs up from his chair, air kissing me from ten feet away. '*Au revoir*, darling!'

''Bye. Oh, where's Victoria?' I shout after him.

'Appointments,' he calls, shutting the door behind him.

I turn to face my desk as Sally places a coffee in front of me. I pick it up immediately, taking a sip while she hovers at my desk nervously.

'Patrick called to remind you that he's not in today,' she says.

'Thank you, Sally. Did you have a good weekend?'

She smiles, nodding enthusiastically as she pushes her glasses up her nose. 'I did, thank you for asking. I finished my cross-stitch and cleaned all of the windows, inside and out. It was wonderful,' she says dreamily as she scurries off to file some invoices.

Cleaning windows? Wonderful? The girl is sweet, but good Lord, she's as dull as dish water.

I spend a few hours working through my e-mail to clear my inbox. I check that the final clean-up of Lusso is complete and grab my phone when it starts dancing across my desk, rolling my eyes when I see who's illuminating my screen. He just will not give up. Yesterday was a relentless bombardment of calls – all of which I rejected – and he's still at it. I've got to speak to the man eventually. He has something I need ... my car.

At one o'clock, I leave the office to meet Kate for lunch.

'Are there any decent men left in the world?' she asks thought-fully, dabbing her mouth with a napkin. 'I'm losing the will to live.'

'It wasn't that bad, was it?' I ask. Her date yesterday evening was a failure. When she walked into the apartment at nine-thirty, I knew it couldn't be good news.

She drops her napkin on her empty plate, pushing it away. 'Ava, when a man gets a calculator out at the end of a meal to work out what you owe, it's usually not a good sign.'

'So, you won't be seeing him again?'

She scoffs. 'No, the bill saga was bad enough. When he dropped me home in the taxi and accepted the twenty I offered him, it finished me off.'

'You were a cheap date.' I giggle.

'Yeah.' She picks up her phone and starts tapping away at the screen, holding it up to show me. 'One BLT and two waters, you owe twelve quid.' We both have a little laugh at Kate's failed date. I love that she can be so lighthearted about it. Kate maintains that it will happen when it happens. I'm with her on this.

'When will your car be ready?' she asks.

I soon stop laughing. She's supposed to be borrowing it to visit her nan in Yorkshire on Saturday, and it's Thursday already. I need to sort this out. 'I'll give the garage a ring later,' I assure her.

'I don't mind taking the van.'

'No, it's fine. I don't think Margo will get you there.' She's a twenty-year-old, hot pink VW camper van that spits and fires all over London on cake deliveries.

My phone shouts and Kate leans over to see who's calling me. I whip it off the table far too hastily, but it's too late. I look at her nervously as I red button him again, before placing it back on the table as casually as I can. My jumpy reaction doesn't get past Kate. Not much does.

'Jesse,' she says with an arched brow. 'What would he want?'

I've not shared any of the hideous events of Tuesday with Kate. I'm too ashamed.

I shrug. 'Who knows?'

'Have there been any more suggestive texts?'

Oh, more than texts. Kate would thrive on my drama, which is exactly why I've not told her. If I don't hear the words out loud, then I can almost pretend it didn't happen ... almost.

'No,' I answer on a sigh.

She looks at me questioningly, making me feel like I'm under examination.

'You deserve some fun,' she says thoughtfully. 'After Matt, you definitely deserve some fun.'

'I know,' I agree. 'I've got to get back to work.' I lean over, giving Kate a peck on the cheek. 'Luv ya.'

'Yeah, ditto. I'll be late tonight. There's a cake convention at the Hilton.' She gets up, waving me away when I try to give her some money for lunch. 'It's my turn.'

We leave each other outside the bar, Kate heading back to her workshop, me back to the office.

When I get home, I change and collapse on the sofa, grabbing my phone up when it rings. It's a number I don't recognise.

'Ava O'Shea,' I announce down the line. There's no reply. 'Hello?'

'Are you alone?'

The voice hits me like a sledgehammer to the gut. Oh, fucking hell. I stand up and sit back down again, visions of him half naked before me, pleading to me with his eyes, starting to assault my mind. This is exactly why I've been avoiding his calls. The influence he has on me is unsettling and most unwelcome. I can't stop shaking.

Why didn't his name come up on my phone? 'No,' I lie, a sweat breaking out across my brow.

I hear him sigh. It's a loud sigh. 'Why are you lying to me?'

I jump back up from the sofa. How does he know? Darting across the lounge, my wine swishing out of my glass, I look out of the window to the road, but I can't see his car. In a panic and with a lump in my throat, I hang up, but it rings again immediately. I chuck my phone onto the couch and let it ring off. And then it rings again.

'Go away!'

I pace the lounge, biting my nails and swigging my wine. Tuesday's events flood back into my mind, but not the bad stuff. Oh, no … it's all the bloody good stuff. How he made me feel, how his hands felt on me – everything before I heard the shrill, cold voice of his girlfriend. I slam a lid on my thoughts immediately and tense when my phone declares a text message. Creeping cautiously toward the sofa, like my phone might launch itself upward and bite me, I swipe it up and open the text.

Answer your phone!

It rings again in my hand, making me jump, even though I completely expected it. He's relentless. I let it ring off again and, quite childishly, text back,

No

I pace some more, up and down, swigging wine and clutching my phone. It's not long before another text arrives.

Fine, I'm coming in.

'What? Oh no!' I shout at my phone. It is one thing ignoring the phone, but it's a whole other level of resistance trying to repel him when he's flesh and blood and looking right at me.

I frantically pull up my call log to call him. It rings once.

'Too late, Ava,' he drawls down the line. I stare at my phone in uncertainty, and then the banging starts.

I run onto the landing, leaning over the banister as he hammers on the door.

'Open the door, Ava.' He bangs again.

What's he thinking? Is he that desperate?

Bang, bang, bang!

'Ava, I'm not going anywhere until you talk to me, please.'

Bang, bang, bang!

'I've got your keys, Ava. I'll let myself in.'

Oh shit. He would as well. Okay, I'll let him in, listen to what he has to say, and then he can leave. Anyway, I need my car back. I'll just have to keep as far away from him as possible, keep my eyes closed and hold my breath so I can't smell him. I must not let him breach my defences. I put my glass down on the table at the top of the stairs and look at myself in the mirror. My hair is piled up on top of my head, but at least I haven't taken my makeup off yet. It could be worse. I mentally slap myself for caring. The worse I look the better, surely? He needs telling to back off.

Bang, bang, bang!

I storm down the stairs in confident, determined strides and open the door on a huff. I'm doomed. I keep underestimating – or forgetting – the effect this man has on me. I'm trembling already.

His hands are braced on the door frame as he looks up at me through hooded lids, panting and looking really quite pissed off. His blond hair is all disheveled, he has his stubble back, and his pale pink shirt is undone at the collar, tucked into grey trousers. He looks delicious.

He punches holes into me with his green eyes. 'Why did you stop it?' His breathing is laboured.

'What?' I ask impatiently. He's here to ask me that? Isn't it obvious?

He grits his teeth. 'Why did you run out on me?'

'Because it was a mistake,' I grate, through equally gritted teeth. My irritation at his audacity is overpowering the other more unwelcome effect he's having on me.

'It wasn't a mistake, and you know it,' he grinds. 'The only mistake was me letting you go.'

I can't do this. I go to push the door shut, but his hand slams against the other side to stop it.

'Oh no you don't.' He pushes against me, easily overpowering me, and steps into the hallway, slamming the door behind him. 'You're not running this time. You're going to face the music.'

With bare feet, I'm almost a foot shorter than him, which makes me feel small and weak as he towers over me, still breathing hard. I back away, but he walks forward, keeping the distance between us minimal.

'You need to leave. Kate will be home in a minute.'

He stops his approach, scowling at me. 'Stop lying,' he snaps, slapping my hand away from my hair. 'Quit the bullshit, Ava.'

I have no idea what to say to him. Defence isn't working – maybe disinterest. He's incredibly thick-skinned and obviously used to getting what he wants.

I turn away to walk back up the stairs. 'Why are you here?' I ask, but before I make it very far, he's behind me, grabbing at my wrist, and I'm spun around to face him. The contact puts me on instant red alert.

'You know why,' he spits.

I yank my wrist from his grip, backing up until my arse hits the wall behind me. 'Because you want to hear how loud I'll scream?'

'No!'

'You are undeniably the most arrogant arsehole I've ever met. I'm not interested in becoming a sexual conquest.'

'Conquest?' he snorts, turning away and commencing pointless pacing. 'What fucking planet are you on, woman?'

I stand frozen in utter shock, reeling at his front. My unease is disappearing and my earlier irritation is swiftly converting into boiling rage. 'Get out!'

He stops pacing and looks at me. 'No!' he yells, recommencing his marching.

I start thinking of how to get him out of the house, but I'm never going to be able to manhandle him and touching him would be a massive mistake. 'I'm not fucking interested! Get out.' My shaky voice lets down my cool front, but I stand firm.

'Watch your fucking mouth!'

Oh, the cheek. 'Get out!'

'Okay,' he says simply, quitting the marching to hammer me with his stare. 'Look me in the eyes and tell me you don't want to see me again, and I'll go. You'll never have to lay eyes on me again.'

The thought of not seeing him again actually sends a nasty ache to my stomach, which is, of course, completely ridiculous.

He's a virtual stranger to me, but he makes me feel … I'm not sure exactly what it is.

When I say nothing, he starts advancing toward me, his long, even strides having him directly in front of me in just a few paces. There's barely an inch between us.

'Say it,' he breathes.

I can't get my mouth to function. I'm aware of my shallow breathing, pounding heart and a dull throb in my groin, and I'm alert to similar reactions emanating from him. I can see his heart hammering under his pale pink shirt. I can feel his heavy, minty breath on my face. I can't vouch for the throb, but I suspect it's there. The sexual tension ricocheting between our close bodies is tangible.

'You can't, can you?' he whispers.

I can't! I'm trying, I'm trying really hard, but the bloody words won't come out. I've been catapulted back to our previous encounter, except this time there's no risk of being interrupted by unfriendly girlfriends. There's nothing to stop me, apart from my conscience, but that's drowning in desire right now.

He places the tip of his finger on my shoulder, his touch sending an inferno racing through me, and slowly, lightly, he drags his finger up the column of my neck until it rests at the sensitive pressure point under my ear.

My heart goes into overdrive.

'Boom … boom … boom,' he breathes. 'I can feel it, Ava.'

I go rigid, pushing myself further into the wall. 'Please, leave.' I barely get the words out.

'Put your hand over my heart,' he whispers, grabbing my hand and placing it on his chest. He needn't have done that. I can see his heart going ten to the dozen under his shirt. I didn't need to feel it to know that. He's just as affected by me as I am by him.

'Why are you trying to stop the inevitable?' Wrapping his fingers around my neck, he tilts my face up so I meet his eyes.

I'm immediately consumed by them. His long lashes are fanning his cheekbones as he leans down so his lips brush my ear. I release a quiet gasp.

'There it is,' he murmurs as he trails feathery light kisses down the side of my throat. 'You feel it.'

I do. I'm incapable of stopping this. My brain has shut down, my body is taking over and as his mouth works its way across my jaw, I resign myself to the fact that I'm lost – to him, I'm lost. But then I hear the sound of a mobile phone ringing. It's not mine, but the interruption is enough to snap me out of the trance he sends me into. Oh God, it's probably Sarah.

I raise my hands to his firm chest and shove him away. 'Stop, please!'

He pulls away, yanking his phone from his pocket. 'Fuck!' He rejects the call and swings furious eyes to me. 'You still haven't said it.'

I'm staggered at my inability to utter some very simple words. 'I'm not interested,' I whisper. I sound desperate, and I know it. 'You have to stop this. Whatever you think you felt, what you think *I* felt, you're mistaken.' I don't mention Sarah because that would be admitting that I can feel something, that she's the only reason I'm stopping this. It's not, of course. There's the obvious age gap, the fact that he has 'heartbreaker' written all over him, and the even more important part … he's a cheater.

He laughs a proper amused laugh. 'Think? Ava, don't you dare try and pass this off as a figment of my imagination. Just then, was that my imagination? Give me some credit.'

'You give me some fucking credit!'

'Mouth!' he shouts.

'I told you to leave,' I say calmly.

'And I told you, look me in the eyes and tell me you don't want me.' He stares at me expectantly, like he knows I can't say it.

'I don't want you,' I murmur, looking straight into his green pools and wincing as the words cause me physical pain.

He inhales sharply, looking wounded. 'I don't believe you.'

'You should.' I define the words clearly, and it takes every bit of strength I have.

We stare at each other for what seems like an eternity, but I'm the first to look away. I can think of nothing more to say, and I silently implore him to leave before I take the dangerous path I know he'll be.

He runs his hands through his hair in frustration, curses profusely, and then stalks out. When the front door slams behind him, I allow air to rush into my lungs as I sag against the wall.

That was irrefutably the most difficult thing I've ever done, which is ridiculous when it should've been the easiest. I can't even begin to understand the whys and wherefores of it. His wounded expression when I denied that I wanted him nearly crippled me. I wanted to scream, 'I felt it too!' but where would that have got me? I know exactly where – against the wall with Jesse buried deep inside me, and while the thought of that makes me shiver with pleasure, it would be a gargantuan mistake. I feel riddled with guilt already at my deplorable behaviour. The man is a cheating arse. An Adonis, but a cheating arse, nonetheless. Everything about this man screams trouble. And he's still got my fucking keys.

Chapter Six

I'm wide awake and my alarm hasn't even gone off yet. I didn't sleep a wink. On a long, drawn-out sigh, I drag myself out of bed and head for the bathroom to take a shower. I've got a busy day at Lusso ahead of me, so I may as well get started.

I'm going to be on my feet all day, traipsing around the complex ensuring everything is just right, so I chuck on some baggy ripped jeans – I can't bear to throw them away – a white burnt-out t-shirt and my flip-flops. Scraping my hair into a loose, messy up-do, I pray it behaves later when I pin it up for the evening. I doubt I'll have time to come home and shower, so I get my mini suitcase and load it with everything I'll need to shower at Lusso later. I retrieve a suit bag and put my knee-length, cherry red pencil dress in, smoothing it neatly while quietly hoping it doesn't crease. Last, I grab my black suede heels and my black onyx studs, and check that my work case is loaded with everything I'll need. It's going to be a ball ache lugging it all on the Tube, but I have no other option without my car. Kate might well be taking Margo to Yorkshire.

As I walk down the stairs, I'm surprised to see my car keys lying on the door mat. So the man's seen sense and freed my car. Does this mean he's also seen sense and given up pursuing me? Has he got the message? Perhaps he has, because there have been no calls or texts since he steamed out last night. Am I disappointed? I don't have time to consider this.

'I'm off,' I shout through to Kate. 'My car's back.'

She pokes her head around the door of her workshop.

'Great, good luck. I'll be there later to drink all of the expensive champagne.'

'Oh, yes. See you later.' I run down the path, halting when I see a cheap mobile phone smashed to pieces in the middle of the pavement. I know immediately where that's come from. I kick it into the gutter and continue to my car, loading my things into the boot and jumping into the driver's seat, only to find myself miles away from the steering wheel.

Laughing, I shift the seat forward so my feet reach the pedals and start her up, jumping out of my skin when the stereo blasts Blur from the speakers. Is his lack of hearing an indication of his age? I turn it down, faltering when the words of the track register. It's 'Country house'. I fight the small part of me that wants to laugh at his little joke and remove the disc from the stereo. I don't think I've ever come across anyone so conceited in all my life. I replace the unwanted CD with a Ministry of Sound *Chillout Sessions* and head for St Katharine Docks.

When I pull up outside Lusso, I present my face to the camera and the gates open immediately, allowing me to park up. I see the caterers unloading crockery and glasses as I get my work case from the boot and head into the building. I've been here a million times, but I'm still completely stunned by the pure extravagance of the place.

As I walk into the foyer, I see Clive, one of the concierges, playing with the new computer equipment. He's part of a team who'll provide a six-star hotel-style service, organising anything from grocery shopping and theatre tickets to helicopter charters and dinner reservations. I cross the marble floor, which has been polished to within an inch of its life, and head toward Clive's huge, curved, concierge desk, spotting dozens of black vases and hundreds of red roses, placed carefully to the side. At least I won't have to chase the delivery of those.

'Good morning, Clive,' I say, approaching his desk.

He looks up from one of the screens, the panic on his friendly face clear. 'Ava, I've read this manual four times in a week and I'm still clueless. We never had anything like this at The Dorchester.'

'It can't be that difficult,' I soothe the old boy. 'Have you asked the surveillance team?'

He throws his glasses down on the desk in exasperation, rubbing his eyes. 'Yes, three times now. They must think I'm daft.'

'You'll be fine,' I assure him. 'When do they start moving in?'

'Tomorrow. Are you all set for tonight?'

'Ask me again this afternoon. I'll see you in a bit.'

'Okay, love.' He turns his attention back to his instruction manual, muttering under his breath.

I traipse across the floor and punch in the code for the penthouse's private elevator, and once I've boarded and been delivered to the top floor, I set about transporting and spreading the vases and flowers between the fifteen floors of the building. Arranging these will keep me busy for a while.

At ten-thirty, I'm back in the foyer and arranging the last of my flowers on the console tables that line the foyer.

'I have flowers for a Miss O'Shea.'

I look up, seeing a young girl gazing around at the impressive lobby. 'Sorry?'

She points to her clipboard. 'I have a delivery for Miss O'Shea.'

I roll my eyes. Don't tell me they've duplicated an order of over four hundred red roses. That really would take incompetence to a whole new level. 'I've already taken delivery of the flowers.' I say tiredly, walking toward her. I notice the van outside, but it's not the florist I ordered through.

'Have you?' She looks a bit panicky as she flicks through the papers on her clipboard.

'What have you got?' I ask.

'A bouquet of calla lilies for Miss ...' She looks at her clip-board again. 'Miss Ava O'Shea.'

'I'm Ava O'Shea.'

'Cool. I'll be two seconds.' She runs off, returning swiftly with the biggest spray of calla lilies I've ever seen – stunning, white, clean flowers surrounded by stacks of deep green foliage. 'This place is like Fort Knox!' she exclaims, handing me the bouquet.

Understated elegance.

My stomach does a few cartwheels as I sign the delivery girl's paperwork and take the flowers from her, finding the card among the forest of green.

I'm so sorry. Forgive me, please. x

Staring at the card, I read it over and over. He's already apologised for his inappropriate behaviour and look where that got me. I start to wonder how he would know I'm here, but then I remember him picking out Lusso in my portfolio. It wouldn't take a lot of effort to find out the launch date and figure I would be here. He's never going to give up, is he?

I place the flowers on the concierge desk. 'Here, Clive. Let's pretty up all this black marble.' He looks up briefly before re-turning to scratching his head, looking overwhelmed. I leave him to it, getting on with my walk-through to ensure everything is in place and ready.

Victoria turns up at five-thirty, looking her usual immaculate self – all blond hair, blue eyes and overdone.

'Sorry I'm late. The traffic's a nightmare and there's nowhere to park.' She gazes around. 'They're all reserved for guests. What can I do? I'm so excited!' she sings at me while stroking the walls of the penthouse.

'I'm all done. I just need you to do a walk-through to make

sure there's nothing I've missed.' I lead her into the main space.

'Oh my God, Ava, it looks amazing!'

'It's great, isn't it? I've never had such a colossal budget. It was fun spending so much of someone else's money.' We giggle together. 'Have you seen the kitchen?' I ask.

'I've not seen it complete. I bet it's incredible.'

'It is; go and take a look. I'm going to get myself ready in the spa. I've done everything in the other apartments so concentrate up here. This is where the action will be. Make sure all of the cushions are plumped and in place. If there's anything you're not sure of, make a note. Okay?'

'Done,' she confirms, disappearing into the kitchen.

An hour later, after utilizing all of Lusso's fancy spa facilities, I'm ready. My dress is creaseless and my hair is behaving. I take a little wander around, a little sad that this will be my last time here. It will soon be crowded with business people and high society, so I make the most of my last opportunity to savour the sheer magnificence of the place. I still can't believe this is my work. I smile to myself as I stand in the colossal open space. Bi-folding doors lead to an L-shaped terrace, with limestone paving, a decked area, sun loungers and a huge Jacuzzi. There's a study, dining room, a huge archway leading into a ridiculously large kitchen, and a back-lit onyx staircase that rises to the four en-suite bedrooms and a massive master suite. The spa, fitness centre and swimming pool on the ground floor of the building are exclusive to the residents of Lusso, but the penthouse boasts its own gym. It's stunning. Whoever's bought this place definitely likes the finer things in life and for a cool ten million, they've got it.

I make my way back to the kitchen and find Victoria.

'All done,' she declares as she hoovers up a stray crumb on the marble worktop.

'Well, let's drink.' I smirk and pick up two glasses of champagne, handing one to Victoria.

'Here's to you, Ava. Stylish in body *and* in mind.' She giggles, raising her glass in a toast, and we both swig then sigh. 'Wow! This is good.'

'*Ca'del Bosco, Cuvée Annamaria Clementi, 1993.* It's Italian, of course.' I raise my brow and Victoria giggles again.

I hear chatter coming from the entrance hall, so I wander out of the kitchen, finding Tom gawping like a goldfish and Patrick smiling proudly.

'Ava, this is some serious special, darling!' Tom runs at me, throwing his arms around my body. He pulls back, looking me up and down. 'Love the dress. Very tight.'

I wish I could say the same for Tom, who takes colour clash to extreme levels. I squint at his bright blue shirt and red tie combo.

'Put the girl down, Tom. You'll crease her,' Patrick grumbles, gently shoving him aside and leaning down to peck me on the cheek. 'I'm very proud of you, flower. You've done a marvellous job, and between me and you,' he leans into my ear and whispers, 'the developers have hinted they want you on board for the next project in Holland Park.' He winks at me, his wrinkled face wrinkling further. 'Now, where's that champagne?'

'This way.' I lead them into the huge kitchen, hearing more cooing from Tom. The place really is that special.

'Cheers!' I announce after handing them all a glass of champagne.

'Cheers!' They all raise their glasses.

I spend a few hours being introduced to high society and explaining my inspiration behind the design. Journalists from architecture and interior magazines swan around taking photographs and generally poking about and, much to my displeasure, hustle me onto a velvet chaise lounge for a shot. Patrick drags me from pillar to post, proclaiming his pride and insisting to anyone who will listen that I've singlehandedly put Rococo Union on the designers' map. I blush profusely, repeatedly playing down his declarations.

I'm thankful when Kate shows up. I usher her into the kitchen, thrust a glass of champagne in her hand, and take another for myself.

'Bit posh, eh?' she muses, gazing around the plush kitchen. 'It makes my place look like a cluttered mess.'

I laugh at the referral to her cute, homely town house that looks like Cath Kidston has vomited, sneezed, and coughed all over it. 'You mean impressive, I'm sure.'

'Yes, that too. I couldn't live here, though,' she says with no shame at all.

I feign a hurt face and wait for her to backtrack, but she doesn't. Instead, she's looking over my shoulder with the biggest smirk on her face. I swing around to find out what's caught her amused attention.

Oh no!

'He's like a bad penny, isn't he?' Kate remarks coolly.

Oh, she has no idea.

Wearing a navy suit and pale blue shirt, one hand in his pocket and the other holding a file, Jesse, as always, looks like a fucking God. He's with the acting estate agent, but not paying a bit of attention. No, his eyes are firmly set on me.

'Shit!' I curse, turning back to Kate. She drags her gaze from Jesse and onto me, her eyes dancing with delight.

'You know,' she sips her drink through her grin, 'this is not the behaviour of someone supposedly unmoved by a certain someone, Ava.'

'I went to The Manor on Tuesday and nearly slept with him,' I blurt.

'What!' Kate splutters, grabbing a napkin to mop up the trail of champagne that's dripping down her chin.

'He apologised for the text he sent. I went back to The Manor and he had the big guy lock me in a room. He was waiting for me half naked.'

'Get out! Oh my God. Who's the big guy?'

The urgency to bring Kate up to speed has me ignoring her question and spitting out facts in a rush. 'It was a disaster. I ran out when I heard his girlfriend calling him. Then Ward turned up at the house last night making demands.'

'Fuck! What sort of demands?'

'I don't know. The man's an arrogant arse. He asked me how loud I'd scream when he fucks me.'

She spits more champagne. 'He what? Fuck, Ava, he's coming over. He's coming over!' She shifts on the spot, her eyes still skipping with amusement.

I start planning my escape, but before my brain can even instruct my legs to move, I feel him behind me; I can smell him, too.

'Nice to see you again, Kate,' he drawls. 'Ava?'

I remain with my back to him, knowing all too well that if I turn to acknowledge him, I'll be hauled into the hazardous place that is Jesse Ward's realm – a place where I struggle to maintain any rational thinking.

Kate's eyes are darting between us, waiting for one of us to say something. I certainly won't be.

'Jesse.' She nods at him. 'Excuse me. I need to powder my nose.' She places her empty glass on the worktop and leaves, and I mentally curse her arse to Hell.

He circles around me so he's facing me. 'You look stunning,' he murmurs.

'You said I wouldn't have to see you again.' I challenge him, ignoring his compliment.

'I didn't know you would be here.'

I look at him tiredly. 'You sent me flowers.'

'Oh, so I did.' A smile tickles the edge of his lips.

I don't have time for his games. 'Please, excuse me.' I go to sidestep him, but he moves with me, effectively blocking my path.

'I was hoping for a tour.'

'I'll get Victoria. She'll be happy to show you around.'

'I would prefer you.'

'You don't get a fuck with a tour,' I snap.

He frowns. 'Will you watch your mouth?'

'Sorry,' I mutter indignantly. 'And put my seat back when you drive my car.'

He grin's a real boyish grin, and I'm even more furious with myself when my heart speeds up. I mustn't let him see the effect he has on me.

'And leave my music alone!'

'I'm sorry.' His eyes flicker with mischievousness. It's so bloody sexy. 'Are you okay? You look a little shaky.' He reaches out, softly running his finger down my bare arm. 'Is something affecting you?'

I jerk away. 'Not at all.' I need to get off this line of conversation. 'Did you want a tour?'

'I would love a tour.' He looks pleased with himself.

On a huff, I lead him out of the kitchen and into the massive living space. 'Lounge,' I wave my hand about in the general space around us. 'You've seen the kitchen,' I say over my shoulder as I walk through the open space and onto the terrace. 'View,' I maintain my tired tone, hearing him laugh lightly behind me.

I lead him back through the lounge to the workout room, not saying a word as we trek through the penthouse. Jesse shakes hands, greeting various people on our travels, but I don't pause to allow him time to stop and chat. I march on in a bid to get this over with as soon as possible. Damn this place for being so big.

'Gym,' I state, walking in and abruptly leaving again when he enters. I head for the stairs, hearing him laugh behind me.

I take the back-lit, onyx staircase, proceeding to open and shut doors, one at a time, while declaring what lies beyond. When we reach the pièce de résistance, the master suite, I wave my hand around at the dressing room and en-suite bathroom. The place really does deserve more passion and time than I'm devoting.

'You're an expert tour guide, Ava,' he teases, regarding one of my favourite pieces of art. 'Care to enlighten me on the photographer?'

'Giuseppe Cavalli,' I toss the name at him, folding my arms over my chest.

'It's good. Is there any particular reason why you chose this photographer?' He's blatantly trying to tempt me into conversation.

I stare at his broad, suit-covered back, his hands resting lightly in his trouser pockets, his lean legs slightly spread. My eyes are very pleased, but my brain is in a jumbled mess. I sigh and decide, wisely or not, to indulge him. Guiseppe Cavalli most definitely deserves my time and enthusiasm. I drop my arms and walk over to join him in front of the piece.

'He was known as the master of light,' I say, and he looks at me with genuine interest. 'He didn't think that the subject was of any importance. It didn't matter what he photographed. To him, the subject was always the light. He concentrated on controlling it. See?' I point to the reflections on the water. 'These rowing boats, as lovely as they are, are just boats, but see how he manipulates the light? He didn't care for the boats. He cared for the light surrounding the boats. He makes inanimate objects interesting, makes you look at the photograph in a different … well, a different light, I suppose.' I tilt my head and observe the picture. I never tire of it. As simple as it seems, the more you look at it, the more you get it.

After a few moments' silence, I rip my eyes away from the picture, finding Jesse staring at me.

Our eyes meet, and he's chewing his bottom lip. I know I

won't be able to say no again if he pushes this. I'm all out of willpower, having used my reserve tank last night. I've never felt more desired than when I'm with him.

'Please don't.' My voice is barely audible.

'Don't what?'

'You know what. You said I wouldn't have to see you again.'

'I lied.' He's not ashamed. 'I can't stay away from you, so you do have to see me again … and again … and again.' He finishes the last part of his declaration slowly and clearly, leaving no room for misunderstanding.

I gasp, instinctively backing away from him.

'You persistently fighting this is only making me more determined to prove that you want me.' He starts slowly pursuing me, taking slow, cautious steps forward, maintaining his deep eye contact as he does. 'I'm making it my mission objective. I'll do *anything.*'

I stop my retreat when I feel the bed at the back of my knees. In two more strides, he'll be upon me, and the thought of imminent contact is enough to snap me out of the trance he sends me into.

'Stop.' I hold my hand up in front of me, halting him in his tracks. 'You don't even know me,' I blurt in a desperate attempt to make him see how crazy this is.

'I know you're impossibly beautiful.' He starts toward me again. 'I know what I feel, and I know you're feeling it, too.' We're body to body now, and my heart is hammering in my throat. 'So tell me, Ava. What have I missed?'

I try to control my rushed breaths, but with my chest heaving and my body physically shaking, I'm struggling. I drop my head, ashamed at the tears gathering in my eyes. Why am I crying? Is he enjoying reducing me to tears? This is hideous. He's so desperate to bed me, he's resorting to stalking me, and I'm crying because I'm so weak. He makes me weak, and he has no right to.

I feel his hand slide under my chin, and the warmth would be welcome if I didn't think he was such an arsehole right now. He tugs at my jaw to raise my head, and when our eyes meet, he winces at my tears.

'I'm sorry,' he whispers softly, sliding his hand around to cup my cheek, slowly stroking the rolling tears away with his thumb. His expression is pure torment. Good. It should be.

I find my voice. 'You said you would leave me alone.' I look at him questioningly as he continues to smooth his thumb over my face. Why is he chasing me like this? He's clearly unhappy in his relationship, but it doesn't make this right.

'I lied, I'm sorry. I can't stay away, Ava.'

'You've already said that you're sorry, yet here you are again. Am I to expect flowers tomorrow?' I don't hide my sarcasm.

His thumb pauses and he drops his head. Now he's ashamed. But then his head lifts, our eyes connect and his gaze drops to my lips. Oh God, I'll never be able to stop this. His lips part and they slowly start lowering to mine. I hold my breath, and as our lips brush, only very lightly, my body gives way, prompting my hands to fly up and bunch his jacket in my fists. He growls his approval as he moves his hands to the base of my spine and pushes my body closer to his, our lips hovering over each other's, our breaths mingling as we both shake uncontrollably.

'Have you ever felt like this?' he breathes, running his lips across my cheek to my ear.

'Never,' I answer honestly. My short, gasping breath is unrecognisable.

He grips the lobe of my ear between his teeth and tugs gently, letting the flesh drag through his bite. 'Are you ready to stop fighting it now?' he whispers, tracing up the edge of my ear with the tip of his tongue, working his way back down and brushing his lips lightly over the sensitive flesh under my ear. His hot breath causes a rush of heat to crash between my thighs. I can't fight this any more.

'Oh God,' I breathe, and his lips return to mine to hush me. He takes them gently, and I accept it, letting our tongues roll and lap together at a steady, non-urgent pace. It's too good. My whole body is on fire.

He moans, releasing my mouth. 'Is that a yes?' He fixes me with his green eyes.

'Yes.'

Nodding his head only very slightly, he kisses my nose, my cheek, my forehead, and returns to my mouth. 'I need to have all of you, Ava. Say I can have all of you.'

All of me? What does he mean by all of me? Mind? Soul? But he doesn't mean that, does he? No, he wants all of my body, and right now my conscience has completely failed me. I need to get this man out of my system. He needs to get *me* out of *his* system.

'Take me,' I say quietly against his lips.

The growl that leaves his lips at my words only heightens my desire, and keeping his lips firmly against mine, he wraps one arm around my waist and splays the other across the back of my head. Lifting me from my feet, he deepens his kiss and walks me across the room until my back is against a wall. Our tongues dance together wildly, my hands moving down his back, but I want closer contact, so I grab the front of his jacket and start pushing it off his shoulders. He keeps our lips locked, stepping back just enough to escape his jacket. I toss it on the floor, grab his shirt and yank him toward me, all my previous battling of conscience long forgotten. I have to have him.

Our bodies smash together and he pushes me up the wall, devouring my mouth.

'Fucking hell, Ava,' he pants through strangled breaths. 'You make me crazy.' He rolls his hips, pushing his erection into me, milking a small cry from my lips, and I fist my hands in his hair, moaning in invitation.

This is way past stoppable now. My body has gone into

cruise control, the stop button lost somewhere in the land of lust. I feel his palms rest on the front of my thighs, and my dress is bunched in his fists and pulled up over my waist in one swift tug. His hips roll again, making me whimper. I need more. I don't know how I've resisted this. He bites my bottom lip and releases me, pulling his face away to look me in the eyes as he delivers another firm grind against my core. My head falls back on a deep moan, giving him open access to my throat, which he takes full advantage of, licking, sucking and lapping at the hollow. I could weep with pleasure, but then I hear voices coming from outside of the room and reality comes crashing down around me. What am I doing? I'm in the master suite of the penthouse, with my dress around my waist and Jesse at my throat. There are hundreds of people milling about downstairs. Someone could walk in at any moment. Someone *will* walk in at any moment.

'Jesse,' I pant, trying to get his attention. 'Jesse, people are coming; you have to stop.' I wriggle a little, causing his erection to hit me in just the right spot, and I bang my head against the wall to try and halt the stab of pleasure it causes.

He groans, long and low. 'I'm not letting you go, not now.'

'We need to stop.'

'No,' he growls.

Oh God, anyone could walk through that door. 'We'll do this later,' I try and pacify him. I need to get him off me.

'That leaves you too much time to change your mind.' He nibbles my neck.

'I won't change my mind.' I grip his jaw, pulling his face to mine so we're nose to nose. I look him squarely in his pools of green. 'I will not change my mind.'

He scans my eyes, looking for the reassurance he needs, but I couldn't be any more resolute. I want this. Yes, I might have time to evaluate the situation, but right now, I'm certain I'll see this through. He's just way too tempting to resist, and God I've tried.

He kisses me hard on the lips and pulls away. 'Sorry, I can't risk it.' He scoops me up into his arms and stalks toward the bathroom.

'What? They'll want to see in there, too!' He can't be serious.

'I'll lock the door. No screaming.' He looks at me on a small smirk.

I'm shocked, but I laugh. 'You have no shame.'

'No. My cock has been aching since last Friday, I finally have you in my arms, and you've seen sense. I'm going nowhere and neither are you.'

Chapter Seven

He kicks the door shut behind him and places me between the sinks on the marble vanity unit before returning to lock the door. My dress is still bunched around my waist, my legs and knickers completely exposed.

I gaze around the vast room that I'm so familiar with, my eyes falling on the gigantic cream marble bath dominating the centre of the room. I smile, remembering the trauma of having to organise a crane to lift it in through the windows. It was a nightmare, but it does look spectacular. The double, open-ended shower on the back wall is made up of floor-to-ceiling sheeted glass and beige Travertine tiles, and the vanity unit that I've been placed on is cream Italian marble, with two sunken sinks and large waterfall taps. A thick, gold-framed, intricately carved mirror spans the entire width of the unit, and a chaise lounge sits at an angle in the window. It really is luxury embodied.

I hear the lock click into place, snapping me from admiring my work and pulling my eyes to the door, where Jesse is watching me closely. As he saunters toward me, he slowly starts unbuttoning his shirt. Anticipation has my stomach churning and my thighs clenching shut. This man is absolutely stunning.

With his final button unfastened, he stands before me with his shirt draped open, and I can't resist reaching up and running my finger down the centre of his hard, tanned chest. He looks down to follow my trail, placing his hands on either side of my hips, nudging his way between my thighs. As he looks back up to me, his lips tip at the edges and his eyes sparkle, the slight creases at the corners softening the usual intensity in them.

'You can't escape now,' he teases.

'I don't want to.'

'Good,' he mouths, dragging my eyes to his lovely lips.

I trail my finger back up his chest, working my way past his throat until my finger rests on his bottom lip. He opens his mouth, biting my finger playfully, and I smile, continuing upward and running my hand through his hair.

'I like your dress.' He drags his eyes down my front.

I follow his stare to the bunched-up material around my waist. 'Thank you.'

'It's a bit restrictive.' He tugs at a piece of material.

'It is,' I agree. The anticipation is killing me. *Rip off the dress!*

'Shall we remove it?' He cocks a brow at me, the corners of his mouth twitching.

I smile. 'If you like.'

'Or maybe, we leave it on?' He breaks into a full-on smile as he holds his hands up.

I melt all over the vanity unit.

His hands are quickly on me again, sliding around my back. 'But then again, I have firsthand knowledge of what's under this lovely dress.' He reaches up, grasping the zipper, breathing into my ear as he does. 'And it's far superior to the dress,' he whispers, pulling it down slowly, teasingly. I'm panting hard and desperate. 'I think we'll get rid of it.' He lifts me off the counter, placing me on my feet before pulling my dress away from my body and letting it drop to the floor. He kicks it to the side without taking his eyes off me.

I frown at him. 'I like that dress.' I couldn't give a toss about the dress. He could have ripped it off and cleaned the windows with it, for all I care.

'I'll buy you a new one.' He shrugs as he places me back on the counter, resuming his position between my thighs. He presses his body up against me and grabs my bum, pulling me in toward him so we're locked tight together. He grinds his hips while staring at me.

The throb at my core is bordering on painful, and I'm at serious risk of falling apart if he continues with that alone. I want to tell him to hurry up; I'm struggling to control myself here.

Reaching up, he unclasps my bra, pulling the straps down my arms and flinging it behind him. I lean back on my hands, exposing my breasts to him, and looking into my eyes he lifts his hand and places it, palm down, under my throat. 'I can feel your heart hammering,' he says quietly. He glides his palm down between my breasts until it rests on my stomach, as he looks at me – all smouldering and delicious. 'You're too fucking beautiful, lady.' He grinds firmly. 'I think I'll keep you.'

I arch my back, thrusting my chest forward, and he smiles before lowering his mouth and taking my nipple deep, sucking hard. When he brings his hand up to massage my other breast, I moan, letting my head fall back against the mirror. Oh, good God. The man is a genius. His arousal is as hard as lead, pressing between my thighs, causing me to roll my hips to ease the throb on a long, drawn-out moan. I don't know what to do with myself. I want to soak up the pleasure because it's so good, but the need to have him is getting the better of me, the pressure in my groin near exploding point. As if reading my mind, he skates his hand up the inside of my thigh, finding the edge of my knickers, and one finger breaches the barrier, lightly brushing the tip of my clit.

'Shit!' I cry, throwing myself up to grab his shoulders, digging my nails into his strained muscles.

'Language, lady,' he scorns, then slams his lips against mine, plunging two fingers into me.

My muscles grab onto him as he works them in and out. I might literally die of pleasure. I feel the fast buildup of an impending orgasm, and I know it's going to blow me apart.

Holding on to his shoulders for dear life, I moan into his mouth as he continues his assault on me.

Oh, here it is.

'Come,' he commands, applying more pressure to the top of my clit.

I fall apart in an explosion of stars, releasing his mouth and tossing my head back in a complete frenzy. I cry out and he grabs my head, yanking it forward to tackle my mouth, catching the tail end of my cries. I'm in pieces. I'm panting, shaking and boneless as I disintegrate all over him, completely uninhibited and unashamed of what he does to me. I'm delirious with pleasure.

His kiss softens and his thrusts slow, easing me gradually down as he scatters tender kisses all over my damp, warm face. Too good, just too, too good.

I feel him brush a stray tendril of hair from my face and I open my eyes, meeting a dark, satisfied stare. He plants a soft kiss on my lips, and I sigh. I feel like a lifetime of pent-up pressure has been extinguished, just like that. I'm relaxed and sated.

'Better?' he asks, sliding his fingers out of me.

'Hmmm,' I hum. I have no energy for speech.

His fingers drag across my bottom lip and he leans into me, watching me closely as he runs his tongue across my mouth, licking the remnants of my orgasm away. His eyes burn straight through me as we gaze at each other in silence and my hands instinctively reach up to cup his face, smoothing down his freshly shaven skin. This man is beautiful, intense and passionate. And he could break my heart.

He smiles lightly, turning his face to kiss my palm before returning his eyes to mine. Oh Lord, I'm in trouble.

We're both cruelly snatched from the intensity of the moment when the door handle of the bathroom is jiggled from the other side. I gasp and Jesse slaps his palm over my mouth, looking at me in amusement. He finds this funny?

'I can't hear anything,' a strange voice says, as the door handle rattles. My eyes bulge in horror.

Jesse removes his hand, replacing it with his lips. 'Shhhhhh,' he mumbles against my mouth.

'Oh God, I feel cheap,' I whine, leaving his lips and dropping my head to his shoulder. How am I going to walk out of this place without burning bright red and looking as guilty as sin?

'You're not cheap. Talk crap like that, I'll be forced to kick your delicious backside all over my bathroom.'

I snap my head up from his shoulder, looking at him in confusion. 'Your bathroom?'

'Yes, my bathroom.' He smirks at me. 'I wish they would stop letting strangers roam around my home.'

'You live here?' I'm puzzled. He can't live here. No one lives here.

'Well, I will as of tomorrow. Tell me, is all this Italian shit worth the outrageously expensive price tag they attached to this place?' He looks at me expectantly.

'Italian shit?' I splutter, completely insulted. He laughs, and I think I might slap him. 'You shouldn't have bought the place if you don't like the *shit* that's in it,' I fire at him, completely outraged.

'I can get rid of the shit,' he quips.

My eyebrows shoot up in a you-didn't-just-say-that expression. I've spent months breaking my back sourcing all of this Italian *shit* and this unappreciative swine is just going to *get rid of it*? I've never been so insulted, or pissed off. I try to wriggle my hands from under his, but he tightens his grip. I shoot him a scowl.

'Unravel your knickers, lady. I wouldn't *get rid* of anything in this apartment.' He kisses me hard. 'And you're in this apartment.' He's taking my mouth again, possessively, greedily.

I won't read into that statement too much. My libido has just jumped to attention and I'm happy to comply. I attack him with equal force, thrusting my tongue into his mouth, circling his with mine as he lifts his grip from my hands. They impulsively fly to those taut, rippling shoulders that I love so much.

Wrapping his arm around my middle, he releases my lips and lifts me up from the counter, leaving me hovering above the surface as his other hand finds my knickers and yanks them down my legs. He rests me back down and removes my shoes, letting them tumble to the tiled floor on a loud clatter. I'm impatient, so I join him in his stripping party, reaching up and pushing his shirt down his broad shoulders, revealing his bare chest in all of its glory. He's cut to complete perfection. I want to lick every square inch of him.

As I trace my eyes down, I recoil slightly at a nasty scar that's running across his stomach and rounding onto his left hip. I never noticed it before. The light at The Manor was dim, but that is one hefty scar. It's slightly faded but bloody big. How did he get that? I elect to not enquire. It could be a sensitive issue, and I don't want anything to upset this moment. I could just sit here and gawp at him forever. Even with the scar that looks so sinister, he's still beautiful.

I scrunch his shirt up between my hands and chuck it on top of my dress, and he raises his eyebrows at me.

'I'll buy you a new one,' I shrug.

He smirks and leans forward, bracing himself on the counter and capturing my lips – all brooding and careful. Reaching for his trousers, I begin unfastening his belt, whipping it out of his loop holes in one swift pull, instigating a snapping sound to erupt around us.

He pulls back on an arched brow. 'Are you going to whip me?'

'No,' I answer uncertainly, throwing his belt to the floor and sliding my hand between his tight, narrow hips and the waistband of his trousers. I wrench him forward so we're nose to nose. 'Of course, if you want me to …' Did I just say that?

'I'll bear that in mind,' he says on a half-smile.

Keeping my eyes firmly on his, I start to undo the button on his trousers, my knuckles brushing over his solid erection, causing him to jerk. He squeezes his eyes shut as I slowly undo his fly, sliding my flat hand into his boxers, grazing across the mass of dark blond hair. He shudders, looking up to the ceiling, the muscles on his chest rolling and undulating. I can't resist leaning forward and flicking my tongue up the centre of his chest bone.

'Ava, you should know that once I've had you, you're mine.'

I'm too drunk on lust to take any notice of that statement. 'Hmmm,' I mumble against his skin, circling his nipple with my tongue and withdrawing my hand from his boxers. I grasp the waistband and ease them down over his tidy, narrow hips until his cock springs free.

My God, it's huge! The involuntary gasp that escapes my mouth is an indication of my shock, and flicking my eyes to his, I find a small smile tickling the corner of his mouth. It's all the mortifying evidence I need to tell me that he's picked up on my reaction.

He steps back, kicking his shoes and socks off before removing his trousers and boxers. I'm instantly drawn to his powerfully lean thighs, and gathering some of my shattered confidence, I reach forward slowly and gently circle my thumb over his tip, watching him as he watches my hand explore him. When I tentatively wrap my hand around the base, I see him struggle with the contact.

'Shit, Ava,' he gasps, resting his hands on my hips. I jerk, and he smiles. 'Ticklish?'

'Just there,' I gasp. Oh, it drives me mad!

'I'll remember that,' he says, taking my lips and working my mouth urgently as I begin slow, even strokes of his hardness, increasing the pace when I feel his mouth getting firmer against mine. His hand disappears between my legs, and with one skim of his thumb over my beating clitoris, I'm suddenly catapulted to Central Jesse Cloud Nine. I gasp into his mouth. He bites my lip.

'You ready?' he asks urgently, and I nod, because speech has completely evaded me.

He rips his hand from the apex of my thighs and knocks me away from his throbbing arousal, and in one measured movement, he moves his hands to my backside, lifts me and impales me onto his waiting length.

I yelp.

'Okay?' he pants. 'Are you okay?'

'Two seconds. I need a few seconds.' I wrap my legs around him, crying out at the mixture of pleasure and pain. I know he's not even all of the way in. Jesus, but the man is enormous.

I'm swung around and thrust up against the wall, the coldness of the tiles not bothering me in the slightest as I try to adjust myself to Jesse's hugeness. He rests his forehead against mine, my hands slipping over his sweat-drenched back as he holds still for a few moments, giving me time to adapt to the intrusion.

Panting, he slowly withdraws from me, re-entering on a deliberate, steady thrust. This time he's in further, and the fullness is making my head spin.

'Can you take more?' he asks urgently.

More? How much more is there? *I can do this, I can do this.* I repeat the mantra over and over as I adjust to his size, taking some calming breaths, and when I know I've got a handle on it, I kiss him slowly, arching my back and pushing my breasts into his chest.

'Ava, tell me you're ready,' he breathes.

'I'm ready.' I've never been more ready for anything in my life.

With my prompt, he extracts himself and drives back inside of me more forcefully. I sigh, tilting my hips forward in acceptance as he growls in appreciation and repeats his swift thrusts, again and again.

'You're mine now, Ava,' he breathes on a deep, delicious plunge. My head drops forward to rest on his. 'All mine.'

In one fast move, he pulls back and pounds home.

I scream.

I'm full to capacity and loving every wonderful bit of it. I grip his shoulders as he increases his thrusts, slamming into me, and hitting my womb every time. I cry in pleasure when he finds my lips, plunging his tongue into my mouth in a desperate claim as our damp, sweat-riddled bodies clash and slide together. I'm about to splinter into a million pieces. Holy shit! I've never come during penetrative sex!

'You're going to come?' he gasps against my mouth.

'Yes!' I shout, sinking my teeth into his bottom lip. He moans. It's animalistic, but I'm losing control here.

'Wait for me,' he demands, pounding harder.

I scream, desperately clenching my muscles around him to try and hold off, but it's not working. How long will he be? I can't hold on.

After three more hard strikes, he shouts, 'Now, Ava!' and I burst at his command, throwing my head back and screaming his name as I feel hot liquid shoot into me.

He grips me hard, pulling me as close as he can get me, holding me there and burying his face in my exposed throat.

'Oh, fucccckkkkk!' he groans against my neck. The long, satisfied moan falling from my own lips is symbolic of how I feel right now.

He slows his thrusts to ease us both down from our incredible highs, and I hold him tight, my inner muscles contracting around him as he lazily circles his hips.

'Look at me,' he orders softly, and I pull my head down to look at him, sighing happily as he searches my eyes. He rolls his hips again and plants a kiss on the end of my nose. 'Beautiful,' he says simply, cupping the back of my head and pushing me toward him so my cheek rests against his shoulder. I could stay like this for ever.

My back peels away from the cold wall behind me and I'm carried to the vanity unit with Jesse still buried deep inside me, pulsating and twitching. He slips out and settles me on the counter, clasping his palms on either side of my face and bending to kiss me, his lips lingering on mine in a total display of affection.

'I didn't hurt you, did I?' he asks, his frown line appearing on his forehead.

I dissolve on the spot. I want to smother him in my arms, so I do. I wrap my whole body around him, arms and legs, and cling on to him like my life depends on it. His face buries in my neck and he strokes my back. It's the most calming sensation I've ever felt. I can't even muster up the energy to feel guilty.

Sarah who?

We remain entwined, a bundle of arms and legs, breathing heavy and holding each other for an age. I want to stay exactly where I am. We could – it is his bathroom. I can't believe he's bought the penthouse.

After far too short a time, he leans back, running the back of his knuckles down the side of my face. 'I didn't use a condom,' he says with genuine regret in his eyes. 'I'm sorry, I got so carried away. You're on birth control, right?'

'Yes, but the pill doesn't protect me from STDs.' I'm such a numb-nut. This man is a God with some serious moves. I dread to think of how many women he's slept with.

He smiles at me. 'Ava, I've *always* used a condom.' He leans forward, kissing my forehead. 'Except with you.'

'Why?' I ask, a little puzzled.

He pulls away and has a little chew on his bottom lip. 'I don't think straight when I'm near you.' He puts his boxers and trousers on, then reaches over me to grab a washcloth from the shelf. I'm about to protest, but then I remember … it's his. Everything in here is his, except for me. Well, not according to him, but that was just an impending orgasm talking. The throes of passion can make you say some funny things. He doesn't think straight? That makes two of us.

He runs the tap, passing the cloth under it and returns to stand before me. I feel exposed sitting here completely naked. This isn't equal ground, so I close my legs to conceal myself, suddenly uncomfortable with my state of undress. But he looks at me, a mystified look flitting across his handsome face as he pouts, reaches between my legs and spreads them gently.

'Better,' he mutters, lifting my arms from my lap and placing them on his shoulders. He rests the warm, damp cloth on the inside of my thigh and begins sweeping it up and down, cleaning the remnants of him away from me. It's a tender act and extremely intimate. I watch his face in fascination, noticing the slight crease across his forehead as he concentrates with his procedure of cleaning me up.

He gazes up at me, his green eyes soft and twinkling. 'I want to toss you in that shower and worship every inch of you, but this will have to do. For now, anyway.' He leans in and kisses me, lingering briefly. I don't think I could ever tire of these simple, affectionate kisses. His lips are so soft, his scent divine. 'Come on, lady. Let's get you dressed.' He lifts me from the counter and helps me into my underwear and dress before zipping me up. My entire body convulses when he rests his lips on the nape of my neck, his warm, soft mouth having the hairs on my neck rising. I don't think he's out of my system – not at all. This is bad news.

I pick his pale blue shirt up from the floor and shake it out before handing it to him.

'There really wasn't any need to screw it up, was there?' He flicks me a grin as he pulls it on, fastening the buttons and tucking it into his navy trousers.

'Your jacket will cov –' I abruptly remember tossing that on the floor in the bedroom. 'Oh,' I whisper, all wide-eyed.

'Yes. Oh.' He arches a brow as he snaps his belt, making me flinch and him grin. 'Okay, you ready to face the music, lady?' He holds his hand out to me, and I take it without a thought. The man is a magnet. 'I'd say quite loud, wouldn't you?'

I gape at him as he gives me a full-on dazzling smile. Then I shake my head, quickly glancing in the mirror. Oh, I'm flushed. My lips are swollen and pink, my hair is still up but with random strands curling down all over the place, and I'm creased. I need five minutes to sort myself out.

'You're perfect,' he reassures me, as if sensing the panic rising in me.

Perfect? Perfect wouldn't be a word I would use. I look thoroughly fucked! He tugs me to the door, unlocks it and strides out, devoid of wariness, while I'm more cautious. I see his jacket still sprawled on the floor, and he scoops it up as we pass.

When we hit the curving staircase, I suddenly register my hand still in his, and I try to ease it from his grasp, but he squeezes it tighter, flashing me a scowl. Shit! He has to let go. My boss and colleagues are down here. I can't go prancing through them holding hands with this strange man. I attempt to free my hand again, but he refuses to let it go.

'Jesse, let go of my hand.'

'No,' he shoots back, short and firm, and without even looking at me.

I stop abruptly halfway down the stairs and scan the room below. No one is looking at us, thank God, but it won't be long before someone clocks us. Jesse turns, looking up at me from a few steps below.

'Jesse, you can't expect me to parade through here holding your hand. That's not fair. Please, let me go.'

He looks at our hands locked together, suspended between our bodies. 'I'm not letting you go,' he murmurs sullenly. 'If I let you go, you might forget how it feels. You might change your mind.'

There is absolutely no chance of me forgetting how we feel flesh on flesh, but that's not the part of his statement that's bothering me. 'Change my mind about what?' I ask, totally perplexed.

'Me,' he says simply.

What about him? My mind hasn't been made up on anything, so there's nothing to change. My mind has just twisted further. I need to focus my attention on persuading him to release my hand before someone spots us, so I'll file that comment, just like I've filed the other strange comments he made upstairs.

Holy shit! I nearly fall down the stairs when I see Sarah breezing across the terrace, reality crashing down around me. Surely when he sees her he'll stop being such an unreasonable fool. She's heading back inside. I don't have time to fuck about, so I narrow my eyes on him and use brute force to yank my hand from his, nearly dislocating my shoulder in the process. He scowls at me, but I don't hang around long enough to soak up his annoyance, taking the stairs fast, down to the vast openness of the penthouse. The woman has made it obvious that she dislikes me, and I can hardly blame her. She saw me as a threat and as it turns out, her fear was warranted.

I hit the bottom of the stairs and see Tom come running through the crowd of people, waving his arms about frantically. 'There you are! Where have you been? Patrick has been looking for you everywhere.' He clasps my shoulders, checking me up and down, ever the drama queen. Noting my disheveled state, he eyes me suspiciously. I feel the heat rise in my cheeks.

'I was giving Mr Ward a tour,' I offer, rather unconvincingly, while waving my hand over my shoulder in the general direction of Jesse. I know he's close behind me; I can still feel him brooding. And I can smell him, too, or that could be his scent all over me. I feel like I've been marked … claimed, even.

With his hands still clasped on my shoulders, Tom looks past me and gasps, yanking me closer, so his mouth is at my ear. 'Darling, who is that divine being growling at me?' he asks, sniffing me.

I struggle out of his hands and turn to see Jesse drilling holes into Tom. I roll my eyes at his pathetic behaviour. Tom's the gayest gay man in London. He can't possibly be threatened by him.

'Tom, this is Mr Ward. Mr Ward, Tom. He's a *colleague*. He's also gay.' I add the last bit sarcastically. Tom won't care – not that it isn't bloody obvious anyway.

I look at Tom, who's grinning widely, then cast my eyes over to Jesse, who's stopped growling but doesn't look any less pissed off. Tom prances forward, grabs Jesse's shoulders and air kisses him. I stifle a laugh, watching as Jesse's eyes bulge and his shoulders tense.

'It really is a pleasure,' Tom sings in Jesse's face while stroking down his biceps. 'Tell me, do you work out?'

A burst of laughter falls from my mouth and, rather immaturely, I decide to leave Jesse to cope with Tom's outrageous flirting on his own. I catch his eyes as I turn to leave, seeing I'm being thrown daggers, but I couldn't care less. He's being stupidly unreasonable.

I find Patrick in the kitchen, and he waves me over, handing me a glass of champagne when I arrive. 'Here she is,' Patrick announces to a tall man, draping his arm around my shoulder and hugging me against his big body. 'This girl has transformed my company. I'm so proud of you, flower. Where have you been?' he asks, his blue eyes twinkling brightly and his cheeks bright red – a clear sign that he's had too much to drink.

'I've been giving a few tours,' I lie, smiling sweetly as I'm squeezed against him.

'I've just been talking about you. Your ears must have been burning,' Patrick says. 'This is Mr Van Der Haus, one of the developers. I was just saying you'll be more than happy to assist on their new venture.'

'My partner has told me lots about you,' Van Der Haus says, smiling broadly. He's very classy – all tall and white blonde, with a bespoke suit and dress shoes. He's quite handsome ... for a mid-forties man ... *Another* older man. 'I'll look forward to working with you.'

I blush. 'I would be delighted, Mr Van Der Haus. What have you got in mind for the next project?' I ask eagerly.

'Please, call me Mikael. The building is nearly complete.' He broadens his smile. 'We have settled on traditional Scandinavian. Being from Denmark, we're going back to our roots.' His mild accent is really sexy.

Traditional Scandinavian? This most definitely panics me. Does this mean I'll be hijacking IKEA? Shouldn't they employ someone Scandinavian for this? 'It sounds exciting,' I say, turning to place my glass on the worktop, spotting Jesse across the room with Sarah as I do.

Oh God. He's drilling holes into me, and Sarah's right bloody there. I swivel back to face my audience. The panic must be clear on my burning face.

'I think so,' Mikael agrees. 'Once I've discussed a favourable fee with Patrick,' he points his champagne glass at my boss, 'we can start building a specification. Then you can get started on some designs.'

'I look forward to it.' I shift on the spot, feeling Jesse's eyes burning into my back.

'She won't disappoint you, Mikael.' Patrick chirps.

He smiles. 'I know she won't. You're an exceptionally talented young woman, Ava. Your vision is impeccable. Now, if you'll excuse me.' I feel the colour deepening in my face as he shakes Patrick's hand and then mine. 'I will be in touch,' he says, holding my hand in his a little longer than necessary before releasing it and strolling off.

I'm still tucked tightly under Patrick's arm as Victoria approaches us and leans against the worktop on a huff.

'My feet are killing me,' she exclaims.

In unison, Patrick and I look down at her six-inch leopard-print platforms with blood red piping. They're ridiculous.

Patrick looks at me, shaking his head, before releasing his hold and declaring his departure. 'Irene will be waiting for me downstairs. I've gotten all the photographs.' He waves his camera at me. 'I'll see you on Monday morning.' He kisses each of us. 'You've both worked hard tonight. Well done.' He takes his big body out of the kitchen, staggering slightly as he does.

Worked hard? I cringe.

'Oh, I nearly forgot.' Victoria drags my eyes away from Patrick's swaying body, back to her. 'Kate said she couldn't wait around for you any more. She said that she hopes you've had fun and she'll see you at home.'

Hopes I've had fun? Sardonic cow!

'Thanks, Victoria. Listen, I think we're done here.' I pick up one more glass of champagne as the waiter passes. I can't drive, so I may as well make the most of it. And damn, I need it. 'I'm heading home. Go when you're ready. I'll see you on Monday.' I kiss her cheek.

'I'm going to hang around for a bit with Tom. He wants to go to Route Sixty for a dance.' She shakes her bum.

'Be prepared for a late one,' I warn. Once Tom's on the dance floor you need a bulldozer to get him off.

'No! I've told him, I can't stay late. I've got too much to do tomorrow. And I can hardly walk in these stupid shoes.'

'Good luck with that. Say bye to Tom for me.'

'I will when I find him.' She limps off in her ridiculous heels, leaving me to finish my last glass of champagne.

I glance around the kitchen, but I don't see Jesse or Sarah.

I'm relieved. I don't think I could look Sarah in the eye. I need to go and kick my loser arse around the flat for being so weak and easy.

I reach the penthouse elevator and punch in the code. It'll be changed tomorrow for the new owner. I huff a little burst of laughter at the thought. Of course, Jesse Ward is the new owner. It's been one hell of a day, and now that I'm alone, I can feel the foreseeable guilt begin to tumble over me. Oh, what a foolish, desperate woman I am.

'Leaving so soon?'

My shoulders raise and I wince at the cold, unfriendly voice. Straightening my expression, I turn to face Sarah. 'It's been a long and tiring day.'

She sips her champagne while eyeing me suspiciously. 'You're quite a surprise,' she purrs.

I really don't know what to say. 'Thank you,' I utter, turning back to the elevator when it opens.

'It wasn't a compliment.'

'I didn't think it was,' I retort without looking at her.

'You know Jesse owns this place, right?'

I want to ask her if she'll be living here, too, but of course, I don't. 'He mentioned it,' I say casually, stepping into the lift and punching the code in. 'It was nice to see you.'

The doors close and I fall back against the mirrored wall.

Shit!

Chapter Eight

After collecting my things from the spa, I wander down to the docks and sit myself on a bench. The hustle and bustle is in full swing as people come and go, all looking happy and content. The flowers are in bloom on the elabourate lampposts, spilling over the baskets and cascading down the ornate iron, and the lights from the building all flicker and glow across the docks, dancing off the rippling waves.

I sigh and close my eyes, listening to the sound of the water lightly lapping at the sides of the boats. It's rhythmic and relaxing, but I don't think anything will make me feel better at the moment. I get my phone out of my bag to call Kate, but when it rings off, I leave a message.

'Hey, it's me.' I know I sound forlorn, but I can't feign chirpiness when I really don't feel it. I groan. 'Oh, Kate … I've made a monumental fuck up. I'll be home soon.' I drop my hand to the bench and look up at the night sky. What was I thinking?

My phone jumps to life in my hand, and I connect the call without looking at the display, assuming it will be Kate. 'Hey.'

'Where are you?' He speaks softly down the phone.

I don't know whether my heart sinks because it's not Kate, or because it *is* Jesse. I'm a firm believer in karma, in which case, I'm in big trouble.

'I'm at home.' I lie again. It's coming naturally these days. I'm twiddling my hair, a sure sign of my Pinocchio behaviour.

'Okay,' he whispers and hangs up.

That was easy. Now he's gotten what he wanted, is that it?

I'm not sure why I feel so neglected. It's what I had expected, and it's no less than I actually deserve. His persistence had worn me down, but now it's out of my system. Now I can get back to my life.

Jesse can continue with his serial seductions and move on to the next lucky woman, for all I care. I'm sure Sarah will find out soon enough, just not now. A woman scorned and after my blood is the last thing I need.

After sitting and musing for a while, I reluctantly get up to go and hail a cab. I need to put tonight behind me fast, but as I turn and look up, I find Jesse standing a few feet away, quietly watching me.

We face each other, still and silent, his face impassive as he studies me. And then I burst into tears. I don't know why, but I put my face in my hands and I sob. I feel his warm body swathe me and my head rests in the crevasse of his neck, my arms on reflex reaching under his to cling onto him. We say nothing for a long time. We just stand there in each other's arms, silent while he massages the back of my head with the palm of his big hand, keeping me tucked tightly against his body. There is only a small part of me wondering where Sarah is, but I don't dwell on it. I feel sheltered and safe, even though I should be running away from these arms, not into them.

'How long have you been here?' I ask when my sobs have finally abated.

'Long enough,' he murmurs. 'What's all this about a monumental fuck up?' He squeezes me tighter. 'I hope to God you weren't referring to me.'

'I was.' I don't beat around the bush. It would be pointless.

'You were?' He sounds surprised, and even a little pissed off, but then a few moments later he follows it up with, 'Will you come home with me?' I feel him tense slightly.

I've just told him that he's my monumental fuck up, and he wants to take me home? What about Sarah? They obviously don't live together then. 'No,' I answer. What I've done already is bad enough.

'Please, Ava.'

'Why?' I ask. I need to know what his fascination is with me, because if I spend any more time with this man, I may be in even more trouble. I can't be getting caught up in sordid affairs with older, unavailable men.

He pulls back to look down at me, his beautiful brow furrowed. 'It feels right. You belong with me.' He says it like it's the most natural thing in the world.

'So who does Sarah belong with?'

'Sarah? What's she got to do with anything?' He looks really confused now.

'Girlfriend,' I remind him. He really has no regard for the poor woman.

His eyes bulge. 'Oh, please don't tell me you've been ignoring my calls and running away because you thought ...' He releases me. 'You thought me and Sarah were ...' He steps back. 'Oh, fucking hell, no!'

'Yes!' I exclaim. 'She's not?' Now I'm really confused. The woman couldn't have made her claim any clearer if she'd pissed all over him.

His hands delve into his hair. 'Ava, whatever made you think that?'

'Oh, let me see,' I smile sweetly. 'Maybe it was the kiss in the hallway of The Manor. Or when she came looking for you in the bedroom. Or it could be her frosty reception to me,' I draw breath. 'Or perhaps it's the fact that she's with you every time I see you.' I can't believe this. I've been beating myself up about this, and over a woman who I really don't like. What a waste of conscience! 'Who is she?' I ask, completely riled.

He holds my hands, leaning down so his eyes are level with mine. 'Ava, she's a little friendly.'

'Friendly?' I scoff. 'That woman is not friendly!'

'She's a friend,' he says soothingly. I don't want soothing. No, I want to pop some pouty red lips! She knew exactly what she was doing. *She* clearly wants to be more than friends.

He brushes his palm down my cheek. 'Now we've clarified Sarah's position in my life, can we talk about yours?'

His previous comments suddenly embed themselves into my mind – all of the *'you're mine'*, *'I'll keep you'* and *'you'll change your mind'*. 'What do you mean?' I ask.

He smirks. 'I mean in my bed, beneath me.' He yanks me into his chest, and I resume my nuzzle, sagging with relief. 'At The Manor?' I ask. It's quite a drive.

'No, I've an apartment behind me, but I can't move in until tomorrow. I'm renting a place on Hyde Park. You'll come.'

'Yes.' I don't hesitate, but I'm aware that it wasn't a question. And I'm also mindful of his previous comments, especially his last one: *'You belong with me.'*

Is that his decision or mine?

After Jesse places me and my bags neatly in his car, we travel in silence, except for the low tones of Massive Attack's *Teardrops* filtering from his car sound system. How fitting after my sobbing fit. I spend most of the journey deliberating on my decision to come home with Jesse, while he repeatedly draws breath, as if intending to say something but deciding against it.

He pulls his Aston Martin into a gated car park, and I let myself out while he grabs my bags.

He takes my hand and leads me into the building. 'I'm on the first floor. We'll take the stairs.' He guides me through a grey fire door, into the stairwell and up a flight of stairs until we exit into a narrow corridor. It looks like a specialist hospital facility. Jesse unlocks the only other door in the long expanse of white and grey, ushers me in, and I'm immediately standing inside a large, open plan area. It's white from top to bottom, with black furniture and a black kitchen, monochrome to the absolute maximum – a real guy's pad. It looks empty, cold and clinical. I hate it.

'It's a pit stop. I bet you're really offended.' His eyes glow and he smiles, no doubt at my critical face.

'I prefer your new place.'

'Me too.'

I wander farther into the apartment, scrutinizing the lack of warmth and cosiness. How does he live here? There are no personal touches, no paintings or photographs. I notice a snow-board propped up in the corner, with various skiing equipment piled around it, and on the sideboard, where I would expect to see vases or ornaments, there's a motorcycle helmet and some leather gloves.

'I don't keep alcohol. Do you want some water?' He strolls over to the huge black fridge and pulls it open.

'Please.' I join him in the kitchen area, pulling out a black barstool from under the black granite worktop of the island. Jesse removes his suit jacket and perches on the adjacent stool, turning to face me and handing me a glass of water before he unscrews the cap of a bottle for himself.

He sips his water, looking at me over the bottle, while I fiddle with my glass. I feel incredibly uncomfortable. Things have become awkward and I'm not sure why.

I hear him sigh as he places his bottle down before taking my glass from my hand and putting it on the island worktop. Then he grasps the seat of my stool and drags it closer to his, turning it to face him and resting his palms on my knees. He leans in. 'Why did you cry?'

'I don't know,' I answer honestly. The whole episode caught me off guard.

'Yes, you do. Tell me.'

I consider what I should say while his eyes probe mine, waiting for me to answer. The light crease appears across his brow, and I realise now that it's a concern frown. What should I tell him? That my trust in men is zero and the fact that he is, quite clearly, a prince of seduction spells trouble for me? But he won't want to hear any of that girly nonsense.

'I don't know,' I repeat instead.

He sighs, his frown morphing into a scowl as he taps his fingers on the granite a few times. I can, quite literally, see the cogs of his mind grinding as he looks at me, chewing his bottom lip. 'Would I be right in saying that your misinterpretation of mine and Sarah's relationship wasn't the only reason you were avoiding me?' he asks, unclasping his Rolex and sliding it onto the worktop.

'Probably.' I look away from him, a little ashamed – I don't know why.

'That's disappointing,' he states conclusively, but I can't hear disappointment in his voice. All I hear is annoyance.

I don't need to tell him that I could, very possibly, fall hard for him. Women must fall hard for him on a daily basis.

Before I know what's hit me, he grabs me and tosses me onto the worktop, sending my glass of water crashing to the tiled floor. My legs are spread with his thighs, causing my dress to ride up, and he attacks my mouth with his inexorable tongue, plunging deeply and meaningfully.

I'm instantly plagued by blazing goose bumps and hot wetness at my core, as he thrusts his hips hard while consuming my mouth. He cups my bum, pulling me closer, keeping his groin tight against me.

Oh, holy shit! I groan as his hips roll, unashamed for him to know that I'm turned on like a thousand-watt light bulb. Releasing my lips, he stares at me, breathing hard with brazen hunger shining from his green pools. I'm certain my eyes are matching his.

'Let's establish some things here,' he pants through short breaths, pulling me off the worktop so I'm straddling his waist. He stares at me. 'You're a shit liar.'

Yes, this I know. My mum and dad tell me all the time. I twiddle my hair when I lie. It's involuntary – I can't help it.

He leans in and kisses my lips, softly stroking my tongue with his. 'You're mine now, Ava.' He rolls his hips, causing me to shift upward and tense to relieve myself of the relentless buzzing at my core. We're face to face. 'I'm keeping you for ever,' he informs me on a thrust of his hips.

I close my arms around his shoulders and kiss him on his lush, moist lips. I'm desperate for him all over again. I'm in so much trouble.

'I'm going to possess every single part of you.' He enunciates each word clearly and sharply. 'There will be nowhere on this beautiful body that won't have had me in it, on it, or over it.' His voice is carnal and deadly serious, which only serves to increase my heart rate a little more.

I'm lowered to my feet and spun around before he yanks the zipper of my poor, mistreated dress down. My bra is removed and tossed aside just as quickly.

Leaning down, he kisses the nape of my exposed neck, blowing his cool, minty breath across it, instigating a delightful shiver from the mixture of heat from his tongue and the coolness of his breath. Christ, I'm buzzing all over. I flex my neck, rolling my shoulder blades to alleviate the tingles that are riddling my entire body.

He moves his mouth to my ear. 'Face me.'

I do as I'm told, turning back around to look at him, finding an expression of pure determination as he lifts me back onto the island. I rest my hands on his shoulders, but he grasps them, and I reluctantly let him guide them down to the worktop so I'm gripping the edge.

'The hands stay here,' he says firmly as he releases them, backing up his demand with that confident tone. He hooks his fingers in the top of my knickers and tugs at them. 'Lift.'

I push my weight onto my arms, lifting my backside off the

worktop so he can draw them down my legs, lowering myself back down when I'm free from the constraints of my underwear. I'm stark naked, and he's still fully dressed. And he doesn't look like he has any intention of removing his clothes any time soon. I want to see that chest, so I move my hands from the edge of the counter to the hem of his shirt.

He steps back, shaking his head slowly. 'Hands.'

I pout, returning my hands to the worktop edge. I want to see him, feel him. This is not fair.

He positions his hands on his top button. 'You want me to remove my shirt?' His low, husky voice is playing havoc with my discipline.

'Yes,' I breathe.

'Yes, what?' he smirks at me, and I narrow my eyes on him.

'Please,' I grate, in a long, drawn-out breath, well aware that he's getting a thrill from making me beg.

He smiles as he slowly unbuttons his shirt, keeping his eyes fixed firmly on me. It takes every bit of effort not to reach forward and yank it open. Why is he making such a meal of this? He knows what he's doing. He's making me wait, and it's torturous.

When he finally gets to the last button, he rolls his shoulders, pulling his shirt off, and for the briefest moment – when both arms are flexed back, his muscles bulging and rippling with his movement – I think I might pass out.

He kicks his brown Grensons off and removes his socks and my eyes run over his perfect physique, my mouth watering, until I see that vicious mar on his abdomen. My eyes pause on it momentarily, but he positions himself back between my legs, snapping me from my curiosity. I fight the urge to grab him. The pressure on my core has me shifting on the counter to ease the immense spasms searing through me, and he's not unaffected himself. His huge erection is straining against the front of his trousers, pressing hard into my thigh.

He rests his hands so they span the tops of my legs, his thumbs on my inside thighs slowly circling, millimetres from my aching core. I'm raw with pure lust, my rapid breathing becoming increasingly difficult to regulate.

He squeezes my thighs. 'Where to start?' he muses, lifting one hand and running his thumb across my bottom lip. 'Here?' he asks. My lips part, and he watches me as he slides his thumb into my mouth. I circle it with my tongue, and his lips lift at the corners in a diminutive smile. Withdrawing his thumb, he runs it across my cheek, then, very slowly, he strokes his flat palm down my neck and onto my pumping chest before cupping my breast possessively. 'Or here?' His husky voice is betraying his calm façade as he raises a questioning eyebrow at me, circling my nipple with his thumb. I gasp.

If he's expecting me to talk, then he can forget it. Speech has totally eluded me, being replaced with short, sharp breaths.

'These are mine.' He gently kneads my breast for a few moments before recommencing his hand stroke down my sensitive skin. He spends a few seconds making big circles on my stomach, and then he continues downward, the heat of his hand when it reaches my inside thigh making me dizzy with lust.

Just when I think he's going to claim me with his fingers, he swiftly changes direction, running his hand around my hip, causing me to jerk. He cups my arse.

'Or here?' He's completely serious. I go rigid. 'Every single inch, Ava,' he breathes. I'm holding my breath, my lungs burning, as he smiles a little, his hand starting to drift back around to my front. He doesn't mess about – he cups me. 'I think I'll start here.'

I release my breath in a thankful rush, relief swamping my entire being, but he taps his finger under my chin so I'm forced to look up into his stunning eyes.

'But I did mean *every* inch,' he affirms coolly before placing his hand on the worktop beside my thigh, his other hand still cupping my core.

Fuck! I'm not sure if I'm up for that. Matt had tried a few times, but it was a flat no fucking way! More pleasurable route, I think he said – yes, for *him*! I don't have long to dwell on it. I feel Jesse's finger run up the centre of my core, generating flashes of pleasure that jet off in a million different directions around my body. I slump forward, resting my forehead on his shoulder as my upper body rolls up and down in time to my thumping heartbeat.

'You're drenched,' he rumbles in my ear as he plunges a finger into me. I immediately tighten my muscles around it. 'You want me,' he states firmly, withdrawing and spreading the wetness over my clit before surging forward again with two fingers.

I cry out.

'Tell me you want me, Ava.'

'I want you,' I pant against his shoulder.

I hear a groan of satisfaction. 'Tell me you need me.'

I would tell him anything he wants to hear at this point – absolutely anything. 'I need you.'

'You'll always need me, Ava. I'm going to make sure of it. Now, let's see if we can fuck some sense into you.'

He withdraws his fingers from me and pulls me down from the worktop, turning me slowly in his arms until my hands find the flat surface of the granite. I'm not happy with this position.

'I want to see you,' I moan, although I don't fancy my chances. He seems like the dominant type.

I feel his body closing in on me, the heat pouring out of him and into me. When the firmness of his chest presses up against my back, I lean on him, the back of my head resting on his shoulder.

He turns his mouth into my ear. 'Shut up and soak up the pleasure.' He pushes his hips into the small of my back and slowly grinds into me as he reaches forward, placing his hands on my wrists. 'No talking unless I tell you. You got that?'

I nod. This is definitely a man who likes to be in control.

He begins a slow, languid jaunt up my arms with his talented fingers, leaving my skin prickling in their wake, spreading fire through my veins. My breasts ache for his touch as he reaches the tops of my arms and moves onto my shoulders. I clamp my lips together, but a moan escapes. I can't help it, not when he's making me feel like this.

His hands span my shoulders entirely, and he begins circling his thumbs into the base of my neck, working out the stiffness that's looming there. The feeling is out of this world. My body is relaxed and my mind serene.

Lowering his mouth to my neck, he brushes his lips over my skin before kissing me gently. 'Your skin is addictive.'

'Hmmm,' I purr. That's not talking.

He laughs softly. 'This good?' he asks, trailing feather-soft kisses up and down my jaw. I turn my face in toward him, meeting him square in the eye. I nod again.

He soaks up my gaze for a few seconds, his expression contented, before planting a soft kiss on my lips and letting his hands work their way down to my hips. I clench my eyes shut, trying my hardest not to jolt forward.

'Keep your hands where they are,' he orders firmly, releasing his hold of me.

I hear the sounds of his trousers being removed before his hands are back on my hips and he's stepping back from me, slowly taking my hips with him. My pulse accelerates and I shift my grip on the worktop to support myself in my braced position, flinching when his hand cups the base of my neck. I feel his erection nudging at my opening, and in an attempt to stabilize my breathing, I draw a long breath, trying to relax as I linger on the brink of penetration. This is the worst kind of torture.

He leans forward, his warm, wet tongue connecting with my

back, licking a straight line up the centre of my spine, finishing with a soft kiss on the base of my neck.

'Are you ready for me, Ava?' he asks against my skin, the vibration of his lips sending tremors of pleasure straight to my core. 'You can answer.'

Despite my breathing exercises, I'm still short of breath. 'Yes.' I'm virtually panting.

The rush of air that escapes his mouth is thorough appreciation. I feel his hand brush against my bum as he positions himself, and then, very slowly, he breaches my pulsing void, plunging in smoothly and controlled. His breathing is laboured, and I want to scream in pleasure, but I'm not sure it's allowed.

Oh, this is good. What will he do if I disobey him, anyway? My loss will be his loss, too. He repositions his hand back on my hip and stills, and my grip tightens on the counter until my knuckles are bloodless. I find myself pushing back against him, taking him to the hilt.

'Fuck, Ava, you turn me inside out,' he groans, his hand tightening around my neck, holding me in place, his other leaving my hip and reaching around to cup my breast. 'I can't do this slow.' He pants as he moulds me, withdrawing slowly and advancing hard and fast in one swift lash, jolting me forward.

'Jesse!' I cry. There is not a chance in Hell I'm going to be quiet if he continues with that. My God, this man is powerful.

He withdraws slowly. 'Quiet, Ava,' he grates and strikes again, knocking my breath right out of my lungs.

I adjust my grip, but it's hard when my hands are sweaty, causing them to slide on the granite. I rid myself of the flex in my arms to prevent him from shoving me forward again, just about managing to stabilize myself in time for his assault. I'm in shock. He hammers back into me tirelessly, leaving no recovering space between hard, relentless pounds. He's unforgiving.

Shifting his hands from my neck and breast, he takes a firm hold of my hips and pulls me back to meet his every hard thrust, slamming into me to the absolute maximum. I've lost all sense of realism. Nothing else exists, except for Jesse, his brutal drive, and my body's craving for it. This is mind-bending stuff.

My stomach coils as I feel my impending orgasm battle its way forward, assisted rapidly by Jesse's ruthless momentum.

'Not yet, Ava,' he warns.

How does he know? I can't sustain this for much longer. I'm going to explode at any moment. I can hear our sweaty bodies colliding on loud blows, along with Jesse's throaty grunts rolling over me. I concentrate on quenching the raw need to let it go, the pleasure verging on the point of pain. But with my thoughts in a million places, except my brain, I'm a slave to my body's need.

And then he pulls out, and I'm left hanging. What's he doing? I whimper as my impending release retreats, and I'm about to yell at him, but then I feel his finger slide down the centre of my backside.

I tense from top to bottom.

Oh no!

'You can do this, Ava.' He slides his fingers down between my thighs and into me, collecting the wetness and slowly dragging it back up to my bum. 'Relax, we'll take it slow.'

Relax? I can't relax! He circles my opening slowly, every muscle in my backside clenching, automatically rejecting the invasion.

'Ava, relax.' He stresses the words.

'I'm fucking trying,' I snap. 'Give me time, damn it!' He can fuck right off if he thinks I'm keeping quiet now! I hear him laugh softly as he takes his fingers back down to my clit, rolling them around, causing spikes of pleasure to bolt through me.

'Watch your mouth,' he warns.

I focus on taking deep, controlled breaths. 'Don't you need some lubricant or something?' I pant.

'You're soaking, Ava. That's enough. You're not very good

under instruction, are you?' He penetrates my opening with his thumb, and I sink my teeth into my lip. 'Relax, woman.'

'Oh God, this is going to hurt, isn't it?'

'Yes, at first. You have to relax. Once I'm in, you'll love it. Trust me.'

Oh, bloody hell!

He continues the massaging of my opening as I drop my head, panting and sweating with nerves, and then I feel his hand wrap around the nape of my neck, gently massaging at my tense muscles as I give myself a mental pep talk. His hand leaves my neck and lands on my backside, and he gently eases me open until I feel the moist head of his erection nudging at my opening.

Oh, fuck!

'Easy, lady. Let it happen,' he murmurs, slowly rolling his wetness around my entrance.

Breathe, breathe, breathe.

Then he advances, the immense pressure on my opening causing me to impulsively jolt forward. His hand comes up to rest over my shoulder, holding me in place, his other continuing to guide himself into me. I'm physically shaking as the pressure builds and builds.

'That's it, Ava. We're nearly there.' His voice is jagged and strained, his palm wet on my shoulder as his fingers flex. And then he surges forward on a strangled growl, breaching my muscles and sliding deep into my forbidden place.

'Shit!' I cry. That fucking hurts!

'Oh God, you're so tight!' he chokes. 'Stop fighting, Ava. Relax!'

I pant as I'm thrown into a place between pleasure and agony. The fullness I feel is indescribable, the pain great, but the pleasure … Oh God, the pleasure is beyond description and completely unanticipated. The tightness of my muscles around him has me feeling every pulsing vein and rolling ripple of his erection. My body releases a little of the tension that it's built up, and in its place … pure pleasure attacks me.

'Jesus, that feels good. I'm going to move now, okay?'

I nod, inhale a deep breath and firm up my grip of the work-top as his hand leaves my shoulder and trails down my back to join his other on my hips. But I don't jerk or jolt when he grips me. I'm too busy preparing myself for what's to come.

'Real slow, Ava,' he moans, slowly pulling out of me.

'Jesus, Jesse!' If he tells me to shut up, I'll get real angry.

'I know.' He starts working himself in and out in slow, meas-ured strokes.

I'm falling apart under him. I never imagined this. I never thought this would feel anything but smutty and wrong. But it doesn't. He's making love to me, and it feels so good. I'm stunned. The power of him claiming me has the ache in my stomach in knots. One touch of my core will have me on the ceiling.

'You feel amazing, Ava.' He growls deeply as he drives for-ward again. 'I could stay here all fucking night, but I'm losing it.'

I find myself pushing back on to his level strokes, inviting him to increase his pace. The unexpected pleasure is unreal, and I'm fast on my way to a furious climax. I'm staggered that I'm even doing this. I need more.

'Keep going.' I utter the words I never thought I would.

'Yes, baby. Are you close?'

'Yes!' I cry, ramming back onto him. I hear his gasps as he moves one hand to my shoulder and the other to stroke my inside thigh. 'Harder!' I scream. I need this.

'Oh fuck, Ava!' he yells, pounding forward, clamping onto my shoulder and cupping my mound, his finger rolling over my pulsating clitoris.

I throw my head back. 'I'm there!' I cry.

'Wait!' he shouts.

I turn light-headed, feeling his cock swell and jerk as he powers on.

I'm delirious with pleasure, and just when I think I might collapse, he bellows, 'Now!' And I let go.

The room starts spinning and I'm lost as I collapse forward onto the bar, my arms spread above my head, taking Jesse with me. He's a weight, but I'm numb from pleasure, aware only of his hard, wet chest pressing me into the granite, his hot, heavy breaths in my hair and his pulsating cock still buried deep inside me. He spasms above me, and my muscles contract on every beat I feel from him, draining every last drop of his seed as he lazily thrusts the last pieces of my orgasm out of me.

I'm floating away.

Chapter Nine

Are you okay?' he whispers in my ear.

'Am I allowed to speak?'

He pushes forward and squeezes my hipbone, sending me on a little jolt across the worktop. 'Don't be smart.'

'I'm well and truly fucked.' I sigh.

'Ava, please watch your mouth,' he cautions, lifting his arms and laying them over mine, softly stroking up and down.

'I am, though.'

'I know, but you don't have to swear. I hate you swearing.'

I frown to myself. 'I have to endure your blue language.'

'My language is only blue, lady, when you make me see red.'

I sigh. 'Okay.'

We lay replete for an age, regaining our breath. I'm pinned under his heavy body, splattered on the granite work surface, the coolness under my cheek a welcome sensation as I watch my hot breath skim the shiny granite, causing it to fog. I'm adrift from reality and drowning in a rush of sentiment. I'm depleted, physically and emotionally, and I'm in even more trouble now.

'Jesse?'

'Hmmm?'

'How old are you?'

He squeezes my arms. 'Twenty-two.'

I roll my eyes. If he's twenty-two, then I'm Mother Teresa reincarnated. I smile to myself. After what I have just partaken in, it's not bloody likely. I feel him pull away from me a fraction, a hollow, empty feeling attacking me when he slips out. He kisses my back and slowly separates us, his skin peeling away from mine gradually. I'm cold.

'Come here,' he whispers, grasping my waist. I notice that it's not my hips.

I brace my flat palms on the granite and lift myself with his slow persuasion, and when I've finally separated my body from the breakfast bar, I turn and face him, my eyes widening when I see he's hard again.

He lifts me onto the counter and muscles between my thighs, picking my arms up and draping them over his shoulders before resting his hands on my waist.

He searches my eyes. 'Are you okay?'

I smile at his handsome face. 'Yes.'

'Good.' He leans in and wraps his arms around me tightly, inhaling in my neck. 'I'm not finished with you yet.'

I curl my legs around his tight waist, squeezing with my thighs. 'I noticed.'

'You have this effect on me,' he tells me on a shrug.

It can't be just me, but I'll take the compliment. I bury my face in the side of his neck and nuzzle. He smells so good.

'Are you hungry?' he asks, pulling back and running his knuckles down my cheek.

'-ish,' I shrug.

'-ish,' he mouths, the corners of his lips twitching. His eyes twinkle and I grin. 'You have a cheeky grin. I love it.' He kisses the corner of my mouth.

'Shit!' As soon as the word falls from my mouth, I wince.

He leans back, eyes wide. 'Mouth!' he grinds, his lips forming a straight line. 'What's the matter?'

'I told Kate I'd be home,' I blurt. She hasn't called, or if she has I've not heard my phone. 'I better call her. She needs my car to visit her gran in Yorkshire.'

I wriggle to free myself, and he begrudgingly lets go on a frown. Retrieving my bag from by the front door, I rummage through, finding my phone to text Kate and explain I'm on my way, adding a *P.S.* on the end to inform her that there's no girl-friend. I pull my jeans out of my overnight bag. 'I've got to go.'

'Go?' he booms.

I flinch. 'I've got one set of car keys and Kate needs them,' I explain. I shake my jeans out and thrust one leg in. No need to bother with underwear.

'Oh!' I yelp as I'm suddenly hoisted into the air and over his shoulder. 'What are you doing?' I'm staring straight at his firm, tanned arse as he turns without a word and stalks across the apartment. 'Shit! Jesse, put me down!' He yanks my jeans off, throws them aside, and slaps my arse. 'Ouch!'

'Mouth!'

I hear the door hit plaster after being kicked open, and we're in a bedroom. It's all black and white in here too. I'm hauled off his shoulder and dropped into a sea of luxurious, white cotton. It smells divine, like fresh water … like him.

I don't have time to get over my disorientation. He's between my thighs in a nanosecond, his hands pinning my wrists on either side of my head, his arms ramrod straight, supporting his upper body. Jesus, the man can move fast. I'm still not quite sure where I am and how I got here. I do, however, recognise that coiling anticipation lingering deep inside me.

The slippery head of his arousal tickles my entrance, leaving my heart sprinting in my chest, while I focus on his eyes above mine, gazing down at me with a mixture of anger and shock. He's mad?

'You're not fucking going anywhere,' he growls, shifting his hips and plunging full length into me, stretching me to the most incredible level.

We both yell in unison at the penetration. He's so deep, and I'm instantly griping onto every inch of him inside me. He holds still for a few seconds, his head hanging and his mouth lax, and once he's gathered himself together, he lifts his gaze to mine and slowly withdraws before ramming straight back in on a loud yell.

I throw my head back on a scream.

'Look at me!' His voice is a carnal growl, not to be ignored.

I return my eyes to his as he holds himself deep inside me. I'm panting like a dehydrated dog.

'That's better. Now, do you need a reminder?' he asks.

A reminder? If he means a reminder of how good he feels inside me, then the answer is yes! I roll my hips to try and get some friction, raging and burning like a wanton hussy.

He stares down at me expectantly. 'Answer the question, Ava.'

'Please,' I breathe. I can't believe I'm begging for him, but he can do what he likes to me, demand anything.

He smiles a knowing, cocky smile, then he lets rip, powering forward. 'You're mine, Ava,' he grunts. I shut my eyes on a yell of pleasure. 'Open your fucking eyes!'

Oh, I don't have the energy. I drag them open as he pounds in and out at an inexcusably hard and forceful pace. It's amazing. Our sweat-ridden bodies are colliding and my breath hitches as I try to control the buildup of pressure that's gathering in my groin. Even amid the disorder of our frantic body movements, his eyes never stray from mine. I wrap my legs around his waist, tilting my hips slightly, sending him deeper and my bordering detonation closer. 'Jesus, Ava. You okay?' He forces the words from his mouth between gruff shouts.

My wrists are freed from his heavy grip, and I feel the thud of his fists punching into the mattress.

'Don't stop!' I scream, flinging my hands up to grab his slippery biceps. I dig my nails in to try and find some grip, prompting him to yell more and pound harder. I throw my head back in despair. The power and control he has is beyond comprehension.

'Damn it, Ava. Look at me!'

My head falls back down and our eyes meet. His pupils are huge and glazed, nearly cancelling out the greenness of his stare, and I notice his frown deepening and sweat dripping down his temples. Shifting my hands to the back of his head, I fist my hands in his saturated hair, pulling his head down so our lips collide and our tongues clash, while he continues his punishing blows.

I can't hold back any more. 'Jesse, I'm going,' I pant against his lips. The tips of my fingers are numb from my stupidly fierce grasp of him.

'Fuck! Together, okay?' he strains through his clenched teeth, driving harder a few more body-blowing, mind-numbing times, before yelling, 'Now!'

I let it go – all of the pent-up heaviness in my groin, the weight in my lungs and the fire in my belly – it all comes out on a massive rush of pressure and a very loud scream.

'Jesus Christ!' he cries, thrusting one last, powerful time before stilling over me.

I feel his scorching release shoot deep inside me, and I sag all around him, closing my eyes in exhaustion. He collapses to his forearms, breathless and soaking wet, as he withdraws fractionally, pushing deep and high a few more times in long, measured strokes. My muscles contract around him, milking every last bit of his release. I can't think straight. This man has given me four incomprehensibly powerful orgasms in less than four hours. I'm never going to be able to walk tomorrow.

I lay there sated and limp, panting and aching from the exertion, my eyes growing heavy. I feel his forehead rest against mine, and I open my eyes to see that his are clenched shut. I wriggle under him to get his attention, feeling his semi-erection twitch inside me. He drags his eyes open, lifting his head so he can focus on me. Searching my face, he settles on my mouth, and leans down to plant the gentlest kiss on my abused lips. I sigh as he drops his torso down to lay flush on my body, his hard chest heavy, but so wanted. The burden is welcome and I reach around to faintly trace my fingers over his back as I rest my chin on his shoulder and stare up at the ceiling. Light shivers ripple through him as he buries his face in my neck, resting his lips against my pulsing vein.

I've never felt so content in all of my life. I know it's only sex and the aftereffects, but this is the finest feeling in the world. It has to be. This man's fierceness is addictive, his tenderness sweet, and his body beyond perfection. He's the perfect mix of maleness.

Tracing my finger across his back, I listen to his breathing, steady and even against my neck. He's asleep, and I'm trapped under his solid body. I stop caressing his back and he shifts his hips, slowly pulling out of me. The feeling is unwelcome, and leaves me wishing I had sustained his weight for longer – maybe for ever.

He pushes himself up on his elbows and stares down at me. 'You sent me to sleep.' His voice is rough.

'I did.'

Picking up a loose piece of my hair, he twirls the shiny, mahogany lock around his finger. 'You're too beautiful,' he whispers.

I stare into his sleepy eyes and run my thumb across his frown line. 'So are you,' I say softly.

He offers a half smile, lowers his head and nuzzles between my breasts. 'Consider yourself reminded, lady.'

Slowly peeling himself away from my body, he rests back on his heels, the cold rush of air that instantly invades me having me wanting to yank him back down. He offers me both of his hands and I take them, letting him pull me up to straddle his thighs, and wrapping one arm around my back, he cradles me to him as he turns, manoeuvreing his body so he's sitting with his back against the headboard, me facing him. He rests his hands on my waist and circles his thumbs on my hipbones, sending a shudder racing through me. I throw my hands over his to still his movements.

He smirks at me. 'Spend the day with me tomorrow.'

Spend all day in bed with this man? After tonight, I need a week to recover – maybe longer. I am, quite literally, fucked.

'I have things planned,' I say warily. I'm being sensible here. I need to keep it casual, or maybe not see him again at all. He's the epitome of bad boy, if slightly older. He's hazardous, enigmatic and completely addictive.

'What things?' he asks on a slight pout.

'I need to sort my stuff out.' I clamp my hands down when I feel him try to move his thumbs again.

'What stuff?' He looks confused.

'Kate's place is temporary accommodation. I've been there for four weeks – everything is everywhere. I need to sort it out for when I get my own place.'

'Where were you four weeks ago?'

'With Matt.'

He recoils. 'Who the fuck is Matt?'

'He's my ex-boyfriend.'

'Ex?'

'Yes, ex.' I see a wave of relief travel across his face. What's the matter with him? 'Jesse, I need to get my car.' I press. 'I can't leave Kate to drive her van all the way to Yorkshire. She rattles and shakes all over the place; it won't be safe.'

'Don't worry. I'll take you to get it in the morning.'

Oh, so I'm staying then? 'She's leaving at eight-ish.' He might not be so keen if I'm dragging him out of bed at the crack of dawn on a Saturday.

'-ish,' he mouths on a smirk. I mirror his smirk, gripping his hands and moving them up to my waist before I reach up to my head, feeling for the grips that are keeping my hair in place, and start pulling at them. He looks up at me with narrowed eyes.

'What?'

'You refuse to spend the day with me, and then thrust those fabulous boobs in my face. That's not playing fair, Ava.' He reaches up and flicks a nipple, causing it to immediately pucker into a tight bud.

I yelp, grabbing my breast. 'Hey! I need to take my grips out. They're digging into my head.' I remove a grip and pop it in my mouth.

He watches me with interest, then leans up, takes the grip with his teeth, and spits it out on the bed. His face plummets, nestling between my boobs, and I smile to myself, smoothing my hands through his damp hair and ignoring the voice in my head that's telling me not to get too contented. He breathes in deeply before pulling back and planting a soft kiss on each nipple. I'm turned around in his lap.

'Let me.' He raises his knees so I'm cradled between them and begins running his fingers through my hair to locate the grips, pulling them out and handing them over my shoulder for me to take.

'How many have you got in here?' he asks as he massages my scalp and finds another stray grip.

'A few. I have a lot of hair to keep up.'

'A few hundred?' he asks doubtfully. 'There, I think I got them all.' He takes the grips from my hand and puts them on the bedside table before sliding his hands over my shoulders and pulling me back so I'm against his chest.

He's so comfortable, and my eyes are incredibly heavy. I've had a stupidly busy day, and I've just finished it off on a marathon of sex with this captivating man. I should go now and avoid the morning awkwardness. But then I feel him wrap his forearms around me and my head automatically rolls back against his shoulder. I'm so comfortable and so sleepy; I'm not going anywhere.

I reach down and start stroking the hair on the outside of his legs. 'How old are you?' I mumble, feeling myself drifting off.

His chest jolts a little, indicating his quiet laugh. 'Twenty-three.'

I sleepily snort my disbelief, but I don't have the energy to challenge him. I'm a slave to sleep and I'm gone.

Chapter Ten

I wake up in the exact same position that I fell asleep in, except the duvet has been pulled up over my waist. Jesse's arms are still wrapped around me, and the heavy scent of sex is in the air.

I scan the room, looking for a clock, hearing Jesse's soft, level breathing in my ear. I'm reluctant to move and wake him, but I need the loo.

I set about gently peeling his arms away from my sticky body. He moans a few times in his sleep, and I smile to myself, surprised at my lack of regret. I've woken with no feelings of remorse or mortification whatsoever. But I also have no desire to outstay my welcome. Oh no, I'm definitely keeping the upper hand here.

Just when I think I've made good progress, I feel his arms clamp around me like a vice, effectively immobilizing me.

'Don't even think about it, lady,' he growls, his voice raspy with sleep.

I grip his forearms with my hands, trying to loosen his hold on me. 'I need to use the bathroom.'

'Tough. Hold onto it. I'm comfy.'

'I can't.'

'I'm not letting go of you.' He states it as a fact, nudging my hand away with a flick of his forearm while maintaining his hold on me.

I flop my head back against his shoulder in exasperation, and his lips turn into my cheek, kissing it sweetly, his overnight stubble grazing me. It feels good, but it wasn't the morning reaction I was expecting.

Once I feel he's relaxed his grip slightly and is busy nuzzling my cheek, I make my move, but no sooner have I tensed my muscles to make my escape, I'm flipped onto my back, my thighs parted and my wrists pinned on either side of my head. He looks down at me, his eyes bright and skipping with enjoyment. Oh yes, he's deeply satisfied with himself, and he looks bloody glorious, with his disheveled hair and dark blond stubble.

My body responds to him automatically, and the pain in my bladder is soon replaced by a distressed ache in my groin, my heart somewhere between my breastbone and my throat. His daybreak smell is a mixture of clean sweat and that heady fresh water scent I love so much. I'm breathless. He must think I'm so easy.

Well, I am … with him.

He rubs his nose over mine. 'Sleep well?'

He wants a chat now? 'Very.' I roll my hips suggestively, and his eyebrows rise, his lips twitching.

'Me too.'

I wait for him to take the lead. He watches me closely as he slowly drops his face to mine, and when our lips finally brush, I moan, opening my mouth invitingly and involuntarily trembling when he skims his tongue gently across mine, taking his time, slowly seducing my mouth and pulling back every so often to kiss my lips gently before he resumes exploring. Oh, I like gentle Jesse very much. This is a million miles away from the dominant sex lord I was faced with yesterday.

When he's happy that he's got me enthralled, he releases my wrists and leisurely strokes down the side of my body with the tip of his index finger. It's enough to have me convulsing and rolling my hips as the pressure in my tummy spirals down to my core.

His touch is addictive. *He* is addictive. I'm totally addicted.

Reaching around to seize his rock-solid arse in my palms, I apply a little pressure, deliberately pressing his hips into mine. We both whimper in harmony against each other's mouths.

'I completely lose myself in you, lady,' he mumbles against my lips as he pulls away, watching my face when he sinks slowly and purposely into me, inch by perfect inch, sending my hands flying to his back and my eyes squeezing shut. I'm full to the hilt.

He remains motionless, letting me adjust around him, his back tense, his breathing shallow. I know it must be taking everything out of him to be so still.

'Look at me, Ava.'

I peel my eyes open. His jaw is tense, his light frown line deeper than usual, and his green eyes are blazing. I roll my hips a fraction to signal I'm okay, and on my invitation, he slowly draws back until I'm sure he's going to pull out, but then, bit by bit, he plunges straight back in to the deepest part of me – in and out, in and out.

'Hmmm.' I moan on a long exhale.

'I love sleepy sex with you,' he breathes.

The deliberate, measured strokes are playing havoc with my self-control. I push my hips up to meet his penetrations, sending him deeper and me higher. The feeling is extraordinary.

'Is that good, Ava?' he asks quietly. He knows it is. His gaze is still locked on mine and I surprise myself that I can maintain the intimacy. It's like we're supposed to be this way.

'Yes,' I breathe.

'Faster?'

'No, just like this, please, just stay like this.' This is perfect. The hard, powerful, commanding Jesse is amazing, but right now, this is absolutely perfect.

His eyes swim as he regards me, continuing his measured dives in and out. I want him to kiss me, but he seems content just looking at me, so I link my legs around his lower back and run my hands up and down his arms in light, feathery strokes.

On a slow withdraw, he pauses, momentarily appearing to gather himself, his eyes probing mine. 'Enough of the sleepy sex,' he murmurs as he surges forward, thrashing me in the deepest recesses of my body, not giving me a moment to adjust.

He cries out and retreats before repeating the delectable move again and again, slowly withdrawing and striking hard. The pleasure washes over me like a storm, sending my mind into orbit. His drives are controlled and exact. I'm reaching my limit. I fist my hands in his hair, pulling his lips down to mine, running my tongue over his bottom lip and biting it lightly, letting it drag through my teeth as I pull away. He bursts forward again, his face tense as he finds my lips and kisses me passionately.

'I'm never letting you go,' he informs me around our kiss.

'I don't want you to.'

He freezes suddenly, stopping the rhythmic drives that had me set to disintegrate in his arms, and I wince at the lack of movement, my orgasm lying in limbo. He's still buried balls-deep inside me as he pulls his head up and looks at me. I'm snapped out of my confusing thoughts immediately by the look of displeasure on his face.

It was the wrong thing to say. I got caught up in the moment, that's all. I look away from him. I've ruined it.

'Look at me now, Ava.' I reluctantly return my eyes to his, finding his face has softened slightly. 'We're going to have this conversation when you're sound-minded and not crazy with lust.' He draws back to the very tip of his thick erection and hovers over me.

He's right; I'm not sound-minded when I'm around him, especially when he has me like this. He cripples me with pleasure, and now he's got me saying crazy shit.

His tongue sweeps his bottom lip and he pants as he pushes

forward, dragging my dormant orgasm back to life. My skin blazes as he pumps slow and hard, and as deep as he can get. Smoothing my palms through his hair, I pull him back down to my lips and devour him while he continues with his deliberate drives.

'I'm going to come,' he mumbles. 'Come with me, Ava. Give it to me.'

And with three more strikes, my mind goes blank and fireworks start exploding in my head. I burst beneath him on a loud cry.

'That's it, baby.' He strains the words, joining me in my pleasure as I rein in my shouts, and moan long and low as his hardness expands, jerking within me, before releasing round after round of his hot, wet seed deep inside me. He collapses on top of me, pushing his hips hard against me, ensuring he empties every last bit of himself. I'm obliterated as both of us lay entangled, panting and struggling for breath.

'I don't know what to say,' he whispers against my ear.

I'm only just cognitive, but I heard that loud and clear, and I'm not quite sure what to make of it. I think we've both said too much already. That's what happens when you get caught up in the moment. Lust and passion take over, and before you know it, ridiculous words are flying out of your mouth.

After a few minutes' silence, I'm beyond uncomfortable, so I shuffle a bit under him. 'Can I use the bathroom now?' I ask.

He slides out, making a huge, exaggerated effort of flopping back on the bed. I've no idea what he's frustrated about.

Without a word, I pad across the white carpet into the bathroom, shutting the door behind me. I know he watched my every step. I could feel his eyes hammering into my naked back. The inevitable awkwardness has been delayed, but it's here now. And it's here with a vengeance.

I use the loo, wash my hands, and take a few moments

to psych myself up before I open the door, finding him still sprawled on his back, unapologetically naked and staring straight at me. I don't know what to do. 'I should go. Kate will be wondering where I am.'

He chews his lips furiously, the cogs firing into action. 'Maybe I'd like to keep you here.'

'She needs my car.' I want to be sensible and leave, but I also don't. 'Will you take me?'

He blasts me back into the bathroom with his smile, making me feel so much better, the awkwardness gone, just like that. 'What do you say?'

'Please.' I grin, and he jumps up from the bed.

'Good girl. Give me five.'

I'm on my knees gingerly plucking up pieces of glass from the kitchen floor when Jesse strolls in from the bedroom. I glance up, finding he's wearing beige board shorts, a white Ralph Lauren Polo shirt – collar turned up – and blue Converse. The blond hairs on his muscled legs are bleached, highlighted by his slight tan. He's not shaved, but his blond stubble doesn't conceal his handsome features. I'm on my knees, lips parted, looking deprived. I feel deprived.

He stops in front of me, looking down with a grin on his face. He looks younger. I want to jump him, but with a hand full of glass shards, us both fully dressed *and* late, I shall resist.

'I need to go,' I press, trying to ignore the mass of male beauty looming over me.

'Here,' he holds both his hands out in front of him for me to transfer the glass. 'You should have left it, Ava. You could've cut yourself.' He empties his hands, tipping the glass into the sink. 'I'll sort it later.' Slipping on his Wayfarers, he collects his keys and my bags before grabbing my hand and leading me to the door.

'Are you working today?' I ask.

'No, not much goes on at The Manor during the day,' he winks, and I melt. He's all roguish, and I love it.

He opens the door and we're immediately met by a couple of scruffy-looking men with clipboards, wearing blue overalls. The embroidered print on their uniforms reads, 'B&C Removals.'

'Mr. Ward?' the one that looks like a trucker asks, his yellow teeth indicating at least fifty cigarettes and twenty cups of coffee a day.

'The boxes in the spare room go first. My housekeeper will be here shortly to assist with the rest.' He pulls me through the corridor, leaving the trucker type and his lanky apprentice to get on with things. 'Be careful with the ski and bike equipment,' he yells behind him.

'You have a housekeeper?' I don't know why this surprises me. The man's bought the penthouse at Lusso for a cool ten million. He's beyond rich.

'She's the only woman I couldn't live without,' he replies flippantly. 'She's off to Ireland next week to visit her family. It'll all fall apart then.'

I make it to my car in record time, after Jesse dipped and weaved through the early morning traffic. Fellow drivers seem to be more accommodating to an Aston Martin and a few hand gestures. He loads my bags into the back of my car while I check my phone. Ten past eight. I fire a quick text to Kate to tell her that I'm on my way and look up, finding him staring at me. Even through his Wayfarers – which he looks tremendous in – I can feel that potent green gaze blazing my skin.

I open the driver's door of my Mini, jump in and start the engine, and Jesse is crouched down by my side in a heartbeat.

'I'll take you for lunch.'

'I told you, I've got stacks to get done.' I'm not being side-tracked by roguish Jesse, although he is very distracting.

'Dinner then.'

'I'll ring you later.' I've spent the whole night with him, he's fucked me into oblivion, and I need some recovery time.

His shoulders sag and he scowls heavily. 'Are you refusing me?'

'No, I'll call you later.'

Leaning in and resting his palm on my thigh, he plants a scorching hot kiss on my lips, leaving me slightly breathless. 'Make sure you do,' he says, strolling away, enhancing that bloody gait. That was a look-what-you're-missing kiss. It worked.

'How old are you, Jesse?' I shout after him.

He turns, walking backward with a fraction of a grin tickling his lips. 'Twenty–four.'

The engine rumbles to life and he roars off like a teenage rally driver. Maybe he is twenty-four. He certainly acts it sometimes.

I fly through the front door and up the stairs, finding Kate drying her hair on the landing. She looks flustered, which means she's running late. When she spots me, she turns the dryer off and grins from ear to ear.

'Good night?' she asks on an arched brow. She doesn't seem in much of a rush now.

'It was okay,' I shrug, reflexively grabbing a tendril of hair. I can't help the smile breaking out across my own face.

'Ha!' she cries. 'Do tell.'

'Yeah, he's a God. I can't lie to you. He's the new owner of the penthouse.'

'Fuck off! He's delicious *and* super rich?'

I smile my agreement. 'Sorry if I worried you when I didn't come home. I left a message on your phone.'

'I've not checked my phone. Anyway, the way he was looking at you, the only thing I was worried about was you not being able to walk this morning.' She starts laughing as she chucks her dryer on the floor and makes her way into her super-tidy bedroom. 'And, if I'm not mistaken, there's a limp!'

I follow her in, flopping on her perfectly made bed. 'Jesus, Kate. The man has experience.' That sudden thought reminds me of all the many conquests that would have come before me. I screw my face up in disgust.

'You wanted uncomplicated fun. It looks like you've got it. High five!' She air slaps me and leaves the room. 'And there's no girlfriend?'

Did I want uncomplicated fun? Will this be uncomplicated fun? 'No, but she wants him. I've worked that much out.'

'Oh well, unlucky for her. I've got to beat feet. I'll be back tomorrow afternoon. What are you up to while I'm gone?'

I roll off her bed and smooth the covers before leaving her immaculate room, shutting the door behind me. 'I'm going to sort my stuff out. Have we got any bin bags?'

'Hurrah! They're under the sink,' She grabs her bag from the top of the stairs and makes her way down to the door. 'Thanks for your car. You're more than welcome to borrow Margo. Bye!'

It's Monday morning again, but unusual in that everyone is here. There's always at least one of us out of the office on site visits or appointments. After Kate returned from Yorkshire late last night, we curled up on the sofa and shared a bottle of wine and a family-size bar of Dairy Milk while I filled her in on my Lord, and she filled me in on her senile grandmother.

Now I'm in the kitchen with Patrick, bringing him up to date on Mrs Kent's new house.

'She can move every year for the rest of her life for all I care, as long as she keeps contracting you to jazz the place up.'

I frown. 'I don't know. I think she loves having the workmen around.' I raise my eyebrows on a laugh.

Patrick laughs with me. 'The old goat is seventy, if a day! Maybe she should get a toy-boy. God knows, Mr K has plenty of young scrumpets scattered around the globe. I have that straight from a very reliable source.' He winks at me, and I smile fondly at him.

I know Patrick's referring to his wife, Irene. If it's happening in this town, Irene knows about it. She's a self-confessed busy-body, know-it-all and gossip. If she doesn't know about it, then it isn't worth knowing about.

'Oh, Van Der Haus wants to meet you on Wednesday,' Patrick continues. 'They really want you, flower.'

'Really?'

He laughs. 'You're too modest, my girl. I checked your diary and pencilled in twelve-thirty. He's at the Royal Park. Is that okay?'

'Absolutely.' I push myself away from the kitchen worktop and head for my desk. 'I'm going to finalise some drawings and e-mail some contractors.'

'Okay, flower.'

I land at my desk and find a text from Kate, asking for a hand after work with a delivery. I quickly reply, telling her to pick me up from the office, then crack on.

As I'm getting ready to run over to the cafe to grab some lunch, Tom prances up to my desk. 'Delivery for Ava!' he screeches, placing a box on my desk.

What's this? I'm not expecting any catalogues or samples. 'Thanks, Tom. Did you have a good night on Friday?'

'Forget my weekend. Tell me who that man was.' He plants his hands on my desk, leaning in toward me.

'What man?' I blurt, far too quickly, retreating in my chair to get some distance from the interrogating presence of my nosy friend.

'Your reaction speaks volumes.' His eyes narrow on me as my face burns up.

'He's just a client.' I shrug.

Tom's scrutinizing stare moves to my fingers, that are

currently playing with a lock of my hair. I release it, quickly picking up a pen. I need to work on this lying business. I'm truly rubbish at it. His tongue moves into his cheek as he straightens himself and walks away from my desk.

What's wrong with me? I yank the box open, finding a single calla lily on top of a book that's wrapped in tissue paper.

Giuseppe Cavalli. Fotografie 1936–1961

I open the cover, and a note slips out.

Ava,
You're like a book I can't put down. I need to know more.
Jx

My eyes drift slowly between the flower and the note, considering what he may want to know. He could start with telling me a few things, like how old he is. Falling into a daydream, I relive every vivid moment of Friday night. Trying to keep myself busy by clearing out my belongings over the weekend did nothing to distract me. I desperately wanted to call him, but that miniscule piece of intelligence I've hung onto kept stopping me, telling me I'll just be setting myself up for disappointment. I don't want to be at the mercy of a man, and Jesse Ward is too easy to surrender to. I reluctantly drag my thoughts away from The Lord and steal a quick inhale of the calla before popping it in my drawer and getting on with some work.

At six o'clock, Margo hisses and bangs up to the pavement to pick me up. I battle with the rusty handle and climb in, pushing a dozen cake magazines and empty Starbucks cups to the floor before I can settle myself on the seat.

'You need a new delivery van.' Considering how crazy tidy Kate is at home, Margo is the pits.

'Shhhh; you'll hurt her feelings.' She grins. 'Good day?' She eyes me warily.

My shoulders slump. I take the book and note from my bag and hand them to her across the van. Uncertainty mars her pretty, pale features as she opens the front sleeve and the note slips onto her lap. She picks it up, scans the words and gapes at me.

'Yikes! The Lord is deep.' She thrusts the book back at me and pulls into the traffic.

'He is.' I start thinking about pillow talk, green eyes and hard warmth.

'Just how good in bed are we talking here?' Kate asks casually, keeping her eyes on the road.

My head snaps to the side to look at her, but she won't return my stare. 'Very,' I reply. The best, amazing, mind-blowing! I want to do it again and again and again!

'Will this be a pinball rebound?'

I sigh, not answering because I'm scared to admit it out loud.

She reaches over and squeezes my knee, smiling thoughtfully. She knows what's happening here.

Chapter Eleven

We slow at the entrance of a residential street, and Kate brings Margo to a stop.

'Right. Get in the back.'

'What?'

'Get in the back, Ava!' She reinforces her instructions with a batting of my knee.

'Why?' I'm frowning heavily.

She points down the street and realisation dawns on me. I look at her, completely wide-eyed.

She has the decency to look a little apologetic. 'I've strapped, padded and cushioned, but this street is a fucking nightmare. That cake took me two weeks to finish. If it goes over, I'm fucked.'

I look down the tree-lined street. Cars are parked on both sides and there is just room for one line of traffic down the middle. That's not what's bothering me, though. It's the vicious, black, rubber speed humps dotted every twenty yards that have my attention. Oh God, I'm going to be tossed about like a penny in a tumble dryer.

'Can't we carry it?' I ask desperately.

'It's five tiers and it weighs a ton. Just hold on to the box. It'll be fine.'

I exhale, unclipping my seatbelt. 'I can't believe you've got me doing this,' I grumble, climbing into the back of the van and wrapping my arms around the tall cake box. 'Couldn't you assemble it on site?'

'Nope.'

'Why not?'

'I just couldn't. Hold the fucking cake!' she yells impatiently.

I tighten my grip, spreading my legs to keep my balance, and lay my cheek against the box. We're positioned at the mouth of the road, engine revving and looking like something out of a comedy sketch.

'Ready?' she calls back.

I hear Margo crunch into gear. 'Just bloody get on with it, will you?' I snap.

She's giggling as she slowly starts creeping forward and it's not long before a car horn starts honking impatiently from behind. 'Fuck off, you tosser!' Kate yells as we hit our first speed hump.

I'm propelled into the air, my face squishing against the box, my heels sliding from under me. 'Kate!' I screech, landing on my arse.

'Don't let go of that box!'

I scramble back to my feet, grabbing the box just as the back wheels jolt down the other side of the hump. 'Will you take it easy?'

'I need a run up, else she won't make it over!' she exclaims, hitting another hump.

'Bloody hell!' I'm catapulted into the air, landing with an almighty thud. 'Kate!'

She's laughing hard now, only serving to piss me off more. 'Sorry!' she gasps.

'No you're not,' I mutter, pulling myself up again. I kick my heels off to try and get a better balance.

'Oh, no.'

I blow my hair out of my face. 'What?'

'I'm not reversing, mister!' she hisses.

I spot a Jaguar driving at us and with only enough width for one vehicle and no space to pull in, it's a standoff. A string of loud car horns start singing out around us as Kate proceeds forward, knocking me all over the place in the back of Margo.

'I'll ram you,' she warns Mr Jaguar, smacking her horn repeatedly. 'Is the cake okay?'

'Yes! Don't you dare let him win,' I yell, landing on my backside again. 'Shit!'

'Hang on, only two more to go.'

'Oh God!'

Two jolts later and probably another two more bruises on my behind, we're double-parked and unloading the stupid five-tier cake. Mr Jaguar is honking, cursing and throwing hand gestures all over the place, but we ignore him. My feet are still bare as I help Kate out with the cake, delivering it into the massive kitchen of Mrs Link, who's throwing a sixteenth birthday party for her daughter. I leave Kate to sort the rest and go back to Margo to wait for her, ignoring the car horns as I look for my shoes in the back.

'Move the van, you stupid bitch!' The violent tone pulls my head from the van to find an overweight, balding, middle-aged businessman approaching with a face like thunder. 'Are you fucking deaf?'

Oh shit, he's going to crack me one. I look toward the steps that lead to Mrs Link's house, but the front door is still firmly closed.

I gasp when I'm shoved in the back. 'Please, give me five minutes.' I plead with the irate twat. If Kate was here, he would be on his arse by now.

'Just move the fucking shed, you dopey cow!' he roars in my face, making me recoil.

I run onto the pavement, stepping on every stray stone on my way, and up the steps to Mrs Link's front door. 'Kate!' I knock frantically, turning and smiling sweetly at Mr Baldy Jag, earning myself another torrent of abuse. This guy needs anger management. 'Kate!' I shout, banging again. Car horns are blaring all around, I've got the angriest man I've ever encountered hurling abuse at me, my arse is sore and my feet are being stabbed by fucking stones! 'KATE!!!' My throat is bloody sore now, too. But then I have a thought. Has she left the keys in Margo? I gingerly run down the steps, back onto the street to check Margo's ignition, going around the back to avoid Baldy.

It would seem that he's not so willing to let me evade him, though, and I collide with his fat, sweaty body as I reach the driver's door. 'Oh!' I cry, getting a waft of stale body odour.

He grabs the top of my arm, squeezing hard. 'If you don't move that fucking thing now, I'll slap your skinny arse all over this street.'

I lean back against the van as he tightens his hold on my arm to a point so painful I want to cry out. I'm going to be bludgeoned on a leafy residential street in posh Belgravia and be plastered all over tomorrow morning's news. I feel my eyes welling up with panicky tears as I'm pinned to the side of Margo with not a clue what to do.

'Get your fucking hands off her!'

The roar that pierces the air around me, blocking out all car horns and London traffic, makes my knees buckle with relief. I turn toward the direction of the most welcome voice I've ever heard and see Jesse running down the middle of the road in his suit, looking murderous.

Oh, thank God! I don't know where he's come from, and I couldn't care less. The relief that washes over me is overwhelming. I've never been so glad to see anyone in my life, and the fact that it's a man I've known barely a week *should* be telling me something.

Mr. Baldy Jag's fat, ugly head snaps up in Jesse's direction, a deep look of panic instantly invading his sweaty features. I feel his grip ease up. Letting go of me and stepping back from Margo, he starts weighing up the mountain of lean tallness that's running at full pelt toward us. The intention to scarper is clear on his ugly face. He doesn't get the chance to, though. Jesse charges him before he sets his short legs to work, taking him clean from his feet and sending him crashing to the Tarmac.

My God! I was wrong. Baldy isn't the angriest man I've ever seen. I watch as Jesse's fist collides with Baldie's face before he kicks him in the gut, causing him to cry out.

'Get off your fat arse and apologise,' Jesse yanks him up from the road, presenting him to me. 'Apologise!' he roars.

I look at Baldy, who's huffing and puffing, his nose clearly broken, blood dripping down his slimy suit. I would feel sorry for him if he wasn't such a nasty bastard. What sort of man does that to a woman?

'I … I'm s … sorry …' he stutters, looking completely dazed.

Jesse's fisted hand in Baldie's jacket shakes him. 'Lay a finger on her again, I'll rip your fucking head off.' His voice is menacing. 'Now, fuck off.' He shoves the crumpled heap of a man out of his hands and grabs me, yanking me into his chest.

I fall apart. I'm a stupid blubbering wreck as I sob all over Jesse's expensive suit while he holds me against his hard, warm chest.

'I should have finished the bastard off,' he grumbles. 'Hey, stop the tears. I'll get crazy mad.' He spreads his palm over the back of my head and sighs into my hair.

'Where did you come from?' I mumble, pulling out of his chest. I don't care; I'm just glad he's here.

He flicks me a look, almost embarrassed. 'I …'

I don't prevent my gasp of shock. 'You followed me, didn't you?'

'And it's a good job.' He dismisses me. 'Where's Kate?'

Yes, where is Kate? Mayhem has broken out and she's still nowhere to be seen. I'm going to kill her – after I've had my fix of Jesse.

'Hey, what's going on?'

I look up and see Kate standing at the front of Margo, looking rather bewildered.

'I think you need to move your van, Kate,' Jesse advises diplomatically. He's not even broke a sweat.

'Oh, okay.' She shrugs, completely oblivious.

Jesse pulls back, running his eyes down my body. 'Where are your shoes?' he asks on a frown, his eyes darkening with rage again, clearly thinking I lost them in the ruckus with Baldy.

'They're in the back of Margo,' I sniffle. 'The van,' I elaborate, when his brow knits in confusion.

He picks me up and carries me around to the pavement, sitting me on a wall outside Mrs Link's house. 'I'm not even going to ask how they got there.'

'I'll get them,' Kate shouts. She bloody should as well. She comes running over with my heels. 'What happened?'

'Where were you?' I ask shortly.

She rolls her eyes. 'I got dragged upstairs for a showing of the party dress. It was way too small and pretty painful to watch. It took them ten minutes to stuff her in the thing.' She glances over at Jesse, who's grabbing my bag from the front seat of Margo. 'What happened?' she asks again on a whisper. 'He looks fuming.'

'I got roughed up by Mr Jaguar,' I brush the gravel from the bottom of my sore soles and put my heels on. 'Jesse ...' I pause, wondering if following could be classed as stalking, 'just happened to be passing.'

'Ava, I'm sorry.' She sits on the wall and puts an arm around me. 'Thank God for the Lord, eh?' I can detect the suggestion in her tone.

'Kate, you need to shift that van before war breaks out.' Jesse strolls over with my bag as I get to my feet. Damn, they hurt. I rest my bum back down on the wall again, wincing when my arse meets the concrete. Jesse frowns when he catches me flinching. 'I'm taking Ava with me.'

'You are?' I blurt.

He raises his eyebrows. 'Yes, I am.' His tone dares me to object.

'I'll see you at home.' Kate kisses my temple and strolls off toward Margo, with absolutely no urgency, looking back and grinning.

I ignore her and gaze up at the tall, handsome beast in front of me – looking edible in his grey suit and crisp white shirt – and find green eyes narrowed on me. 'Why are you flinching?'

I stand up, wincing again when my feet take my full weight. 'My backside hurts,' I rub my battered bum and reach to take my bag from him. 'I was holding Kate's cake up in the back of Margo.'

'You didn't have a seatbelt on?'

'No. You don't get seatbelts in the back of vans, Jesse.'

He shakes his head and picks me up, cradling me in his strong arms, before striding off down the street. I sigh heavily and let him do his thing, resting my head against his shoulder and wrapping my arms around his neck.

'You didn't call me. I told you to call,' he grumbles accusingly.

'I'm sorry.'

'So am I.'

'What are you sorry for?'

'For not being here sooner, Don't do stupid shit, Ava. And call when I tell you to.'

I frown into his shoulder and he looks down at me as if sensing my response to his scold. He grins, brushing his lips on my forehead. My eyes close. I can't ignore it. There's definitely something here and it's knocked the wind right out of my singleton sails.

He pulls up outside Kate's, and I'm not surprised that Margo's not arrived home yet. The man drives like a loon. I let myself out of the car, but I'm soon scooped up and carried up the path to the front door.

'I can walk.' I laugh, but he ignores me, taking my keys from my hand when we reach the door and opening it himself before kicking it shut behind us. I wriggle and he places me on my feet, his hand wrapping around my waist, pulling me into him.

I'm lifted until my lips meet his, and I sigh, linking my arms around his neck, letting his tongue roll around my mouth slowly and calmly. I'm screwed if I even *think* I can resist him.

'Thank you for the book,' I say against his lips.

He leans back, gazing at me, his green eyes twinkling with pleasure. 'You're more than welcome.' He drops a chaste kiss on my lips.

'Thank you for saving me.'

He smiles that cheeky, roguish smile. 'Anytime, baby.'

The front door flies open and Kate bowls in, clocking us in our embrace.

'Sorry,' she mouths, hastily retreating upstairs to the flat.

Jesse laughs lightly and rolls his hips into me, unearthing a delightful drum deep in my stomach. My breath hitches as his forehead meets mine. 'If we were alone, you would be against that wall and I would be fucking you stupid.' He rolls again, dragging a whimper from me as the drumming moves into my core. I mentally curse Kate to Hell.

'I can be quiet,' I whisper. 'Gag me if you must.'

He smirks. 'Trust me, you'll be screaming. No gag will stifle it.' My body convulses. 'Now, tomorrow,' he says assertively, 'I'd like to make an appointment.'

'An appointment to fuck me?'

'Mouth!' he laughs. 'I want you back at The Manor so you can take the details you *really* need to start working on some designs.'

My mouth forms an O and he leans down, plunging his tongue in, attacking me with passion. I let him take me with everything he has, my knees buckling when he rolls those damn, delectable hips again.

I feel lost when he breaks away, panting, his eyes briefly clenching shut. 'I don't make appointments to fuck you, Ava. I'll be doing that when I please.'

Removing his hooded eyes from mine, he glances up the stairs, and I know he's cursing Kate for being home, too.

'The Manor at noon,' he states, reaching up and running his finger down my cheek. I nod. 'Good girl.' He smiles, pushes his lips against my forehead before turning and striding out.

I sag against the wall, trying to catch my breath, my mind racing. I'm falling. I'm falling hard and fast.

And I'm scared.

Chapter Twelve

The next morning, I land in the office with an almighty crash – quite literally. I'm sprawled across the wooden floor, surrounded by boxes, with Tom running toward me, horror plastered all over his baby face.

'Oh God. Are you okay?' He reaches down to help me up, brushing down my black, fitted skirt before beginning on my sleeveless blouse. 'I'm so sorry. I was just moving them into storage.' He flaps around me like a mother hen, babbling about health and safety and accident books.

'Tom, I'm fine. Get your hands off my tits!'

He quickly withdraws his flapping hands from my breasts, giggling. 'Oh, and what lovely breasts they are, Red Riding Hood!'

'If you weren't gay, I would have slapped you by now.'

'Morning,' I hear Victoria before I see her. 'Tom, I'm never going out with you again,' she hisses at him, perching herself on her chair.

I look to each of them in turn. 'What's going on?'

'He dumped me again!'

I drop my bag by my desk and watch as Victoria fires all sorts of accusations at a very guilty-looking Tom. With no desire to get involved, I get my phone from my bag and find a text from Kate.

Left early, didn't want to wake u in case u were dreaming of all things Lord like ;-)

Baroque at 1? Have to be back for 2:30 xxx

Yes. And daydreams too. My confused mind homes straight in on the thoughts that kept me awake most of the night – the thoughts that are making my heart and head squabble relentlessly. He's taken me, fought and won, but I'm not sure I'm ready to give myself to a man again, and especially to a man who demands so much. I'm a sensible girl, except, it seems, when it comes to Jesse. I need time to think about this, without him close by to distract me with his touch.

I try to busy myself with e-mails and checking up on contractor progress, while at the same time thinking of all sorts of excuses I can feed Jesse. I should arrange a meeting, make it business and ensure it stays that way, which is far easier said than done when I'm in close proximity to him.

Patrick comes rolling in at eleven with Starbucks. I could kiss him.

'Cappuccino, extra shot, no sugar or chocolate for you, flower.' He clucks my cheek, placing my coffee on my desk. 'Don't forget your appointment with Mikael tomorrow,' he perches on my desk and I hold my breath as it creaks.

'No, I haven't.' I push my diary across my desk for Patrick to see the big, bold print.

'Good girl. How did you get on at The Manor?'

I blush instantly. I didn't tell Patrick about my second appointment, but he only has to flick through my diary to see – which he obviously has.

'Fine,' I squeak, my voice a few notes higher than my typical tone.

'Jolly good. Keep me posted.' He lifts himself up from my desk and goes about handing out the rest of the coffees. I instinctively check underneath for splintered wood or loose screws, puffing my cheeks out in relief for both his lack of interrogation and for my desk's well-being. With all of my distractions,

I hadn't considered the possibility of Patrick finding out about my extracurricular activities with Mr Ward. This could have a very detrimental effect on my career. I can't risk that as well as a broken heart. In a moment based on pure instinct, I text Kate a yes to her lunch offer and follow it up with a message to Jesse.

I'm sorry. I need to cancel.

I can't even see him on a professional level right now. He'll push and I'll cave. No sooner have I placed my phone back on my desk and untangled my finger from my hair, the office door opens and a spray of calla lilies are carted in. It's the delivery girl from Lusso. I see Tom point to my desk, and I'm instantly flooded with guilt. I slump in my chair. I've just stood him up and he's sent me flowers. I accept the bouquet, signing the delivery girl's paperwork before finding the card.

> *I'm very much looking forward to my appointment.*
> *You should be too.*
> *Jx*

I drop my arms on the desk and bury my head in them, telling myself that this is the right thing to do – the sensible thing. His written word has just confirmed that this meeting will not be in the least bit business-related. Fuck!

My phone starts ringing. I don't have to look at it to know who's calling. He was never going to accept a brush-off via text, or *any* brush-off for that matter. It stops, but almost immediately blurts the arrival of a text.

Cancel for what?

I read the three-word, simple question a dozen times and come up with nothing that'll appease him, so I bite the bullet and text him back.

Just give me some time. This is really intense, really fast.

I leave at twelve-forty-five to go and meet Kate, after ignoring ten missed calls from Jesse, who's clearly not prepared to give me the time I'd like.

When I arrive, the bar is busy, but I spot Kate in the corner with drinks already on the table. She detects my despondency immediately. 'Should I ask what the matter is?' she says, just as my phone starts screaming again and I let out an almighty sigh. 'Who's that?'

'Jesse.'

She frowns. 'Aren't you going to answer?'

I lean back in my chair, letting it ring off. 'I cancelled my meeting with him.'

Kate's jaw drops open. 'Why?'

I think real hard, but it hurts too much. 'I'm not sure …' My shoulders sag. 'I don't know.' I was so overwhelmed yesterday, I let a firm chest, hypnotic voice and soft, lush lips derail my cognitive thinking.

She gives me a sympathetic look, but it quickly transforms into one of immense interest when something catches her eye. 'Hello, hottie at three o'clock! Oh, and he's looking. How's my hair? Have I got any icing on my face?' Kate starts frantically brushing her cheeks with her palms.

I turn to three o'clock and see the guy from the bar at The Manor, Sam. He has a big smile on his cheeky face as he raises his bottle of beer to me. I raise my hand and turn back to Kate.

'You know him?' she asks incredulously.

'Sam. He was at The Manor. He's a friend of Jesse's.'

'Fucking hell! Jesse's a member of the hot gang.' She giggles, her eyes widening with excitement. 'Hey, he's coming over. Introduce me, please!'

I shake my head at her. It's one more first date for her to get her teeth into. Sam reaches the table, still smiling and flashing that dimple. He really is very cute, with his unkempt hair and twinkling eyes. He's in jeans and a t-shirt again. Casual must be his thing.

'Ava, how are you?'

'I'm good, Sam. You?'

'Great. How's Jesse?' he enquires on a grin.

I feel my face blush, even though I've reached the swift conclusion that he's playing with me. He's Jesse's mate; he should know how he is. I shrug, because I really don't know what to say. When I left him yesterday, he was firing on all sexual cylinders, and I was panting like a desperate, wanton loser. Now, I expect, he's slightly irate that I've cancelled our meeting. No, scrap that. I *know* he's irate. His persistent calls tell me so.

I feel a sharp crack on my shin and look up to see Kate scowling at me. 'Oh, Sam, this is Kate. Kate, meet Sam.' I wave my hand between the two of them, watching as Kate turns all angelic, putting her hand out to Sam, who grins before clasping it.

'Nice to meet you, Kate,' he says smoothly, maintaining his grin and running his free hand through his mousy waves.

'You, too.' She giggles as Sam compliments her wild, red hair, their hands still linked.

My phone declares a text, and to escape the blatant flirting going on in front of me, I pick it up and open the message with one eye closed.

There better be a GOOD fucking reason for you standing me up & needing time isn't one! Someone had better be dying. I'm going out of my fucking mind, lady. NO KISS

My poor bloody brain feels like it could explode. What's happening to me? I put my phone on the table and look up to see Kate performing the best flirting act I've ever witnessed. And their hands are still clasped.

She drags her attention away from Sam to look at me. 'Jesse?'

'Jesse?' Sam repeats, turning his gaze to me.

'Yes,' I reply off-hand, like it doesn't matter, taking a needed swig of my lunchtime wine.

I sit forever, ignored by Kate and Sam while they chat and laugh. It suits me fine, but it also gives me too much time to think. But it's no good. I need quiet. Peace. Silence around me and a bottle of wine while I let my heart and brain loose on each other.

I stand, keen to get back to work and attempt to busy myself. 'Kate,' I smile sweetly as she finally drags her greedy blue eyes away from Sam. 'Haven't you got a two-thirty appointment?'

'Nope.' She smiles back, trumping my sweetness level.

I narrow my eyes on her playfully, picking up my bag and phone. 'I'll see you later then. It was nice to see you again, Sam.'

He kisses me on the cheek. 'Yeah and you, Ava. Keep it real.'

I turn to leave and find Jesse standing behind me, glaring at me like a rabid dog, but looking delicious in a charcoal suit.

'Who's dead?' he barks.

I shrink on the spot, as he scowls at me, good and proper. 'You don't get to fuck me off, Ava.'

Kate starts looking anywhere and everywhere but our direction, and Sam does a really rubbish job of looking uninterested. Jesse looks like he's about to hit something.

'I have to get back to work,' I say quietly, sidestepping him and leaving the bar.

I walk out onto Piccadilly and into the lunchtime crowd, knowing he's following me. I can feel his penetrating green eyes stabbing at my back, so I quicken my pace, intent on making it to my office where I'm safe from his wrath and interrogation.

I make it through the office door, but no sooner have I made it to my desk, I'm hauled from my feet on a squeal, and I'm on my way back out.

'What the bloody hell are you doing?' I shout at him, but he ignores me, carrying on with his long, even strides out of my office. I brace my hands at the bottom of his back and look up to see Tom, Victoria, and Sally with their faces pushed up against the window, gawping as I'm manhandled into the street. Oh God, please let Patrick be out of the office.

'Jesse, fucking hell! Put me down now!'

He lets me slide down his front – purposely slow so I feel every hard muscle of his delicious chest – stopping me before my feet hit the ground. He holds me around my waist so my lips are level with his, his blatant erection rubbing me in just the right spot. He's mad *and* turned on?

A treacherous moan escapes my lips as he pushes himself against me, breathing his hot, minty breath on my lips. My senses have been hijacked again, just from contact, as he holds me in place in front of all my colleagues, who are all squashed at the office door, fighting for the best view.

'Mouth. You stood me up.' He presses his lips to mine before he pulls away, his eyes softening as he looks at me expectantly.

'I'm sorry.' I divert my eyes from his penetrating stare, not knowing what else to say. My conflicting thoughts are becoming frustrating. When he's still silent a few moments later, I slowly lift my gaze back to him. This could be a mistake.

He shakes his head mildly, and then he attacks my mouth, right in the middle of Bruton Street. He's reminding me. My fingers thread through his hair as I surrender to his impossibly addictive mouth and he unashamedly consumes me, oblivious to the hustle and bustle of lunchtime pedestrians passing and staring.

'What do you need time for?' He thrusts his groin forward aggressively, coaxing a moan to escape my mouth.

'To think.'

'Don't think, Ava,' he orders, in a tone that dares me to defy him. 'This is how it is. Accept it.' He releases me from his grip and my feet hit the ground, the loss of support causing me to stagger forward.

He grabs the top of my arm to steady me, causing a slight stab of pain to radiate through me, snapping me out of my spellbound state on a sharp inhale. I'm dropped from his hold and he stands back, his soft eyes raging and focused on the scatter of bruises at the top of my arm, courtesy of Mr Baldy Jag. His jaw starts ticking, his chest puffing, as he stares at my arm.

'I'm fine,' I cover my arm with my palm in the hope that concealing the offending area might snap him out of his fuming state. He looks positively homicidal. 'I need to get back to work.' My voice is small, nervous even. I'm not at all comfortable with the darkening of his green eyes.

Eventually, he shakes his head lightly and stalks off, without another word, leaving me standing on the pavement wondering what in the world just happened. I look down to the ground, my eyes darting about, like I might find the answer written in chalk on the slabs.

Is that it? Is it over? The look on his face said it is, but I'm not sure how I feel about that now. One second he's thrusting his hips into me on a moan, the next he's looking at me in pure irritation. What am I supposed to make of this? I really don't know, so I shake myself out of my reverie and head back into the office.

The silence is awkward, everyone obviously pretending to look busy.

'You okay?' Tom asks, slowly passing my desk. I look up, seeing his usual nosy expression is dotted with concern.

'I'm fine. Not a word to Patrick.' It comes out harsher than I intended.

'Of course, I'll say no more.' He holds his hands up in defence.

Fuck! All I need is Patrick to find out that I've been caught up with a client. I should have been stronger and resisted his advances. I'm really not very comfortable with how I feel right now. I think … I think it's somewhere in the realms of … abandonment.

I practically crawl through the front door in an exhausted heap, finding Kate in the kitchen, hanging out the window having a cheeky cigarette.

'You need to pack that in,' I scold her. She doesn't smoke much, just a couple here and there, but it's a bad habit, nevertheless.

She takes a last drag and throws it out of the window before hastily climbing down from the worktop. 'It helps me think.' She defends herself. 'Where's the wine?' She grabs my bag from me, pulling it open, before looking at me in disgust. I've just committed a cardinal sin – I've forgotten the wine.

I shrug. I've had other things on my mind. 'Sorry.'

She looks at me in sympathy. 'I'll go to the shop, you get changed. Fish and chips?' She grabs her purse from the table as she shoves her feet in her flip-flops.

'Just chips.' I make my way down the hall to my bedroom, feeling completely deflated.

I sit with Kate on the couch, picking at the chips on my plate. I have absolutely no appetite, and I'm only half watching the re-run of *Friends*. My mind is all over the place, and I'm so furious with myself for letting it be.

'Come on then, spit it out,' Kate demands.

I turn to face my fiery friend with a chip halfway to my mouth. I was an idiot if I thought I could get away with sulking in peace. I give her a non-committal shrug, popping the chip in my mouth and chewing lazily. Talking about it will only emphasize the fact that I am actually sulking over it – 'it' being a man.

'You like him.'

Yes, I do. I don't want to, but I do. 'He's bad news. You saw him today.' I grumble.

She makes a dramatic display of rolling her eyes and throwing herself back on the sofa. 'Ava, what I saw was a man who's crazy about a woman,' She puts her plate on the coffee table in front of the sofa.

I frown at her. 'Then why did he abandon me?'

Her pale brow furrows. 'Abandon?'

I realise my error immediately. 'I didn't mean it like that. He followed me back to the office, told me he wasn't giving me any space, then stalked off.'

'Have you called him?'

'No,' I answer quietly. This is the space I asked for and it's also what I need. I didn't think I'd feel so empty, though. I go for a subject change. 'You should know that Dan's coming home.'

The groan that fills the room is exactly what I expected. 'That's fine, as long as I don't have to see him.'

'He's going down to Mum and Dad's first, so you're safe for a while.'

'Good,' she spits harshly, drifting into thought.

I need to pull her back around quickly. 'Sam?' I ask on a raised brow. It does the job. She's immediately animated.

'Isn't he yummy? He took my number.'

'You're a tart, Kate Matthews.' I laugh.

'I know!' she shrieks and turns serious again. 'Hey, you're crafty.'

'What?'

'We were talking about you.'

'I'd rather not.' I lean back and get comfy. 'Let's watch this.'

Kate slowly turns back to the television. 'I like him,' she says quietly, almost like she's afraid to admit it, like it's wrong to like him. 'I'm just saying. He's rich, steaming hot and obviously well into you. A man doesn't behave like that when he's just fucking about, Ava.'

Well, that may be so, but it doesn't change the fact that he's cleared off and my phone hasn't rung since. It's undoubtedly a good thing; I have to keep telling myself that. 'Do you fancy a proper night out on Saturday?' I ask. It's a stupid question that I already know the answer to.

The look she fires me is mischievous. I grin back at her.

Chapter Thirteen

The next day, I breeze into the Royal Park hotel at twelve-fifteen, all set for my appointment with Mikael Van Der Haus. I'm directed into a snug sitting area with plush sofas, gilded frames swamping the walls and a carved fireplace dominating the space. It's typically regal. I'm offered tea, which I decline in favour of water – it's bloody hot, and my black pencil dress is clinging to me – and twenty minutes later, Mr Van Der Haus enters looking impeccable. He's really very handsome. He smiles brightly at me, revealing a perfect row of white teeth. What is it with me and older men at the moment? I hastily bat away my wayward thoughts.

'Ava, please accept my apologies. I never like to keep a lady waiting.' His mild Danish accent is only just detectable but really sexy.

I rise from my seat as he approaches, putting my hand out to him with a smile, and he takes it but shocks me when he leans forward and kisses me on the cheek. Okay, that's slightly inappropriate, but I'll go with it. Maybe it's a Danish thing.

'Mr. Van Der Haus, it's not a problem. I've not long arrived myself.' I reassure him.

'Ava, this is our second project together. I know you dealt with my partner on Lusso, but I will be involved in The Life Building a lot more, so please, call me Mikael. I hate formality.' He takes a seat in the chair opposite me, crossing his long legs. 'So, I'm looking forward to going through some designs with you soon.'

'Yes, I'm looking forward to getting some ideas rolling.'

'Me, too,' he laughs. 'I'm being very rude dragging you here at such short notice, but I'm flying back to Denmark on Friday. I have your e-mail and I shall send you the specific requirements. You did such a good job at Lusso. It really does lighten the pressure when you work with proficient people.' He smiles.

Isn't he going to give me the specifics now? That's why I'm here, isn't it? 'We could have a quick chat now.' I prompt, waving my pad at him.

He sits for a while, regarding me quietly, before leaning forward in his chair. 'Ava, I hope you don't think I'm being audacious, you see ... Well, how can I put it?' He drums his fingers on his chin. I'm a little worried. 'I'm afraid I've brought you here under false pretenses.' He laughs nervously, shifting in his chair.

'Oh? How so?' I ask, forcing my own awkward laugh.

'I would like to ask you to join me for dinner.' He looks at me expectantly, and I'm sure my face must resemble that of complete horror. I'm burning up. 'Tomorrow evening, if it's convenient with you, of course,' he adds.

Shit! What do I say? If I say no, he might withdraw his business from Rococo Union and Patrick will go spare.

'Mr. Van Der Haus ...'

'Mikael, please,' he interrupts me with a smile.

'Mikael, I'm not sure mixing business with pleasure is a good idea. It's kind of a rule for me. I'm very flattered.' I laugh at my own audacity. Since when has that been an issue of late? And why did I say pleasure? I've assumed, and suggested, that it would be pleasurable to have dinner with him. It might not be, or it very well could be. Oh God! I mentally throw myself into the lovely fireplace.

'Oh, that is a shame, Ava,' he sighs.

'Yes, it is,' I agree, re-launching myself back into the hearth when he looks up in surprise.

He leans forward. 'I admire your professionalism.'

'Thank you.' I'm bloody blushing again.

'I hope this won't affect our business relationship, Ava. I very much look forward to working with you.'

'I'm looking forward to working with you, too, Mikael.'

He lifts himself from the couch, approaching me with his hand stretched out. Thank God! I take it, letting him gently shake it. Did he really just drag me here to ask me to dinner?

'Once I return from Denmark, I would like to show you around the building. Until then, you can draft some schemes. I'll have the drawings sent to your office, and I'll e-mail you the specifics.'

'Thank you, Mikael. Enjoy your trip.'

'Good-bye, Ava.' His long legs take him out of the snug, leaving me to finish my water.

By two-thirty, I'm back in the office. I don't mention to Patrick the strangeness of my meeting with Mikael Van Der Haus, mainly because I'm concerned that in the name of business he'll demand I go to dinner with him. Patrick will assume it would be a business dinner, but Mikael made it perfectly clear that there would be no business involved. Instead, I just mention e-mails, drawings and his intention to show me the building upon his return from Denmark. This seems to keep Patrick happy.

I get busy and start making a few notes on Scandinavian design. I know I'll be basing my plans around clean, white, easy living, but I'm comforted by the fact that it will be tranquil and warm, not sparse and cold.

My phone rings and I grab it, way too hastily. It's Kate.

'Hi,' I greet in an over-the-top, chirpy voice. I don't know why I bother. She sees straight through it.

'Faking detachment, are we?'

'Yes.'

'I thought so. Have you not heard from him?'

'No.'

'Liking monosyllables today, huh?'

'Yes.'

She sighs heavily down the phone. 'Whatever. Have you asked Victoria and Tom if they're up for Saturday night?'

'No. I will, though. I've just got back from a very strange meeting.' I open my top drawer to grab a paperclip, noticing the calla lily squished down by the side of my stapler.

'Strange how?' She's intrigued.

'I went to meet the developer of Lusso. Well, one of them. He asked me to dinner. It was really uncomfortable.' I grab the lily and chuck it in the bin, resisting the urge to smell it again.

She laughs down the phone at me. 'How old is this one?'

'Mid-forties I guess, but extremely handsome, in a Scandinavian kinda way.' I shrug to myself while guiding my mouse aimlessly around the screen.

'You're like a mature man magnet at the moment. Are you going?'

'No!' I screech. 'Why would I?'

'Why not?' I can't see her, but I know she has a questioning eyebrow arched. 'It might help you get over a certain other client. If you want to get over him, I mean.'

'No, I can't, because I have a new rule … no mixing business with pleasure.'

'MOVE!' she screams, making me jump at my desk. 'Sorry, some prat just cut me up. No mixing business with pleasure, ah?'

'Yes. Are you driving and talking on your mobile, Miss Matthews?' I challenge her. I know Margo doesn't have a hands-free kit.

'Yeah, I'd better beat feet. See you at home. And don't forget to tell Tom and Victoria the plans for Saturday.'

'What are the plans?' I blurt before she hangs up.

'Get drunk, Baroque, eight o'clock.'

Get drunk. Yes, that's a very good plan.

'Morning.' I know I sound like a miserable cow, but I'm trying really hard not to be.

Tom looks up from his copy of *Interiors Weekly* and lowers his glasses to the end of his nose. 'Darling, why the long face?' he asks. I can't even muster up the energy to plaster on a fake smile. I slump in my chair, and Tom's sprawled across my desk like mature ivy within a second. 'Here, this will cheer you up.'

He presents me with a feature in the magazine he's reading and there, sitting casually on the velvet chaise lounge at Lusso, is me. 'Wonderful,' I sigh. I don't even bother reading it. I need to eradicate all things relating to Lusso from my mind.

'Man trouble?' He gives me a look of sympathy.

No, not man trouble – there's no man to be having trouble with. I sulk and reluctantly admit ... I really miss him. 'I'm fine.' I find the strength to slap a smile on my face. 'It's Friday, I'm looking forward to getting plastered tomorrow night. I need a good night out.'

'Are we really getting plastered? Fabulous!'

Patrick comes barrelling into the office. 'Guys, have we any work to do, or is it fart-around Friday?' He passes us swiftly, heading into his office and shutting the door behind him.

'Let's get on with some work, shall we?' I shoo Tom away from my desk.

'Oh, I forgot.' Tom swings around. 'Van Der Haus called to say he'll be back in London on Monday. He'll call you upon his return. He's e-mailing you the specifics and had these sent over. Is he hot?' His eyebrows jump up suggestively as he hands me an envelope.

Tom's the biggest gay tart, but I'll humour him. 'Very.' I take the drawings, widening my eyes for effect.

His baby face screws up in disgust. 'How come you get all

the dishy clients?' he asks as he walks back to his desk. 'What I wouldn't give to have an Adonis walk in here and throw *me* over his shoulder.'

I wince at Tom's referral to Jesse's performance the last time I saw him and start to work my way through heaps of quotations, delivery schedules and contractor requirements, before calling my live clients to check all is well. An e-mail lands from Mikael, and I scan it quickly, deciding to look at it in more detail on Monday.

Sally comes scuttling up to my desk with a delivery. 'Um … I think this may be for you, Ava.' She shifts from side to side with a box in her hand. 'Do you want it?'

If it's a delivery for me, then I guess I want it. Oh, this girl is painfully anxious. I take the box from her hands.

'Thank you, Sally. Will you make Patrick a coffee?'

'I didn't know he wanted one.'

The panic on her face has me wanting to make *her* a coffee. 'Well, he doesn't look right. Let's look after him.'

'Is he okay? He's not ill, is he?'

'No, but I think he could do with a coffee,' I press, trying my hardest not to lose my patience.

'Of course.' She scuttles off, her brown plaid skirt swishing around her court shoes. I couldn't even hazard a guess at her age. She looks about forty, but intuition tells me she'll shock me and be nearer my age. I open the box and find all of the material swatches I ordered for The Life Building, but I throw the box under my desk, set to deal with them on Monday, too.

On Saturday, I stand in my bedroom ready to go. My hair is behaving – happy that it's been blow dried into tumbling waves, courtesy of Philippe, my hairdresser – and the new dress I picked up from Selfridges to make me feel better fits perfectly. It's black, short and very tight. With dramatic, smudged eyes and nude lips, I'm looking pretty sultry.

I walk into the kitchen, finding Kate hanging out of the window having a sneaky cigarette. What's she thinking about now? She looks her usual lovely self in a cream backless dress.

'Wow!' she blurts. 'Someone's out to impress tonight.' She jumps down from the worktop, slipping her feet into her gold heels. 'Short enough?'

I arch an eyebrow at her, running my eyes down her dress. 'Pot …'

She laughs her carefree laugh that never fails to bring a smile to my own face. 'Here.' She hands me a glass of wine, and I take it gratefully, pretty much necking it. It's very welcome. 'The taxi's here. Let's go have fun.'

We walk into Baroque, spotting Tom and Victoria at the bar immediately.

'What the hell?' Tom exclaims, running his eyes up and down my black-clad body on a grin. 'Ava, you look lethal!'

'Really good, Ava,' Victoria adds.

'Thanks,' I shrug, pulling the hem down.

'What are you having?' Kate asks.

'Rosé, but make sure it's Zinfandel, please.'

Kate orders the drinks, and we make our way to a table near the DJ. As the wine flows, my troubled thoughts ebb away. We're laughing and chatting, and I'm beginning to feel normal again. My mum has always said, 'Alcohol makes for loose lips and loose lips sink ships,' This, I have just discovered, is most certainly true because I'm totally lit up, and I've filled everyone in on recent events. Considering I wanted to forget about it, I'm doing a bloody good job of hanging on to the memories.

Tom is thrilled about all of the rebound sex I've had. 'So, he just stalked off and you haven't seen him since?' he asks critically.

Victoria pipes up. 'That's really un-cool.'

Kate rolls her eyes, looking at the pair like they're a sandwich short of a picnic. 'Isn't it obvious?' she huffs. Tom and Victoria look at each other, then to me. I shrug. Is what obvious? Kate shakes her head. 'You lot are dense. It's simple ... he *wants* her. No man behaves like that over a quick screw. I've told you this, Ava.'

'Why would he disappear then?' Victoria leans in, truly captivated by Kate's explanation for Jesse's behaviour.

'I don't know! I'm just saying. I've witnessed the chemistry. It's way off the scales.' Kate flops back in her chair in complete exasperation.

I laugh. I'm not sure if it's too much wine, but that's just ... funny. 'It doesn't matter. He was a rebound fuck and that's it.' My explanation doesn't seem to satisfy because they all carry on studying me with doubtful looks on their faces. I don't even think *I'm* satisfied with my explanation, but it's been four days and I've resisted the overwhelming temptation to call him, and he hasn't called me. I'm moving on. 'Can we change the subject, please?' I groan. 'I'm out to enjoy myself, not to analyse the details of my rebound fuck.'

'Rebound fuck?' Kate asks on a raised brow. 'Is that what we're calling him now?'

'Yes,' I reply conclusively.

Tom stirs his piña colada. 'You know, everything happens for a reason.'

'Oh, don't start with all that airy fairy crap!' Kate chides him.

'It does. I'm a firm believer in it. Your rebound fuck is a stepping stone to the love of your life.' He winks at me.

'And Matt was a four-year stepping stone,' Kate points out.

'To stepping stones,' Tom sings, raising his glass.

Kate joins the toast. 'And shots!'

I finish my wine and raise my glass in agreement.

'Yes, shots!' Tom shouts, dancing off to the bar.

We sway down the road to our next destination, The Blue Bar, making it past the doormen, although one does eye Tom's shirt suspiciously. Tom and Victoria charge for the dance floor when they hear Flo Rida and Sia singing about Wild Ones, leaving Kate and I to get the drinks.

I order a round and take Tom and Victoria's over, putting them on a ledge nearby where they're getting down with some serious dance moves. When I join Kate back at the bar, she's talking to a man. She doesn't know him, and I can tell because she's notched up her flirting by a few gears.

As I approach, she raises her voice over the music. 'Ava, this is Greg.'

I smile, putting my hand out politely. He looks normal enough. 'Hi, nice to meet you.'

'Yeah, and you.' He immediately turns his attention back to Kate, resting his palm on her backside and leading her into a corner. She doesn't stop him.

'Ava!'

I turn toward the familiar voice, spotting Matt heading straight over to me, and it takes every ounce of my drunken willpower not to groan. He grabs me, squeezing me to his chest, throwing me out completely. Never has he hugged me like this, even when we were together.

He pulls away and plants a kiss on my cheek, lingering longer than is necessary. 'How are you?'

'Fine.' I break away from him.

'You look nice,' he says cheerfully. 'Do you want a drink?'

'No, I'm fine.' I frown at him, completely flummoxed. There's been no contact since we split and while everyone claims they can remain friends, it never works, especially when one half shagged half of London behind the other's back. He starts fidgeting, acting shifty and nervous, and it's making me incredibly uncomfortable. I take a sip of my wine, watching him over my glass as he twitches and plays with the rim of his pint. What's eating him?

He eventually draws a deep breath 'I've missed you,' he says, firmly and concisely.

My glass is hovering at my lips as he continues. 'I was a total twat. I don't deserve any second chances ...'

I scoff, nearly spitting my wine all over him. 'Second chance?'

He drops his head in defeat. 'Yeah, okay. I take your point.' He lifts his head, his face all genuine and soppy. 'It would never happen again, I promise you.'

Is he having me on? How many times have I heard the same old bullshit? He's a serial cheater. 'Matt, I'm sorry, but it's never going to happen.' I tell him evenly and calmly. His eyes widen with surprise, and I shake my head lightly to re-affirm my statement. I watch as he drifts into thought, and then his hand lifts and he strokes my arm gently.

'We were so good together.'

'No we weren't,' I laugh, not meaning to sound so condescending, but it comes naturally. The only person our relationship was good for was *him*, and that's because I was a blind twat.

I turn to place my empty on the bar, mainly to get Matt's hand off me without having to shrug it off, and when I turn back, Matt has moved from in front of me. It takes me a few seconds to piece together the events that are unfolding before my eyes, but when I do, I'm appalled.

Jesse has him in a firm grip around his neck and pinned up against a pillar.

Chapter Fourteen

Keep your fucking hands to yourself,' Jesse snarls in a startled Matt's face. Where did he come from? This is all I need on my night out, supposedly free from arrogant men and now I have two.

'Jesse, let go of him. He wasn't doing anything.' Matt looks at me gratefully, knowing I'm stretching the truth. I gently stroke Jesse's arm in an attempt to calm him down, ignoring his warm firmness. He looks like he could explode with anger.

'Who the fuck is this?' he yells, making both Matt and me wince. I don't want to tell him. Jesus, he looks capable of murder.

'What's going on?' Kate arrives next to me, quickly assessing the situation and gasping at the sight of my ex being restrained. 'Oh …'

'Jesse, let him go.'

He doesn't appear to be listening. What am I supposed to do with this? I'm feeling derailed already, and he hasn't even looked at me yet. I can hardly walk away and leave Matt to bear the brunt of Jesse's unjustified rage, even if I do think he's a complete tosser.

I'm beyond relieved when Sam turns up on the scene. 'Sam, please sort your twat of a friend out.' I turn toward Kate. 'Come on.'

Kate's eyes light up like the Blackpool illuminations at Sam's unexpected arrival, and I hear Sam calmly coaxing Jesse from Matt's throat as I drag Kate away, heading for the dance floor.

'What was all that about?' she asks.

'Don't.' I groan. If I tell Kate what just went down, she'll probably fight Jesse off and choke Matt herself. 'What happened to Greg?'

'He was a total dick. Come on,' she takes over the lead, 'let's dance.'

Tom and Victoria welcome us with waving arms as we join them on the dance floor, my earlier relaxed state hijacked and drowned out by unease. I've been thrown off completely by Jesse turning up, more so than Matt.

After half an hour and a string of some great tracks, I haven't seen or heard from Jesse. Sam must have ejected him, or maybe the doormen did. I couldn't care less about Matt. I'm free to resume the great night it had been up until Jesse crashed in, with any pangs of Jesse withdrawal now extinguished by his unreasonable behaviour.

I signal to Kate that I'm going to the bar, smiling when she acknowledges with a shimmy and a laugh.

As I wait to get served, that unease increases and I know it's because he's still here. Every fine hair on the back of my neck prickles when I turn and see Jesse leaning against the very pillar he had Matt pinned up against not an hour ago. His severe stare is piercing me, while Sam and the other guy from The Manor, Drew, are busy chatting and drinking. Jesse's not engaging in the conversation, though. No, he's standing there looking as angry as he did earlier, drilling holes right into me.

The barman knocks my arm to get my attention, and I turn, accepting the drink being held across the bar. I pay him and try to leave, but I can't move. I can feel his eyes burning into my back. I know I should just walk away, but the magnet effect he has on me sets my body turning toward him instead. I'm instantly swallowed up by his eyes, completely immobilized. All I can think about is his voice, his smell, his touch. The unforgiving power he holds over me trumps my intelligence, and my heart is hammering a wild, uneven beat in my ears.

He starts toward me, and I see Sam look in my direction as Jesse leaves their group, Drew flipping his eyes up, too. They both look uneasy at Jesse's obvious target.

I momentarily recapture my senses when Sam grabs Jesse's arm to pull him back but gets shoved out of the way. I plead with my legs to listen to the sensible side of my brain and take me away from here before my stupid side allows me to fall victim to his physical magnetism again. I abandon my drink on the bar and bolt through the crowd, knocking people out of the way as my retreat becomes fraught.

Stumbling out onto the street, I waste no time trying to flag a taxi down, but when I hear him shouting after me, I make a desperate run for it instead. I don't get far. He captures me easily, lifting me clean from my feet before carting me into a close-by side street as I shout and bash my fists on his lower back – for what use it does.

I'm lowered to my feet, and resting my back against the wall I try to get some air into my lungs. I can't look at him; I'll cave. I need *not* to be in this fucking position! How did I get myself in this situation?

'Ava, look at me.'

I shake my head and make to escape, but I'm pinned in place with ease.

'Goddamn it, Ava.'

'Go away, please.' I whimper, pushing his hands away from me.

'No, fuck! Ava!'

I just have to leave. He won't restrain me in such a public place. I need to walk away, block it out ... block *him* out. But my second attempt to escape is just as fruitless as the first. I notice his rapid breathing, his black shirt lifting with the rise and fall of his chest. Then I desperately drop my stare to his jeans, knowing that if I look up at his handsome face, I'm at an instant disadvantage.

'Ava, look at me,' he demands harshly. I clap my hands over my ears, lowering myself so I'm squatting on the floor. 'Ava, why are you doing this?' he asks.

I start humming in my head as I stare down at the floor, but then I feel his palms clamp around my wrists and he pulls my hands away from my ears. 'I don't want to do this here, Ava.'

'Then don't.' I try to regain possession of my hand. 'Please, just let me walk away.'

He slowly crouches down in front of me, still holding my wrists. 'Never,' he whispers.

The tears in my eyes spill over, splashing the tops of my bare knees. 'Why are you doing this to me?'

Releasing one of my hands, he clenches my jaw, pulling it up so I have no choice but to look at him. His eyes are glazed. 'Doing what?'

Oh, the arsehole. His impudence knows no bounds. I use my free hand to roughly brush the dampness away from my cheeks, suddenly horrified that I am, yet again, crying all over him.

'You persistently pursued me, bombarded me with calls and texts, fucked me into oblivion, and then stormed off for four days. I don't even know why!' I pull my other hand from his grasp. 'Now you turn up, trampling all over my night.'

He's the one to look away now, ashamed. 'Watch your mouth,' he murmurs. 'You asked for space.'

'But you weren't prepared to give it to me. What changed so suddenly?' I look at him, and he scowls at me, his frown line deep on his forehead. I can't cope with this.

I stand up, leaving him crouching, but he reaches up and clasps behind my bare legs. The fear of his evocative touch is completely warranted. I'm immediately on guard as the heat emanating from his palms spreads like wildfire through my bloodstream.

'Let me go, Jesse,' I grate, with all the firmness my quivering vocal cords will allow.

He looks up at me. 'No.'

'You seemed to manage just fine on Tuesday.'

He pushes himself up to his feet, sliding his palms up the backs of my legs as he does. It sparks a vicious bang between my legs. 'I was mad,' he says quietly as he looms over me.

'You're still mad.'

'I just found your ex-boyfriend dribbling all over you!'

'He wasn't dribbling!' I retort, thanking everything holy that he didn't hear the conversation. 'And how do you know who he is?'

'Because I strangled it out of him!' he yells. 'You won't see him again, Ava.'

I ignore his stupid demand. He has no right to enforce rules and regulations on me. The fact that I'll go out of my way to avoid Matt is beside the point. 'Did you know I would be here?' I ask. He stares down at me, but he doesn't answer. 'You knew I would be here, didn't you?' I push.

'Sam,' he offers, completely unashamed.

'Sam?'

His face is poker straight. 'He rang Kate.'

The devious cow! I can't believe she's done this to me. There will be some seriously strong words exchanged when I get my hands on her.

'I'm going to kiss you now.' It's that tone, and I know I'm doomed. 'You're lucky, because if I had you anywhere else, you would be getting a reminder … right … about … now.'

I gasp as he takes the one step forward that's needed to close the gap between us, and with the wall behind me, there's no retreating space.

'I like your dress,' he murmurs, stroking my bare arm with his fingertip. 'It's too short, but I like it.' He leans down, nuzzling my neck on a groan. My knees buckle. Damn him. And damn me, too.

My eyes close without command, my head turning into his

hot breath on my neck, my willpower scattered to the wind, just like that. It's impossible. *He's* impossible.

I feel him crouch slightly, his arm creeping under my backside, and with one effortless pull, he straightens his legs and lifts me from the ground. I'm secure against his chest and looking down into glittering green eyes.

Game over.

'Do you have any idea what you do to me?' His husky voice breaks as he looks up at me. 'I'm a fucking mess, Ava.'

He's a mess?

He releases his grip on me slightly, causing me to slide down his body until our lips meet and I'm pushed up against the wall. I don't have time to be concerned by our location; I'm too busy searching for the willpower to stop this. His tongue brushes across the seam of my closed lips, tempting them open, and I'm furious with myself for responding. But I should know by now … it's unavoidable. I open to him like I always do, meeting his tongue with mine, clamping my hands in his hair.

Groaning deep and low, he locks his free hand around the base of my neck to hold me in place as he pushes his body further into mine, our mouths fused and our tongues colliding, rolling and stabbing together. This is a possessive, demanding kiss, and I'm back to square one. With just one kiss, I've surrendered. I'm weak with this man. Helpless.

Breaking away, he leaves me panting and feeling the violent rise of his chest pressing against my breastbone. His forehead meets mine and my nostrils are instantly invaded with his minty breath.

'There she is,' he pants surely.

'You've got me again.'

He smiles slightly, circling his nose with mine. 'I've missed you, baby.'

'Why did you go then?'

'I've no idea.' He plants a lingering kiss on my lips and lets me slide down his body. I feel the undeniable hard ridge of an arousal as I slip past his groin and look up at him, finding a dark smile playing at the corners of his lips. 'I should force you to sort this out.' He places his hand over his crotch and my eyes widen in shock. Fuck, I probably would as well. He bashes down all of my defenses and tramples my rational thinking. He has a frightening effect on me. 'But I'm not having you on your knees out here. We'll make friends properly later.'

I'm not sure if I'm disappointed or relieved.

He holds his hand out on a smile, and, of course, I take it, letting him lead me back into the bar. 'What do you want to drink?' he asks, tucking me under his arm and getting the barman's immediate attention when we arrive at the bar.

'Zinfandel, please.' I inch closer to him. I can't get near enough.

He gives me a quick scan over with his enquiring eyes, pursing his lips. 'Your friends?'

'Oh, Kate's a wine, vodka and tonic for Victoria, and a piña colada for Tom.'

His eyes widen. 'Tom?'

I smile. 'You met him at Lusso, remember.'

Realisation dawns on his handsome face, and he shakes his head in dismay, releasing me and turning back to the barman, who's waiting patiently for Jesse to order the drinks.

Kate and Tom approach us, laughing and eyeing me up, but I shoot her down by flashing her a look.

'Jesse's ordered your drinks,' I inform them.

'Oh … a god *and* a gentleman,' Tom gushes, blatantly eyeing up Jesse's arse. I don't blame him; it's a very attractive denim-clad arse.

Jesse presents the drinks to Kate and Tom, and I watch in stunned silence as Kate leans in to give Jesse a kiss on his cheek. What is wrong with that woman? I'm even more shocked when

Jesse smiles brightly at her before whispering something in her ear. What's going on?

She turns, winks at me and leads Tom back to the dance floor as Jesse hands me my wine, opening a bottle of water for himself. He slips his free arm around my waist to pull me close, and I look up at him questioningly.

'Hey, my man,' Sam comes barrelling over with Drew, both taking the beers that Jesse hands them. 'Ava, where's the love?' He leans down so I can peck his cheek, flashing me his cute dimple as he does. Drew holds his bottle up as his hello, ever the standoffish one.

I smile and lean up to Jesse's ear. 'I'm going to join the others.' He's with his mates and this is supposed to be a girly night out – Tom doesn't count. He turns his face into my neck and steals a cheeky nuzzle, taking full advantage of my position.

'I'll be watching,' he warns in my ear, nipping my lobe and slapping my backside. The soreness has abated, but there's still evidence of my tumble around in the back of Margo. I pull away and pout playfully, earning me a huge smile and a wink.

Leaving him at the bar, I find the others on the dance floor, all happily lapping up the music and drinks. I laugh at Tom, who's in a world of his own, and as Justin Timberlake's 'LoveStoned' comes through the speakers, I'm welcomed to the dance floor with gasps and whoops.

In my semi-drunken state, I stupidly down my wine and discard my glass on the designated drinks ledge. If there was ever a track to pull me out of my despair, even if it's just for a few moments, it would be this one. The timing is impeccable. All bags are thrown unceremoniously into the middle, Justin shouts 'Hey', and the crowd is thrown into a delirious frenzy.

I'm happily enjoying some moves and laughs with Kate when I'm grabbed by the waist and spun around, finding Sam grinning at me and nodding over my shoulder.

'Here he comes. I hope you're ready for this,' he says.

'What?' I shout over the music.

Sam's grin widens, displaying his dimple at its deepest. 'He thinks he owns JT.'

He clasps my shoulders, rotating me on the floor, and I spot Jesse striding toward me. I'm suddenly worried that he's going to cause a scene and drag me from the floor. For what, I don't know, but he's famous for flinging me over his shoulder as he pleases.

I watch him nearing, slowing my movements down as I concentrate on his approach. I'm not sure what to make of this. His expression is dark and hungry, and I'm completely engrossed by his tall, lean body getting closer. By the time he's standing before me, as close as he can get but without touching me, I've stopped moving completely. My breathing is heavy as he snakes his arm around my waist and hauls me up to his body, prompting my hands to fly up and grasp his flexing biceps as he rests his forehead against mine.

'You're going to get a lot of men dropped if you keep dancing like that. You like a bit of JT?'

'Yes,' I breathe.

He smiles that delicious, melt-worthy smile, reserved only for women. 'Me too.' He drops a kiss on my lips, then, to my utter shock, he grasps my hand and flings me out on a spin before yanking me back into his arms. He's not going to dance, surely? 'And it's the extended version.'

I look at Sam, who rolls his eyes on a shrug, then back to Jesse, who has the biggest self-assured smirk on his face. He *is* going to dance.

I don't know if it's the fact that I've drank my own body weight in wine, or if it's Jesse's cocksure demeanor – it's probably the former – but whichever, it's got me performing an indecent shimmy down Jesse's body, while my palms drag, damn right obscenely, from his chest, all the way down to his thighs. There I am, squatting in front of him with my palms partly spanning the front of his magnificent thighs, looking up at the most handsome man I've ever laid my eyes on. My dress is probably riding up my bum cheeks in the crudest fashion, but I'm oblivious. All of my attention is on the Godlike creature staring down at me with a filthy, promising look on his face. I smile boldly, making a point of smoothing my palms closer to his groin area, before slowly pushing myself up his body, ensuring maximum contact between us. As my face passes his groin, I run my nose up the fly of his jeans, feeling him shudder and jerk before he reaches down, grabs my arms and hauls me up the rest of the way. My heart is hammering as he breathes in my ear – long, hot, heavy breaths.

'I should bend you over here and fuck you until you scream. That dress is absurd.'

I don't have time to say 'yes, please!' I'm spun out, and I watch as Jesse makes a mockery of Mister JT himself. I'm completely astonished at what's unfolding before my eyes. Jesse Ward can *dance* – and dance well.

He moves around me, his rhythm flawless, drawing the attention of many delighted women. I snatch quick glances at the others, all sharing in Jesse's delight, and I laugh. I laugh at the sexy, confident, fluid movements that have come as such a pleasant surprise. This man doesn't only have moves in the bedroom. Does he do anything badly?

Leaning into me, he gives me a teasing circle of his hips before he sends me on a full three-sixty spin under his arm, pulling me back into his chest and thrusting his hips into my lower stomach, his erection still evident. I cheekily reach down to stroke his denim-clad crotch, raising my eyebrows when he shakes his head in warning.

He starts to lower himself down my body, grinning as he clasps my hips and I jerk. I look at him watching me as he drifts down, landing on his knees in front of me, moving his glorious hips in time to the beat.

All of his attention is on me and me alone, and nothing or no one else exists. I love that he has no misgivings; he doesn't care what anyone thinks. He's confident, masculine and unashamed. It's refreshing. I'm falling really hard for this man. And I don't think there's much I can do about it ... or want to.

I glance at the others, seeing Sam flinging Kate around and Drew homing in on Victoria. Drew, in all his smart finery, seems a bit too up his own backside for sassy, sometimes a bit dense, Victoria, but drink has clearly loosened him up because he's laughing and the suit jacket's been removed. Tom is just being Tom, throwing himself around like a deranged maniac.

I turn my attention back to Jesse when he grasps my hips and plants a long, languid kiss on my stomach, gazing straight into my eyes before springing to his feet in front of me and dropping his lips to mine. I wrap my arms around his neck, sighing into his mouth.

'It seems I have competition,' he mumbles against my lips.

'No, you win.'

He pulls back, hitting me with his roguish grin. 'I've won all right, lady.' He releases me and I toss my hair over my shoulder, letting him take me on the floor. We move in complete harmony together. It's perfect. *He's* perfect, and all conflicting thoughts are forgotten as he drowns me in his attention.

As the energetic beat slows down, drifting into the smooth, powerful drones of violins and a slow intense beat, I'm short of breath and swathed in Jesse's body. He thrusts his thigh between my legs and sways us both to the echoes of the extended piece.

I look up at his beautiful face as he sings to me, and I have a frightening moment of pure lucidity. *Holy shit, I think I love this man.* I know next to nothing about him, but despite my lack of knowledge, he's completely taken me. I can't fight this any more. It just is.

I lean up and place my lips on his, and within a few seconds, when he's moaned into my mouth and tightened his grip on me, we're entwined in a deep, passionate embrace.

The music starts to fade out, drifting into another track, and I start leaning back in his arms. He bends with me, supporting my back, refusing to break the contact of our lips. Moaning disapprovingly, he finally and reluctantly breaks our kiss but keeps me suspended. It's not uncomfortable; he's holding all of my weight, like I'm no more than a feather.

His green eyes twinkle as they penetrate my heart and soul, and he lowers his face to mine so our lips brush lightly.

'You've got me, baby.'

Well … that statement is just playing havoc with my drunken mind.

I make my way from the dance floor with Jesse's palm placed in the small of my back, guiding me as he moves people out of the way with his spare arm. He leads me over to a table, but all the stools have been claimed elsewhere.

'Wait here.' He positions me by the table and wraps his palm around my neck, pulling me in and planting a kiss on my forehead. 'Don't move.'

I dump my clutch on the table, watching him as he disappears into the crowd, but I don't have much time with my thoughts – it's probably a good thing because I have no idea what to make of them – Kate and the others come crashing through the crowd, laughing and sweating, with Sam and Drew in tow.

Sam eyes me on my own. 'Where's Jesse?'

I frown. 'I don't know.' I point in the direction that Jesse left in, just as he reappears back through the mass of people carrying a barstool over his head.

He places it down on the ground. 'Sit,' he commands, lifting me onto the stool. 'Drinks?' he asks. Everyone nods, throwing their orders his way, leaving him looking slightly harrassed as he leans in to listen to what everyone wants.

Sam steps up to the plate. 'I'll give you a hand.'

'Yeah, I'm coming.' Drew follows Jesse and Sam to the bar, leaving the three remaining pairs of eyes on me.

'What?' I ask. I know what. My head is suddenly swimming in wine.

Kate arches a well-plucked eyebrow at me, folding her arms over her chest. 'Looking a bit cosy,' she fires.

Tom strokes the oversized lapels of his coral shirt. 'Cosy? No, no, no. That wasn't cosy. That was guaranteed hot sex tonight, darling!' He raises both hands, and Kate and Victoria comply, slapping a hand each in unison.

I scowl lightly at Kate. 'Me and you, later.'

She inhales sharply. 'Oh, feisty!'

'Did you see him move?' Victoria pipes up.

'He weren't bad,' Tom pouts, and we all laugh. Someone's stolen Tom's dance floor thunder.

'So – ' I'm firing this right back at Kate. 'Talking of cosy?' I nod at Sam as he walks back through the crowd, balancing three drinks between his hands.

'A bit of fun,' she shrugs.

'And you?' I look at Victoria.

She looks shocked. 'Me?'

'Yes, I saw you shaking your thing at Drew.'

Tom throws his hands up in the air in exasperation. 'I'm a huffing gooseberry! I want to go to Route Sixty.' He turns to Victoria. 'Darling, please!'

'No!' she exclaims, and I don't blame her. It makes a change for Victoria to be having the male attention, possibly the action, too.

Sam plants the drinks on the table and Drew follows suit, brushing suspiciously close to Victoria. She giggles, fluffing her hair.

Sam grins. 'Wine for Kate.' He bows as he hands her the glass. 'Vodka for Victoria and I've no idea what this is, but it looks camp, so it must be yours.' Sam hands Tom a piña colada on a wink.

My gay friend blushes a bright shade of red and flops a limp wrist at Sam. I don't believe it. For the first time in his life, Tom is rendered shy! Oh, this is too good an opportunity to miss. 'Tom, your face is clashing with your shirt!' I splutter through a helpless fit of laughter.

Everyone turns to stare at Tom, only serving to intensify his blush and, subsequently, his mortification. An eruption of howling laughter breaks out, prompting Tom to huff a few times before storming off.

'What's so funny?' Jesse asks when he reaches us, placing my wine and a bottle of water on the table. I can't talk. I'm still recovering from my fits of giggles, frantically wiping at my leaking eyes.

'We've just found Tom's Achilles heel,' Kate volunteers when she sees I'm no closer to composure. Jesse looks perplexed as he gazes around at the recovering hyenas that he's returned to. I see Sam shrug, swigging his beer.

'Sam,' I offer through my abating giggles.

'Sam?' Jesse frowns.

Victoria jumps in. 'Tom fancies Sam!' she cries cheerfully.

Jesse shakes his head and reaches for his water, undoing the screw cap and taking a swig. 'Here, have some.' He thrusts the bottle under my nose demandingly, and I take it willingly, despite the harshness of his demand. I'm feeling dehydration beginning to set in. I soon return to my wine, though, making quick work of the whole glass.

I sit quietly, vaguely aware of conversation going on around me, but my head is suddenly very foggy. That was the last drink you should never have had. The voices begin to muffle and double vision sets in.

Yep, mission accomplished ... I'm plastered.

I feel Jesse's hand at the base of my neck, massaging me over my hair as he chats to Sam, and I close my eyes, absorbing his firm touch as he works my muscles for an eternity.

When I open my eyes, he's leaning down, looking into my drunken eyes and shaking his head. 'Come on, lady. I'm taking you home.'

I don't argue. I'm too drunk to do anything ... even stand.

I'm presented to everyone in turn, all of them planting a kiss on my cheek, while Jesse props me up. Once he's ensured I've said all of my good-byes, he guides me out of the bar, and I'm ashamed to admit it, but if Jesse's arm wasn't wrapped around my waist holding me up, I would be flat on my face.

The fresh air hits me, causing me to stagger slightly, but I'm swiftly scooped up from the pavement, feeling the familiar comfort of Jesse's chest against my cheek as he carries me to his car.

'You're not going to throw up on me, are you?' he asks.

'No,' I scoff on a slur.

'Are you sure?' he laughs, and I feel the vibrations from his chest pass through me.

'I'm fine,' I garble against his shirt. He sounds like my dad. Is he old enough to be my dad?

'Okay, a few seconds' warning would be nice, though. I'm putting you in my car now.'

'I'm not going to throw up,' I insist.

I feel myself being lowered into his car and the sensation of cold leather on the back on my legs as I come to rest in the seat. He leans in over me and fastens my seatbelt, his fresh water smell and minty breath invading my nostrils. I recognise it, even in my inebriated state. As he pulls back, hovering in my line of sight, there are two of him. I try to focus, eventually homing in on a huge smile.

'You're adorable, even when you're legless,' He leans in, giving me a chaste kiss on my lips. 'You're coming home with me.'

'You're bossy,' I complain.

'Get used to it.' He starts the car and the vibrations from the engine instantly play havoc with my wine-filled stomach. I hear him laugh to himself.

'Jesse?'

'Yes, Ava?'

'How old are you?'

I definitely hear him sigh. 'Twenty–five.'

I really am very drunk and car spin is beginning to set in, even though my eyes are closed. 'It doesn't matter how old you are,' I mumble.

'It doesn't?'

'No, it doesn't. Nothing matters – I still love you.'

I hear a sharp intake of breath before I pass out.

Chapter Fifteen

Ouch!

I squint at the bombardment of light that's hammering at my sensitive eyes and snap them shut again, shuffling onto my side. I immediately realise that I'm not in my own bed. My eyes fly open, and I sit up. *Oh, ouch!*

My hands grip my head to try and ease the pain, but short of shooting my brain out, nothing is going to alleviate the thumping. This is a non-curable hangover. I know it.

I gaze around the room, recognizing my surroundings immediately. I'm in the master suite of Lusso, but I'm at a total loss at how I came to be here. I've never been so drunk that my memory has failed me. I try retracing my night, instantly remembering the bar and Jesse ...

I grasp the bedding, lifting the sheets to look under the covers, finding I have my bra and knickers on, so I can't imagine any Jesse-style fucking went down. I smile.

Oh Lord, I need a toothbrush and some water, pronto. I gingerly push myself up, untangling myself from the bedding as I go, revelling in the waft of Jesse's scent as it hits my nostrils. Every slight movement crashes into my poor head and when I'm on my feet, standing in just my underwear, I stagger. I'm still drunk.

'And how is my lady lush this morning?' Jesse saunters over to me, looking too fucking delicious in his tight, white boxer shorts, with his morning messy hair. I know I probably look awful, with my loose hair and crusty make-up.

'Terrible,' I confess moodily. I hear him chuckle to himself. If I could coordinate my movements, I would swing at him. His arms wrap around me, and I'm thankful for the support, burying my head in his chest.

'Do you want some breakfast?' he asks, stroking my hair. Even his soft rubs against my skull are unbearably loud, and I nearly vomit at the thought of food. He must feel my dry heaves and body jerks because he laughs again. 'Just some water then?'

'Please,' I mumble into his chest.

'Come here.' He scoops me up and carries me downstairs to the kitchen, placing me on the worktop gently.

'Oh!' Shit, that's cold!

He laughs, easing his grip away slowly, like he's afraid I might fall off. I might. I feel god-awful. I grab the edge of the worktop to steady myself and watch through half open eyes as Jesse opens almost every cupboard in the kitchen before he finds the one with the glasses in it.

'You don't know where you keep your own glasses?'

He rummages through a drawer, pulling out a white sachet. 'I'm learning. My housekeeper tried to tell me, but I was a little distracted.' He rips open the sachet and tips it into a glass. The muscles of his back roll as he gets a bottle of water from the fridge, filling the glass quickly, before walking back over to me. 'Alka-Seltzer. It'll sort you out within half an hour. Drink.'

I reach to take it from him, but my arms won't liaise with my brain, so without a word, he moves between my thighs and lifts the glass to my lips for me. I guzzle the lot.

'More?'

I shake my head. 'I'm never drinking again,' I mumble, falling forward onto his chest.

'That would please me to no end.' He strokes my back. 'Promise me you won't get in that state when I'm not around to look after you.'

'Did we argue?' I ask, remembering our dispute outside, but we were friends after that.

He sighs. 'No, I submitted power temporarily.'

'That must have been a challenge,' I reply dryly.

He reaches up, snapping my bra strap. 'It was, but you're worth the effort.' He turns his face into me, kissing my hair before pulling back and focusing his stare on my semi-naked state. 'I love you in lace,' he says softly, tracing the top of my knickers. 'Shower?' I nod, wrapping my arms and legs around him as he slides me from the counter.

I'm carried back through the penthouse, upstairs into the bathroom and put on my feet outside the shower. I'm left feeling wobbly as he turns the shower on, and as soon as he's in front of me again, I flop forward onto his chest.

'You *are* feeling sorry for yourself, aren't you?' He picks me up and places me on the vanity unit. 'I have fond memories of you sat exactly here.'

I frown to myself, but then realise ... our first sexual encounter happened in here on the launch night of Lusso. I look up into hazy green eyes staring down at me. 'You finally got me where you wanted me, didn't you?'

He cups his hand on my cheek. 'It was always going to happen, Ava.' He grabs his toothbrush, squirts some toothpaste on and runs it under the tap. 'Open,' he orders.

He sets about brushing my teeth gently, holding my jaw in his free hand. I watch him concentrate on his small, circling movements around my mouth as my dance floor revelation comes back to me – the moment that I finally admitted to myself that I have, most definitely, fallen in love with this man. I wasn't so drunk when that little realisation crashed into my wine-drenched brain.

I reach up to cup his stubbled cheek in my hand, and his eyes jump to mine, his lips parted ever so slightly. He stops brushing and turns his face into my palm, kissing it tenderly. Yep, I love him. Oh God, what am I going to do?

'Spit,' he says quietly against my hand.

I drop my hand from his face and lean over the sink to rid my mouth of toothpaste before returning to face him. 'Thank you,' I utter through my cracked voice.

The corner of his mouth cocks into a half-smile. 'It's just as much for my benefit as it is for yours.' He leans in, kissing me soft and slow on the lips, his tongue sweeping through my mouth tenderly. 'You're rubbish at hangovers. Is there anything I can do to make it better?' He pulls me off the unit, so I'm standing before him, and reaches around to clinch my bum, effectively holding me up.

'Have you got a gun?' I ask him seriously. That would cure my pounding head.

He laughs, a proper belly laugh. 'That bad, huh?'

'Yes; why is it so funny?'

'It's not. I'm sorry.' He straightens his face and runs his middle finger down the side of my cheek. 'I'm going to make it all better now.'

Oh? Alcohol, quite clearly, has not killed off my libido because every dehydrated nerve ending has just sprung to life. I must look hideous, and he's getting all fresh with me?

He reaches around my back, unclasps my bra and removes it before leaning down and giving each one of my nipples a quick peck. They harden instantly under the brief contact from his lips, my breasts becoming heavy burdens on my chest. My body has been completely distracted from the after-effects of alcohol and is now buzzing all over in anticipation of his touch.

As his head raises and his lips find mine, my hands slide up his arms and delve into his soft, blond mass of hair. Oh God I've missed this. It's only been four days, but I've missed it so much it frightens me.

'You're addictive,' he breathes against my mouth. 'We're going to make friends properly now.'

'Are we not friends?' I ask. My voice is breathy and desperate.

'Not properly, but we will be soon, baby.'

A wave of tremors fly through me as he kisses my nose gently and drops to his knees in front of me, spanning my hips with his big palms, hooking his thumbs into the top of my knickers.

I tense and wait, but he makes no attempt to remove them. I look down at him and watch him kneeling there, his forehead resting on my stomach, as I weave my fingers through his dark blond hair. We remain like that for an eternity, trapped in our own little dream state, just me watching him as he rolls his forehead across my tummy, back and forth.

Eventually, he takes a deep breath and leans in, placing his lips below my bellybutton, letting them linger there for a few seconds, before slowly dragging my knickers down my legs. He taps my ankle – a wordless instruction to lift – and repeats the same on my other foot.

I look down at him knelt before me, his head lowered, and I know something's playing on his mind, so I tug on his hair to snap him out of his daydream, and he turns his face up to me, his eyes meeting mine. His frown line is heavy on his forehead as he reaches up, spreads his palms on my backside and dips his head, kissing my stomach again. He's behaving peculiarly.

'What's wrong?' I can't keep my concern to myself any longer.

He smiles, but it doesn't reach his eyes. 'Nothing,' he says unconvincingly. 'Nothing's wrong.'

No sooner am I preparing to challenge him, his face is buried in the apex of my thighs and my legs have buckled.

'Ohhhhh!' My head flies back and my grip on his hair tightens. In one delicious lick, he has me lock, stock, and the niggling urge to press him is forgotten.

He moves his grip to my hips, causing me to jerk wildly. He's the only thing holding me up. I feel his hot, skillful tongue circle my hypersensitive nub of nerves, rounding with slow, precise movements before delving deep into my core. There is not a single bit of me he's not exploring.

'I need a shower,' I complain.

'I need you,' he mumbles against me.

I'm sent into a melting mess as he increases the pressure, digging his fingers into my hips as I grind against his mouth. It's only a matter of seconds before I'm falling to pieces, the surging pressure crashing down into my groin having me holding my breath, with my heart jumping into my throat.

'You taste incredible. Tell me when you're close.'

'I'm close!' I gasp on a long rush of breath. Holy shit, I'm close!

'Someone's keen this morning.' A hand is removed from my hip and two fingers plunge into me, sending me into orbit.

'Oh, shit!' I shout. 'Please!' I must be ripping his hair out.

'Watch … your … fucking … mouth,' he scolds me, between powerful, even strokes. He can't tell me off for swearing during these moments. It's his fault for putting me through this.

He stretches my opening with his fingers, circling and thrusting, while working my clit with his thumb and lapping at my sensitive lips with his tongue. It's a torturous pleasure that I could endure forever, if it wasn't for the increasing pressure weighing down on me, demanding release.

'Jesse!' I shout desperately.

With a few more measured strokes of his fingers, thumb and tongue, I'm hurled off the edge of a cliff and freefalling into nothing, the banging of my dehydrated brain replaced with sparks of pleasure. I'm cured.

He laps and sucks, slowly and gently, easing me down at a steady rate, my body relaxing and my heart rate levelling out as I trace slow, light circles in his hair.

'You're the best hangover cure.' I exhale on a long, satisfied breath.

'You're the best *everything* cure,' he counters, his tongue tracing up the middle of my stomach, between my breasts as he rises to his feet. He continues the trail up my neck, tilting my head on a groan as he laps up my taut throat. 'Hmmm, now,' he kisses my chin softly, 'I'm going to fuck you in the shower.' He tugs my chin so my head comes back down, giving him access to my lips. 'Deal?'

'Deal,' I agree. What a stupid question. I've not had him for four days.

I take my time running my palms down his lovely chest, settling my eyes on his evil scar.

'Don't even ask. How's your head?'

I snap my eyes from his scar, back up to his, finding he's looking at me with a warning look. Yeah, I won't be challenging that tone, or that face. 'Better,' I answer. His face softens, and he looks down at his boxers.

I take the hint, slipping my hand into the waistband, brushing his hair with the back of my hand and skimming over his morning erection. I flick my eyes to his and find them regarding me carefully, and when I move in closer, he takes the opportunity to lower his forehead onto mine, blessing me with his signature minty breath.

We're surrounded by steam now, condensation settling all over us as I slip my hands around the back of his boxers, smoothing my palms over his tight, extraordinary arse.

'I love this,' I whisper, moulding my palms over his cheeks.

He rolls his forehead against mine. 'It's all yours, baby.'

I smile my approval and smooth my palms back to the front, grasping his thick, pulsing arousal at the base. 'I really love this.'

He groans in appreciation, swooping down to claim my lips, raiding my mouth possessively, forcing me to release my grip of his hard length and take my hand back to his arse. I'm yanked into his chest, getting a full impact blow of his hardness pushed into my groin. The urgent need to have him inside me has me breaking our kiss and tugging at his boxers to get them down his long, lean legs. He releases one hand from my bum to assist, his boxers soon rid of, his massive erection pointing straight at me. This is going to be a shock and awe moment.

I'm right. I'm swiftly grabbed around the waist and pulled upward against his heaving body.

'Get your thighs around my waist,' he growls against my neck, as he sucks and bites at me. I comply without a thought, wrapping my legs around his waiting body when he lifts me, his arousal slipping over my swollen entrance, causing a desperate cry to escape my mouth.

'Oh God,' I gasp.

He crashes his lips against mine, moaning as our tongues perform a ceremonial dance in our mouths, my hands smoothing down his stubble as he holds me with one arm wrapped around my waist and walks us into the shower. I'm immediately pinned against the tiles, his palm slapping into the wall above my head as he worships my mouth, hot water raining down all around us.

'This is going to be hard, Ava,' he warns. 'You can scream.'

Oh Lord, help me. I'm burning all over, and it has nothing to do with the hot water pouring all over us. I move my hands around to grip his back when I feel him rear back, ready to enter me, my thighs relaxing to give him room. Bringing his hand down from the wall, he guides himself to my entrance, looking straight into my eyes as the head of his erection probes at me. I shiver.

'You and me,' he says as he lowers his lips to mine, kissing me ravenously. 'Let's not fight it any more.' And on a sharp shift of his hips, he thrusts upward, filling me to the absolute hilt, slamming his hand back into the wall beside my head on a roar.

'God!' I scream.

'No, baby, that's me,' he strains between powerful thrusts, pushing me farther up the tiled wall. 'Feels good, doesn't it?'

I claw at him, trying to get some grip, but the pounding water at his back is making it impossible to hold him.

'Ava?'

'Yes!' I throw my head back, panting and crazy with pleasure, as with each hard strike he pushes me further toward absolute ecstasy. I feel his lips close around my exposed throat, the water making them skim and slide over my flaming skin.

'You feel so fucking perfect,' he groans against my throat, continuing with his strong, voracious tempo. 'Remember yet?'

Oh, this is a reminder fuck! He has no need to worry. There's not a chance I could ever forget.

'Ava, have you remembered yet?' he barks, making a point of slamming out each word.

'I never forgot!' I cry, helpless to his punishing crashes against my body. I release his back, knowing he'll hold me in place, and pull his face up to mine, my hands brushing away the pouring water that's trailing down his face. His eyes lift to find mine. 'I never forgot,' I cry through hard slams.

Feeling him move inside me, feeling him tremble with the intensity of our joined bodies moving together, has my emotions tackling me from every angle. He gasps, tilting his head to claim my lips. It's a kiss of significance, and I melt into it. He moans into my mouth as I hold onto his face, soaking up the passion radiating from every pore of his body. He pounds on, hard and fast, and as our mutual hunger assails us and I reach the point of no return, I lock my thighs around his narrow hips, every muscle in my body bracing for the snap and release that's on the horizon. He shudders, mumbling incoherent words against my lips.

Oh, fucking hell!

He throws his head back. 'Jesus *fucking* Christ!'

'Jesse, please!' I cry. This is bordering on unbearable. I don't know what to do with myself.

He brings his eyes back down to mine. They're dark and hooded. I'm slightly concerned. 'Harder, Ava?'

What? Oh God, he's going to rip me in half.

'Answer the question,' he demands.

'Yes!' I scream. Can this get any harder?

He growls deep in his throat, increasing his thrusts to an even more determined, purposeful pace – a pace that I never would have thought possible. I tighten my thighs to the point of pain, but that just increases the friction and, subsequently, my pleasure.

'Jesse!' I'm thrown over the threshold, erupting around him on a scream, the loud groan that bursts from his lips signaling he's with me as he holds himself deep inside me, his big body jerking as he bellows my name. I feel the warm sensation of his release within me, and I drop my head to his shoulder, my heart beating a fast staccato in my chest.

Oh my God! I'm held in place with one arm, the forearm of his other resting against the wall, his face buried in my neck. He's breathless, and my muscles are naturally bonding to his beating length as he rocks gently into me. The shower is pouring down on us, but I can still hear our ragged breaths over the pounding water.

'Holy shit,' he whispers through his suppressed breathing.

I sigh. Yes, holy shit, indeed. That was beyond intense. My mind is like jelly, and I know I won't be able to stand if he tries to put me down.

As if reading my mind, he turns us so his back is against the tiles and slides down the wall, taking me with him so I'm straddling his lap on the shower floor. My face is planted on his chest, and I can still feel him pulsing inside me.

I'm totally wrecked. My hangover has been chased away, but it's been replaced with complete exhaustion. I close my eyes as I lay peacefully, stuck to his sharp body.

'Lady, you're mine for ever,' he says softly as he strokes my wet back with both hands.

My eyes open and many thoughts invade my recuperating brain, but the loudest one is screaming *I want to be*. I don't say it, though. After having my realisation, I'm petrified I'm going to be left restoring a broken heart. My damn willpower sucks, but I can't resist him.

'Are we friends?' I ask, resting my lips on his chest and kissing my way around his nipple.

'We're friends, baby.'

I smile into his chest. 'I'm glad.'

'Me too,' he says quietly. 'So glad.'

'Where have you been?'

'It doesn't matter, Ava.'

'It matters to me,' I argue quietly.

'You asked for space. I'm back. That's all that matters.' He clinches my bum and pulls me closer to him, his softening length of muscle stroking me deliciously.

I sigh and peel myself from his chest, lifting my heavy eyes to his. 'I need to wash my hair.'

He pushes my wet locks away from my face and drops a gentle kiss on my lips. 'Are you hungry yet?'

I am actually. Hangover sex has built me up an incredible appetite. 'Very.' I climb off him, reaching for the shampoo. 'Is this it?' I look at the shampoo, then to Jesse. 'No conditioner?'

'No, sorry.' He pushes himself up from the shower floor, taking the bottle from my hand and squeezing some into my hair. 'I want to do it.'

I relinquish hair-washing duties, letting him lather my hair, his big palms gently sweeping over my head. I close my eyes, let my head fall back and absorb the rhythmic movements of his hands, but all too soon, he's positioning me under the shower to rinse away the suds. 'What the fuck are they?' he splutters.

'What?' I turn to find out what he's talking about and catch a glimpse of a shocked expression as he grabs me, turning me so my back is to him again.

'Them!'

I look over my shoulder, finding him gawking at my bum and the faded bruises from my little jaunt in the back of Margo. 'I fell over in the back of Margo.'

'What?' he snaps impatiently.

'I was holding up the cake in the back of Margo,' I remind him. 'I got chucked about a bit.'

'A bit?' he gasps, running his palm across my bum. 'Ava, you look like you've been used as a rugby ball.'

I laugh. 'It doesn't hurt.'

'No more cake propping,' he demands. 'I mean it.'

'You're overreacting.'

He grumbles some inaudible words and kneels, planting his soft lips on each of my cheeks. I close my eyes and sigh.

'I'll be having a word with Kate, too,' he adds, and I highly suspect he will.

Standing again, he turns me back around to face him, sweeping the water from my face. I open my eyes, finding him staring down at me, his face expressionless, but his eyes telling a different story. He's mad because of a few bruises?

He leans down and rests his lips on my collarbone before running his tongue up my neck and clamping his teeth on my earlobe, tugging gently. His hot breath in my ear has me shuddering. Bloody hell, I could go again!

'Later,' he whispers, and I moan in disappointment. I can't get enough of him. 'Out,' he demands, turning me and clenching my waist from behind to guide me from the shower.

I stand quietly, letting him run the towel all over my body and through my hair to soak up the excess water. He's being so attentive and caring. I like it. In fact, I like it way too much.

'All done.' He wraps the towel around his waist without drying himself.

The temptation to lean up and lick off the beads of water that are dripping over his shoulders is impossible to resist, but my hand is grasped and I'm pulled back into the bedroom before I can follow through on my intent.

I look around the room for my dress, returning to Jesse when I don't see it. I drool, watching him pull on some jeans.

'No boxers?' I ask.

He tucks himself in and gingerly zips himself up on a dark grin. 'No, I don't want any unnecessary obstructions.' His tone is suggestive and very confident.

I frown. 'Obstructions?'

A crisp white t-shirt is pulled over his wet hair and down his rippling abdominals. I'm gawping. 'Yes, obstructions,' he confirms in a low husk. He strides over to my naked form and wraps his palm around my nape to pull my face close to his. 'Get ready,' he whispers, pressing his mouth hard on mine.

'Where's my dress?' I ask against his lips.

He releases me. 'I don't know,' he says dismissively, casually striding out of the room.

What? He must have taken it off because I was in no fit state to coordinate a strip. I go into the bathroom to get my underwear. At least I know where that is … no, I don't. My bra and knickers are gone.

Okay, he's playing games. I go to his walk-in-wardrobe and find what I expect to be the most expensive shirt on the rail and slip it on before making my way downstairs, finding him in the kitchen. He's sitting at the island, dipping his finger in a jar of peanut butter. My nose wrinkles in distaste.

His smile dazzles me as he looks up, his lips wrapped around a peanut butter-covered finger. 'Come here,' he orders.

I stand in the archway, naked except for a white dress shirt, and frown at him. 'No.' I decline, watching as his smile dulls into a straight line.

'Come … here,' he punctuates the words slowly.

'Tell me where my dress is,' I challenge.

He narrows his eyes on me and places his jar of peanut butter calmly and precisely on the work surface. Those cogs are working hard again, and his finger is tapping ferociously on the counter as he stares me down.

'You have three seconds,' he declares, his voice dark, his face straight.

I raise my eyebrows. 'Three seconds for what?'

'To get your arse over here.' It's that fierce tone. 'Three ...'

My eyes widen. Is he serious? 'What happens if you make it to zero?'

'Do you want to find out?' He remains completely impassive. 'Two ...'

Do I want to find out? Fucking hell, he's not given me much time to run this over.

'One ...'

Shit! I bolt toward his outstretched arms, colliding against his hard body. There was no mistaking the dark look of satisfaction I got a glimpse of before my head was buried in his neck. I don't even know what happens on zero, but I do know how much I love his arms around me, so it's a no-brainer really. As my face nuzzles between his pecs and I trace my fingers over his back, I can hear his heartbeat slow and steady under my ear. He exhales and stands, placing me on the island, working his way between my thighs. He rests his palms on the tops of my legs.

'I like your shirt.' He skates his palms over my thighs.

'Is it expensive?' I ask on a pout.

'Very.' He smirks. He knows my game. 'What do you re-member about last night?'

What do I remember? I was ridiculously drunk, shockingly brazen on the dance floor, and I admitted to myself that I'm in love with him. He doesn't need to know the last revelation. 'You're a good dancer,' I say instead.

'What can I say? I'm a sucker for JT,' He shrugs it off swiftly. 'What else do you remember?'

'Why?' I ask on a frown.

He sighs. 'Do you remember seeing your ex?'

'Yes,' I confirm, not relishing the reminder.

'Do you remember my request?'

'Yes.' There's little point in challenging him. I don't want to see Matt.

'And at what point do you draw a blank?'

'I don't remember getting home, if that's what you're getting at. I do realise I was stupidly drunk and highly irresponsible.'

'You don't remember anything after the bar?'

'No,' I admit. That's never happened to me before.

'That's a shame.' His green eyes search mine for something, I've no clue what. He leans down, kissing me tenderly on the lips, smoothing his palms over my face.

'How old are you?' I ask as I look him straight in the eye.

He dips his lips to mine again, coaxing them open and slowly swirling his tongue around my mouth before biting my bottom lip and tugging gently. 'Twenty-six.' he whispers, planting soft, skimming kisses all over my mouth.

'You missed twenty-five,' I mumble, closing my eyes in complete contentment.

'No, I didn't. You just can't remember asking me.'

'Oh. After the bar?'

He rubs his nose against mine. 'Yes, after the bar.' He pulls back and runs his thumb across my bottom lip. 'You feeling better?'

'Yes, but you need to feed me.'

He laughs, planting a chaste kiss on my lips. 'Are you making demands?'

'Yes,' I say haughtily. 'Get me my clothes.'

He narrows his eyes on me, making a play for my hipbone, squeezing it hard and sending me on a jolt across the worktop.

'Who has the power, Ava?'

'What are you talking about?' I laugh around his torturous squeezes.

'I'm talking about how much easier we'll get along if you accept who holds the power.'

Oh, I can't bear it any more. 'You do!'

He releases me immediately. 'Good girl.' He grabs my hair and yanks me forward, landing me with a hard, forceful kiss. 'Don't forget it.'

I melt into him, absorbing his so-called power on a long, drawn-out sigh, but all too soon, he leaves me on the work-top and returns a few minutes later with my underwear, dress, shoes, and bag. I scowl at him as I take them.

'Don't look at me like that, lady. You won't be wearing that dress again, I can assure you. Put the shirt over it.' He gives the dress a disapproving look before leaving the kitchen to take a call.

I laugh to myself. Who holds the power? Me, that's who! I throw my clothes on and rummage through my bag to try and find my contraceptive pills, but after searching my makeup bag and tipping the rest of my bag's contents out, I find no pills.

'You ready?'

I turn to see Jesse in the archway to the kitchen with his hand held out. 'Two seconds.' I stuff my things back in my bag and walk over, taking his outstretched hand.

His eyebrows rise. 'It's a good job Cathy isn't here. You would give her a heart attack in that dress.'

'Cathy?'

'My housekeeper,' He looks down at my dress disapproving-ly and sets about fastening the buttons of his shirt. 'Better,' he concludes on a small, satisfied smile.

We exit the lift and I'm pulled through the foyer of Lusso, Clive doing a double-take as we pass.

'Morning, Mr Ward,' he greets cheerfully. 'You look better this morning, Ava.'

Jesse nods at Clive but doesn't slow his long strides. I blush profusely, smiling sweetly as I scuttle along, keeping up with Jesse.

I'm bundled into the Aston Martin and driven home at the usual hair-raising speed, while Ian Brown soothes my ears.

Chapter Sixteen

Outside Kate's, I let myself out of his car and meet him on the pavement. He looks down at me with those glorious green eyes. I don't want him to go. I want him to take me back to his tower in the sky and hide me there for ever, in his bed – with him in it, too. I'm a slave to this man. I've been completely and utterly taken.

I step forward, pushing into his chest and tilting my head up to him, but he stands casually, with his hands resting lightly in his jeans pockets, his twinkling eyes watching me as I reach up on my tiptoes and brush my lips over his. That's all it takes for him to remove his hands from his pockets and heave me to his chest, plunging his tongue into my mouth, fiercely taking whatever he wants. It's totally fine. He can have it. My arms find their way around his neck, and I absorb it all as he completely consumes me, but he soon pulls away on a long exhale, leaving me breathless and wanting so much more. I turn on my unsteady legs, taking myself up the path to Kate's front door, mind racing, heart beating relentlessly.

When I reach the front door, I pivot to watch him drive off but find him close behind, looking down at me. My brow furrows. 'What are you doing?' I ask.

'I'm coming in to wait for you.'

'Where am I going?'

'You're coming to work with me,' he replies, like I should know this.

He's going to work? Of course, hotels don't close on

weekends, but what am I going to do while he's working? Do I care as long as I'm with him?

'You just kissed me good-bye.'

A smile plays at the corners of his mouth. 'No, Ava. I just kissed you.' He brushes a damp lock of hair from my face. 'Get ready.'

'Okay.' I relent far too easily. There will be no complaints from me.

I walk into the lounge with Jesse in tow to find Kate and Sam sprawled across the sofa, a tangle of semi-naked arms and legs, eating cornflakes. Neither of them makes any urgent attempt to cover up.

'Hey, my man,' Sam exclaims when he looks up and sees Jesse.

Jesse's eyes travel over Sam's half-nakedness, a look of disapproval clear on his face.

'How are you feeling, Ava?' he asks.

'Good.' I glance at Kate with a get-in-my-room-NOW look. 'I'll be as quick as I can.' I leave Jesse in the lounge and retreat to my room, pacing while waiting for Kate.

She swans in, looking all roughed up. 'Someone looks thoroughly fucked!' she laughs and gives me a mischievous grin that I match with my own.

'Don't look at me like that, Kate Matthews. What's going on with you and Sam?'

'Adorable, isn't he?' She winks. 'It's just a bit of fun.'

I pull Jesse's shirt and my dress over my head, flinging them both to the floor. 'Just fun?'

Kate rolls her eyes and scoops them up, placing them on my bed before flopping down on my duvet, her red hair fanning around her pale face. 'Yep. You're not the only one getting a good seeing to,' she says seriously. I gape at her. 'It's written all over your face, Ava.'

'I'm going to work with Jesse.' I grab my dryer to try and

salvage the damp mess that is my hair.

'Have fun,' I hear her call as she sashays out of my room. I flip my head upside down and rough dry my hair, ignoring the fact that I'm rushing to get back to Jesse.

When I flick my head back up to the mirror, an image of Jesse propped up against my headboard smacks me in the face. His arms are casually braced behind his head. He practically fills my double bed. I flick my dryer off, turning to face green eyes burning holes into me. I want to crawl up that bed and into him.

'Hey, baby.' He looks me up and down.

'Hey, yourself.' I grin. 'Comfortable?'

He bounces himself lightly. 'No, I'm only comfortable with one thing under me these days.' His eyebrows raise suggestively.

That look and those words have my knees quivering and coils of craving springing into every crevice of my body. I watch as he pushes himself up from my bed and walks slowly over to me, turning me to face my wardrobe. Reaching over one of my shoulders, he flicks through the rails of clothes, pulling out my cream shirt dress.

'Put this on,' he breathes in my ear. 'And make sure there's lace underneath it.'

I clench my eyes shut and reach forward, taking the hanger from him and moaning when his hand falls down and brushes over my breast, his hips rolling forward into my lower back.

Oh, good Lord, STOP!

'Be quick.' He slaps my bum lightly and stalks out, leaving me a wobbly mess and holding onto my cream dress for support.

Once I'm dressed in what Jesse has chosen, I pull out every handbag I own, searching for my pills, but they're nowhere to be found. I find Kate in the kitchen making tea, still in just a t-shirt.

'Have you seen my pills?' I rummage through the junk

drawer in the kitchen, housing everything from batteries and phone chargers to lipsticks and nail polish.

'Nope.'

I slam the drawer on a frown. 'I always keep them in my makeup bag.'

'Problem?'

I look up, finding Jesse filling the doorway. 'I can't find my pills.'

'Find them later. Come on.' He puts his hand out. 'I like your dress,' he says softly, running his gaze up and down me as I walk toward him.

Of course he does; he picked it.

He reaches under the hem to run his forefinger up the inside of my thigh, watching me as my lips clamp together and my hands fly up to his chest. He smirks dirtily and sweeps his finger under my knickers seam, brushing my sex softly. I sigh.

'Wet,' he whispers, circling me slowly. I could weep with pleasure. 'Later.' He withdraws his finger and licks it clean.

'You have to stop doing that.'

'Never.' He grins, yanking me out of the kitchen.

We drive out of the city, toward the Surrey Hills. I catch a glimpse of him every now and then, watching me instead of the road. Each time, he smiles and squeezes my knee, which has had his palm spread on it for most of the journey.

'How long have you owned The Manor?' I ask.

He throws me a curious, arched eyebrow and turns down the music. 'Since I was twenty-one.'

'That young?' I blurt, my tone clearly displaying my shock at his answer.

He smiles brightly at me. 'I inherited The Manor from my Uncle Carmichael.'

'He died?'

His smile disappears. 'Yes.'

'I'm so sorry.'

'Me too,' he muses thoughtfully.

I reach over and rest my hand on his knee, giving it a little squeeze of comfort. He smiles at me, and I reflect it with my own. 'How old are you, Jesse?'

'Twenty-seven,' he says, completely impassive.

I sigh. 'Why won't you tell me how old you are?'

'Because you might think I'm too old for you and run a mile.'

'Do *you* think you're too old for me?' Given what he has done to me, I'm guessing the answer is no, but as it seems like such an issue, it's worth an ask.

'No, I don't.' He keeps his eyes on the road. 'My issue is your issue.'

I frown. 'I don't have an issue.'

He turns his handsome face toward me, all smoky eyed and glorious. 'Then stop asking me.'

I scowl my annoyance, but decide to change the subject. 'What about your parents?'

The straight line his lips form has me immediately regretting the question. 'I don't see them.'

I sit back and say no more for the rest of the ride. His contemptuous approach makes me all the more curious, but it also makes me shut my trap.

When we pull up at The Manor, Jesse flips a switch on the dash, opening the gates. I see Big John getting out of his Range Rover in his usual black suit and wraparound sunglasses. He nods in greeting as I get out of the car and walk around to Jesse's side.

'What's happening, John?' Jesse asks, taking my hand and leading me up the steps to The Manor's entrance. I shiver, thinking about the last time I was here. I never thought I would be back, but here I am. I look up at Jesse as he claps hands with Big John. He's turned all businesslike.

"S'all good,' John rumbles, allowing Jesse and me to pass

before following us through to the restaurant. For ten o'clock on a Sunday morning in a hotel, it's surprisingly quiet.

Jesse orders breakfast, smiling at me when he confirms they serve my favourite – Eggs Benedict with salmon – and gives instructions for it to be sent to his office with a cappuccino made to my liking – no chocolate or sugar. Then grabbing my hand, he hauls me through The Manor, and as soon as the door to his office has shut, I'm thrust up against the back of it, my dress around my waist.

He buries his face straight in my neck, my arms flying up to grip his t-shirt. I'm caught off guard by his ferociousness. Slow, prepared build-up, or hard, fast pounce – the result is still the same. I'm sucking in short, sharp breaths and ready to beg.

The pressure of his body pushing me up against the door increases and his mouth crashes to mine. He bites my lip. 'Are you wet?'

'Yes,' I pant, grappling at his t-shirt. I only have to look at him and I'm turned on.

His hands leave my breasts, disappearing south, and I hear the sound of his fly zipper being undone, his *no obstruction* comment now perfectly clear. My knickers are yanked to the side.

I have no time to brace myself for the hard and fast that's coming. He tugs one of my legs up to his waist, positions himself and slams into me, thrusting me up the door on a loud shout. I scream.

'Quiet,' he barks.

He gives me no time to adjust. He pounds into me repeatedly, punishingly, over and over, sending me skyward in pleasure. I press my lips together to refrain from shouting out, dropping my head onto his shoulder in delirious despair.

'Do you feel me, Ava?'

Lord give me strength, I think I'm going to pass out. He's working into me like a madman, urgently thrusting and gasping.

'Answer the question!'

'Yes! I feel you.'

He hammers on, pushing me further and further into a mind-spinning despair. I'm a second from bursting, the one leg I was standing on now off the floor from being pushed up the door.

'Does it feel good?'

'Oh God, yes!' I scream as all breath leaves my lungs and I'm assaulted by his greedy mouth.

'I said, quiet.' He bites at my lip, the pressure bordering on painful.

The blazing fire attacking my core cracks, fizzles and ruptures, pushing me into a fevered bliss as I climax on a loud cry, his mouth capturing my screams as my mind goes blank. I shake uncontrollably against him, but he drives on, shouting on his own explosion, his erection pulsing and jerking as he spills himself deep inside me.

Oh, good Lord. My head is spinning wildly. I'm in complete awe of what this man does to me.

'I might bring you to work every day,' he breathes against my neck as he slowly pulls out of me, letting me slide down the door. 'Are you okay?'

'Don't let go of me,' I mumble into his shoulder. I can't find my balance.

He laughs lightly, wrapping his arm around my waist to steady me. I blow my hair out of my face and find his stunning eyes in my field of vision.

I smile. 'Hi.'

'She's back.' He presses his lips to mine and picks me up, carrying me to the sofa and placing me down before he sets about tucking himself in and refastening his fly.

I rearrange my dress and flop back on the sofa, a smile tickling the corners of my lips. The contrast of his persona from wild and demanding to tender and attentive is a real brain burner. But I love both sides.

He comes and sits next to me, pulling me onto his lap. 'I thought you could go up to the extension and start drafting some ideas.'

'You still want me to design?'

'Of course I do.'

'I thought you just wanted me for my body,' I tease, earning myself a flicked nipple.

'I want you for a lot more than your body, lady.'

At the sound of a knock at the door, I remove myself from his lap, instantly missing the feel of his firm body beneath me.

'Come in,' he instructs.

The chap from the restaurant walks in with a tray and places it on the coffee table.

'Thanks, Pete.'

'Sir.' He nods at Jesse and flicks a friendly smile in my direction before leaving.

'Eat your eggs, baby,' Jesse instructs, and I waste no time diving in, passing some to him on a fork when he demands it.

Once I've cleared the plate, he smiles and reclaims me, yanking me over to his side of the couch and pinning me under his hulking body.

'I want to devour you, but I have to fucking work.' He hits me with a lasting kiss before growling his frustration as he lifts and collects a pad and pencil from his desk drawer.

'I'll head up to the extension.' I remove myself from the couch, batting away his grappling hands on a laugh when I take the pencils and try to pass him.

'Kiss me.'

'I just did.'

'Don't make me ask again, Ava.'

I smile and give him what he's demanded before I'm allowed to leave his office.

When I open the office door, Big John is waiting to escort

me upstairs. 'I know where I'm going, John,' I offer. He doesn't have to flank me all of the way.

"S'all good, girl,' he continues his long strides beside me.

When we reach the stained-glass window at the bottom of the stairs to the third floor, I glance up the wide staircase. At the top, there's a set of wooden doors with pretty circle symbols carved into the wood. They're closed and quite intimidating, but I'm distracted from the imposing vastness of wood when I hear a door open. I look over the landing, seeing a man walking out of a guest suite doing his fly up. He looks up, catching me staring and my face flames as I look at John, who's eyeing up the guy, shaking his head menacingly. A wave of worry washes over the guest's face, and I scuttle off through the archway that leads to the extension to try and escape the embarrassing situation.

I let myself into the farthest room, and with the lack of furniture, I slide down the wall to my bum.

John pokes his head around the door. 'Ring Jesse if you need anything,' he grunts.

'I can go find him.'

'No; ring Jesse,' he affirms, closing the door, leaving me frowning at nothing. So, if I need the toilet, have I got to ring Jesse then?

A few hours later, my arse is dead and I have a rough draft of an amazing bedroom. I flick the pencil over the paper, shading and blending here and there. He said a big bed was essential, and the huge four-poster, positioned in the middle of the room, screams luxury and sensuality. I study the picture, blushing at my own work. Jesus, it's almost erotic. Where has that come from?

My line of thought is interrupted when the door opens and I'm presented with Sarah's pouty face. I inwardly groan. The woman is everywhere – everywhere Jesse is.

'Ava, what a pleasant surprise.' She shuts the door softly

behind her before walking into the middle of the room. My unkind thoughts have me wishing she would take a tumble in those ridiculous heels. I really don't like this woman. She brings out my inner bitch better than anyone I've ever known. Pleasant surprise? Sure.

'Sarah. It's nice to see you.' I clasp a lock of my hair and start fiddling with it, thinking her red lips look super inflated today. She's definitely had work there.

My sitting position, in relation to her standing position, has me feeling inferior to her. I'd get up, if my backside wasn't numb and I could be sure I wouldn't crumble back down to the floor in a heap.

'Working on a Sunday,' she muses as she gazes around the empty room. 'Do all of your clients get the same special treatment you offer Jesse?'

'No,' I smile. 'Just Jesse.'

She folds her arms under her ample chest. She's probably had those done, too. 'So, what is it about my Jesse that has you giving up your free time to work?'

My Jesse?

'I'm not sure what business that is of yours.' My hackles rise.

'Maybe it's his money?'

'I'm not interested in Jesse's wealth,' I retaliate shortly.

'Of course you're not.' She wanders over to the window before turning back to face me, her face as cold as her voice. 'Be warned, Ava. Jesse is not the sort of man you build your dreams on.'

I stare her straight in the eye, trying to mimic her cold face and tone. It's not hard – it comes naturally with this horrible woman. 'Thank you for the warning, but I think I'm grown up enough to decide who I build my dreams on.'

She scoffs mildly. It's in pity, and it makes me feel like crap. 'Little girl, jump out of your fairy tale and open your e—'

The door opens and Jesse strides in, looking at me slumped

on the floor before turning his eyes to Sarah. 'All right?' he asks.

I recoil on the inside. Why the hell is he asking her? It's me he ought to be asking. I'm even more stunned when she plasters on a ridiculously fake smile and walks over to him – all straightbacked with her chest thrust forward.

'Yes, sweetie. Ava and I were just discussing the new rooms. She has some fabulous ideas.' She rubs his shoulder.

I want to pry her fake nails off her fingers. The bloody lying bitch! He's not going to fall for that, surely? The satisfied smile he gives her, before turning it on me, tells me he has. The blind twat!

'She's good,' he says proudly. He's making me feel like a fucking kid.

'Yes, very talented,' Sarah purrs, smiling slyly at me. 'I'll leave you to it.' She leans up and kisses his cheek. I burn with rage. 'Ava, it was lovely to see you again.'

I muster up the decency to smile at the beast. 'And you, Sarah.'

She leaves the room and Jesse and I are alone. What role does that woman play in Jesse's life? She's been here every time I have, and she was at the Lusso launch, too. She wants me gone, and there is only one reason she would want that ... she wants Jesse. The thought of him being with anyone else makes my heart constrict in pain – makes me want to hurt someone. I've never been the jealous type, nor clingy or needy. But I can feel all of these new feelings racing to the surface, swamping my entire being. I'm not comfortable with it. I'm in big trouble here – big, fucking trouble. She said Jesse isn't the sort of man you build your dreams on. I think I already know that.

'Let's have a look then, lady.' He slides down the wall next to me, reaching over for the pad. 'Wow! I love that bed.'

'So do I,' I admit sullenly. The enthusiasm for my idea has been sucked right out of me.

'What's all this?' He points to the canopy on the bed.

'It's a lattice design. All the wooden beams overlap to form a gridlike effect.'

'So you can hang things from them?' He looks at me inquisitively.

'Yes, like material, or lights, maybe.' I shrug.

His mouth forms an O as he grasps my concept. 'What colours did you have in mind?'

'Black and gold.'

'I love it.' He brushes his hand over the drawing. 'When can we start?'

Huh? 'It's only a draft. I have to do some mood boards, scale drawings, lighting plans, that sort of thing.' I don't know if I'll be doing any of those things. I've fallen into a deep state of depression after being warned off by Sarah. I've got to seriously re-think what I'm doing here. 'Will you take me home?'

His head shoots up, his green eyes laced with concern. 'Are you okay?'

I push my numb backside up from the floor, using every ounce of strength I have to plaster a smile as fake as Sarah's onto my face. 'I'm fine. I've got some work stuff to sort out for tomorrow.' I smooth my dress down.

'Okay.' He gets up from the floor with ease and hands me back the pad. 'Are you sure you're okay?' he presses.

I maintain my fake smile. 'I'm fine. Why wouldn't I be?' I fight my hand back to my side when it reaches up to grab a piece of hair.

He eyes me suspiciously. 'Come on then.' He takes my bag and fills my empty hand, leading me out of the extension into the main house.

As we land in the entrance hall, Jesse glances around nervously. 'Wait here, I need to get my phone and keys. Actually, go and get in the car. It's open.' I frown as he ushers me out of the door before he jogs off toward his office.

I take myself down the steps of The Manor, across the gravel to the DBS, but before I make it to the car, I hear the laughter of a certain acid-tongued, pouty-faced beast. I tense from top to toe and swivel on the gravel, only to find her standing at the top of the steps with Jesse.

'Okay, sweetie. See you later.' She reaches up and kisses his cheek. I heave. 'Hope to see you again, Ava,' she calls.

Her icy stare penetrates me as Jesse approaches and gives me my bag before taking my hand again. I'm put in the car, and as soon as the engine is started, my ears are invaded with Radiohead's 'Creep'. I think to myself. Yes, why am I here?

Chapter Seventeen

I leave Jesse with a chaste kiss and a look of trepidation all over his stunning face. 'I'll call you.' I shut the car door and hurry up the path to Kate's house, and I don't look back, shutting the door swiftly behind me and sagging against it.

'Hey!' Kate appears at the top of the stairs with a towel wrapped around her. 'You okay?'

I can't plaster the fake smile on any more. 'No.'

She looks at me with a mixture of confusion and sympathy. 'Tea?'

I nod, peeling myself away from the door. I knew this would happen. Not this soon, but this nasty aching heart business was inevitable. I drag myself up the stairs and collapse in one of the mismatched chairs while Kate makes tea. 'Has Sam gone?'

She spoons three sugars into her mug, and even though her back is turned away from me, I know she's grinning. 'Yeah,' she says, way too casually.

'Good night?'

She turns, narrowing her bright blues on me before she grins. 'The man's an animal!'

I scoff at her description of Sam. There's a certain someone else I could nail that descriptor to. 'Good?'

She pours boiling water into the mugs and adds milk. 'He's all right.' She shrugs. 'That's enough about me. Why did you leave this morning looking like you'd had a similar night to me, and return a few hours later looking like you've been slapped?' She takes a seat, handing me my tea.

I sigh. 'I'm not going to see him again.'

'Why?' she cries.

'Because, Kate, without a shadow of a doubt, I'm going to get stung, really nastily. He's hazardous.'

'How do you know that?'

'He's a mature businessman, way beyond rich and confident. I'm just a little plaything to him. He'll get bored, toss me away, and move onto someone else.' I sigh dejectedly. 'Trust me, there won't be a shortage of women throwing themselves at his feet. I've seen the reaction he draws, I've experienced it. He's incredibly fierce in the bedroom – and bloody good with it – and that tells me he's not short of sexual conquests.' I draw breath, while Kate looks at me agape. 'He's a woman magnet, possibly a womanizer. I'm already getting a reaction from Sarah, the woman I thought was his girlfriend.' I slump back in my chair, grabbing my mug of tea.

'You're not seriously jumping ship because of a few bitchy words from a woman scorned? Tell her to fuck off!'

'No, it's not just that, although I really don't need claws digging in my back.'

Kate rolls her eyes. 'My friend, you're blind!'

'No I'm not. I'm sensible,' I defend myself. 'And why do you like him so much?'

'I don't know.' She shrugs. 'There's just something about him, isn't there?'

'Yes, and it's dangerous.'

'No, it's the way he looks at you, like you're the centre of his universe or something.'

'Don't be stupid! I'm the centre of his sex life,' I correct her, suddenly considering the fact that I could, quite possibly, be one of many women he's showing a good time to. The thought is painful and another reason to walk away while I'm still partly intact. Who am I kidding? I'm already in pieces, but it's only going to get worse the longer I let this go on.

'Ava, you're the master of denial,' she scorns me lightly.

'I'm not in denial.'

'Yes, you are,' Kate states firmly. 'You've fallen in love with him. It's easy to see why.'

Is it that obvious? I should deny it, but I won't insult Kate's intelligence. 'I'm going to lie down.' I push my chair away from behind my legs and it scrapes along the wooden floor, making me wince at the piercing sound. The hangover's back with a vengeance.

'Okay,' Kate sighs.

I leave her in the kitchen to retreat to the sanctuary of my room, flopping on the bed and pulling a pillow over my head. I hate to admit it, but that pouty bitch is right. I can't build my dreams on Jesse Ward, and the thought is like a knife through my splitting heart.

I walk into the office for a fresh week, feeling anything but fresh. 'Morning, flower,' Patrick calls from his office.

'Hi.' I try to sound chirpy but fail miserably, throwing my bag by my desk and sitting down to fire up my computer.

Within five seconds, my desk is screaming in protest as Patrick takes his usual pew. 'What's the state of play with Van Der Haus?'

I reach under my desk to retrieve the small box of material samples that I abandoned on Friday. 'These came on Friday,' I say, laying some on my desk. 'He's e-mailed me the specifics and sent the drawings over.'

Patrick flicks through the pile of swatches – all in neutral tones of beige and creams, some patterned, some not. 'They're a bit boring, aren't they?' he grunts disapprovingly.

'I don't think so.' I pull out a lovely, thick-striped piece. 'Look.'

He turns his nose up. 'Not my cup of tea.'

'It doesn't have to be,' I remind him. He's not going to be

buying a posh apartment in The Life Building. 'Mr. Van Der Haus is back from Denmark today. He said he would call about a site visit. I'm going to crack on, if you don't mind.'

Patrick stands, and I perform my usual wince as the desk creaks. 'Yes, you carry on.' He eyes me suspiciously. 'Tell me to mind my own if you like, but you don't seem yourself. Is there anything the matter?'

'No, I'm fine, honestly.'

'Are you sure?'

'Yes, Patrick.' I try and fail terribly to sound sure. My phone starts jumping around my desk and Sam Sparro's 'Black and Gold' blares around the office. I frown, picking it up to see Jesse's name flashing on the screen. He's been messing with my phone again. My heart flutters and not in a good way. I can't speak to him. Hearing his voice will knock me back too many steps.

'I'll let you get that, flower. Keep that pretty little chin up. That's an order!'

Patrick leaves me as I silence my phone, but no sooner has it stopped, it starts replaying again. I push the button to shut it up, placing it on my desk and throwing myself into some work, finding the e-mail from Mikael. It's brief, but there's enough information for me to start compiling my designs.

Fifteen minutes later, my phone is still ringing and my text alert starts chiming, too, but instead of deleting it – which would be the sensible option – I open it.

ANSWER YOUR PHONE!

Sam Sparro starts playing up again, and I silence my phone … again. I'm never going to get any work done at this rate. Then there's another text.

Ava, speak to me, please. What have I done?

I put my phone on silent and try to forget about him. What has he done? Nothing really, but I'm sure if I give him the opportunity he will. Or will he? Oh, I don't know. But instinct tells me to walk away.

'Sal, if anyone calls the office I'm on my mobile, okay?' I know that will probably be his next move.

'Okay, Ava.'

I start cracking on with my mood boards and drawings for Mikael. I've not even seen the apartments yet, but I have a good idea of where I'm going with this and, surprisingly to me, I'm quite excited.

I pop to the cafe at lunch time to grab a sandwich, returning to the office to eat it. I'm informed by Sally that a man called while I was out, but he didn't leave a message. Of course I know who it is.

I persistently ignore my phone, except when Mikael calls to arrange a meeting for tomorrow. He's stuck in Denmark for the rest of the week, so I'm meeting his PA at The Life Building at nine in the morning. As six o'clock hits, I'm satisfied with my productive day and glad I knuckled down. The day has flown by.

I arrive at The Life Building the next morning bang on time, but in a bit of a fluster after waking late. My rush was a waste of time. Mikael's PA is running late, so I sit myself down and take the opportunity to call my mum and check all is well in Newquay. It is, and Dan's arriving on Monday, which lifts my spirits. When I hang up, I gaze down at my phone and finally muster the strength to acknowledge the mass of missed calls and messages – all Jesse, except a message from Kate last night telling me she was staying at Sam's. In my rush this morning, I didn't notice she was missing. I quickly reply, explaining I fell into bed. I can still mentally hear his persistent banging at the door last night as I hid under the covers like a scared child.

'You must be Miss O'Shea.' I look up and see a petite blonde holding her hand out to me. 'I'm Ingrid. Mikael advised you that I would be here, yes?' Her Danish accent is very strong.

'Ingrid, call me Ava, please.' I stand and take her hand, shaking it lightly. She looks so fragile.

She smiles and nods. 'Ava, of course.'

'Mikael called me yesterday to tell me he's held up in Denmark.'

'Yes, he is. I'll give you the tour. Works are not quite finished so you'll need to put these on.' She hands me a yellow hard hat and hi-visibility vest. I slip on the safety kit, while she presses the button for the elevator. 'We'll start in the penthouse. It's very similar to the layout of Lusso.' The elevator arrives and we step inside. 'You're familiar with Lusso, of course.' She smiles.

'Yes, I'm familiar with Lusso.' I return her friendly smile. *More familiar than you know!* I snap a lid on my drifting thoughts immediately and start digging through my bag for my file.

'Here we are.' The elevator opens straight into the penthouse. 'After you, Ava.'

'Thank you.' I walk into a vast space, immediately noting that the size of this penthouse must be almost exactly the same as the penthouse in Lusso.

'You can see we used oak here. All of the windows and doors are bespoke and made using sustainable wood. I'm sure Mikael has advised you of this part of the specification in the e-mail that he sent you.' I glance at her, and she must catch my blank expression because she laughs, shaking her head. 'He didn't mention it in his e-mail?'

'No,' I reply, praying that I read it properly, and in full.

'You'll have to forgive him. He's slightly sidetracked with his divorce.'

Divorce? Oh, is that what's held him up in Denmark? I think it slightly inappropriate that she's told me such a private part of Mikael's personal life.

'Consider me advised.' I smile.

Over the next few hours, Ingrid walks me through the entire building. I take photographs of the space, making notes en route. Mikael and his partner certainly know how to deliver on modern, luxury living. The views over Holland Park and the city are incredible.

Eventually we find ourselves back in the main foyer. 'Thank you for the tour, Ingrid.' I remove my fetching hat and vest.

'You're welcome, Ava. Do you have everything you need?'

'Yes. I'll wait to hear from Mikael.'

'He said he would call you on Monday,' she says as she shakes my hand.

We say our good-byes and I head back to the office, calling my doctor on the way. I need to replace my pills. I get an appointment for four o'clock today, which is a relief. Not that I plan on having much sex anytime soon. I've had enough lately to see me through for a while.

'Afternoon,' I sing to Tom and Victoria as I walk into the office.

Tom frowns and glances at the clock. 'Oopsie! I'm late for Mrs Baines. She'll be having kittens! I'll be back after I've pacified the loopy old bird,' he chants, collecting his man-bag and dancing out of the office.

'You okay, Victoria?' I ask as I land at my desk. She's day-dreaming. 'Hello?' I call.

'Huh? Oh, sorry. I was miles away. What did you say?'

'Are you okay?'

She smiles brightly, flicking her blond locks over her shoulder. 'I couldn't be better.'

'And why is that?' I ask on a raised brow.

She giggles like a little girl. 'I have a date with Drew on Friday night.'

I knew it, although I still can't wrap my brain around ditsy Victoria and serious Drew. 'Anywhere nice?'

She shrugs. 'He didn't say. He just asked if he could take me out.' Her mobile rings and she excuses herself, just as my own phone chimes the arrival of a text. It's Kate.

Just turned our phones on. Was ... busy. Have you seen Jesse?

Busy? Sam and Kate being 'busy' is probably a Godsend.

No.

I don't need to say any more than that, and I hope Kate doesn't find the need to text me back and tell me what I already know. Wishful thinking.

Ok. I get the picture. Just so you know, between Sam and I ... 30 missed calls. And Sam has spoken to him. Not happy, but at least he knows you're alive now.

What does he think could've happened to me? I turn my attention to my computer, silencing my phone again when it starts blurting 'Black and Gold', but after it's shouted at me three times on the bounce, I turn the sound off altogether. The man is a persistent pain in the arse.

'I'm off,' Victoria calls, getting up from her desk.

I wave good-bye and start filtering through my e-mails, and then take some copies of drawings to send to my contractors.

When it hits three o'clock, I go to make the coffee.

'Ava?' I hear Sally call me. I poke my head around the kitchen door, seeing her waving the office phone. 'A man on the phone for you, but he won't say who he is.'

My heart jumps into my throat. I know damn well who it is. 'Is he on hold?'

'Yes. Shall I put him through?'

'No!' I yell, and poor nervous Sally flinches. 'I'm sorry. Tell him I'm out of the office.'

'Oh, okay.' She looks all wide-eyed and confused as she pushes a button on the phone that will connect her back to Jesse. 'I'm sorry, sir. Ava is out of the offi—' She jumps a metre into the air, dropping the phone onto her desk with a loud clatter. She scrambles to pick it up again. 'I ... I ... I'm ... I'm ... sor ... sorry, sir ...' Poor Sal stutters and stammers all over the place, a good indication that Jesse is yelling down the phone at her. I feel riddled with guilt for putting her through this. 'Sir, please ... I ... I assure you ... she's ... she's not here.'

I watch as she freaks out at her desk, looking at me wide-eyed and stunned as she's verbally assaulted by Mr Neurotic. I smile apologetically. I'll buy her some flowers.

The phone is dropped back into the cradle, and she looks at me in shock. 'Who was that?' She's going to cry.

'Sally, I'm so sorry.' I quickly grab the coffees from the kitchen – the only peace offering I can lay my hands on at the moment – and take Sally's to her desk.

She blows out a long, exasperated breath. 'Someone needs a cuddle!' She starts giggling.

I'm completely stunned on the spot. I was expecting tears and a nervous breakdown, but instead, dull as dishwater Sally has just cracked a joke. I look at the mousy, plain Jane chuckling, and I start laughing, too – a proper bendover, tears-in-my-eyes, stomach-cramping belly laugh. Sally joins me in my hysteria as we both fall apart all over the office.

'What's going on?' Patrick's voice calls from his desk.

I wave my hand in the air to him and he rolls his eyes, returning to his computer on an exasperated head shake. I couldn't tell him, even if I was in a fit state to talk. I leave Sally crying and head for the toilet to sort myself out. Oh, that feels so good. I've seen Sally in a whole new light. I like sarcastic Sally.

When I've gathered myself together and dabbed my running

mascara, I let Patrick know that I'm off for a doctor's appointment. 'I'm sorry, Sally. I can't look at you!' I splutter as I pass her desk and leave the office, hearing her laughing again. I compose myself and make my way to the Tube.

Chapter Eighteen

After receiving a lecture about carelessness from Doctor Monroe, our lifelong family doctor, I collect my new prescription and head over to the chemist to collect my pills. I get home just before six, and am surprised to find Kate isn't there.

I shower, change, and grab my phone from my bag, rolling my eyes at the twenty missed calls. I delete five more texts without opening them, knowing it would be a mistake to read them, and enter the kitchen, just as my phone starts flashing in my hand.

Pulling the fridge door open, I grab some wine and decide some bravery and resilience is required. This is getting stupid. I answer my phone.

'Hello.'

'Ava?' He sounds fraught and out of breath.

'Jesse,' I take a deep breath of confidence. 'I can't see you again.'

'No! Ava, listen to me ...'

My bravery is short-lived. I hang up, taking deep breaths as I pour my wine but clatter the bottle against the glass when there's an almighty bang on the front door.

'Ava!'

I close my eyes, looking for strength. I was tortured last night by his relentless beating of the door. The neighbours will be calling the police.

'Ava!' he roars, banging again.

Walking calmly through to the lounge, I look out of the

blind to see Jesse staring up at the window. He looks frantic, but I'm not answering the door. Being face to face with him will be a huge mistake. I watch as he holds his phone to his ear and mine starts flashing in my hand again, but I reject it and look on as he glances at his mobile in disbelief.

'Ava! Answer the fucking door!'

'No,' I whisper, like he might hear me. I nearly have heart failure when I spot Sam pulling up in his Porsche.

Kate gets out and approaches Jesse, who's waving his arms around like a loon, as Sam joins them on the pavement and rubs his shoulder in a gesture of comfort. They talk for a few moments before Kate leads them up the path to the front door.

'Oh God, Kate!' I stand like a complete lemon in the lounge, hearing the front door swing open, smashing against the wall behind it, and then the stamping of heavy feet flying up the stairs. He crashes through the lounge door, the anger on his face turning to relief before reverting back to pure fury again. His grey suit looks perfectly smooth and unaffected, unlike his dishevelled hair and sweaty brow.

'Where the FUCK have you been?' He blasts me with his shout, his breath, literally, breezing past my ears. 'I've been pulling my fucking hair out!'

I stand staring at him with no idea what to say. Is he under some sort of illusion that I'm answerable to him? Kate and Sam approach behind him, all quiet and apprehensive. I look at Kate, shaking my head, dying to ask if she likes *this* Jesse.

'We're just gonna pop down The Cock for a drink,' Sam says quietly, grabbing Kate's hand and pulling her down the landing. She doesn't try to stop him. I watch them leave, mentally cursing their chicken arses for leaving me alone to deal with crazy man here.

He seems to take a few calming breaths, looking up at the ceiling in weariness, before returning his blazing gaze to mine. It penetrates me deeply. 'Does someone need a reminder?'

What? I think I must have a carpet burn on my chin because my jaw has just plummeted to the rug.

'No!' I shout, steaming past him into the kitchen. I need that drink! I hear him follow me, watching as I chuck my phone on the worktop and yank the bottle of wine up. 'You're a complete bastard!' I yell, pouring my wine with shaky hands. I'm boiling mad. I swing around and fire him my most evil look. He actually winces slightly, which fills me with immense satisfaction. 'You've got what you wanted. So have I. Let's not fuck about,' I spit. I haven't got what I wanted, not in the least bit, but I ignore the voice in my head screaming that at me. I need to stop this before I get dragged any further into the intensity that is Jesse Ward.

'Watch your fucking mouth!' he shouts. 'What are you talking about? I haven't got what I wanted.'

'You want more?' I quickly swig my wine. 'Well, I don't, so stop hounding me, Jesse. And stop shouting at me!' I go for brutality, but I fear I probably sound pretty pathetic in my attempt. Something's got to work. I take another huge gulp of my wine, jumping when it's swiped from my hand and tossed in the sink. I wince at the shattering of glass that cracks through the air.

'You don't have to drink like a fucking fifteen-year-old!' he yells.

My fists ball at my sides as I use all of my willpower to calm myself down. 'Get out!' I scream. My attempts are failing miserably. I'm becoming frantic – desperate.

I shrink on the spot when he roars in frustration, throwing his fist into the kitchen door, leaving a huge dent in the wood.

Eyes bulging and lips sealed firmly shut, I can do no more than watch his fierce reaction to my rejection. He turns to face me, shaking his hand a little, and looks me square in the eyes, his green stare attacking me.

Fuck me, that's gotta hurt. I'm about to go to the freezer to get some ice, but he starts to stalk toward me. I brace my hands on the edge of the worktop behind me and watch him approach until we are front to front, his hands laying over mine, effectively trapping me.

Breathing heavily in my face, he scowls at me, and then smashes his lips onto my mouth. My breath is literally sucked out of me as I writhe under him, trying to free myself. What's he doing? Actually, I know exactly what he's doing. He's going to hit me with a reminder fuck. I'm so screwed.

He pushes his lips harder against mine, but I don't accept his kiss. I keep telling myself that this is bad, so bloody wrong. I'm going to hurt even more if I accept this, I know I will. I half-heartedly try to free myself, but he growls, his hands tightening on mine. I'm not going anywhere. My desperate attempts to halt this are being seriously hindered by his sheer determination to break me down.

His tongue skims my bottom lip as I continue to deny him access, shuddering in an attempt to fight off the reactions he's drawing from me. I know that if he gains entry, it will be game over, so I stubbornly keep my lips locked shut while mentally pleading for him to give up.

When he releases one of my hands, I instantly grab his bicep to push him away, but it's no good. He's a powerhouse of a man and a determined one at that. He's not affected in the slightest by my feeble attempts to free myself.

He grabs my hip tightly and I jerk under him, but I'm pressed back into the worktop. I'm completely trapped, but I still defiantly reject his kiss, keeping my lips shut tight. I turn my head away when he eases up a bit.

'Stubborn woman,' he mutters, pressing his lips against my neck, licking and nibbling his way down to the hollow, circling long, wet strokes before working his way up to my ear and biting at my lobe.

I squeeze my eyes shut, pleading with my self-control to

resist his irresistible touch. My fingernails are digging into his tense upper arm and my lips are locked shut for fear of letting out a cry of pleasure.

His hand leaves my hip and moves slowly across my stomach, skimming the waistband of my shorts.

'Please. Please, stop.'

'You stop, Ava. Just stop.' Slipping his index finger under the material, he traces left to right, in slow, soft, measured strokes while continuing the invasion of his lips on my ear and neck. I could cry with frustration.

The warm friction buckles my knees, sending violent quivers over my entire body, and I hear him laugh lightly, deep at the back of his throat, sending vibrations down my spine and a slow steady beat to my core. I clamp my thighs together, moving my hand from his arm to his chest and pushing in total vain. I don't even know why I'm bothering now. I'm a heartbeat away from surrendering to him. My head feels like it could explode, and I'm not sure if it'll be in pleasure or confusion.

And then his hand is delving into my knickers, his fingers separating me, causing electricity to spark violently through me. He brushes over my clitoris, so very gently, and I jerk, my mouth opens and I let out a cry of pleasure. He takes full advantage of my lapse in willpower, thrusting his tongue into my mouth, exploring and lapping every corner, his thumb slowly circling my burning core.

I kiss him back.

'Let my hand go,' I pant, flexing the muscles in my arm.

He must know that he's got me because my hand is released on a moan and he's gripping the nape of my neck immediately. I throw my arms around his neck to pull him closer to me – just like that. I orgasm on a shout that's a mixture of pure Jesse bliss and infuriating frustration.

'Remember yet?' he whispers softly against my lips, pulling his hand free. I sigh, dragging my heavy eyes open to meet his green gaze. I don't answer him; he doesn't demand it. He just leans down, dropping a gentle kiss on my mouth.

He lifts me onto the worktop. 'Why do you keep running away from me?' His eyes search mine as he rests his hands on either side of my thighs, bending his body, leaning in.

I drop my head. I can't look at him. What can I tell him? That I've fallen in love with him? No, so I shrug instead.

He places his index finger under my chin and tips my head back up so I'm forced to confront his achingly handsome face.

He raises his eyebrows at me expectantly. 'Talk to me, baby.'

I sigh. 'You're distracting me. I don't want to get hurt.'

I look at him as he chews his bottom lip, the cogs of his mind going into overdrive. He doesn't know what to say to that. 'I'm a distraction?'

'Yes.'

'What am I distracting you from?'

'Being sensible,' I reply quietly. The intoxicating effect he has on my body is settling deeper. He said he would make me need him, and he's keeping true to his word.

'Ava, know one thing. I'll do anything to avoid hurting you. Please don't run away from me.' He leans in and pecks my lips. 'I'm going to distract you some more now. We need to make friends.' His low voice is sparking off my desire for him all over again, his words comforting as he grabs me under my bum and slides me off the worktop to straddle his waist.

I wrap my arms around his back as he walks us out of the kitchen, into my bedroom, kicking the door shut behind him, and then placing me on the end of the bed, pulling my vest up over my head. My bare breasts spring free, prompting a smile from him as he looks down into my eyes. My vest is tossed on the floor and the waistband of my shorts grasped, encouraging me to lift my bum so he can draw them down my legs, taking my knickers with them.

'Stay there.' he orders, reaching up and pulling at his tie.

Sparks of anticipation ricochet all around my body as I watch him slowly undress in front of me, my eyes automatically drawn to the sight of his scar. I'm desperate to know where it came from.

'Look at me, Ava.'

His tone pulls my eyes to his as he drags his boxers down his legs, his erection springing free at eye level to me. If I reach forward and open my mouth, I'll have the upper hand. That would make a nice change. I glance up at him, catching a wicked grin and blazing eyes.

'I'm desperate to be inside you,' he says darkly. 'I'll look forward to fucking your mouth later. You owe me.'

A powerful thud crashes into my core as he leans down and curls his arm around my waist before crawling up the bed above me and placing me down gently beneath him. My thighs are spread by his knee, and he cradles himself between them, resting his forearms on either side of my head as he looks down at me with soft eyes. I could weep.

'We don't run any more, Ava.' he says, holding my gaze as he slowly draws back and drives forward, plunging deeply into me. I moan and adjust my grip on his shoulders, shifting under him. The fullness is incredible. He blows out a long, controlled breath of air, the concentration frown flickering across his brow, shiny with sweat and heavy on his forehead.

I resist the urge to contract around him – he needs a moment. His eyes close, his long lashes fanning out against his cheeks, his head dropping to mine as he battles to compose his erratic breathing. I wait patiently, running my hands up and down his firm upper arms, more than happy to lay here looking at this beautiful man so closely. He knows I need gentle Jesse right now.

After a few moments, he gathers himself together and lifts his head back up to look at me. My heart constricts in my chest. I'm so in love with this man.

He lifts his upper body to brace his arms, then lazily drags back and gradually drives forward.

I purr. Oh, good God. He repeats the delectable move, over and over, watching me the entire time.

'Ava, when you're tempted to run again, think about how you feel right now. Think about me.'

'Yes,' I breathe, struggling to dampen down a fast buildup of pressure. I do think, though. That's the problem and an unavoidable one. He invades every corner of my mind.

I rock my hips up to meet his every thrust, and he lowers his mouth to mine, taking my lips leisurely and lazily, matching his blazing hip rhythm with his tongue.

I whimper, digging my nails into his arms as he drives slowly forward, circles deeply and withdraws lazily, time and time again. I can't hold out for much longer. How does he do this to me?

'Does that feel good?' he whispers.

'Too good,' I gasp on a lazy grind.

'It does. Are you there, lady?' he asks against my lips.

I nip his tongue. 'I'm there.'

'I've got you, baby. Let it go.'

The racking shudder that courses through my body has me clenched around Jesse's arousal, shaking wildly against him as I moan my release into his mouth. The last, deep thrust, followed by a jerk and hot sensation flooding me, signals Jesse's release. He holds himself deep and clenches his eyes shut, while paying loving attention to my mouth, moaning low, the pulsating of him triggering my muscles to tense around him, all in time to his throbs. I'm draining him dry.

'God, I've missed you,' he whispers, burying his face in the crook of my neck and nuzzling before rolling onto his back. He holds his arm up, and I move into his warm, firm chest, resting my cheek on his pec.

'I love sleepy sex with you,' I muse dreamily.

'That wasn't sleepy sex, baby.' He brushes my hair from my face with his spare hand.

'What was it, then?'

He kisses my forehead gently. 'That was catching-up sex.'

Oh, a new one. 'I like catching-up sex then.'

'Don't like it too much. It won't happen very often.'

A stab of disappointment pierces me. 'Why?'

'Because, lady, you won't be running away from me again, and I don't plan on being away from you very often either.' He inhales in my hair. 'If ever.'

I smile to myself, throwing my leg over his thighs. He clasps my knee, rubbing circles over my skin with his thumb while I trace my fingers across the surface of his scar. 'How did this happen?' I ask as I follow the line around to his side.

He inhales tiredly. 'How did what happen, Ava?' His words leave no room for movement or interrogation on the matter. He doesn't want to talk about it.

'Nothing,' I whisper softly, making a mental note not to ask again.

'What are you doing tomorrow?'

'It's Wednesday. I'm working.'

'Take the day off.'

'What, just like that?'

I feel him shrug. 'Yes; you owe me two days.'

He makes everything sound so straightforward. It's okay for him, with his own business and no one to answer to. I, on the other hand, have clients, a boss and a pile of work to do.

'I have too much to do. Besides, you abandoned me for four days,' I remind him.

'Come with me now, then.' He squeezes me in a little bit more.

'Where?'

'I've got to shoot over to The Manor, sort a few things out with John. You can have some dinner while you wait for me.'

Not a chance! I'm not going to The Manor and risk bumping into old pouty lips. 'I think I'll stay here. I don't want to get in your way.' I say quietly, hoping he doesn't push this. Another standoff with Sarah will not be a good way to end the day.

I'm rolled onto my back with my wrists pinned to the sides of my head as Jesse looms over me. 'You won't ever be in my way.' He rests his lips between my breasts and trails kisses across to my nipple. 'You'll come.'

My nipple hardens under his gentle, swirling tongue, my breathing fluttering. 'I'll see you tomorrow.' I force the words through pants.

His teeth clamp lightly onto my nipple as he looks up at me, grinning. 'Hmmm, sense fuck?' he offers through a mouthful of breast.

I hear the front door crash open and the laughter of Kate and Sam coming up the stairs, and I look down at Jesse still clamped around my nipple, the frustration marring his face leaving me secretly pleased. While I'd take a sense fuck any-time, the sense he aims on fucking into me on this particular occasion makes no sense at all. Why would I want to set myself up for a verbal spar with Sarah?

He huffs childishly, releasing my nipple. 'I don't suppose you can keep your mouth shut while I fuck some sense into you?'

I raise my eyebrows. He knows that's impossible.

'For fuck's sake,' he grumbles, pushing himself up, making a point of brushing his knee up the inside of my thigh and over my moist centre. The friction has me wanting to yank him back down to me. I don't want him to go. He leans down and kisses me hard and purposefully. 'I've got to go. When I call you to-morrow, you'll answer the phone.'

'I will,' I confirm obediently.

He smiles darkly and grabs my hip, making me squeal like a little girl and flip myself onto my front. Then I feel the sting of his palm meeting my backside.

'Ouch!'

'Sarcasm doesn't suit you, lady.' The bed shifts as he gets up.

When I turn over, his shirt is on his back and he's working the buttons. 'Will Sarah be at The Manor?' I blurt, before my brain filters the stupid question.

He pauses briefly before picking up his boxers and stepping into them. 'I hope so. She works for me.'

What? 'You said she was a friend.' I sound whiny, and I mentally slap myself for it.

He frowns. 'Yes, she's a friend and she works for me.'

Marvellous. I roll out of bed and find my vest and shorts. No wonder she's always loitering around. God, I hate that woman. I yank my vest and shorts on, and turn to find Jesse pulling his suit jacket over his shoulders. He's watching me thoughtfully. Does he know what I'm thinking?

'Are you going to put some clothes on?' he asks, looking me up and down.

I look down at my shorts and vest combo and back up to him. His eyebrows are raised. 'I'm at home.'

'Yes, and Sam's out there.'

'Sam doesn't seem to think anything of walking around in his pants. At least I'm covered.'

'Sam's an exhibitionist,' he grumbles, walking over to my wardrobe and flicking through the rails. 'Here, put this on.' He hands me a chunky knit, oversized cream jumper.

'No!' I splutter in disgust. I'll pass out of overheating!

He thrusts it closer to me with a determined, dirty look. 'Put the jumper on.'

'No.' I say it slowly and concisely. He's not dictating my wardrobe, especially not when I'm at home. I snatch the jumper from him and throw it on the bed, watching as he follows its path through the air. He looks at it sprawled on the bed, then slowly returns his eyes to mine. His teeth are going ten to the dozen, chewing his bottom lip.

'Three,' he grates.

My eyes widen. 'Are you winding me up?'

He ignores me. 'Two.'

'I'm not putting the jumper on.'

'One.' His lips press into a straight line of displeasure.

'Do what you like, Jesse. I'm not putting that jumper on.'

His eyes narrow. 'Zero.'

We stand opposite each other, him with an expression of genuine fury mixed with a bit of delight, and me wondering what the hell he's going to do now.

He shakes his head, exhaling a long lungful of air, and then he makes his move. I dart across the bed to escape, getting caught up in the mountain of sheets and squealing when I feel his warm palm wrap around my ankle. He yanks me across the bed.

'Jesse!' I cry as he flips me over and straddles me, pinning my arms under his knees. 'Get off!' I blow my hair out of my face, finding him looking down at me, his face deadly serious.

'Let's clear something up.' He removes his jacket, throws it on the bed and picks up the jumper. 'If you do what you're told, our lives will be a lot easier. All of this,' he strokes his palms over my torso and pinches my nipples through my vest, 'is for my eyes only.' He moves his hand behind him and digs his fingers into the hollow above my hipbone.

'NO!' I scream. 'Please, no!' I start laughing. Oh God, I'll pee myself!

He continues with the digs and squeezes, sending me on a wild bucking mission. I can't breathe. I'm between laughter and crying at his torturous touch.

'That's better.' I hear him say through my bucking frenzy. I feel my hair being brushed away from my face, then his lips pressed hard on mine. 'You could have saved us both a lot of trouble if you'd have just put ... the ... fucking ... jumper ... on.'

I look up at him and scowl as he lifts his heavy weight from me and puts his jacket back on. I sit up, finding I'm wearing the stupid jumper. How did he manage that? I turn my fierceness onto him. He's regarding me intently, not a hint of amusement on his face.

'I'll just take it off,' I spit.

'No, you won't,' he assures me on a grin.

I get off the bed, heading for the bathroom in the ridiculous jumper. 'You're an unreasonable arse,' I mutter, slamming the door behind me.

I go for a wee and make a mental note never to let him get to zero again. That was my worst nightmare. I rub my poor abused hips, the sensitive flesh above my bones still tingling.

When I'm done, I find Jesse in the kitchen with Sam and Kate, who both run their eyes over my jumper-clad body. I shrug, pouring myself another wine.

'Made up?' Kate asks, perching on Sam's lap. He separates his thighs, causing Kate to slip between his legs on a squeal. She playfully slaps him before looking at me for an answer.

'No,' I mutter, throwing Jesse a disgruntled look. 'And if you'd like to know who has put a hole in your kitchen door, look no further.' I point my glass at Jesse. 'He also smashed your wine glass.' I add, like the pathetic snitch I am.

I watch as Jesse reaches in his pocket, palms off a pile of twenties and slaps them on the table in front of Kate. 'Let me know if it's any more.' he says, keeping his eyes firmly on me. I look down at the table. There must be at least five hundred quid there. And I notice he didn't apologise, the arrogant arse.

Kate shrugs and scoops the money up. 'That should cover it.'

Jesse shoves his hands back in his pockets, saunters over to me and bends so his face is level with mine. 'I like your jumper.'

'Fuck off,' I mouth, before taking a huge swig of wine.

He grins, kissing my nose. 'Mouth,' he warns, grasping the back of my head and bunching my hair in his fist, pulling me forward so we're nose to nose. 'Don't drink too much,' he orders, and then lands me with a searing hot kiss. I try to resist ... a little. I don't at all.

'You might need to remind me of that.' I grin around his lips and he laughs a little.

When I'm free and have regained my senses, I take another glug as I watch him over the rim.

He shakes his head mildly, inhaling deeply, before turning away from me. 'My work here is done.' he says smugly as he leaves.

'Bye,' Kate sings on a laugh.

'My man.' Sam holds his hand up on a grin. 'Ava, where's the love?'

'Up his arse,' I mumble, discarding my wine glass and collecting my phone before traipsing back to my room. I hear Sam and Kate laughing as I crawl into bed with my jumper on.

Chapter Nineteen

I sit at my desk in a complete daydream, my mind racing with thoughts of comforting words and fuckings of various degrees. If – in my perfect little world – I end up in a relationship with Jesse, would this be how it is all of the time? Jesse making commands and me obeying them? It's that or receiving some sort of fuck, or being subjected to some kind of countdown and torture until I relent, or he manhandles me into complying. I'm not denying the certain element of fun in the fucking side of things, but there has to be give and take. And I'm not sure Jesse knows how to give – unless it's a Jesse-style fucking. Am I already in a relationship with this man?

'Ava, you're here early.' Sally walks into the office, and I immediately giggle to myself. I saw Sally in a different light yesterday.

'Yes, I woke up early.' I say, wanting to add that it's because a neurotic arse made me wear a winter jumper in bed, causing me to wake up in a pool of sweat.

She settles herself at her desk. 'I tried calling you yesterday after you left.'

'You did?'

'Yes, that angry man came into the office shortly after you left.'

'He did?' I should have known.

'He did. And his mood had not improved,' she says dryly.

I can imagine. I smile. 'Did you give him a cuddle?'

Sally snorts, flopping back in her chair in another fit of

laughter, and I join her, laughing helplessly as I watch Sal fall apart all over her desk.

Patrick walks in and looks at both of us in exasperation before making his way to his own office, shutting the door behind him.

Oh, shit! 'Was Patrick here?' I ask.

She takes her glasses off and starts cleaning them with the hem of her brown polyester blouse. 'What? When the lunatic came in? No, he was collecting Irene from the train station.'

I let out a sigh of relief. What's Jesse thinking? He's a client. He can't come into my office and start throwing his weight around. I can hardly pass off Jesse's temper as a normal client grievance scenario. He's already heaved me out of the office once.

The office door opens and the flower delivery girl – Lusso girl again – trundles in with two lavish sprays. 'Flower deliveries for Ava and Sally?'

I watch as Sally nearly passes out at her desk. I bet she's never had flowers bought for her. I already know who they're from, though, the smooth bastard. 'Me?' Sally gushes, grabbing the colourful bouquet from the delivery girl and shooing her toward my desk.

'Thanks.' I smile, taking the simple spray of calla lilies before signing on behalf of Sally and myself. 'What does the card say, Sal?' I call, watching her eyes dart from left to right across the words.

She leans back, placing her hand over her heart. 'It says ... "Please accept my apologies. That woman makes me crazy" Oh, Ava!' She looks up at me all soppy. 'I would love to make a man that crazy!'

I roll my eyes, retrieving the card from my own flowers. I bet I don't have an apology. And Sally wouldn't be saying that if she was on the receiving end of Jesse's unreasonable, neurotic behaviour. I make him crazy? What a joke.

I open my card.

You're the one I've been waiting a long time for ...
Jx

My soppy side swoons slightly, but then the sensible side of my brain – the part that's not completely consumed with Jesse – is screaming that *The One* is actually someone who drops to their knees and obeys his every command, demand and instruction. While I'm fully aware that I've done exactly that, on numerous occasions, I also need to keep a hold of my identity and my mind. It's bloody hard when I'm so affected by this man. I'm *The One*. Is he *The One*? Oh heck, I really want him to be.

After leaving work late, I wander down our street and see Kate in the distance, jumping around in the middle of the road like the redheaded nutter that she is. As I near, I do a double-take, seeing a bright pink van parked up next to Margo, but this one's brand spanking new. So, Kate's finally invested in some new wheels.

'Nice wheels,' I say as I approach.

She spins around, her blue eyes dancing, her pale cheeks flushed. 'Do you know anything about this?'

I shake my head. 'Why would I?'

'I just got home and it was parked here. I admired it for a bit, walked through the front door and trod on the keys. Look.' She thrusts the keys under my nose, prompting me to look at the note attached to a piece of string on the key ring.

No more bruised butts, please.

No! He wouldn't have, surely? I think back to his fierce reaction to my battered bottom.

'Have you spoken to Sam?' I ask.

'Yep. He said I should speak to Jesse.'

'Why would he say that?' I ask.

'Well, obviously, because he thinks Jesse is the mystery van buyer.' She rolls her eyes. 'If he's bought *me* a van so *you* don't bruise your arse again, then I'll … Well, I'll love the fact that you bruise like a peach!'

'Kate, you can't accept it.'

She looks at me in disgust, and I know that there's not a hope in hell of her returning the van. I can see it in her delighted eyes.

'No fucking way! Don't you dare make me give it back. I've already christened her.'

'What?'

She spreads her long, pale fingers over the bonnet. 'Meet Margo Junior.' She lays her torso down on the pink metal.

I shake my head in exasperation, making my way up the path to the house.

'I'm taking her for a spin!' Kate yells.

I don't reply. Instead, I take myself up the stairs and throw myself in the shower, taking my time to wash the day away. As I turn the water off, I hear a Stone Roses track, 'The One', and nearly break my neck scrambling out of the shower to sprint across the landing. He's been messing with my phone again, but I couldn't give a damn. The phone rings off, the screen clearing to reveal eight missed calls.

Oh no, he'll be ripping his hair out. I dial him as I walk across the landing and into the lounge, looking out of the window to see if Kate's back.

She's not, but Jesse is pacing up and down the garden path, looking his usual Godly self, in jeans and a thin, knitted navy jumper. I smile, tingling from top to toe at the sight of him. He's frantically punching buttons on his phone and, just like I knew it would, my mobile lights up in my hand.

'Hello?' I say, all cool and casual.

'Where the hell are you?' he barks down the phone.

'Where are you?' I counter. Of course, I know damn well where he is. I stand at the window, watching him rake his hand through his hair, but then he disappears from view into the recess of the front door.

'I'm outside Kate's kicking the door down,' he snaps. 'Is it too much to ask that you answer your phone the first time I call you?'

'I was in the shower,' I say, making my way down to the front door.

'Take your phone with you!' He's completed exasperated, making me smile. I love every crazy element of him.

'You don't need to shout at me.' I look out of the viewer, dissolving on the spot when I see him leaning against the wall in the open porchway.

'I'm sorry,' he says softly. 'You make me crazy. Where are you?'

I watch him slide down the wall until his arse hits the floor, knees bent, head dropped. Oh, I can't see him like that.

I open the door. 'Here.'

He looks up and drops his phone from his ear, but makes no attempt to get up. He just looks at me, relief flooding his handsome face. I step out and slide down the wall opposite him so we're sitting across from each other, knee to knee. I half expect him to throw me inside because of my half naked state, but he doesn't. Instead, he reaches forward and places his big hand on my exposed knee, and I'm less than surprised when it sends hot sparks of fire flying off all over me.

'I thought …'

'I'd run again,' I finish for him, resting my hand over his on my knee. 'I was in the shower.'

'Where are your clothes?' He runs his green eyes over my towel-clad body.

'In my wardrobe,' I answer dryly.

His hand disappears under my towel, clasping me above my hipbone, prompting a jerk and the loosening of my towel. 'Sarcasm doesn't suit you, lady.'

'Sorry!' I splutter, relaxing when he releases me. 'Sally loved her flowers.'

'Did you love yours?'

'I did. Thank you.'

'My man!'

I look down the path and see Sam walking up, and when I return my eyes to Jesse, he looks like he may very well have a seizure now. His eyes are wide as he jumps to his feet and yanks me up, doing a spectacular job of keeping me covered by the towel.

'Sam, don't fucking move!' he yells. I'm scooped up and bundled through the door at breakneck speed, hearing Sam laughing as Jesse jogs up the stairs with me in his arms, muttering about ripping prying eyes out. I'm tossed on the bed. 'Get dressed. We're going out.'

I snap my head up. *I'm not going to The Manor*, I think as I get up from the bed, minus one towel, and go to my dressing table. 'Where?'

His gaze travels down my naked form. 'Well, it occurred to me when I was out running that I've not taken you for dinner yet. You have the most incredible legs. Get dressed.' He nods at my wardrobe.

If he means dinner at The Manor, then I'm not game. I'll avoid that place at all costs if she's there. And the chances are – given that she works for him – she will be.

'Where?' I ask again as I start rubbing cocoa butter into my legs.

'A little Italian place I know. Get dressed before I collect on my debt.'

I stand, slowly massaging my cream in. 'Debt?'

His eyebrows rise. 'You owe me.'

'I do?' I frown, but I know exactly what he's talking about.

'Oh, you do. I'll wait outside at the risk of cashing in sooner.' He gives me his roguish grin. 'I wouldn't want you to think this was *all* about sex.' He leaves me with that little comment before stalking out.

Those few words have just made my day. Maybe tonight I'll find out what goes on in that beautiful, complex mind of his.

We pull up outside a small Italian restaurant in the West End. I get out of the car and Jesse comes to collect me, grabbing my hand and pulling me into what can only be described as a sitting room. Dimly lit and with Italian paraphernalia in every nook and cranny, it's like I've stepped back in time to the eighties in Italy.

'Sir Jesse, how very good it is to see you.' A small Italian man approaches. He has a naturally happy face.

Jesse clasps his hand. 'Luigi, good to see you too.'

'Come, come.' Luigi gestures us farther into the room.

He settles us at a little table in the corner. The tablecloth is cream and embroidered with the *Italia Turrita*. It's very pretty.

'Luigi, this is Ava.' Jesse introduces us.

Luigi bows at me. 'Ah, a beautiful name for a beautiful lady, yes?' I smile, blushing slightly at his forwardness. 'What would Sir Jesse like?'

'May I?' Jesse asks, nodding at the menu.

He's asking me? 'You usually do,' I mutter. His eyebrow arches as he puffs his lips slightly, in a don't-push-it gesture. I let him get on with it. He obviously knows what's good on the menu.

'Okay, Luigi. We'll have two of the fettuccine, with yellow squash, parmesan and lemon cream sauce, a bottle of the *Famiglia Anselma Barolo* 2000 and some water.'

Luigi scribbles frantically on his pad, backing away. 'Yes, yes, Sir Jesse.'

Jesse smiles fondly. 'Thank you, Luigi.'

The Italian scurries off, leaving us alone in the quiet corner of the restaurant. 'You come here often?' I ask.

His smile broadens into knee-trembling territory. 'Are you trying to chat me up?'

'Of course.' I smile as he shifts in his chair.

'Mario, the head barman at The Manor, insisted I try it, so I did. Luigi's his brother.'

'Luigi and Mario?' I snort, rather rudely. Jesse raises his eyebrows at me. 'I'm sorry, that really tickled me!'

'I can see that.' He frowns as Luigi returns with the drinks. Jesse pours me some wine and himself some water.

'You didn't get a whole bottle for me?' I blurt. 'Are you not having any?' Christ, I'll be on my back.

'No. I'm driving.'

'And I'm allowed?'

His lips press into a straight line, but I can see that he's trying to suppress a smile at my cheekiness. 'You may.'

I grin, picking up my glass and sipping carefully as he watches me. It's lovely. 'You bought Kate a van.'

'I did.'

'Why?'

'Because I don't want you being tossed around in the back of that jalopy.'

I shake my head a little at his candidness, and as I gaze over the table at the beautiful, neurotic man, my brain is suddenly bombarded with questions.

'I want to know how old you are.' I state confidently. This whole age thing is really quite stupid.

He circles the rim of his glass with the tip of his finger as he watches me. 'Twenty-eight. Tell me about your family.'

'I asked first.'

'And I answered. Tell me about your family.'

I shake my head in despair. 'They retired to Newquay a few years back,' I sigh. 'Dad ran a construction firm, Mum was a housewife. My dad had a heart attack scare so they took early retirement to Cornwall. My brother is living the dream in Australia. Why do you not speak to your parents?' I watch carefully, almost apprehensively, for his reaction.

He takes a sip of water, and I'm more than surprised when he launches into his answer. 'They live in Marbella. My sister's there, too. I've not spoken to them for years. They didn't approve when Carmichael left me The Manor and all of his estate.'

'He left it *all* to you?'

'He did. We were close, and he didn't talk to my parents. They didn't approve.'

'They didn't approve of your relationship?'

'No, they didn't.' He starts chewing his lip.

'What was not to approve of?' I'm completely intrigued now.

He sighs. I can tell he's not comfortable talking about this. 'As soon as I left school, I spent all of my time with Carmichael. Mum, Dad, and Amalie moved to Spain, and I refused to go. I was eighteen and having the time of my life. I stayed with Carmichael when they left. They weren't happy about it.' He shrugs. 'Three years later, Carmichael died and I was left to run The Manor.' He tells the story with no emotion and takes another swig of water. 'The relationship was strained after that. They demanded I sell The Manor but I couldn't. It was Carmichael's baby.'

I'm stunned. I've found out more about this man in five minutes than I have since I've known him. Why is he so talkative tonight? I decide to take advantage – I don't know when I'll get another chance.

'What do you do for fun?'

His green eyes flash black and he grins wickedly. 'Fuck you.'

My eyes widen at his crass answer, but I keep my cool, even

though I've caved a little on the inside. 'You like power in the bedroom,' I state without a trace of a blush. I'm proud of myself. His skill and influence on my entire being has me nervous.

'I do.' His face is completely impassive.

'Are you a dominant?' I blurt, and then mentally stab myself with the fancy silver fork at my place setting. Where did that come from?

He coughs, nearly spitting his water all over me.

Placing his glass down, he picks up his cloth napkin to wipe his mouth as he shakes his head on a half-smile. 'Ava, I don't need that sort of arrangement to get a woman to do what I want her to do in the bedroom.'

'You're very controlling,' I state coolly, observing the swirling of my wine. I'll get that one out there, too.

'Look at me,' he demands softly, and like the slave to him that I am, I look, finding his green eyes have softened as he sits back, relaxed in his chair. 'Only with you.'

'Why?'

'I don't know.' He has a quick chew of his lip. 'You make me crazy.'

I sigh wearily into my wine glass. I make him crazy? *Right back attcha, Ward!*

'Here's your pasta.' I look up and see Luigi singing as he approaches.

'Lovely people.' He places two considerable bowls in front of us. *'Buon appetito!'*

'Thank you, Luigi.' Jesse smiles politely.

I stir the pasta with my fork and play with it for a few moments, then I try a bit.

'Good?' Jesse asks.

I nod and we eat in a comfortable silence for a while, occasionally tossing stares at each other.

'When did you buy the penthouse?' I ask.

He pauses with his fork halfway to his mouth. 'March,' he

answers, taking his last mouthful of food and pushing his bowl away before picking up his water.

'You never told me why you requested me personally to work on the extension of The Manor.' I give up on my pasta, pushing it away.

Jesse looks at the half-eaten dish and returns his eyes to mine. 'I bought the penthouse and loved what you did with it. I can assure you, I didn't expect you to come rocking up, with your perfect figure, olive skin and big brown eyes.' He shakes his head, as if shaking off the memory. I feel somewhat better knowing he was as shocked to see me as I was to see him.

'You weren't exactly the Lord of the Manor I was expecting, either.' I do my own little shiver when I recall the effect he had on me; the effect he still has on me. 'How did you know where I was on that Monday lunchtime when I *bumped* into you at the bar?'

He shrugs. 'Lucky guess.'

'Of course,' I scoff. Followed me, more like.

I look up and see a smile tickling the edge of his luscious lips. 'I couldn't think of anything else after you left The Manor. I had to have you.'

'Do you always take what you want?'

He watches me across the table, his face completely straight as he leans forward. 'I can't answer that, Ava, because I've never wanted anything enough to pursue it so relentlessly. Not like I wanted you.'

'And now you have me.' I pause and force myself to ask the one question I can't shake. 'So, with the chase over, do you still? Want me, I mean.'

He sits back in his chair and studies me, stroking his glass of water. 'More than anything.'

A little gush of air escapes my mouth. I'm not sure if it's relief or desire. 'Then I'm yours.'

His tongue slowly sweeps across his bottom lip. 'Ava, you've been mine since you turned up at The Manor.'

'Have I?'

'Yes. Will you spend the night with me?'

'Are you asking or demanding?'

'I'm asking, but if you give me the wrong answer, then I'm sure I can think of something to change your mind.' He smiles slightly.

'I'll spend the night with you.'

He nods in approval. 'Tomorrow night?'

'Yes.'

'Take the day off,' he demands.

'No.'

His eyes narrow. 'What about Friday evening?'

'I've arranged to go out with Kate on Friday night,' I inform him, resisting the temptation to reach up and twiddle my hair. He can't assume I'm there whenever he demands. I hope Kate's free.

His narrowed eyes instantly darken. 'Cancel.'

Now this is something I *do* need to clear up, pronto – his neurotic unreasonableness. 'I'm going out to have a few drinks. You can't stop me from seeing my friends, Jesse.'

'How many is "a few drinks"?'

I can feel my brow knitting. 'I don't know. That depends on how I feel.' I look at him accusingly.

He starts chewing his bottom lip again, and I can see the cogs of his mind going into overdrive. He's trying to work out how he's going to get around this. I haven't done myself any favours by getting in such a state last Saturday.

'I don't want you out drinking without me,' he says firmly.

'That's a bit of bad luck, isn't it?' God, I'm being rather brave.

'We'll see,' he muses to himself.

We sit quietly, looking at each other across the table, him scowling, me hiding a small smile. After a few moments, he leans back casually in his chair at a slight angle, his eyes rapt with intention. I don't shy away from his concentrated stare. I meet it with equal intent, in a barefaced come on. I want him desperately, despite his challenging ways.

Luigi comes over and clears our plates, intruding on our moment. 'You like?' he sings.

Jesse doesn't fracture the connection. 'Great, Luigi. Thank you.' His voice is throaty and he's tapping the table with his middle finger. I feel his leg brush against mine, and that's all it takes to hitch my breath up several notches and spring my nerve endings to life. I'm blazing from head to toe … and he knows it.

'The bill, please, Luigi,' he demands, his friendly tone altering into one of urgency.

Luigi seems to get the message because he doesn't offer us the dessert menu. He just scuttles off, returning almost immediately carrying a black plate filled with mints and a piece of paper. Without looking at the bill, Jesse stands and pulls a wad of notes from his jeans pocket, slapping some down on the table.

He reaches over and seizes my hand. 'We're going.'

I'm hauled from my chair and rushed to the door. 'Are you in a hurry?' I ask as I'm guided to the car by my elbow.

He makes no attempt to slow down. 'Yes.'

When we reach the car, I'm whirled around and shoved up against the door. His forehead meets mine, our heavy breaths merging together in the small space between our mouths. His erection is painfully hard against my lower stomach.

Oh God, I want him to take me here and now. Damn anyone who wants to watch.

'I'm going to fuck you until you're seeing stars, Ava.' His voice is harsh as he grinds his hips against me. I whimper. 'You won't be going to work tomorrow because you won't be able to walk. Get in the car.'

I would, but I already can't walk. Suspense has rendered me immobile.

After a few seconds have passed and I've still not convinced my legs to shift, he pulls me out of the way, opens the door, and gently shoves me into the passenger seat.

Chapter Twenty

Our journey back to Lusso is the longest I've ever endured. The sexual tension bouncing around in his car is excruciating, and Jesse is almost violent when he gets stuck behind a Sunday driver.

He skids to a halt outside the electronic gates of Lusso and presses a remote to open them, his hand drumming on the steering wheel as he waits impatiently for them to shift.

I smile. 'You're going to have a seizure if you don't calm down.'

He pauses with the drumming and looks at me, all smoky-eyed. 'Ava, I've had a fucking seizure every day since I've met you.'

'You're swearing a lot,' I muse as the gates open and he pulls into the car park, fast and carelessly.

'And you're going to be screaming a lot. Out,' he orders.

I've no doubt I will be, but I do love it when he's in these frenzies. I take my time getting out of the car, and when I'm finally vertical, I glance up to find him in front of me with a very irked look on his face.

'What are you doing?' he asks incredulously at my leisurely pace.

I gaze around at the black nighttime sky and down to the docks before returning my eyes to him. 'Do you fancy a walk?'

His mouth drops open. 'Do I fancy a walk?'

'Yes, it's a lovely evening.' I'm doing a rubbish job of hiding my smug smile.

'No, Ava, I fancy fucking you until you beg me to stop.' He bends, grabs me around the back of my thighs and hoists me over his shoulder, kicking shut the door of his ridiculously expensive car.

'Jesse!' My stomach catapults into my mouth at the swift movement. 'I'll walk!'

He strides into the foyer of Lusso determinedly. 'Not fast enough. Good evening, Clive.'

I brace my hands on Jesse's lower back, craning my head up to find Clive observing me draped over Jesse's shoulder. What must he think of me? The last time I entered Lusso I was being carried too. 'I'm not drunk!' I yell, watching Clive disappear from sight as Jesse carries me into the elevator and punches the code in harshly. In my sassy state, I slide my hands beneath his jeans, onto his fantastic, tight arse to feel the tense and swell of his muscles and smooth, warm skin as he strides out of the lift.

'No fucking about. I want inside you now. You fuck about, I swear to God ...'

'You're so romantic.'

'We've got all the time in the world for romance, lady.'

I smile to myself as he barges into the penthouse, slamming the door behind him. I'm a touch disorientated when he lowers me to my feet in the kitchen, leaving me standing before him, my hands resting on his shoulders, trying to get my bearings.

'You know, you're really not going to be in a fit state to work tomorrow.' His hot breath touches my face. 'Strip, now.'

I'm shaking – visibly shaking. I try to pull myself together, but it's impossible when he's looking at me like this. I feel his hands lay over mine and peel them away from his shoulders. He places them on my stomach.

'Start with the shirt.' His voice is throaty, tinged with a bit of desperation.

I can do this; I can be audacious. 'So, am I in charge?' I ask, inwardly bracing myself for his scoff.

It doesn't come. He looks at me, the slight surprise at my question clear, but he doesn't laugh. He can't be in control all of the time.

'If it makes you happy.' He unclasps his Rolex and slides it onto the island.

I take a deep breath and staring him boldly in the eye, I raise my hands to my top button, willing my fingers to cooperate. Every button I undo, his face strains harder, and I become bolder. If this isn't fucking about, then I don't know what is.

I release my shirt, letting it hang open, and watch as he scrapes his eyes down my torso, his tongue running across his parted bottom lip. Then taking my hands to my shoulders, I pull my shirt away, accentuating the slow push forward of my breasts when I lower it down my arms, and like the wanton sex fiend I am, I hold it out to my side for a few seconds while his eyes travel back up my body. When our eyes meet again, I dramatically open my palm and let it fall to the floor, leaving my arm outstretched and hovering at my side for a few seconds. His eyes are blazing, his forehead damp.

'I love you in lace,' he whispers.

Smiling, I lower my hands to the fly of my trousers and lazily undo one button at a time as he watches, his panting increasing by the second. The drain on his self-control has him chewing his lip to the point of drawing blood.

Once all the buttons are undone and my trousers are gaping open, I stand with my hands tucked in the front, ready to drag them down my legs, but I don't. I'm too enthralled by his reaction to my shameless strip.

He looks up at me, his eyes blazing and desperate. 'I could rip them off in two seconds flat.'

'But you won't.' My voice is husky and alluring. I'm stunned by my own brashness. 'You'll wait.' I kick my shoes off, sending them flying a few yards across the kitchen.

He follows their course before looking back at me with

raised eyebrows. 'Taking this a bit far, aren't you?'

I smile sweetly as little by little, inch by inch, I slide my capri pants down my legs and kick them off until I'm standing in my coral lace underwear before this glorious man. I've lost all my inhibitions. It's an eye-opener.

He lifts his hand to stroke my breast. 'No,' I utter firmly, his hand floating over my breastbone. It's not touching me, but the heat emanating from it has me hyperventilating. My self-control is wavering, but I really love this power.

'Fuck you,' he mumbles, dropping his hand.

'Please do.'

He lifts me from my feet, paces toward the kitchen island, and sits me on the cold marble. Nudging my thighs apart, he edges between them with his hands on my waist and pulls me forward to meet his groin, his erection rubbing me in just the right spot. I moan, placing my hands around his neck.

'I thought I was in charge.'

'Wrong.' He pushes back just enough to pull his jumper up over his head, and then kicks his Grensons off, before making quick work of his jeans and boxers. I sit patiently, more than happy to watch him undress. This man is a God. I drag my eyes down the full loveliness of him, briefly faltering on his scar and settling on his thick, pulsing erection.

'It's rude to stare,' he says softly.

My eyes jump to his, uncertain as to whether he's referring to me looking at his scar or his beautiful manhood. He doesn't elaborate. He moves back into me, reaching around my back to unhook my bra, slowly drawing it down my arms and tossing it behind him.

Resting his hands on the edge of the worktop, he watches me as he leans down and takes a nipple in his mouth, slowly swirling and flicking it with his tongue.

In pure, unashamed bliss, I sigh, reaching up to lace my fingers in his hair as he divides his attention between each of my breasts. My head falls back and I close my eyes, absorbing his attentive mouth.

His tongue starts a lazy trail up the centre of my body, finishing with a soft kiss on my chin. 'Lift,' he commands, grasping my knickers. I brace myself up on the worktop, letting him pull them down my legs. 'I'll be back. I'm a bit peckish.'

He wanders boldly and with poise over to the fridge-freezer, completely butt naked. I sit rapt by the tremendous view of his impossibly taut arse, long, lean legs and powerful, smooth back, his gait all the better when he's naked.

'Enjoying the scenery?'

Looking up, I see him standing watching me. I don't know how long I was daydreaming. I could watch him for ever. He holds up a can of squirty cream, grinning, before taking the lid off, giving it a little shake and squirting some in his mouth. I watch him carefully. He looks very pleased with himself.

'And that's a staple food in your world?' I ask.

He saunters back toward me, shaking the can. 'Absolutely,' he says seriously, replacing himself between my legs, nudging my chin upward with the tip of his finger. 'Open.'

I open my mouth, and he rests the nozzle on my tongue, watching me as he presses the notch, releasing a blob of cream into my mouth. I lick my lips and the cream disintegrates in my mouth instantly.

Placing my hands behind me, I lean back as he runs his eyes down my front. 'Do your worst, Mr Ward,' I tease.

His eyes sparkle and he grins that roguish grin. 'This might be a little cold,' he warns as he squirts a long trail straight down my middle. I inhale quickly at the initial shock of the freezing cold cream, running from the hollow of my throat all the way down to the juncture of my thighs. He smirks, squirting a little extra where it counts. I look down at the long path of white puffs, feeling my nipples pucker tighter at the chilliness close by. He stands back, his eyes dancing with delight.

'It's a bit of a *cliché*, isn't it?' I grin.

He squirts some in his own mouth. 'The old ones are the best.' He starts walking away again. Where's he going? I sit on the breakfast bar coated in cream, watching as he riffles through cupboards. 'Here it is.'

Here's what? He opens a drawer, pulls out a spatula and walks back over, tapping a jar of chocolate spread mischievously. As he arrives back between my legs, he unscrews the lid and tosses it on the marble counter.

I arch a brow at him questioningly, even though I know damn well what his intent is. The spatula is dipped and twirled, and he scoops out a big dollop, abruptly slapping it onto my breast.

'Ouch!' My skin stings from the smack.

He smirks as he starts circling the chocolate around my nipple, the sting mixed with the rhythmic swirls leaving me purring deep in my throat. I soak it all up, and when the jar is completely empty and he's satisfied he covered every part of my torso, he puts his instruments down and stands back to admire his handiwork. The smile that spans his handsome face makes me want to dive on him and tackle him to the floor. He looks thoroughly thrilled with himself.

'My very own Ava éclair,' he declares, licking his lips.

I look down at my coated body and back up to his dancing eyes. 'I guess now you've had your fun, I should go take a shower.' I make to move and he's on me in a flash, grasping me in his arms as I knew he would. I'm locked to his chest, sliding all over the place. I give a little shimmy on a laugh, just to rub it in.

'Sneak,' he mutters, pulling away, the chocolate and cream stringing between our bodies. He takes my hands, gently pushing me back until I'm flat on my back and looking up at him. 'I've not even started with the fun part, lady.'

I grin. 'I'm filthy.'

'Oh, I love that grin. You won't be filthy for long.' He leans over me, rubbing his erection against my core, scooping a trail of chocolate from my nipple with his index finger and keeping his eyes firmly on mine as he slides it between his lips and licks it off in the most spectacular fashion. 'Hmmm, chocolate, cream, and sweat.'

I shudder under his piercing eyes, the light throb at my sex kicking into high gear, as I writhe on the bar under his intoxicating stare. I reach up to pull him down onto me. I need contact. He lets me take him, dropping his lips to mine and resting his chest on me so we slip and slide all over again. The warmth of his body all over mine catapults me straight to Central Jesse Cloud Nine.

My tongue gently coaxes his from his mouth with small butterfly flicks, and I smile against his lips as he moans and snakes his arm under my lower back, tugging me up from the counter. My arms remain around his neck, working my fingers through his hair as he continues to ravish me, and I continue to writhe.

Straying away from my lips, he begins kissing his way up my cheek to my ear, making a point of grinding his everloving hips against me, instigating the familiar heaviness in my groin. I groan as my fingers curl tightly in his hair and he bites my lobe, slowly dragging it through his teeth.

'Jesse,' I pant, arching myself into him.

'I know,' he hums against my ear. 'You want me to take care of it?'

'Yes!'

He drops a tender kiss on the hollow of my ear, easing me down onto my back.

With his upper body braced on one arm at the side of me, he gently brushes the hair from my face. I watch as he studies me thoughtfully, his green pools swimming, the cogs of his mind turning.

'Everything is so much more bearable with you around, Ava,'

he says softly, his eyes searching mine.

I absorb his words. What's more bearable? I can't cope with the vagueness of this statement, especially not now. There is so much more than meets the eye with this man. I want answers, but as I draw breath to speak, he drops his head to my breast, flicking his tongue over my already taut nipple, circling it and licking the chocolate away. I buck when his teeth clamp over my tight bud, the sharp stab arching my back and pushing my breast up, forcing him to pull away slightly to accommodate me.

'Feel good?'

'Yes!'

'You want more of my mouth?'

'Jesus, Jesse!'

He hums in satisfaction, spreading his attention between my breasts, lapping, nipping and sucking the chocolate, gradually and meticulously, away.

I moan. I'm a sweating mess. My fingers are clawed in his hair as I squirm under his expert tongue. One touch of my core and I'll be propelled into a despairing stupor.

'All clean,' he drawls as he lifts his body, his eyes locking with mine. 'But she wants more of my mouth.' He licks his lips and backs away from me, my stomach performing a full three-sixty spin.

Oh, Christ. I won't last a second.

He looms over me, looking straight down to the apex of my thighs, and then eases his palms onto my legs and slowly pulls them farther apart. 'Fuck, Ava. You're weeping.' He breathes in deep, and I see the rise and fall of his chest speed up as he flicks one last gaze up at me before his head drifts down, slowly and provocatively. I clamp my eyes shut, tensing my whole body, as I wait for that first dash of contact.

And there it is – one long sweep of his tongue, straight up the centre of my core, with a little dance on my clit to finish off.

'Oh … *God!*' I groan, and I'm rewarded with two fingers thrust straight in to maximum capacity. I buck and squirm involuntarily as Jesse lays an arm across my stomach to hold me down.

'You want me to stop?' he asks. His voice is gravel, my reaction violent. He swiftly returns to my sex, plunging his fingers in deep while lightly stroking my clitoris with his tongue.

In seconds, I feel the peak of an explosion on the horizon, and with one last casual sweep up the very centre of my most sensitive place, I burst apart under him. I'm lost. I thrash my head from side to side, a rush of breath escaping my burning lungs on a long, peaceful sigh as my thumping heart works its way back down to a steady, safe rate.

He laps gently, helping me ride out the pulses of my orgasm, letting me drift delicately down as I moan in pure satisfaction. He has the most incredible mouth.

In my sublime state, I feel him shift from between my legs. 'You're amazing. I need to be inside you.'

He moves quickly, and in one measured movement, he yanks me forward and impales me on his waiting arousal. I cry out at the shocking invasion, my abating climax resurrected.

'My turn,' he gasps, pulling out and firing forward again. I cry out, throwing my arms over my head as he clamps onto my thighs tightly, pulling me back and forth on the marble to match his momentum. I peel my eyes open and find him sweating, his jaw clenched.

The remnants of the cream and chocolate has me sliding to meet him with ease, tingling sensations attacking me between my thighs, the delicious full drives of his powerful body set to blow my brain clean out of my head.

'Does that feel good, Ava?' he shouts over my cries.

'God, yes!'

'You won't run away from me again, will you?'

'No!' *Never!*

I'm hauled up onto his body and swung around to meet the wall, my back crashing against it, causing a shocked yell to burst from my mouth. I lied. I'm not used to him, not at all. And I'm not sure I ever will be. He's so incredibly powerful, forceful and large. I endure his determined, unrelenting pounds as I'm pushed up the wall on cry after cry, and in my desperation to control my rolling orgasm, I find his shoulder and latch on with my mouth, sinking my teeth into his flesh.

'Oh, FUCK!' he roars. I hear his forehead collide into the wall behind me, his hips powering forward.

That's it.

I release his shoulder, throw my head back on a harsh cry and erupt into a splintering follow-up orgasm.

He stills suddenly, his breathing ragged and violent, and then he thunders forward one last, powerful time. 'Jesus!' he barks, jerking against me, inside and out. I'm convulsing in his arms with my own fitful breathing, trying to gulp down some valuable air into my overworked lungs.

I clench my arms and legs tighter around him, close my eyes and melt into his body.

I'm only dimly aware of being transported back to the kitchen island in his arms, the movement causing his semi-erection to stroke me inside as I cling onto him, revelling in his heat. I lay back as he lowers me, feeling the comfort of his solid chest rest onto mine, and instinctively curl my arms around his back as he showers my face with tender kisses.

Oh God, I feel so overwhelmed. I've never felt so needed or wanted. My time with Jesse, good and bad, strops and affection, has blasted any other feelings I've had well and truly out of the water.

I open my eyes, knowing he's looking at me.

'You and me,' he whispers, gazing down at me.

I close my heavy lids and pull his head down to bury my face in his neck, completely losing myself in him.

'We need a shower.'

I drag my eyes open as I'm being lifted from the breakfast bar. My body is wrapped around Jesse and I have no intention of letting go. 'Let's stay,' I murmur dreamily. I'm so tired.

He chuckles. 'Just hold on. I'll do all the work.'

So I do. I hold on tight, my legs wrapped around his waist, my arms around his shoulders, as he carries me through the penthouse, up the stairs and into the bathroom.

'Put me in bed,' I gripe as he deposits me on the vanity unit.

'You're sticky, *I'm* sticky. Let me wash us both, then we can get in bed and snuggle. Deal?' He goes to turn the shower on.

I look up at him through sleepy eyes. 'No, put me in bed.'

'Ava, you're adorable when you're sleepy.' He scoops me up from the unit and carries me into the shower. I rest my head in the crook of his neck, making no attempt to free myself from his warm body. The water is blissful. 'I'm going to put you down,' he says, and I tighten my grip around him. He laughs. 'I can't wash you without any free hands.'

'I want to stay stuck to you.'

Turning his face into mine, he drops a tender kiss on my forehead, humming against my skin. One arm releases me, his knee rising to meet my backside, while he leans over and grasps the shower gel from the shelf, dropping it to the floor before doing the same with the shampoo. He lowers his knee, slips his arm back under my bent legs and slowly slides down the wall, holding tightly onto me until I feel the firmness of the shower floor beneath him as we come to rest on the floor.

I know I'm restricting him with my arms clenched around his neck, but I don't move them, and he doesn't complain. He works around me, holding me with one arm, washing and rinsing my hair with his free hand as best as I'll allow. His task is unhurried as he cleans away the leftovers of cream and choco-late from my body, his hand gliding over me tenderly in slow, careful circles, wheedling me into a slumber. I keep my hold of him. I don't want to ever let go.

'I want to look after you for ever,' he whispers, pressing his lips against my temple.

I release a hand from his neck, brushing down his chest to his abdominals, slowly circling his belly button. 'Okay,' I agree. I'm more than happy with that. I can't think of anything more natural to me – I doubt I ever will.

He lets out a long, tired breath. 'Come on, let's get you out.'

I lean in to drop a chaste kiss on the centre of his chest, and look up at him to find his eyes are squeezed shut, his face turned up toward the ceiling. Reaching up, I kiss his throat to get his attention, but a few seconds pass before he brings his face down to mine.

I smile at him, and he offers a little one in return. It's not con-vincing, and it has me wondering what's causing his anguish.

'What's wrong?' I ask nervously.

'Nothing's wrong. Everything is right.' He cups my cheeks in both of his hands, giving me a half-smile, his eyes running all over my face before he turns the shower off and lifts us to our feet, wrapping a towel around his narrow waist.

I walk out behind him, and I'm immediately engulfed in a soft bath sheet. He rubs me from top to toe, working the excess water from my hair.

'You want me to carry you?' he asks.

I nod and he smiles approvingly, scooping my naked body up into his arms and carrying me to the bed. I crawl under the sheets, inhaling deeply as my head rests on the pillow, the delicious waft of Jesse swamping my senses. I'll sleep well here.

As soon as he's dropped his towel and is close enough, I crawl into his chest, burying my face under his chin, my hot breath ricocheting off his neck back into my face. I draw my leg up, resting my upper leg between his thighs. I'm completely swathed in him, and it's the most soothing place in the world.

'Go to sleep, baby.' He drops a kiss on top of my head and squeezes me to him.

There is no space welcome between us.

Chapter Twenty-one

I regain consciousness with Jesse lying between my thighs, rubbing his nose against mine.

'Morning, lady.'

I groan, extending my arms above my head in a long, satisfying stretch. I feel Jesse's morning hard-on nuzzling between my thighs, a flicker of a smile playing at the sides of his mouth.

I wiggle under him. 'Morning, yourself.'

In one swift movement he drives deep into me, and it's already a great day. I hold onto his tight biceps as he rests on his forearms and works up into a firm, steady rhythm.

He opens his eyes. 'I love sleepy sex with you.'

I stare into his calm, peaceful face and let him take me to paradise, but I'm abruptly snapped out of my dreamy state when Jesse rolls us both over, keeping us connected, so I'm straddling him. The sudden gravity sensitizes me to his invasion.

'Ride me, Ava.' His voice is raspy, his hunger-filled eyes glistening in the morning light. He grasps my thighs, and I plant my palms on his pecs.

'I'm in charge?'

'Do your worst, baby.' He flicks his hips up, prompting me to instigate some movement, so staring him squarely in his sleepy eyes, I slowly and carefully rise from his hips, bracing myself up for a few seconds, teasing and watching his face blaze for friction. Then I lower myself back down with equal precision, grinding as far as possible. It sends him into a tailspin.

He throws his head back, moaning so loudly it echoes around the bedroom.

'Again?'

'Fuck, yes!'

'Mind your language, please,' I taunt him as I slowly rise and fall with complete precision, grinding myself against him again. I repeat the torturous move over and over, watching as he crumbles beneath me.

His hands shoot up to cup my breasts, his thumbs working small circles around my tight nipples. I rise again, pausing at my peak. His eyes are skipping, his mouth parted. I'm struggling to keep control above him.

'Down?'

'Oh God, yes.'

I descend and watch his face distort. He won't endure this for much longer. I can see the strain carved in his tense jaw and creased forehead. He groans, holding my breasts tighter, sending a sharp, shooting pain directly to my core. *I'm* not going to be able to endure this for long. I'm on the crest of release, and I need him to be there when I fall.

I lift myself up, knowing he expects me to slowly lower myself, but I don't. Instead, I knock the wind right out of him and crash down, completely impaling myself on him. I grind down hard.

'Jesus fucking Christ!' he roars, sweat instantly breaking out across his brow. I roll my hips, ensuring optimum penetration, forcing myself down onto him. 'Fuck fuck fuck. Ava, I'm going to come!'

'Wait,' I demand.

His eyes snap open in shock, desperation filling them. I roll again, watching as he squeezes his eyes shut, his frown line the deepest I've ever seen it. This is taking everything out of him. I just need one more …

'Ava, I can't.'

'Shit! Wait.'

'Watch your mouth!' he yells, his eyes still closed in concentration. It's killing him.

'Fuck off, Jesse!'

Those greens fly back open in warning at my crass words, but I couldn't give a damn. I clamp my hands over his and use my leg muscles to lift myself again, hovering above him and crashing down so he completely spears me.

I lift again. 'Now!' I cry, smashing back down. My body explodes, sending me soaring right into orbit, and I'm only vaguely aware of Jesse's strangled moans as I feel hot moisture invade me, warming my entire being. I collapse onto his chest in an exhausted heap – job done.

I lay sprawled across him, melting into the rhythm of his fingers circling my back, his semi-erection drumming steadily inside me, our heartbeats clashing together between our chests as we try to regulate our breathing. We're both totally replete.

'I love sleepy sex with you.'

He kisses the top of my head. 'Except for your filthy mouth.' His voice is full of scorn.

I laugh and look up at him, reaching to run my fingers down his stubbly cheek. I love his stubble. He turns his face into my touch, kissing my fingers and returning my smile.

'I don't think we can call that sleepy sex, baby.'

'No?'

'No. We'll think of a new name for that one.'

'Okay,' I agree, completely contented. I rest my cheek back onto his chest and trace small circles around his golden nipple. 'How old are you, Jesse?'

'Twenty-nine.'

I scoff, but it occurs to me very suddenly that I won't have a clue when we finally reach his real age. I'm plumping for thirty-four. That's eight years past me – I can live with that.

I sigh. 'What's the time?' I could do with another hour.

He shifts me from his chest. 'I left my watch downstairs. I'll go take a look.'

'You need a clock in here,' I grumble as he gets out of bed, leaving me cold and bare without him.

'I'll put in a complaint to the designer,' he replies dryly.

I ignore him, turning over to snuggle down, making do with the pillow. This bed is the most comfortable I've ever slept in.

'Seven-thirty,' I hear him shout from downstairs.

I bolt upright in bed. 'Shit!' I jump out and race downstairs to the kitchen. 'You'll have to drop me at home.'

He sits, dead cool and casual on the barstool, completely bare arsed naked, scooping peanut butter from a jar with his finger. 'I'm a bit busy this morning,' he says without looking at me.

Oh, the irritating pig! This is, without a doubt, a ploy to keep me here. I'll get the Tube, it's no bother. I scan the floor where I dropped my clothes – no clothes.

'Where are my clothes, Jesse?'

He sticks his peanut butter-covered finger into his mouth, sucking it off and pulling it slowly from his mouth on a little pop. 'I've no idea.'

Where has he hid them, the little shit? They can't be far. I stalk around his apartment, huffing and puffing, pulling open cupboard doors and looking behind furniture, but when I find nothing, I march back into the kitchen, finding him still sitting there, looking infuriatingly naked and handsome, and completely unaffected by my frenzy.

Oh, I've not got time for this. I can't be late for work. 'Where are my fucking clothes?' I shout.

'Watch your fucking mouth!'

I shake my head at him. He'll have a bar of soap in my mouth next. 'Jesse, I never swore out loud before I met you … Funny, huh? I need to get home so I can get ready for work.'

'I know you do.' In goes another peanut butter-covered

finger.

'So, where are my clothes?' I try calm, but if he doesn't give me my clothes *now*, I'll soon revert back to madwoman. I can't be late.

'They are … somewhere.' He grins around his finger.

'Where is somewhere?' I ask, while thinking about how much I dislike roguish Jesse today.

'If I tell you, you have to give me something in return.'

I feel madwoman coming on. 'What?'

'Don't drink tomorrow night.' His face is deadpan.

I scowl at him as I watch him fighting to control a smirk from breaking out. The conniving pig. He's got me cornered, naked, late for work and in need of a lift.

I stand, pondering his trade. If I'm honest, I wasn't planning on getting particularly drunk, especially after my performance on Saturday. I've not even asked Kate if she's free yet, but I don't want Mr Control Freak thinking he can dictate my every move. Give him an inch and all that.

'Fine.' How will he know if I have a drink, anyway?

He looks shocked. 'That was easier than I thought. What about lunch later?'

'Okay, get my clothes.'

'Who holds the power, Ava?' he asks.

I don't have time to challenge him on that. 'You do. Get my clothes!'

'Correct.' He struts over to the fridge – with a little extra swagger for my benefit – and opens the door. 'Here you are, lady.'

They were in the fridge? I snatch them from his hand, and he raises a warning brow at me. I don't care. I'm going to be so late. He watches me frantically yank my capri pants on and laughs as I hop around gasping when the freezing cold material rests on my skin.

'Have I got time for a shower?' he asks seriously.

'NO!'

He laughs, slaps my bum and saunters out of the kitchen.

Jesse drives me home in his usual driving style – frighteningly fast and ever impatient, but today I'm grateful.

He waits for me in the car, making a few calls while I shower and get ready in record time. I shove on some black, fitted ankle grazers, a white shirt and my red Dune ballet pumps. I'm dressed for speed today. My hair is having a strop for not being blow-dried last night, so I pin it into a messy up-do. I'll put my makeup on in the car.

As I rush across the landing, I collide with a half-naked Sam. Has he moved in?

'You're always in a rush, chick,' he laughs as I sidestep him, darting into the kitchen to get a glass of water and swallow my pill. 'Good night?'

I nod over my glass as he stands, bold as brass in the kitchen doorway, looking all roughed up. I won't ask if he's had a good night. That much is obvious.

'Where's Kate?' I ask.

He grins. 'I've tied her to the bed.'

My eyes widen. I have no idea if he's serious or not. He's such a joker. 'Tell her I'll call her later.' I wait for Sam to budge and let me out. 'See ya!' I call, running down the stairs.

'Hey, tell Jesse I'm not running today!' he shouts after me.

I rush down the path and onto the street, where Jesse is illegally parked and flipping off a traffic warden from his driver's seat. I wait for the warden to finish lecturing Jesse, but he seems to be on a roll.

'Move so the lady can get in the car,' Jesse growls, but the warden ignores him, launching into a speech on verbal abuse and lack of consideration for other road users.

'Excuse me.' I try for polite as opposed to Jesse's aggression. I get ignored. Damn, I'm going to be super late.

'For fuck's sake!' Jesse swings his door open and strides around the car to meet the warden on the pavement. The poor man visibly shrinks at Jesse's presence, moving away hastily. He opens the door, deposits me in the car before slamming it, cursing some more and sliding back behind the wheel. We roar off down my street, way too fast.

'They're just doing a job, you know.' I flip the mirror down to sort my makeup out.

'Power hungry failures who didn't make cops,' he grumbles. He looks at me and smiles. 'You look lovely.'

I snort. 'Watch the road. Oh, Sam said he can't make your run.'

'Lazy bastard. He's still there, then?' he asks, overtaking a taxi. I grab the side of my seat. My makeup is going to be everywhere.

'He's got Kate tied to the bed,' I mumble, flicking my lashes with my mascara wand.

'Probably.'

I swing my head around with my wand halfway to my eyes. 'You don't sound shocked.'

'That's because I'm not.' He looks at me out of the corner of his eye.

He's not? Sam's into kinky shit? 'I don't want to know,' I mutter, returning to the mirror.

'No, you don't,' he says quietly.

We pull up near my offices, but far enough away so I'm not spotted getting out of Jesse's Aston Martin. I'm still trying to figure out how Patrick might react to all of this. Jesse hasn't mentioned the extension since Sunday, and I can't imagine a pleasant reaction from my boss if I tell him that I'm not designing for Mr Ward; I'm dating him instead.

'What time's your lunch?' he asks, stroking my thigh, generating the familiar stabs of pleasure. Now is not the time to get horny, and that touch does it for me.

'One,' I squeak.

He rubs circles on my thigh. I stiffen slightly. 'I'll be here at one then.'

'Right here?' I breathe.

'Yes, right here.' His hand drifts between my legs.

'Jesse, stop.' I close my eyes, trying to fight off the sparks of pleasure.

He runs his hand up my centre, over my trousers.

I whimper.

'I can't keep my hands off you,' he says in that low hypnotising voice – the one that knocks all sense and reason out of me, 'and you're not going to stop me, are you?'

Leaning over, he wraps his hand around the back of my neck and pulls me toward him, increasing the strokes of my core, and when his lips find my mouth I moan. I'm being worked up into a blissful rhythm as he caresses my tongue with his, slowly and surely, guaranteeing optimum pleasure. I can't believe I'm letting him do this in his car in broad daylight, but he's triggered something now, and I can't walk into that office with the ache of an abandoned orgasm lurking inside me. I need relief, or I won't concentrate all day.

Coils of craving spread out and build up, my concern at the possibility of being captured indecently disappearing, just like that. I'm all over him. He just does it for me in so many earth-shattering ways.

'Let it go, Ava,' he says into my mouth. 'I want you in that office thinking of what I can do to you.'

I hit my climax, crying out as he presses his lips harder on mine, stifling my moans and alleviating the pressure of his hand to slowly work me down again.

'Better?' he asks as he pecks light kisses over my mouth.

'I can work in peace,' I sigh.

He laughs and releases me. 'Well, I'm going home to think

of you and sort this out.' He cups himself where his running shorts are tenting.

I smile, leaning into him, kissing him chastely on the lips. 'I could do that for you,' I offer, reaching down and grazing my palm over his arousal. His eyes widen, sparkling with pleasure as I reach into his shorts and release his throbbing length, squeezing the base and drawing a couple of lazy strokes.

His head falls back against the headrest. 'Oh, fuck, Ava. That feels so good.'

It does feel good, but in my mouth it would feel better. I continue with a few more controlled strokes, the tip glistening as he shifts and moans in his seat. He must be close, so I lower my head into his lap and flick my tongue across the pulsing head of his glorious cock, tracing slow circles on his wet tip. His hips buck, he grabs the steering wheel and he moans deep, long and low.

Smiling to myself, I lazily slide my wet tongue down his shaft, causing him to buck some more before I wrap my lips around his head and slowly take it all the way to the back of my throat.

He gasps. 'That's it, baby. Take it all the way.'

I pause, feeling the throb beating against my tongue, and on a slow exhale, I work slowly back to the top. He sighs in pure gratification.

'Keep going, just like that,' he encourages me, running his hand over the back of my neck.

I grin around him, releasing his erection from my mouth, letting it spring against his tight stomach. His eyes widen as I straighten up in my seat and wipe my mouth.

'I'd love to, but you've already made me late for work.' I jump out of the car, yelping when he makes a grab for me.

'What the fuck? Ava!'

I cross the road quickly, suddenly considering the possibility of him chasing me down and tossing me over his shoulder. Would he?

I turn around when I reach the pavement, seeing him standing by his car rubbing his groin, a dark smile on his face. I feel untold relief.

'How old are you, Jesse?' I shout across the road.

'Thirty. That wasn't very nice, you little temptress.'

I blow him a kiss and curtsy sweetly, watching as he puts his hand out to catch it, that dark smile ever present. I can see those cogs flying around from here. I turn on my heels and sashay off down the road, feeling rather pleased with myself – for now, anyway. After all, he holds the power.

'Meeting at twelve,' Victoria calls as she totters out of Patrick's office.

I start sifting through my current clients, making notes on current statuses.

'Sally?' I call down the office. She looks up from her computer screen, acknowledging me by removing her glasses. 'Can I have a list of payment statuses on clients, please?'

'Of course, Ava.'

'Oh, and me,' Victoria shouts.

Sally looks at Tom, who nods, too. It's rare to have to chase payment, but highly embarrassing when you do. Patrick's a stickler for payment deadlines.

The morning passes quickly and just before twelve, Sally places a box on my desk. 'This came for you.'

Oh? 'Thanks, Sal.' I look down at the white box. Of course, I know who it's from. I open the box, secretly excited, while glancing around the office to make sure no attention is aimed in my direction. Inside is a chocolate éclair. I laugh out loud, and Tom's head whips up from his desk. I wave my hand in a dismissive gesture, and he rolls his eyes, returning to his sketching.

I grab the note and open it.

Revenge is sweet.
Jx

I smile, pick up the éclair and sink my teeth in as I grab my folder and head for Patrick's office, Sally following behind with a tray full of tea and cakes.

Victoria and Tom join us as Sally hands out a spreadsheet of clients' invoice statuses before pouring the tea and settling down. I scan the list of invoices – all marked 'Paid' or 'Not due' and run my finger across the page when I come across the highlighted 'Overdue' section. There's one client in the column – just one.

Chapter Twenty-two

What?

I inwardly cringe. Any hope I had of evading any reference to The Manor and Mr Ward has just been spectacularly dashed. The idiot hasn't paid his initial consultation fee. What's he thinking? I glance up, seeing Patrick running through the same list as me, along with Victoria and Tom, who both look up at me in unison with the same expression. It's an, *oh dear* look. I sag in my chair, waiting for it.

'Ava, you need to contact Mr Ward and give him a nudge. What's the current position?' Patrick asks.

Oh … dear. I've completed no client forms – apart from the initial briefing sheet – I've sent no quotations, I've not established my role in the project, whether it be to design or design and manage. I've done nothing. Well, I have, but nothing you can class as work related. I've not even submitted an invoice request for the second *so-called* meeting that had me running away without my bra. Where is that bra?

Oh, fucking hell. I clear my throat. 'I'm compiling the consultation breakdown and quotation as we speak.'

He looks up at me, frowning in disapproval. 'Your first meeting was nearly two weeks ago and you've had a second since. What's taking so long, Ava?'

I break into a cold sweat. A list of my fee structure is a simple task to complete, according to individual contracts, and usually done before the second meeting. I have absolutely no excuse. I can feel Tom and Victoria staring at me.

'He's been away,' I blurt. 'He asked me to hold off with any correspondence.'

'When I spoke to him last Monday, he was very keen to get cracking.' Patrick counters as he checks his diary. Damn him for making notes on everything!

I shrug. 'I think it was a last-minute business thing. I'll give him a call.'

'You do that. And I don't want you spending any more time on it until he's coughed up. Now, what's the current status with Mr Van Der Haus?'

I exhale in relief, launching into an enthusiastic update on The Life Building, glad to be off the subject of The Lord of the Manor. I'm going to kill him!

I leave the office and walk down the street to where Jesse dropped me off this morning. As I approach Berkeley Square, I'm scared half out of my skin by some prat on a motorbike screeching past me. I compose my racing heart and carry on, coming to a stop and leaning against a wall, as I pull my phone out of my bag to check my messages. There are two from Kate.

I need some help. Can u pop home & untie me plz?

I gape at my phone, quickly looking at the message details and noting it was sent at eleven. Is she still there? I open the next.

Don't panic! Sam's being a knob. I would love 2 c your face. xxx

Oh yes, Sam the comedian. But a small part of me wonders if there's an element of truth in his joke. Jesse wasn't at all surprised when I mentioned it to him. *Fun*, Kate said. Hmmm. I bet.

I look at the time, noting it's five past one. He's late and I'm offended. As I'm debating how long I should wait, I glance up and see the handsome face I love so much. He's straddling the screeching motorbike that nearly knocked me down. I feel my lips curve into a semi grin as I push myself away from the wall and walk over to him. He's just beyond sexy on that death trap.

'Good afternoon, lady.' He sits on the bike with his helmet resting between his thighs, wearing no leather, just jeans and a white t-shirt. I can't help but think how irresponsible it is. He looks delicious, though.

'You're a menace,' I scorn, coming to a stop in front of him.

'Did I scare you?' He secures his helmet on the handlebars of his bike.

'Yes. That thing needs a noise risk assessment,' I complain.

'This *thing* is a Ducati 1098.' He slips his arms around my waist and yanks me onto his lap. 'Kiss me,' he breathes, claiming my lips, making a dramatic display for all to see. I hear jeers and taunts from passersby, but I don't care. I wrap my arms around his neck and let him have me. It's only been a few hours, but I've missed him.

Suddenly, it occurs to me that we're a hundred yards from my office and Patrick could breeze out at any moment. If he sees me cavorting with Mr Ward, he'll jump to the obvious conclusion: I'm giving special treatment at the expense of his profitability.

I wriggle to free myself, but he just increases his hold on me, pressing his lips harder to mine until my attempted escape becomes fraught and desperate. Placing my hands into his chest, I push against him, and he eventually frees my lips, but not my body.

He narrows fierce eyes on me. 'What do you think you're doing?'

'Let me go.' I strain against him.

'Hey. Let's get one thing straight, lady. You don't dictate

when and where I kiss you, or for how long.' He's deadly serious.

'Jesse, if Patrick sees me with you, I'm in all kinds of shit. Let me go!' To my utter shock, he releases me, and I scramble onto the pavement to straighten myself out. When I look up, I'm met with the filthiest scowl I've ever encountered.

'What the fuck are you talking about?' he shouts. 'And watch your mouth!'

'You,' I start accusingly, 'have not paid your bill, and now I'm supposed to be giving you a polite reminder. I was forced to give some spiel about you being away.' Could a full-on kiss be considered a polite reminder? Jesse would probably think so.

'Consider me reminded. Now get your arse here.'

'No!' I say incredulously. I'm not risking my job security, just so I don't upset Mr Control Freak here.

He looks at me in complete disbelief, dismounting his bike in the most spectacular fashion, his jeans stretching tightly over his magnificent thighs. I shift on my feet. I'm way too affected by this man.

He glares at me. 'Three ...'

I gape. He wouldn't. Not in the middle of Berkeley Square. It would look like I'm being abducted, raped and murdered all at once!

His lips spread into a straight line of displeasure. 'Two ...'

Think, think, think. 'Oh, I'm not getting into a row with you in the middle of Berkeley Square. You're a child sometimes!' I pivot and start walking away. I don't know why I'm doing this; he's like an unexploded bomb, but I've got to hold my own here. He's being stupidly unreasonable, and I'm putting my foot down.

I feel him close behind me as I stalk toward Bond Street, but I charge on. There's a cute boutique up here. I'll escape in there.

'One!' he yells.

I carry on walking. 'Fuck off! You're being unreasonable

283

and unfair.' I know I'm pushing my luck now, swearing *and* disobeying.

'MOUTH! What's so unreasonable about wanting to kiss you?'

'You know damn well what's unreasonable about it. And it's unfair because you're trying to make me feel shitty about it.' I enter the store, leaving him pacing up and down on the pavement, looking through the window every now and then. I knew he wouldn't come in, but I'm not oblivious to the fact that he looks raging mad and I have to leave the shop at some point. I need a few moments alone to collect myself, though, so I start mooching about.

An overdressed, overly made-up girl approaches me. 'Can I help you?'

'I'm just browsing, thanks.'

'This section is all new season stock.' She runs her arm along a suspended rail of dresses. 'We have some beautiful dresses. Please, just ask if you need another size.' She smiles.

'Thank you.'

I start cruising through the rails, spotting some truly gorgeous dresses – albeit stupid prices, but gorgeous, nevertheless. I pick up a fitted, cream silk, sleeveless affair. It's shorter than I usually wear, but lovely.

'You're not wearing that!'

I snap my head up and see Jesse standing in the doorway, looking at the dress like it could spit poison. Oh, how embarrassing! The sales assistant looks wide-eyed at Jesse and back to me, and I half smile at her. I'm horrified. Who the bloody hell does he think he is? I throw him my dirtiest look, mouth *fuck off* and watch as the proverbial steam fires out of his ears.

I turn to the assistant. 'Have you anything shorter?' I ask sweetly.

'Ava!' he barks. 'Don't push me.'

I ignore him, keeping my eyes on the assistant expectantly.

The poor girl looks like she could have a panic attack, her gaze flicking, very nervously, from me to Jesse and back again.

'No, I don't think so,' she says quietly.

Okay, now I'm feeling sorry for her. I shouldn't be dragging her into this pathetic disagreement over a dress. 'Okay, I'll take this one.' I smile, handing her the dress.

She looks at me, then at Jesse. 'Er ... is this the correct size for you?'

'It's a ten?' I ask. I can literally feel the shop shaking under his wrath.

'It is, but I would recommend you try it on as we don't offer refunds,' she advises me.

Well, I was going to risk it not fitting, but at that price, maybe not. She shows me to a changing room and hangs the dress on a fancy hook for me.

'Just call if you require any help.' She smiles, pulling the velvet curtain across, leaving me and the dress alone.

I'm being as pathetic as Jesse by doing this; I'm purposely pushing him. We're talking about the man who made me sleep in a winter jumper in the middle of spring because another male was in the flat. Is this necessary? I decide it is – he can't behave like this.

I fight my way into the dress, struggling with the zipper where it meets the seam on the bust line. I'm not giving up. I know if I can just get it over that line of stitching, it'll be just fine. I smooth down the front of the dress. It feels lovely.

Pulling the curtain across, I stand back from the floor-length mirror to take a good look, smiling when I get the full impact.

'Oh, Jesus, Mary and Joseph!'

I swivel, finding Jesse gripping his hair, pacing up and down. He stops, looks at me, opens his mouth, snaps it shut and starts with the pacing again. I'm quite amused.

He halts stalking and gawps at me, all wide-eyed and trau-matized. 'You're not ... you ... you can't ... Ava ... baby ... oh, I can't look at you!' He walks out adjusting his groin, muttering some crap about an intolerable female and heart attacks. Then I'm alone with the dress again.

The assistant approaches with caution. 'The dress looks incredible,' she says quietly, looking over her shoulder for Jesse's whereabouts.

'Thank you. I'll take it.'

When I exit the changing rooms, Jesse is inspecting some very high heels. The look of mystification on his beautiful face makes me melt slightly, but then he spots me, shoves them back and scowls at me. And I remember … I'm furious with him. I get my purse from my bag and hand my credit card over, wincing at the thought of five hundred quid for a dress. It is way too extravagant, but I'm being defiant.

The assistant begins wrapping the dress in all sorts of fancy tissue paper. I want to tell her to shove it in a bag and be done with it before Jesse resorts to ripping it apart, but I fear the poor girl might lose her job if she did something as common as that, so I resign myself to shutting up and waiting patiently while she does her thing.

After an age of wrapping, folding, tucking in and punching in my pin number, the assistant hands me the bag. 'Enjoy the dress, madam. It really did look lovely on you.' She flicks a cautious glance at Jesse.

'Thank you,' I smile. Now, how to get out of the store? I turn, finding Jesse filling the doorway, still scowling and still brooding. I walk with purpose I don't really feel and stop in front of him. I'm really crapping myself, but I won't let him see that. 'Excuse me.'

He looks at me, then at the bag. 'You've just wasted hundreds of pounds. You're not wearing that dress,' he says emphatically.

'Excuse me, please.' I accentuate the *please,* and his lips press into a straight line as he shifts his tall, lean body to the side, leaving a gap for me to pass.

Stepping out onto the street, I head toward the office. I've only had forty minutes, but I'm not spending the rest of my lunch break arguing over touching in public and my wardrobe choice. Today started so well … when I was complying.

I feel his hot breath on my neck. 'Zero.'

I yelp as I'm yanked into an alleyway and shoved up against a wall. His lips smash to mine, his hips grinding against my lower stomach, his raging arousal evident beneath the button fly of his jeans. He's turned on by getting cranky over a dress? I try and resist the invasion of his tongue … a little.

Damn, it's no good! I'm instantly consumed by him and the need to have him all over me. I link my arms around his neck, accepting him willingly, absorbing his intrusion and meeting his tongue, stroke for stroke.

'I'm not going to let you wear that dress,' he moans into my mouth.

'You can't tell me what I can and can't wear.'

'Stop me,' he challenges.

'It's just a dress.'

'It's not *just* a dress on you, Ava. You're not wearing it.' He pushes his groin into my lower stomach, a clear demonstration of what the dress does to him, and I know he's thinking that other men will have the same reaction.

Crazy man.

I exhale wearily. Buying the dress is one thing. Putting it on and making it to the pub is another challenge entirely. I'm twenty-six years old, and he said himself that I have great legs. I decide I'm not going to get anywhere with this. Not now, anyway. I do, however, intend to discuss in full detail his illusions that he has control over my wardrobe. In fact, we need to talk about his unreasonableness full stop – but not now. I only have twenty minutes left of my lunch break, and I highly expect *that* conversation to take considerably longer.

'Thank you for the cake,' I say as he kisses every inch of my face.

'You're welcome. Did you eat it?'

'Yes, it was delicious.' I kiss the corner of his mouth, rubbing my cheek up his stubble. A low rumble escapes his lips as I hum in his ear and nuzzle into his neck, inhaling his lovely fresh water scent. I just want to crawl inside him. 'I'm not supposed to be spending any more time on you until you've settled your bill.' I hold onto him, squeezing a little tighter as he nibbles at my earlobe.

'I'll trample anyone who tries to stop me.'

I've no doubt he will. The man is crazy beyond crazy. 'Why are you so unreasonable?'

He pulls back and looks at me, surprise at my question evident on his stunning, stubbled face. 'Can I ask you the same question?'

My mouth falls open. Me? This man is crazy delusional. His list of misdemeanors goes on and on. I shake my head on a frown. 'I'd better get back to the office.'

He sighs. 'I'll walk you.'

'Halfway. I can't be seen to be entertaining clients for lunch without Patrick knowing, especially ones in debt,' I grumble. 'Pay your bill!'

He rolls his eyes. 'God forbid Patrick should find out that you're having your brain fucked out by a non-paying client.' A small smirk breaks the corners of his mouth as I gasp in shock at his crude summary of our relationship. That's the second time he's done it.

We walk toward my office, and the silence is uncomfortable – for me, anyway. Is that how he sees me? Like a little plaything he gets to fuck and control? I wilt on the inside and contemplate the agony that I'm setting myself up for. Just thinking about the possible pain hurts.

I feel his hand brush against mine, and I automatically pull it away, but on a slight growl, he tries again. I say nothing but pull my hand away ... again. I'm in a mood and want him to know it. When I think he's got the message, he grabs my hand again, holding it in a vice grip, to the point of pain. It's what I would have expected. I'm beginning to read this man like a book. I flex my fingers, looking up to see his fixed glower fade into contentment as I give up fighting and let him keep hold of me. Let him? Like I have any other option.

As we near my office, he stops and gently presses me up against the wall with his body. He lowers his face to mine, his hot, minty breath warming my cheeks. 'Why are you sulking?'

'No reason,' I say quietly.

He reaches up, grasping my wrist to pull my hand down from my hair. 'Tell me the truth.'

How has he picked up on my bad habit so quickly?

'Answer me, Ava.'

I don't. I keep my mouth shut and my eyes down.

'Is this over a dress? Because you'd better get used to that. My eyes only, Ava.'

This lunch hour has been a massive eye opener. He wants complete control of me, and I get absolutely no say in it – none at all. Is this what I want? My head is a riot of mixed feelings and doubts. Why did I have to go and fall in love with the ultimate, unreasonable, challenging control freak?

I push myself away from the wall with some determined effort. 'What do you care? After all, you're just fucking me.' I don't hang about. I leave him on the pavement and walk back to my office as fast as my shaky legs will carry me.

Pushing my way through the office door, I'm met by Tom and Victoria's inquisitive faces. I must look as terrible as I feel. I hope they don't start asking questions about Mr Ward, or about anything, actually. I think I'll fall apart. I shake my head at them both as I make my way to my desk.

Sally walks out of the kitchen with a tray full of coffees. 'Ava,

I didn't realise you were back. Do you want a tea or coffee?'

I want to ask her if she has any wine stored away in the kitchen, but I refrain. 'No, thank you, Sal,' I murmur.

I focus my full attention on my computer screen, trying to ignore the ache dwelling deep inside me. Jesse has some serious issues with control – or power, as he calls it, but stupidly or not, I'm willing to accept that if I get him – all of him, not just his body. I'm addicted to every crazy element of him. And that's annoying as well as unsettling.

My mobile rings and I'm grateful for the distraction from my turmoil. It's Mr Van Der Haus. 'Hello?'

His light Danish accent rolls down the telephone. 'Hello, Ava. How did you find The Life Building? Ingrid has advised me your meeting went very well.'

'Yes, very well.'

'I do hope that lovely head of yours is swimming with ideas. I'm looking forward to meeting upon my return to the UK.'

'Yes, I received your e-mail. I'll have some schemes ready for you.' I've practically finished the mood boards and drawings. It just came to me all of a sudden – at a moment when my brain wasn't consumed with a certain other client.

'Excellent! I shall be back in London next Friday. Can we meet?'

'Yes, of course. Any particular day?'

'I will have Ingrid contact you. She arranges my diary.'

'Okay, Mr Van Der Haus.'

I hear him tut. 'Ava, please. It's Mikael. Good-bye.'

'Good-bye, Mikael.' I hang up and retrieve my drawings for The Life Building, spreading them out on my desk. I hear the office door open in the background, but I don't look up. I'm on a roll with additional ideas. It's a welcome and very needed distraction.

'Ava,' Tom calls. 'It's someone for you-hoo!'

I look up, nearly falling off my chair when I see Jesse standing as bold as brass at the front of the office. Oh, good God, what is he doing?

He walks with complete confidence over to my desk – all godly in his faded jeans, white t-shirt and ruffled hair. I notice Tom and Victoria tapping their pens casually on their desks as they follow his path to me, and even Sal has paused mid-scan, looking slightly confused. He lands at the foot of my desk, my eyes travelling up his body to meet his green gaze, the semblance of a smug, satisfied smile tickling the corners of his mouth.

'Miss O'Shea,' he says softly.

'Mr. Ward,' I greet hesitantly. I glance across the office, spotting three pairs of eyes flicking toward me at regular intervals.

'Aren't you going to ask if I would like a seat?'

I snap my eyes back to Jesse. 'Please.' I indicate one of the black tub chairs on the other side of my desk, and he pulls one out, lowering himself slowly into the chair. 'What are you doing?' I whisper, leaning across my desk.

He smiles that self-assured, melt-worthy smile. 'I'm here to settle an invoice, Miss O'Shea.'

'Oh.' I lean back in my chair. 'Sally?' I call. 'Can you deal with Mr Ward, please? He would like to settle his outstanding account.' I watch as Jesse shifts in his chair slightly, throwing me a critical look. I'm not being defiant. It's not my job to take payment; I wouldn't know where to start.

'Of course,' Sally calls. I see realisation hit her. Yes! It's the same man who screamed at you down the phone, bulldozed the office, and sent you flowers. I throw her a don't-ask-just-do look, prompting her to scuttle off toward the filing cabinet.

'Sally will look after you, Mr Ward.' I smile politely.

Jesse's eyebrows shoot up, his frown line jumping into position. 'Only you,' he says softly, for my ears only.

The familiar thump of Patrick's approaching footsteps nearly makes me snap my pencil. This day just keeps getting better and better.

'Ava?'

Glancing nervously up, I see my boss standing at the side of my desk, looking at me expectantly, so I wave my pencil in the general direction of Jesse. 'Patrick, this is Mr Ward. He owns The Manor. Mr Ward, meet Patrick Peterson, my boss.' I throw Jesse a pleading look.

'Ah, Mr Ward, I know your face.' Patrick puts his hand out.

'We met briefly at Lusso.' Jesse says as he stands and clasps Patrick's hand.

I see the pound signs ping into Patrick's delighted blue eyes. 'Yes, you bought the penthouse,' he chirps, and Jesse nods his confirmation. I notice Patrick isn't so worried about his outstanding bill now. Sally approaches with a copy of Jesse's invoice and jumps a mile when Patrick snatches it from her dainty, pasty hand. 'Have you offered Mr Ward a drink?' he asks a stunned Sally.

'I'm fine, thank you. I've just come to settle my account.' Jesse's husky tones reverberate through me as I sit, stuck like Velcro to my chair, watching the polite exchange going on before me.

How can he be so calm and collected? I'm tense from top to toe, twiddling my pencil nervously in my hand and keeping my mouth firmly shut. It must be obvious that I'm uncomfortable, but Patrick seems oblivious.

Patrick waves Sally away. 'You shouldn't have rushed in just for this.' He flaps the outstanding invoice in the air.

I scoff, following it up with a cough to disguise my reaction to Patrick's casualness regarding the invoice he huffed about only a few hours ago.

'I've been away. My staff overlooked it,' Jesse explains. I release a thankful rush of air.

'I knew there would be a perfectly reasonable explanation. Was it business or pleasure?' Patrick sounds genuinely interested. I know differently. He's mentally calculating how much money he might be able to make out of Jesse. He's a dear man, but he's mad about turnover.

Jesse turns his eyes on me. 'Oh, definitely pleasure.'

I shrink further into my swivel chair, feeling my face turning a thousand shades of red. I can't even look him in the eye. What is he trying to do to me?

'I'd like to make some appointments with Miss O'Shea while I'm here. We need to get a quick turnaround on this.'

Ha! I very nearly remind him that he supposedly doesn't make appointments to fuck me. But if I did that, then I suspect I would firstly get the sack, and secondly receive a sense fuck to rival all others. So I keep my mouth firmly shut.

'Absolutely,' Patrick rumbles. 'Are you looking for a design, or a design consultation and a project manage?'

I roll my eyes. I know the answer to this question. After my perfectly exasperated eye roll is executed, I lift my eyes to Jesse and find him watching me, clearly struggling to maintain his serious face.

'The whole package,' Jesse answers.

'Super!' Patrick claps his hands together. 'I'll leave you with Ava. She'll take good care of you.' Patrick offers his hand and Jesse takes it, keeping his eyes right on me.

'I know she will,' He smiles, turning his green pools back to Patrick. 'If you give me your company bank details, I'll arrange an immediate bank transfer. I'll also make an advanced payment on the next stage. It will save any future delays.'

'I'll get Sally to note them down for you.' Patrick leaves us, but I don't relax.

Jesse sits back down in front of me, his irritatingly handsome face displaying an abundance of joy at my nervousness. The full package? Definitely pleasure? I should bash him around the head with my paperweight!

Dragging myself out of my dumbstruck state, I shift all of

the drawings that are littering my desk and pull my diary over. 'When are you free?' I know I sound highly unprofessional and terse, but I don't care. He's taking his power trip too far now.

'When are you?'

I look up, finding a green, satisfied stare. I lean in. 'I'm not talking to you,' I spit, rather immaturely.

'What about screaming for me?'

My eyes widen in shock. 'Neither.'

'That may make business a little tricky,' he pouts, his lips dancing at the corners.

'Will it be business, Mr Ward, or pleasure?'

'Pleasure, all the way,' he answers darkly.

'You do realise that you're paying for me to have sex with you,' I whisper on a hiss. 'That, in effect, makes me a hooker!'

I watch as a flash of anger passes over his face and he shoots forward in his chair. 'Shut up, Ava,' he warns. 'And just so you know, you will be screaming later,' he leans back again, 'when we make friends.'

I sigh heavily. It would be better all-round if I dropped this contract right now. Patrick will keel over with shock, but either way, I'm totally knackered. I'm losing control here. Losing control? I laugh to myself. Have I ever had control since this beautiful man trampled into my life?

'Is something funny?' he asks seriously.

I make a meal of flicking though the pages of my diary harshly. 'Yes, my life,' I mutter. 'When shall I pencil you in?'

'I don't want to be pencilled in anywhere. Pencil can be erased.' His tone is smooth and confident, and I look up from my diary to find a large, permanent black marker pen being waved under my nose. 'Every day,' he states calmly.

'Every day? Don't be so stupid!' I blurt a bit too loudly.

He gives me his roguish grin as he removes the lid from the marker, and reaching over, making a point of brushing his fingers over my hand, he pulls my diary away from me. I shiver, and he gives me that knowing look. Turning to tomorrow's page in my diary, he coolly runs a line through the middle, writing 'Mr. Ward' across the page in big, black letters. He then skims past the weekend. 'You're mine then anyway,' he muses to himself.

I frown, but dare not say anything, mainly because of our location and the fact that he has absolutely no concern. He arrives at Monday's page and finds my ten o'clock appointment with Mrs Kent. Locating an eraser from my desk tidy, he slowly rubs it out, looking up at me when he leans down to blow the fragments of rubber from the page. He's really enjoying this, while I'm sitting back in my chair watching him trample all over my work diary, at the same time trying to gauge how serious he is. I fear he's completely serious.

He proceeds to put a big, black line through Monday as well. What is he doing? I glance around the office, noticing my colleagues have gotten bored of the Jesse and Ava show, knuckling down with some work instead.

'What are you doing?' I ask calmly.

He pauses, looking up at me. 'I'm making my appointments.'

'You're not happy enough controlling the social aspects of my life?' I'm surprised at how calm I sound. I feel completely ram-raided. This man has untold front and confidence. 'I thought you didn't make appointments to fuck me?'

'Watch your mouth,' he cautions me. 'I've told you before, Ava. I'll do whatever it takes.'

'For what?' My voice is barely a whisper.

'To keep you.'

He wants to keep me? What, to fuck me? I don't ask that, though. 'What if I don't want to be kept?' I ask instead.

'But you do. By me. This is why I'm having such a hard time trying to figure out why you keep fighting me off.' He returns his attention to my diary and sets about putting a line through every day for the rest of the calendar year.

When he reaches the end, he slams it shut and stands. His

confidence knows no bounds. And how does he know I want to be kept by him? Maybe I don't. Christ, I'm trying to lie to myself now. I'm going to have to buy a new diary. I mentally applaud myself for backing up my appointments on my e-mail calendar, a precautionary measure in case I lost my diary, not because some unreasonable control freak might erase them all.

'What time will you be finished with work?'

'Six-ish.' I can't believe I've just answered that without a second's hesitation.

'-ish,' he mouths, putting his hand out over my desk. He wants me to shake his hand? I reach up, mentally demanding my hand not to tremble, and place it gently in his. The familiar fizzle flies through me when our hands connect, his fingers brushing gently over my wrist as he slowly strokes down the centre of my palm.

My eyes fly up to his. 'See?' he whispers, before pulling away and striding out of my office, collecting an envelope from Sally's outstretched hand on the way.

I collapse back in my chair, my heart convulsing in my chest. I'm breaking out in an uncomfortable sweat as I sit at my desk, frantically fanning my burning face with my coffee coaster. How does he do these things to me? Tom looks over at me with wide eyes and I blow out a long lungful of air in an attempt to regulate my hammering heart. He wants to keep me? What? Keep me and control me, keep me to love me or keep me to fuck me senseless? He's already fucked me pretty senseless. He must have, because I keep going back for more.

I start folding away my drawings of The Life Building before pulling up my e-mail calendar so I can start transferring my appointments back into my diary.

Oh, I'm in some major deep shit. But he's totally right ... I do want to be kept by him. I'm completely addicted.

I need him.

Chapter Twenty-three

I'm the last to leave the office. I set the alarm, lock the office door behind me and jump out of my skin when I hear the familiar scream of a high-powered engine. I turn around, seeing Jesse pull up to the kerb on his bike. He takes his helmet off, dismounts and approaches me looking like he's had a perfectly normal day. 'Good day at work?'

I gape. 'Not really,' I answer on a frown, my tone dripping with sarcasm.

He observes me for a while, chewing his bottom lip, the cogs kicking into action. I hope he's thinking about how unreasonable he's been.

'Can I make it better?' He reaches for my arm and slides his warm palm down until he's clasping my hand.

'I don't know; can you?'

'I think I definitely can.' He smiles, and I drop my head. 'I'll always make it better, remember that,' he adds confidently.

I give myself whiplash when I snap my head up to look at him. 'But you made it shitty in the first place!'

He pouts, hanging his head. I think he's ashamed. Good. He should be. 'I can't help it.' He shrugs guiltily.

'Of course you can!'

'No, with you, I can't help it,' he states in a matter-of-fact tone – a tone that suggests he completely gets it. I, however, never will. 'Come here.' He pulls me over to his bike and presents me with a large paper bag.

'What's this?' I peek into the bag.

'You'll need them.' He reaches in and pulls out a pile of black leather.

Oh, no! 'Jesse, I'm not getting on that thing.'

He ignores me, unfolding the trousers and kneeling in front of me, holding them open for me to step into. He taps my ankle. 'On.'

'No!' He can give me a sense fuck or the countdown all he likes – it's not happening. No way. Hell will freeze over. He's trampled all over my day, and now he wants to kill me on that death trap?

He heaves a tired breath and rises to his feet. 'Listen to me, lady.' He cups my cheek with his palm. 'Do you honestly think I would let anything happen to you?'

I look at his soft eyes, seeing he's clearly trying to reassure me. No, I don't think he would let anything happen to me, but what about all of the other road users? They don't give a toss about little old me on the back of that death trap. I'll fall off, I know it.

'They scare me.'

He bends down, getting nose to nose with me, his minty breath soothing me. 'Do you trust me?'

'Yes,' I answer immediately. I trust him with my life. It's my sanity I don't trust him with.

He nods, dropping a kiss on the end of my nose before kneeling back down in front of me. He removes my ballet pumps, feeds my feet into the trousers, and pulls the leathers up my body, fastening them swiftly. Next, he pulls out a fitted leather jacket and takes my bag before putting the jacket on me, followed by a pair of boots.

'Take the pins out of your hair,' he orders, putting my pumps and my new, taboo dress in my oversized work bag. I'm surprised he didn't throw it to the ground and trample all over it.

I reach up and start removing my grips. 'Where are your leathers?'

'I don't need them.'

'Why, are you indestructible?'

He holds the helmet above my head. 'No, lady, self-destructible.'

'What does that mean?'

'Nothing.' He dismisses my question and pushes the helmet onto my head, effectively shutting me up, and starts adjusting the chin strap, leaving me feeling like my head's been squeezed into a condom. I flex my neck from side to side, and he flips the visor up.

'You should wear protective clothing,' I admonish him. 'You're making me.'

'I'm not prepared to take any risks with you. Anyway ...' he smacks my arse, 'you look fucking hot.' He lengthens the strap on my bag, putting it across my body and around my back. 'When I'm on, put your left foot on the peg and swing your right leg over, okay?'

I nod and watch admiringly as he puts his own helmet on, then swings his long leg over the bike, starts it up and stands it between his powerful thighs. He looks at me and nods his instruction for me to climb on, so I reluctantly step forward, place my hand on his shoulder and vault my right leg over, soon finding myself straddling his waist.

'I feel too high.'

He turns his head. 'You're fine. Hold on around my waist. When I lean, gently lean with me and don't put your feet down when I stop. Keep them on the pegs. Clear?'

I nod.

'Put your visor down,' he orders, flipping his own into position.

I do as I'm bid and lean forward, hugging my arms around his chest and squeezing my knees on either side of his hips.

The vibrations of the engine travel through me as Jesse revs the bike, backing onto the road with his feet. Then, slowly and smoothly, he pulls into the traffic. My heart is hammering in my chest, my thighs gripping his hips tightly, but he's obviously taking it easy with me on board, and I love him all the more for it. He brakes lightly, takes corners smoothly, and I find myself naturally mimicking the bike's movements. As we break the city limits, I have no idea where we're going, but I don't care. My arms and legs are wrapped around my solid hunk of male, and with the rush of air speeding past me, I feel completely exhilarated. Until I recognise the road leading to The Manor. My joy instantly dampens. After the day I've had, it would be just perfect for it to end on a helping of old pouty lips. I give myself a mental pep talk, telling myself to rise above her obvious jealousy and bitterness. What I would like to know most, though, is why she's behaving like this.

The iron gates at the entrance of the grounds open as Jesse pulls off the main road, and he proceeds down the gravel driveway to The Manor, braking gently until we come to a stop.

He flips his visor up. 'Off you get.'

I swing my leg over, rather elegantly, soon finding myself to the side of the bike. Jesse kicks the stand down and shuts the bike off before dismounting with complete ease. He removes his helmet, his blond hair all rough and disheveled from the friction, and he runs his hands through it as he places his helmet on the seat before taking mine off.

Hesitancy is marring his perfect features when my face is revealed. He's worried I didn't like it. I grin, launching myself at him, wrapping my legs around his waist and my arms around his neck.

He laughs. 'There's that grin. Did you enjoy that?' He holds me with one arm, placing my helmet next to his, then clasps me with both hands.

I lean back to get his face in my line of vision. 'I want one.'

'Forget it! Not a fucking chance in Hell. Never, no way.' He shakes his head, his expression pure dread. 'Only ever with me.'

'I loved it.' I tighten my grip around his neck, pulling myself back into him and lowering my lips to his. He moans approvingly as I coax his mouth open, landing him with a deep, moist and passionate kiss. 'Thank you.'

He bites lightly on my bottom lip. 'Hmmm. You're more than welcome, baby.'

I've completely lost sight of my doubts. When he's like this, it kind of trumps his unreasonable, controlling ways. It's crazy. 'Why are we here?' I ask. I can't help the pang of disappointment at ending my amazing bike ride at The Manor.

'I've got a few things to sort out. You can have something to eat while we're here.' He lowers me to the ground. 'Then I'm taking you home, lady.' He brushes my hair from my face.

'I've got nothing with me.' I'll need to shoot home and pick some things up.

'Sam's here. He brought some of your stuff from Kate's.' He grabs my hand, pulling me toward The Manor. Sam brought my stuff? That was very forward thinking of him. Oh, please tell me that Kate packed it! The thought of Sam's cheeky grin as he ploughs through my underwear drawer has me blushing on the spot.

Jesse leads me up the steps, and through the doors into the entrance hall. It sounds busy tonight, with laughter and chatter coming from the restaurant and bar, but we bypass both, heading straight for Jesse's office. I'm relieved. Avoiding a certain acid-tongued pout is top of my list of things to achieve this evening.

As we pass through the summer room, a few groups of people are gathered, relaxing on the plush sofas, drinks in hand. All conversation halts as soon as they spot us. The men raise their drinks and the women smooth their hair, straighten their backs and plaster ridiculous smiles on their faces, but the smiles soon disappear when their stares land on me, fully clad in leather, being pulled behind Jesse.

'Good evening.' Jesse nods as we pass swiftly.

A chorus of greetings flood my ears, all of the men acknowledging me with a smile or a nod, all of the women throwing suspicious glares. I'm placing my bets that the luxurious accommodations and surroundings aren't the only reasons women like The Manor.

'Jesse.' I hear Big John's low rumble up ahead, and I drag my eyes from the crowd of angry women to find him coming out of Jesse's office. He nods at me and I nod back.

'Any problems?' Jesse asks, leading me into his office.

John follows and shuts the door behind him. 'Small issue in the communal room, now resolved.' His deep voice is monotone. 'Someone got a bit excited.'

I frown, looking at Jesse. What's a communal room? I see Jesse mildly shake his head at John before flicking cautious eyes to me.

"S'all good. I'll be in the surveillance suite.' He turns and leaves.

'What's a communal room?' I can't keep the interest from my tone. I've never heard of such a thing.

Jesse yanks me toward him by the collar of my leather jacket and removes my bag, taking my mouth possessively, completely distracting me from my question. 'I like you in leather,' he muses as he unzips the jacket, pushing it down my arms slowly and chucking it on the sofa. 'But I *love* you in lace.' He undoes the zipper of the leather trousers as he circles my nose with his. 'Always in lace.'

I watch his hands work the fastener, my pulse quickening. 'I thought you have work to do,' I whisper.

He picks me up, walks me over to his big desk and places me on the edge. Both boots are removed and tossed on the sofa before he bends down, braces his hands on the edge and leans forward so our faces are close.

His green pools of lust are penetrating me. 'It can wait.' He snakes his arm around my waist and lowers me to the desk surface. 'You drive me crazy, lady,' he says, reaching down and unbuttoning my white shirt as he stands between my open thighs.

'You drive *me* crazy,' I breathe, arching my back when his hot touch skims my breastbone.

He smiles darkly at me. 'So we're made for each other.' He yanks the cups of my bra down, running his thumbs over my nipples, sparking endless shots of pleasure throughout me.

Our eyes connect and lock. 'Probably,' I agree. I really want to be made for him.

'There's no "probably" about it.' He hooks his forearm under my waist and pulls me up from the desk, resting his mouth on my throat. Then circling his tongue, he works his way up my jawbone as I lace my fingers through his soft hair and exhale a contented lungful of air. Perfect. We're making friends.

The office door flies open, and Jesse yanks me into his chest protectively, and probably to conceal me, too.

'Oh, sorry.'

'For fuck's sake, Sarah! Knock!' he yells. I'm secretly delighted at the tone he's taken with her. I might be half-naked and sprawled across his desk, but Jesse is concealing me just fine. He doesn't let me go as he shifts slightly so he can land Sarah with a filthy look. I catch a glimpse of her in the doorway, wearing a red dress to match her lips, her sour face as plain as the obvious boob job.

'Finally got her in leather, then?' she says on a sly smile, turning on her heels and leaving. The door shuts with a loud bang, and Jesse rolls his eyes in frustration. I don't think I've ever disliked someone so much.

'What did she mean?' I ask, feeling like I'm the butt of a private joke.

'Nothing. Ignore her. She's trying to be funny,' he grumbles. His mood has changed dramatically.

Well, I don't find her remotely funny, but his short, abrupt answer makes me think twice about pushing it. Damn, I want him to finish what he started.

I'm lifted from the desk and placed on my feet and after he pulls the cups of my bra back over my breasts, he starts to button up my shirt and peel the leathers down my legs. I'm going to look like a crumpled mess. He fetches my bag from the floor, putting my ballet flats at my feet for me to step into while I start tucking my shirt in, trying to make myself more presentable. I watch as Jesse takes a seat in his huge brown leather swivel chair. He's gone quiet. Resting his elbows on the arms and letting his fingertips meet in front of his lips, he watches me thoughtfully as I finish sorting myself out.

'What?' I ask. He looks deep in thought.

'Nothing. Are you hungry?'

I shrug. '-ish.'

A smile tickles the corner of his mouth. '-ish,' he counters. 'The steak's good. Do you want that?' I nod. Yes, I could eat a little steak. He picks up his office phone and dials a few numbers. 'Ava would like the steak.' He puts the phone to his shoulder. 'How do you like your steak?'

'Medium, please.'

He returns to the phone. 'Medium, with new potatoes and a salad.' He looks at me with raised eyebrows. I nod again. 'In my office … and bring some wine … Zinfandel. That's all … yes … thank you.' He hangs up and dials again. 'John … yes … I'm ready when you are.' He hangs up before picking up again. 'Sarah … fine, don't worry. Bring me the latest attendance figures.' He puts the phone down again. 'Sit,' he orders, pointing at the sofa in the window.

Okay, I'm getting an uncomfortable feeling, my small appetite fading fast. Damn it, I hate coming here. 'I can go if you're busy.'

He frowns, throwing me a questioning look. 'No, sit.'

I take myself over to the sofa to settle myself in the soft brown leather. I feel like a spare part, uncomfortable and awkward and with little else to do, I grab my diary from my bag and start making some notes on the extension of The Manor. I glance up every so often and catch him gazing across his office at me, and each time he lobs me a reassuring smile but it does little to ease my discomfort.

After twenty minutes or so, there's a knock on the door and Jesse calls an okay for whoever it is to enter. Pete walks in with a tray and follows Jesse's pointed pen over to me.

'Thank you, Pete.' I smile as Pete places the tray down in front of me and hands me some cutlery wrapped in a white material napkin.

'My pleasure. May I open your wine?'

'No,' I shake my head. 'I've got it.'

He nods before leaving the room quietly.

I remove the lid from the plate and a delicious smell invades my nostrils, dragging my appetite back. Unwrapping my knife and fork, I stab at the separate bowl of salad, the most colourful I've ever seen – peppers, red onion, and a dozen varieties of lettuce leaf, all drenched in infused oil. I could eat this alone. It's wonderful.

Crossing my legs, I place the tray on my lap and slice into the steak, humming a satisfied moan around my fork. The Manor does food very well.

'Good?'

I feel Jesse's chin resting on my shoulder. 'Very,' I mumble around my steak. 'You want to try?'

He nods, opening his mouth. I slice a piece of steak and hold it over my shoulder for him to take. 'Hmmm, very good,' he says around his chew.

'More?' I ask. His eyes widen in appreciation, so I cut him another piece, passing it over my shoulder again. He watches me as he wraps his full lips around my fork and slowly pulls the steak off. I can't help the big smile that breaks out across my face. His eyes sparkle with pleasure and he struggles to prevent his own smile as he chews and clamps his hands on my shoulders, burying his face in my neck from behind.

He nips playfully at my neck. 'You taste better.'

My smile broadens as he makes a meal of chewing at my throat, growling and nuzzling to his heart's content. I laugh, raising my shoulder when he latches onto my ear, his hot breath causing shudders to course through me. He entices so many extreme reactions from me – extreme frustration, extreme desire and extreme happiness are just a few.

'You eat,' he says as he kisses my temple tenderly. He starts circling his thumbs into the top of my back. 'You're tense. Why are you tense?'

I roll my neck in gratitude. I'm tense because I'm here – it's the only reason. How can one woman make me feel so uncomfortable? There's a knock on Jesse's office door.

'Yes?' He carries on working my shoulders as Sarah walks in.

Speak of the Devil. The atmosphere instantly cools as she clocks Jesse massaging my shoulders, her facial expression altering significantly. I notice it, but Jesse seems oblivious to the chilly undertones of her presence. I tense further, suddenly wanting Jesse's hands off me.

'Your figures,' she grumbles, waving the folder and walking casually over to Jesse's desk to place them in front of his chair. She turns to face us, throwing daggers at me.

'Thanks, Sarah.' He leans down and brushes his lips over my cheek, inhaling deeply before releasing me. 'I have to work now, baby. Eat your dinner.' I see Sarah scowl briefly before reinstating the fake smile on her pouty face when Jesse turns toward her. He reaches into his jeans pocket. 'Have one hundred thousand transferred into this account ASAP,' he instructs, handing her an envelope.

'One hundred?' Sarah blurts, glancing down.

'Yes. Now, please.' He leaves her staring at the paper, taking his seat behind his desk, completely ignorant to her gaping mouth. She flicks me a murderous look. It's then I realise that it's the envelope Sally gave him.

One hundred thousand? That's way too much! What's he thinking? Should I say something? I look at Sarah, finding her scrutinizing me, pursing her red lips. I don't blame her. Christ, she already thinks I'm after his money.

'That's all, Sarah.' Jesse dismisses her and she turns to leave, but not before throwing a scowl in my direction.

She saunters over to the door, meeting John at the threshold. The big guy nods at her before moving to the side to let her pass, shutting the door behind her. He then flicks me a nod, and I smile before resuming picking at my salad and steak. My appetite has run for the hills. One hundred thousand? I place the tray back on the coffee table to pour some wine, but I notice Pete's only brought one glass, so I take myself over to the sideboard, collect a tumbler for myself and return to the sofa to pour the wine. When I place the glass on Jesse's desk, John stops talking and they both look at the glass, then at me.

Jesse picks it up, handing it back to me. 'I'm fine. Thank you, baby.' He smiles. 'I'm driving.'

'Oh,' I take the glass back. 'Sorry.'

'Don't be; you have it. I got the wine for you.'

I take my place on the sofa, picking up a magazine called *SuperBike*. It's the only one so it will have to do.

I have no idea how much time passes. I'm completely lost in details of four-stroke engines, horsepower ratings, and the approaching Milan Motorcycle show when I feel warm hands wrap around my neck from behind. I drop my head back to look at his upside-down features.

'I've started something, haven't I?' He bends and drops his lips onto my forehead.

'Why haven't you upgraded to the 1198?'

He smiles. 'I have, but I prefer the 1098.'

'Oh; how many do you have?'

'Twelve.'

'Twelve?' I gasp. 'Are they all superbikes?'

He laughs lightly. 'Yes, Ava, they're all superbikes. Come on, I'm taking you home.'

I place the magazine back on the table and begin to unravel my folded body. 'You know, you should be wearing leathers,' I push casually.

'I know I should.' He takes my hand, leading me to the door.

'So why don't you?'

'I've ridden bikes since I—' he halts mid-sentence and glances down at me, 'for many years.'

'You're going to have to reveal an age at some point.'

I smile brightly, earning myself a return beam from Jesse. 'Maybe,' he says quietly.

We walk through The Manor, finding Sam and Drew at the bar. Sam's obviously not seeing Kate tonight. He looks his usual self, as does Drew, with his black suit and perfectly placed black hair.

'My man!' Sam cheers. 'Ava, I love your Little Miss knickers.' He hands me a familiar gym bag.

I die a thousand deaths on the spot, feeling my face flame as I glance up at Jesse and see anger pouring from his entire being.

'Don't push your fucking luck, Sam,' he warns, his tone super-serious. Sam's grin fades as he puts his hands up in submission, and Drew exhales, shaking his head as he places his beer on the bar.

'There's a line, Sam,' he says in agreement to Jesse's reaction toward Sam's inappropriate comment.

'Hey, I'm sorry,' Sam grumbles, looking at me with a hint of a grin breaking free.

I glance around the busy bar, seeing plenty of people milling about, all chatting, many putting their hands up to acknowledge

Jesse, but none of them approach him. I feel the same animosity from the women in here as I did in the summer room. Is Jesse aware of all these admirers? I feel like I've poached him, and now I'm certain that their business is based solely on The Lord of the Manor and his devastating looks.

'I'm taking Ava home.' Jesse takes the gym bag from me. 'Are you running tomorrow?' he asks Sam.

'Nah, I might be tied up.' He grins at me.

I feel my colour deepen. I'll never get used to his forwardness and lurid comments. 'Where's Kate?' I ask. I should call her.

'She had a few deliveries to do. She got all excited about taking Margo Junior out on her maiden voyage. I've been dumped for a pink van.' He takes a swig of his beer. 'I'm heading over when I'm done here.'

'Done what?' Drew asks on a raised brow.

'Fuck you,' Sam spits.

I frown, and Jesse starts pulling me out of the bar. ''Bye, lads. Tell Kate Ava's with me,' he calls over his shoulder. I wave my free hand to them as I'm hauled from the bar, and they both raise their bottles in good-bye, both grinning.

I'm escorted out of The Manor to Jesse's Aston Martin, really rather quickly. He opens the passenger door for me to get in.

'I want to go on the bike,' I complain. I'm addicted.

'Right now I want you in lace, not leather. Get in the car.' His eyes have turned wickedly dark and promising. When did that happen?

I get in the car, clenching my thighs together, and wait for him to slide in next to me. He quickly flies off down the driveway toward the gates, clearly on a mission. I glance over at the gorgeous profile of the man next to me, all relaxed as he drives, his eyes flicking to me before returning them to the road. I can tell he's trying his hardest not to smile.

'One hundred thousand pounds is a massive overpayment,' I say coolly.

'Is it?'

'You know it is.' I look at him challengingly as he fights the smile threatening to break out across his lovely face.

'You're underselling yourself.'

'I must be the most expensive hooker ever,' I flip, watching his lips press into a straight line.

'Ava, if you refer to yourself in that way again ...'

'I was joking.'

'Do you see me laughing?'

'I have other clients to deal with,' I inform him bravely. He can't expect me to devote all of my working time to his extension, or to him. I highly doubt he'll let me get on with it undisturbed, and Patrick will get massively suspicious if I'm never in the office.

'I know, but I'm a special client.' He reaches over, squeezing my knee, and I look up to a dark grin.

'You're special all right!' I laugh, earning myself a dig in the soft void above my hipbone.

He cranks the volume up, and Elbow settles me back in my seat as I watch the world go by. I'm really in love with him right now, as opposed to *just* in love with him. Despite the lapse in the middle, it's turned out to be a beautiful day.

Chapter Twenty-four

The gates to Lusso slowly shift open and Jesse pulls in, parking the car swiftly and accurately. He wastes no time collecting me from my side of the car and dragging me through the foyer toward the elevator.

'Evening, Clive,' I call as I'm hauled past and stuffed into the penthouse lift. 'Are you in a rush?'

'Yes,' Jesse answers decisively, punching in his code. The doors of the lift close and I'm swiftly thrust up against the mirrored wall. 'You owe me an apology fuck,' he growls, attacking my mouth.

'What's an apology fuck?' I pant as he thrusts his knee between my thighs, moving his mouth to my ear. I could make a list as long as my arm of all the apologies he owes me. I can't think of anything that I should be apologizing for.

'It involves your mouth.'

I shake off a tremble as he pushes himself away from me, leaving me a raging bag of hormones, panting and holding myself up by leaning against the wall.

He steps back until his back meets the opposite wall of the lift, his hooded eyes watching me closely as he removes his t-shirt and begins working the button fly of his jeans. My lips part to allow air into my lungs as I wait for instruction. I'm a quivering mess. He's perfection incarnate, every sharp muscle flexing and rippling with his movement.

His jeans gape open, revealing his mass of hair, his erection falling out into his waiting palm. He isn't wearing boxers. No obstruction. I flick my eyes up to his, but he's looking down, observing himself.

Following his eyes with my own, I watch as he draws long, slow strokes over his arousal, his breath hitching slightly on each draw. Seeing him work himself has pins and needles stabbing at my groin and my body temperature swiftly rising. Good God, he is way past perfect. My gaze travels back up his body, finding the most erotic sight I've ever seen. His stomach muscles are tense, his eyes hooded and lust-filled, and that full bottom lip is parted and moist.

He's staring at me, carefully watching me from across the lift. 'Come here.' His voice is hoarse, his eyes dark. I walk slowly toward him. 'On your knees.'

I steady my breathing and slowly lower myself to the floor, sliding my hands down the front of his tight thighs, maintaining our eye connection as I do. He looks down at me, his arousal still being worked slowly in his hand. I'm absolutely transfixed by this beautiful man looming over me, working himself.

He uses his free hand to caress the side of my face as he pants short, strained breaths through his parted lips, and then he taps my cheek with his middle finger. 'Open.' I part my lips, running my hands around the backs of his legs to grip the tops of his thighs as he strokes the side of my face in approval and positions himself at my lips. 'You'll take it all the way, and I'm going to come in your mouth.' He runs his moist head over my bottom lip, and my tongue darts out to lap up the bead of creamy cum escaping. 'You'll swallow.'

My stomach twists, my breath catching in my throat as he rears back and slowly plunges into my mouth. I watch as he squeezes his eyes shut, clenching his jaw so hard, I think he could burst a vein in his temple. In my pent-up state, I tighten my grip on the backs of his thighs and pull him forward.

'Fuuuuuck,' he sighs, his fist still wrapped around the base, preventing me from taking him all the way. He moves his other hand to the back of my head as he stills, drawing urgent breaths. I can feel the pressure he's applying to his thick length, no doubt to prevent himself from climaxing immediately.

After a few moments, he's regained his composure, and he slowly peels his hand away from his base, placing it on the back of my head to join the other. I watch him puff out a few hard breaths. He's psyching himself up. I better make this good then.

I draw my mouth back and wickedly skate my hand around to the front of his thigh and between his legs to glide under his heavy sacks, delighting when his grasp on my head tightens as he moans a prayer to the ceiling, his hips shaking. He's fighting to keep control.

It emboldens me, so, very lightly, I trace the tip of my finger back and forth over the seam of his sack and watch as the cords in his neck tighten to snapping point. I'm enjoying this. He's defenseless, vulnerable, and I'm in total control. Despite his earlier demands to 'kneel' and 'open', he's at my complete mercy. It makes a nice change, and I want to please him.

I'm dimly aware of the elevator doors opening, but I ignore it, completely engrossed in what I'm doing to him. Moving my hand to his base, I hold him firm as I run my tongue over his tip and plant a soft kiss on the end. I look up and see him lower his head, searching for my eyes. When he finds them, he begins working slow circles with his hands in my hair as I lap at his entire length, paying special attention to the underside and taking immense pleasure when he jerks a few times, pushing rapid bursts of air through his teeth.

Refusing to close his eyes and determined to see me work him, he watches as I trail the entire length of him, pushing the tip of my tongue into the slit when I reach his broad head. He gives me that roguish grin, but I wipe it from his face and knock the air clean out of his lungs when I return my hand to the back of his thigh and yank him forward into my mouth.

'Oh Jesus, Ava!' he barks.

I can feel him brushing the back of my throat, and it takes every effort not to retch at the invasion. He feels so thick in my mouth. I start to retreat, but he knocks the wind out of *me* by thrusting back in, robbing me of breath. His fingers curl in my hair as he slowly withdraws and drives forward again, letting out a long moan of pure pleasure. Any illusion that I was under of me being in control is long forgotten. He knows what he wants and how he wants it. Yet again, he has the power.

'You have a fucking incredible mouth, Ava.' He surges forward again, holding me in place with his strong hands, but calmly caressing and stroking my hair at the same time. 'I've wanted to fuck it since I laid eyes on you.'

I'm not sure if I should be offended or delighted by that statement, so instead of pondering it, I un-sheath my teeth and drag them over his taut skin as he withdraws.

'Christ, Ava. Take it deep,' he shouts, powering forward again. 'Relax your jaw.'

I close my eyes and absorb his assault on my mouth. If it wasn't so damned erotic, it would be pretty brutal. He's aggressive with his power but tender with his hands. He's in complete control.

After a few more incredible strikes, I feel him swell and pulsate in my mouth. He's tipping the edge. One of his hands moves from my head to the base on his length, and he withdraws slightly, taking a firm grip, working back and forth urgently. I circle, lap and suck his swelling head as he sucks in a sharp, short breath.

'In your mouth, Ava,' he yells, and I take his cue, wrapping my lips around his jerking erection and placing my hand over his as he spills hot, creamy cum into my mouth. I take it – all of it. I swallow around him, glancing up to see his head thrown back as he yells into thin air, a throaty cry of satisfaction, his hips slowing their thrusts to a more level, lazy pace as he rides out his climax and I lick and suck the tension away. My debt is settled.

His chest is heaving as he looks down at me with a foggy green gaze, and he bends to drag me up his body, smothering my lips with his in a complete appreciation kiss. 'You're amazing. I'm keeping you for ever,' he informs me, showering my face with kisses.

'That's nice to know,' I snap sarcastically.

'Don't try and pull a hurt with me, lady.' He rests his forehead against mine. 'You left me high and dry this morning,' he says quietly.

Oh, I'm apologizing for leaving him hanging. That makes perfect sense, but how will he repay me for all of his transgressions?

I lift my arms and rest my palms on his chest, smoothing over his toned pecs. 'I apologise,' I murmur, leaning in to rest my lips over his nipple.

'You have lace on.' He wraps his arms tightly around me. 'I love you in lace.' I'm lifted, my legs automatically curling around his narrow waist before he scoops up my bag and his t-shirt and carries me out of the lift.

'Why lace?'

'I don't know, but always wear lace. Keys, back pocket.'

I reach under his arm, feeling in his pocket to drag his keys out before he turns slightly to give me access to the door. It's soon kicked open and closed again before he throws my bag down and carries me all the way upstairs. I could get so used to this. He hoofs me about like I'm little more than a t-shirt on his back. I feel weightless and completely safe.

I'm placed on my feet. 'I'm taking you to bed now,' he whispers softly.

My ears are suddenly invaded by the low sounds of Massive Attack's 'Angel'. My body goes rigid. This is music to make love to. I start burning up as he slowly starts undressing me, his soft green eyes remaining locked with mine.

The diversity of this man staggers me completely. This man is a brutal, demanding sex Lord in one breath, and a tender, gentle lover in the next. I love all elements of him, every single one. Well, almost every single one.

'Why do you try to control me?' It's the only element of him that I'm struggling to deal with. He's beyond unreasonable.

He pushes my shirt from my shoulders and down my arms. 'I don't know,' he says on a frown, his perplexed expression having me believe that he really doesn't, which is of no help to me in trying to understand why he's like this with me. He's known me for a few weeks. It's crazy behaviour. 'It just feels like the right thing to do.' He offers the explanation like it should explain everything. It doesn't in the slightest.

He unfastens the zipper of my trousers and slides them down my thighs, lifting me out of them and leaving me standing before him in my underwear. Stepping back, he takes a good look at me as he removes his shoes and jeans, kicking them off to the side.

He's hard again. I run my appreciative eyes over his loveliness, finishing back at his twinkling green pools. He's like a science project of perfection – God's masterpiece. My masterpiece. I want him to be just mine.

He reaches across to me and pulls the cups of my bra down, one at a time, brushing the back of his hand over each of my nipples, hardening them further. My breath skips, and he flicks his gaze to mine.

'You make me crazy,' he says, completely expressionless. I want to scream at him for being so thick-skinned. He keeps saying this.

'No, you make *me* crazy.' My voice is a breathy whisper. I mentally plead for him to acknowledge that he's an unreasonable control freak. He can't believe this is normal behaviour.

His lips curve, his eyes twinkle. 'Crazy,' he mouths.

I'm lifted against his chest and laid on the bed, his body spreading down the length of mine. Once he's swathed me, his mouth lowers and his lips take me worshipfully, softly working their way over me, his tongue sweeping through my mouth slowly.

Oh God. I love you. I could weep at this moment. Should I tell him how I feel? Why can't I just spit the words out? After today and his performances, you would think I would be running as fast and as far as I can. I can't, I just can't do it.

I feel my knickers being drawn down my legs, and my thoughts well and truly scatter when he shifts his body up to sit on his heels, pulling me up to straddle his waiting lap. He reaches under us to position himself at my opening.

'Lean back on your hands,' he orders softly, his voice like gravel, his eyes intense. I do as I'm bid, his spare arm wrapping under my waist to support me.

He enters me slowly on a rush of air, his lips parted and moist. I moan in pure, delighted pleasure as he fills me completely, my arms shifting a little as I lock my legs around his waist. He feels so good inside me. I could die now a very happy woman. His other hand joins the one wrapped around my waist, his big hands nearly encompassing me, as he starts directing my hips around in slow, grinding circles, lifting me up slowly before pulling me back down and swivelling again. He's working us in perfect time to the music. Christ, he's good. I sigh, long and breathy, at the exquisite sensations he's creating as he lifts, pulls me back down and circles, his own hips following the movements that he has complete control over.

'Where have you been all my life, Ava?' he moans on a long, grinding circle.

I gasp as I'm lifted and lowered again, the shimmer of a slow-building, highly satisfying climax beginning to gather force. I'm hypnotised by him – completely rapt as I watch his face burning with passion, his chest muscles undulating as he guides my body on his. This is slow, meticulous lovemaking, and it's doing me no favours with regards to my feelings for him – none whatsoever. I'm as addicted to gentle Jesse as I am to dominant Jesse.

His tongue sweeps across his moist bottom lip and his eyes flicker, his frown line working its way across his brow. 'Promise me something.' His voice is soft as he swivels his hips on another mind-numbing grind.

I moan. He's taking advantage of my mesmerized state by asking me to make promises now. But then again, that was more of a demand than a question.

I study him, waiting for his request. 'You'll stay with me.'

What? Tonight? For ever? Elaborate, damn it! That definitely wasn't a question, it was an order. I nod my head as I'm pulled back down and he mumbles incoherent words.

'I need to hear the words, Ava,' he says, circling his hips, penetrating me to the deepest part of my body.

'Oh God, I will.' I exhale around the scorching infiltration, my voice quivering from pleasure and emotion as the forceful throb at my core takes over and I tremble in his hands.

'You're going to come,' he pants.

'Yes!'

'Jesus, I love looking at you when you're like this. Hold it, baby. Not yet.'

My arms start to buckle under me, prompting him to shift his grip to the middle of my back and pull me up so we're front on front. I cry out as our chests collide and my new position has him penetrating me further. My hands fly up to grasp his back.

He searches my eyes. 'You're painfully beautiful and all mine. Kiss me.'

I obey, moving my palms to cup his handsome face and lowering my lips to his, soaking up his moans as I plunge my tongue into his mouth.

'Jesse,' I plead. I'm going.

'Control it, baby.'

'I can't.' I pant into his mouth. I'm helpless to his invasion of my mind and body as I tense my thighs around him and shatter all over him. I cry out and trap his bottom lip between my teeth, biting down.

He shouts, rises to his knees, rears back and slams into me on his own release, clenching me to his chest and spilling himself inside of me, thrusting up one last, powerful time. I cry out.

'Jesus, Ava! What am I going to do with you?'

His face plummets into my neck as he pumps his hips slowly, back and forth, milking every ounce of pleasure from me. I'm dizzy, my head spinning wildly as his heavy, hot breath spreads across my neck and travels down my chest. Every internal muscle I possess grips him as he pulsates inside me. He's shaking – proper trembling shakes.

I wrap my arms around him and squeeze him to me. 'You're shaking.' I mumble the words into his shoulder.

'You make me so happy.'

'I thought I made you crazy.'

He pulls back and looks me in the eyes, his forehead shimmering with sweat. 'You make me crazy happy.' He kisses my nose and sweeps my hair away from my face. 'You also make me crazy mad.' He gives me an accusing look. I don't know why. It's his own unreasonable, neurotic behaviour that makes him crazy mad, not me.

'I prefer you when you're crazy happy; you're scary when you're crazy mad.'

His lips twitch. 'Then stop doing things to make me crazy mad.'

I gape at him, but he presses his lips to mine before I can challenge him on that accusation. The man is crazy deluded, on top of everything else.

He rests back down on his heels. 'I would never hurt you

intentionally, Ava.' The uncertainty is clear in his voice as he brushes a stray hair away from my face.

I'm absolutely certain of it, but only in the physical sense. It's the emotional sense that scares me to death. And the fact that he added 'intentionally' should be cause for concern.

I look into the hazy green pools of this beautiful man. 'I know,' I sigh, but I really don't. And it scares me to death.

He swivels around onto his back, taking me with him so I'm sprawled across his chest, and I shift slightly so I can trace a figure eight on his stomach, lingering longer over his scar than anywhere else.

It fascinates me in a morbid kind of way, and it's another mystery behind this man. It's definitely not a war wound from an operation, and it's not a puncture wound or a slice. It looks far more sinister than that. The thick, jagged wave looks like someone has literally plunged a knife into his lower stomach and dragged it all the way around to his side. I shudder. I wouldn't have thought anyone could survive a wound like it. He must have lost a heap of blood. 'Were you in the army?' I ask quietly. This could explain it, and I've not asked directly.

He pauses from stroking my hair briefly but continues shortly after. 'No,' he answers. He doesn't ask me why I would think that. He knows what I'm getting at. 'Leave it, Ava,' he says in that tone – the one that makes me shrink on the spot.

'Why did you disappear on me?' I ask a little apprehensively. I need to know.

'I told you. I was a mess, and you asked for space.'

'Why?' I press. I feel him tense beneath me.

'You spark feelings in me,' he answers softly.

'What sort of feelings?'

'All sorts, Ava.' Now he sounds irritated.

'Is that a bad thing?'

'It is when you don't know how to deal with them.' He lets out a long, tired breath of air, making me stop with my strokes.

He doesn't know how to deal with the feelings he's having, so he tries to control me? How will that help?

'You think I belong to you.' I start circling my finger again, hoping he'll confirm it.

'No. I know you do.'

I'm deliriously happy. 'When did you establish that?'

'When I spent four days trying to get you out of my head.'

'It didn't work?'

'No. I was even crazier. Go to sleep,' he orders.

'What were you doing to try and get me out of your head?'

'It doesn't matter. It didn't work, end of. Go to sleep.'

I pout to myself, thinking I've probably extracted as much information as I'm going to get. Crazier? I don't think I ever want to meet that man. All sorts of feeling? That, I think, I like the sound of.

I continue with my swirling patterns over his chest, while he strokes my hair and drops a kiss to my head every now and then. The silence is comfortable and my eyes are getting heavy.

Pulling myself further into him, I rest my leg over his thigh. 'Tell me how old you are.' I garble into his chest.

'No,' he replies flatly.

I screw my face up in sleepy disgust. I didn't even get a fake age. I doze off into a peaceful slumber, dreaming of all things crazy.

Chapter Twenty-five

I wake up feeling exposed and cold, and I know immediately why. I sit up, blowing the hair from my face, to find Jesse on the chaise lounge, bending down.

'What are you doing?' My throat is hoarse, not yet broken in.

He looks up and dazzles me with his smile, reserved only for women. How come he's all bright-eyed and bushy-tailed? 'I'm going for a run.' He bends back down and I notice he's tying his trainers.

When he's finished, he stands up, the full six-foot-three-inches of lean loveliness, all the more lovely in loose black running shorts and a marl grey vest. I lick my lips and smile admiringly. He has stubble. I could eat him.

'I'm quite enjoying the view too,' he says cheerfully, staring at my chest with an arched brow and a half smile on his handsome face. I follow his gaze and find the cups of my bra are still sitting under my boobs. I leave them as they are, rolling my eyes.

'What time is it?' I suddenly have a stomach-turning panic moment.

'Five.'

I gape at him before dramatically collapsing back onto the bed. Five? I have at least another hour of sleep. I pull the sheets over my head and close my eyes, but I only get roughly three seconds of shut-eye before the sheets are whipped off me and Jesse is in my face, a wickedly mischievous grin plastered all over his face. I wrap my arms around his neck, trying to pull him down to me, but he pulls against me, and I end up in a standing position before I realise what's happened.

'You're coming,' he informs me, snapping the cups of my bra back over my boobs. 'Come on.' He turns, heading for the bathroom.

I scoff indignantly. 'No, I'm bloody not.' He must be mad. I don't mind a run, but not at five in the morning. 'I run in the evenings,' I advise his back, falling back to the bed. I crawl to the top and snuggle back down into the pillows, locating the one that smells the most of fresh water and mint, but I'm rudely interrupted from my peace when he grabs my ankle and yanks me to the bottom of the bed.

He leans over, whips the pillow away and narrows his eyes on me. 'Yes, you are. Mornings are better. Get ready.' He flips me over and smacks my backside.

'I don't have my running kit,' I say smugly, just as a sports bag lands on the bed next to me. 'You bought these for me?' I ask incredulously as I sit up. That's a bit presumptuous. Maybe I don't like running.

'I saw your trainers in your room. They're wrecked. You'll damage your knees if you keep running in them.' He stands with his arms folded, waiting for me to change.

It's the crack of dawn. I'm not even awake yet, and he wants me pounding the pavement and puffing myself out through the streets of London?

Unreasonable!

He sighs, walking over to the sports bag, and starts pulling out all sorts of running paraphernalia. He hands me a sports bra on a smirk. Oh, he really has thought of everything. I snatch it from his hands and remove my lace bra, replacing it with a reinforced Shock Absorber. Next, he passes me a pair of black running shorts – the same as his but the ladies' version – and a fitted pink running vest. I put it all on under his watchful eye.

'Sit.' He points to the bed, and I sigh dramatically, plonking myself on the end. 'I'm ignoring you,' he grumbles as he kneels in front of me, lifting one foot at a time to put breathable running socks on and a rather swanky pair of black Nike running shoes. He can ignore me all he likes. I'm not happy, and I want him to know it.

When he's done, he pulls me up, stands back and runs his gaze up and down my sporty-gear clad body. He nods his approval. Yes, I certainly look the part, but I've always just thrown on my baggy sweatpants and an oversized t-shirt. I don't want to look better than I actually am.

'Come on then, lady. Let's start the day how we intend to finish it.' He takes my hand, leading the way downstairs.

'I'm not running again today!' I splutter. This man really is mad.

He laughs. 'That's not what I meant.'

'Oh, what did you mean?'

He flashes me a dark, dirty grin. 'I mean by being out of breath and sweaty.'

I gasp a little. I know which way I would prefer to get out of breath and sweaty, morning, noon and night, and it doesn't involve this get-up. 'You're not seeing me tonight,' I remind him. His hand tightens around mine and he grunts a few times. 'I need a hair tie,' I say, spotting my bag by the door.

He releases me and goes into the kitchen, leaving me to retrieve a hair tie from my bag. I scoop my hair up into a high ponytail, and he's soon back to collect me. We make our way down to the foyer, finding Clive with his head in his hands.

'Morning, Clive.' Jesse nods formally as we pass, far too alert for this time of day.

Clive grumbles to himself, waving an absentminded hand at us. I don't think he's getting the hang of all that equipment.

Jesse stops us in the car park. 'Stretch,' he instructs, releasing my hand and pulling his lower leg up to his backside to stretch his quad. I watch as it bulges under his running shorts and cock my head, more than happy to stay right here and watch him do that. 'Ava, stretch,' he orders.

I throw him a disgruntled look. I've never stretched in my life – only in bed – and it's never done me any harm.

On an overexaggerated sigh, I turn my back to him and spectacularly, and oh so very slowly, spread my legs and bend down to touch my toes, thrusting my backside in his face.

'Oh!' I feel his teeth sink into one of my cheeks, followed by the swift sting of his hand colliding with my bum. I turn back around and find an arched brow on a peeved face. The man is serious about his running, whereas I just do a few miles now and again to keep the wine and cake from creeping onto my hips. 'Where are we running?' I ask, mirroring Jesse stretching his thighs.

'The Royal Parks,' he answers.

Oh, I can do that. It's roughly six miles around the circumference and one of my regular runs. No sweat.

'Ready?' he asks.

I nod and make my way over to Jesse's car, while he makes his way to the pedestrian gate. 'Where are you going?' I shout over to him.

'For a run,' he answers coolly.

Realisation dawns on my waking brain. He's going to make me run all the way to the parks, around them and back again? I can't do that! Is he trying to kill me off? 'Er … How far is it to the parks?' I try to sound completely blasé, but I'm not sure I'm pulling it off.

'Four miles.' His eyes are dancing with delight.

That's a fourteen-mile round trip! He can't seriously run that far on a regular basis; it's over half a bloody marathon. I choke slightly and disguise it with a cough, determined not to give him the satisfaction of knowing that I'm disturbed by this. I pull my vest down and walk over to the cocky, smug Adonis of a man who has my heart in a tangled mess.

He punches the code in. 'It's eleven, twenty-seven, fifteen.' He glances at me with a small smile. 'For future reference.' He holds the gates open.

'I'll never remember that,' I call over my shoulder as I pass him, starting my jog toward the Thames. I can do this, I can do this. I repeat the mantra – and the code – over and over in my head. I've not run for three weeks now, but I refuse to let him get the better of me.

He's caught up with me and running alongside me within a few yards. I look up to his lean loveliness, wondering if this man does anything badly. He runs like his upper body is disconnected from his lower body, his legs transporting his tall, lean frame with ease.

I get into my stride and we run along the river in a comfortable silence, throwing each other glances every now and then. Jesse is right – running in the morning is really relaxing. The city isn't quite in full swing, the traffic is mainly delivery vans, and there are no horns or sirens ringing in my ears. The air is surprisingly fresh and cool, too.

Half an hour later, we hit St James's Park and follow the green lushness at a steady pace. I feel surprisingly good, considering I've run somewhere near four miles already. I glance up at Jesse, who's putting his hand up to every fellow runner as they pass – all women – who smile brightly at Jesse and eye me suspiciously. I roll my eyes and glance up to gauge his reaction, but he looks completely unaffected by both the women and the running. That was probably just his warm up.

'Okay?' he asks on a half-smile as he looks down at me.

I'm not talking. That's a sure way to puff me out, and I'm doing really well at the moment. I nod and return my focus to the path ahead of us, willing my muscles not to give up. I have a point to prove.

We maintain our steady pace, making our way around St James's Park, eventually reaching Green Park. When I glance up again, I still see a completely unaffected, virtually refreshed face and body running next to me. I'm feeling it now, and I don't know whether it's my fatigue, or the fact that crazy man here is increasing his pace, but I'm struggling to keep up. We've got to be knocking on nine miles now. I've never ran nine miles in my life. If I had my iPod with me I would be hitting the button for my power track right about now.

We hit Piccadilly and I start to feel my lungs burning, my breath getting harder to keep steady and constant. I think I may have hit the proverbial runner's wall. I've never ran far enough to hit it before, but I can now completely appreciate the meaning of the statement. I feel like I'm pushing against a ton of bricks wedged in sand.

I must not give up.

Oh, it's no good. I'm bloody shattered. I detour off the road and into Green Park, collapsing unceremoniously onto the grass in a sweaty, overheated heap. I lay spread-eagled, dragging valuable air into my overworked lungs. I don't care that I've given up. That's my Personal Best. Man, he can run.

I close my eyes and concentrate on taking in deep breaths. I feel sick. The cool morning air invading my sprawled body is most welcome, until it's swallowed up by a hunk of leanness closing in on me from above. I open my eyes, finding a gaze so green it could rival the trees surrounding us.

'Baby, did I wear you out?' He grins around his words.

Jesus, he's not even broken a sweat. I, on the other hand, can't even talk. I heave underneath him like the running loser that I am, letting him smother my face with kisses. I must taste god-awful.

'Hmmm, sweat and sex.' He licks my cheek and rolls us over so I'm sprawled across his stomach, and I proceed to pant and wheeze all over him as he runs his firm palms all over my sweaty back. My chest feels tight. Can you have a heart attack at twenty-six?

When I've finally got my breathing under control, I push my hands into his chest and straddle his hips, sitting up on his body. 'Please don't make me run home,' I plead. I think I could possibly die. He places his hands under his head, all casual and amused by my laboured breathing and sweaty face. His toned arms look edible as they flex. I could just about muster up the energy to lean down and take a bite.

'You did better than I expected,' he says on a raised brow.

'I prefer sleepy sex,' I grumble, falling forward onto his chest.

His hands come around to secure me against him. 'I prefer sleepy sex, too.' He traces circles across my back.

Okay, today, I really, *really* love him. And it's only six-thirty in the morning. But I should bear in mind that a lot can change and very quickly with Mr Jesse Ward. Give it an hour and I might have disobeyed, and then, very suddenly, I'd be dealing with crazy, mad Mr Unreasonable Control Freak and being given the countdown or a sense fuck – I'll take the sense fuck; I'll leave the countdown.

'Come on, lady. We can't frolic in the grass all day; you have work to do.'

Yes, I do. And we're miles from Lusso. I heave myself up from his chest and stand. I'm slightly wobbly, but Jesse, of course, rises to his feet like a dolphin gliding across the calm ocean. He makes me sick.

He wraps an arm around my shoulder and walks us onto Piccadilly, flagging a taxi down and bundling me in.

'You brought money for a taxi?' He knew I wouldn't make it?

He doesn't answer. He just shrugs and yanks me across the taxi into his arms.

I feel a little guilty for cutting his run short, but I'm too beat to dwell on it for long.

I'm dragged, quite literally, through the foyer of Lusso and into the lift. I feel like I've been awake for a month, when in reality it's not even been two hours. I've no idea how I'm going to make it through the day.

When we reach the penthouse, I collapse on a barstool in the kitchen, resting my head on my arms. My breathing is only just returning to normal.

'Here.'

I look up and find a bottle of water being waved under my nose, and I take it gratefully, swigging the lovely ice liquid and wiping my mouth with the back of my hand.

'I'll run a bath.' He looks at me in sympathy, but I detect a little enjoyment mixed in there too. *The smug bastard!* I'm lifted from the stool and carried upstairs in my usual chimplike manner.

'I don't have time for a bath. I'll have a shower,' I say as he places me on the bed. What I would do to crawl under the covers and emerge sometime next week.

'You have plenty of time. We'll grab some breakfast and go to The Manor mid-morning. Now, stretch.' He drops a kiss on my sweaty forehead and turns toward the bathroom.

We'll go to The Manor? Oh, bloody hell. He was completely serious when he permanently marked out my diary for the rest of the calendar year? The one hundred grand is to keep Patrick quiet while he gets his fix of me, morning, noon and night. What about my other clients – Van Der Haus being *the* most important other client? He alone will boost Patrick's turnover tenfold. Oh God, I feel a trample coming on.

'Jesse, I need to go to the office.' I try for a calm and reasonable tone.

'No, you don't. Stretch,' is the straight, flat answer, followed by a terse demand that I get thrown back at me from the bathroom.

What am I going to do? I'm too exhausted to run away at the start of a countdown – not that I would get very far, even firing on all cylinders. And a sense fuck will probably finish off my already strained heart.

'All of my equipment is at the office. My computer programmes, reference books, everything.' My voice is small.

He presents himself at the doorway of the bathroom, chewing his lip. 'And you need all that stuff?'

'Yes, to do my job.'

'Okay, we'll stop by your office.' He shrugs and returns to the bathroom.

I throw myself back on the bed in exasperation. What in God's name am I going to say to Patrick? I exhale a weary sigh. He's led me into a false sense of security by bringing me home in a taxi and carrying my tired body up the stairs when my legs felt like they could give out. I'm just as deluded as he is. I'm never going to be in control.

'Bath's ready,' he whispers in my ear, snapping me from my unrest.

'You were serious, weren't you?' I ask as he lifts me up from the bed and carries me into the bathroom. The enormous bath dominating the room is only half full.

'I was serious about what?' He places me on my feet and starts peeling off my wet running gear.

'About not sharing me.'

'Yes.'

'What about my other clients?'

'I said I don't want to share you.' He pulls my shorts down my legs and taps my ankle. I do as I'm bid, lifting my feet in turn.

'I don't need to be at The Manor to collate designs, Jesse.'

He lifts me into the bath and starts undressing himself. 'Yes, you do.'

The water is a welcome relief for my screaming muscles. It's a shame it won't relax my screaming brain. 'No, I don't,' I affirm. I'm attempting to put my foot down again.

I look up to a very disgruntled face as he climbs in behind me and pulls my back against his chest. He's silent for a short while before he takes a deep breath. 'If I let you go to the office, you have to do something for me.'

If he lets me? This man is beyond self-assured and arrogant. But he's negotiating, which is an improvement on demanding or forcing me. 'Okay. What?'

'You'll come to The Manor's anniversary party.'

'What? Like a social event?'

'Yes, exactly like a social event.'

I'm glad he can't see my face, because if he could, he would see a screwed-up contortion of displeasure. So now I'm between a rock and a hard place. I get out of going to The Manor today, but I'm negotiating delaying the chore, not completely avoiding it. And for a social event? I would rather boil my head!

'When?' I sound less enthused than I feel, and that's saying something.

'Two weeks today.' He wraps his arms around the tops of my shoulders and nuzzles his face into my neck.

I should be dancing around the bathroom in joy. He wants to take me as a date. It doesn't matter that it's the posh hotel that he owns; he wants me there. But I'm not sure I'm prepared to spend the evening under the unfriendly, watchful eye of Sarah. And it's a dead cert that she'll be there.

'You'll come.' He thrusts his tongue in my ear, swirls it around a few times and kisses under the hollow of my lobe before thrusting it back in my ear.

I squirm under his hot tongue, my body slipping over his. 'Stop!' I shudder.

'No.' He squeezes me to him as I writhe, water splashing everywhere. 'Say you'll come.'

'No!' I laugh when his hand moves to my hip. 'Stop!'

'Please,' he purrs in my ear.

I stop struggling. Please? Did I hear him right? I'm stunned on the spot. Jesse Ward said *please*? Okay, so he's brokering a deal, and he said *please*.

'Okay, I'll come,' I sigh, earning myself a super-tight squeeze and an over-the-top nuzzle. I reach up and wrap my hands around his forearms. I've made him happy, and that, in turn, makes me *very* happy.

So I'm going to be his date. That will please Sarah no end. Actually, I will go, and I'll look forward to it, too. He wants me there, and that has to signify something. I can't help the little satisfied smile playing at the corners of my mouth. I'm not usually the competitive type, but I really dislike Sarah and I *really* like Jesse, so it's a no-brainer, really.

'I've never had a bath before,' he says quietly.

'Never?'

'No, never. I'm a shower man. But I think I might be a bath man now.'

'I love having a bath.'

'Me too, but only if you're in it with me.' He squeezes me. 'It's a good job the designer of this place anticipated the need for a big one.'

I laugh. 'I think she did well.'

'I wonder if she ever considered being in it?' he muses.

'No, she didn't.'

'Well, I'm glad she is.' He tugs at my earlobe with his teeth as I feel his feet slide down my shins, rubbing across the tops of my feet above the bubbly water.

I close my eyes and rest my head against his chest. Perhaps I should ditch work and stay with him all day, after all.

In my sleepy bath-time slumber, I decide that tub-talk with Jesse is one of my new favourite pastimes. And I might even start running in the morning. Not crazy distances, but around the Royal Parks once or twice every other morning. I must remember to stretch.

'You're going to be late for work,' he says softly in my ear.

I pout to myself. I'm way too comfortable. 'Just think … if you didn't go to the office, we could stay longer.' He kisses my temple and rises to get out, leaving me silently wishing I had relented to his insistence on staying with him all day.

Chapter Twenty-six

After I get myself dressed, I pad back downstairs and find Jesse at the kitchen island on his mobile, dunking his finger into a jar of peanut butter. He glances up at me, nearly knocking me off my heels with his roguish smile.

I run my eyes over his grey-suited, black-shirted physique and sigh in admiration. His dirty blond hair has been ruffled with wax and set in a messy array to one side, and I'm super appreciative that he's not shaved. He looks rugged and mind-bogglingly handsome.

'I'll be there after I've dropped Ava at work.' He turns himself on the stool, cocking his head to the side. 'Yes, tell Sarah I want it on my desk when I get there.' He pats his lap, and I make my way over, fighting the scowl from my face at the mention of *her* name. 'We revoke his membership, simple.' I lower myself onto his knee, smiling when he buries himself in my neck and inhales deeply. 'He can kick off all he likes. He's gone, end of,' he spits harshly. What's he on about? 'Get Sarah to cancel it … yes … okay … See you in a bit.'

He hangs up, tosses his phone on the worktop and snakes his arms under my knees to pull me up from the floor, greeting me with a greedy, full-on kiss. 'Breakfast?' he asks.

I glance at the clock on the cooker. 'I'll grab something at the office.' I can't be late. I jump down and grab my bag to get my pills. 'Can I have some water?'

'Knock yourself out, baby.' He returns to his jar of peanut butter.

I walk over to the huge fridge, slap my bag onto the worktop and remove everything, but I find no pills. Nowhere.

'What's up?' he asks.

'Nothing,' I mutter, dumping everything back into my bag. 'Fuck.' I curse under my breath, but then mentally applaud myself for separating the packets and putting some in my underwear drawer.

'Watch your mouth, Ava,' he rebukes me. 'Come on; you'll be late.'

'Sorry,' I mutter. 'This is your fault, Ward.' I swing my bag onto my shoulder.

'Mine?' he blurts, all wide-eyed. 'What's my fault and how?'

'Nothing, but it's your fault because you're distracting me,' I accuse.

He looks down at me, his lips twitching. 'You love me distracting you.'

I can't deny it. So I don't.

I'm delivered to Berkeley Square in record time. He really is a menace on the roads, in his stupidly expensive car. He parks illegally on the corner and turns himself to face me.

'I love waking up with you,' he says gently, reaching over and running his thumb across my bottom lip.

'I love waking up with you, too. But I don't like being run ragged at five in the morning.' My legs are really feeling it, and it's only going to get worse.

'You would prefer to be fucked ragged?' He grins that roguish grin, running his palm down the front on my dress.

Oh, no, you don't! 'No, I prefer sleepy sex,' I correct him, leaning over and planting a chaste kiss on his mouth. I get out of the car, leaving him and his frown line alone. 'I'll be seeing you tomorrow. Thank you for exhausting me before work.' I shut the door and walk off on my abused legs and in the most uncomfortable shoes I own.

*

I spend the morning checking on my clients and schedules. I'm pleased everything is running smoothly. I pencil in a few site visits for next week, smiling as I write between the diagonal lines of permanent marker pen. I need to replace my diary before Patrick cops a load of my daily appointments with the Lord.

I gladly accept the cappuccino and muffin that lands on my desk, courtesy of Sally, and frown when I hear a commotion of car horns coming from outside the office. I look up, spotting a pink van double-parked and Kate frantically waving to get my attention. I lift myself from my chair, groaning as my muscles scream in protest, and hiss on every step I take until I'm standing at the side of Margo Junior, smiling fondly at my friend's excited face.

'Isn't she pretty?' Kate lovingly caresses the steering wheel of Margo Junior.

'Beautiful,' I agree, shaking my head, but then I remember something. 'What are you playing at, letting Sam have free rein on my underwear drawer?'

'I couldn't stop him!' Her voice is high-pitched and defensive. It bloody well should be. 'He's a cheeky swine.' She grins.

I've no doubt that he is. The thought instantly reminds me about the whole tying-up charade. I'm tempted to ask Kate, but I quickly decide that I really don't want to know.

'How's Jesse?' Her grin widens. 'Have fun?'

'Well, I had a wild ride on a Ducati 1098, had daggers thrown at me by Sarah and ran nine miles this morning.' I reach down, rubbing my hands over my aching thighs.

'Fuck; is she still at it? Tell her to take a leap.' She frowns. 'You ran nine miles? Wow! And what the hell is a Ducatsiwhatevery?'

'A superbike,' I shrug. I wouldn't have known that myself a few days ago. 'He's deposited a hundred grand into the Rococo Union bank account.'

'What?' she shrieks.

'You heard.'

'Why?'

I shrug. 'To keep Patrick quiet while he hogs me. He doesn't want to share me.'

'Wow! That man's crazy.'

I laugh. Yes, crazy man, crazy deluded, crazy rich, crazy challenging, crazy loveable … 'Are we out tonight?' I ask. I've rebuffed crazy man on the assumption that Kate's free.

'Absolutely!'

I sag in relief. 'Aren't you seeing Sam then? He's becoming a bit of a permanent fixture at your place.' I arch a brow. He's actually a semi-naked permanent fixture, but I don't point that out.

'It's just a bit of fun,' she replies haughtily.

I laugh at her casualness. I know different. We're talking about the girl who hasn't been on a second date for years. Sam's cute. I can certainly see the appeal.

A car starts honking its horn from behind Margo Junior. 'Oh, fuck off!' Kate yells. 'I'm off. I'll see you at home later. You're in charge of getting the wine.' The window starts to rise and she grins from ear to ear. I still can't believe he bought her a van.

I suddenly remember the deal I brokered in exchange for my clothes … no drinking tonight. I smile to myself. He'll never know.

Kate zooms off down the road and I return to my desk, stretching my legs back out. Yes, I'm really feeling it now. Standing back up, I pull my heel up to my backside, letting out a long, grateful breath when my quad muscle stretches most satisfyingly. My phone starts jumping around my desk and Placebo starts crooning about 'Running up that Hill'. I don't even have to look at the screen to know who it is. He has amazing taste in music.

'I like,' I say, by way of greeting.

'Me too. We'll make love to it later.'

'You're not seeing me later,' I remind him again. He's doing this on purpose.

'I miss you.'

I can't see him, but I know he's pouting. And as for the 'make love' part ... well, it's a massive improvement on 'fucking'. I smile, my heart performing jumping jacks in my chest. 'You miss me?'

'I do, I miss you,' he grumbles. I glance at my computer. It's one o'clock. It's not even been five hours since I left him. 'Don't go out tonight,' he says. It's not a plea, it's a demand.

I flop in my chair. I knew this was coming. 'Don't,' I warn, in the most assertive voice I can muster. 'I've made plans.'

'You know, you may be at work, but don't think I won't come down there and fuck some sense into you.' His voice is deadly serious and even a little angry.

He wouldn't, he couldn't. Or could he? Bloody hell, I'm not even sure. 'Knock yourself out,' I respond, very lightly.

He laughs. 'I was serious, lady.'

'I know you were.' I've no doubt about it, but he will have to wait until tomorrow to do any sort of fucking.

'Do your legs ache?' he asks, just as I'm stretching them under my desk again.

'-ish.' I'm not giving him the satisfaction of knowing that I'm actually in pain. I'll have a Radox bath before I go out. Hold up ... Was he trying to cripple me so I can't go out?

'-ish,' he replies, humour clear in his husky voice. 'Remember our deal?'

I roll my eyes to myself. I was kidding myself if I thought he would forget about his little deal. And now I'm certain he had me running a marathon at the break of dawn in an attempt to immobilize me. *Control freak!*

'No reminder fuck required,' I mutter, standing back up and yanking my heel to my arse. He'll never know. I'm not going to get so drunk that I have a raging hangover – it's too soon after my last performance.

'Watch your mouth, Ava,' he sighs, tiredly. 'And I'll decide *when* and *if* a reminder fuck is necessary.'

'Roger that,' I confirm with all the sarcasm it deserves.

'When will I see you?' he sighs.

'Tomorrow?' I really *do* want to see him.

'I'll pick you up at eight.'

Eight? It's a Saturday; I want a lie-in. *Eight?* I really won't be getting drunk, not if Jesse is going to be rocking up at eight. 'Noon,' I counter.

'Eight.'

'Eleven.'

'Eight!' he barks.

'You're supposed to meet me halfway!' The man is impossible.

'I'll see you at eight.' He hangs up, leaving me on one leg with my phone hanging from my ear. I look at my mobile disbelievingly. He can turn up at eight all he likes; I won't be awake to let him in, and I seriously doubt Kate will be, either. I sink my achy body back into my chair on a few sharp inhales of breath. I'm never running again.

'Tom,' I call. 'We're out tonight; you coming?' I don't bother asking Victoria because it's her date night with Drew.

He looks up with a dirty great big grin on his baby face. 'I shall decline graciously.' He bows his head like the gentleman I know he's not. 'I have a date!'

'Another?'

'Yes! This one is definitely a keeper.' Tom nods with the biggest smirk on his face.

I leave Tom with his grin, returning to my computer. They're all keepers.

I leave the office at six, heading straight to the shop to get some Radox and a bottle of wine before making my way to the Tube.

I fight off the temptation to open the wine here and now. It's Friday; I'm catching up with Kate tonight and spending the day with my challenging control freak tomorrow. Perfect.

I walk through the front door, finding a half-naked Sam walking out of Kate's workshop, followed by a fully dressed Kate with a highly satisfied smile on her face.

'Seriously?' I splutter, as I try to direct my eyes anywhere except on Sam's fine physique.

He blinds me with his ultimate cheeky grin and turns to face Kate, giving me a rear view of his bare back and baggy-jeaned arse. It's then that I notice a lump of cake mixture at the nape of his neck.

'You missed a bit.' I point to the offending smear of mixture.

Kate swivels Sam back around to face me and licks up the centre of his back toward his neck. He smirks at me and I laugh. What a pair of exhibitionists.

Making my way up to the flat, I hiss at the stabbing pains travelling down my legs with every step I take. I go straight to the bathroom to run the bath, pouring in half the bottle of muscle-relaxing bath soak. Then I take myself to the kitchen to take care of special requirement number two; I pour myself and Kate a glass of wine each and gasp my appreciation as I take my first sip.

Five minutes later, I'm flinging every garment in my underwear drawer over my shoulder in a panic. 'KATE!' I know I put them in here, so where the hell are they? If this is Sam's idea of a joke, I'll wring his fucking neck!

Kate breezes into my room. 'I've turned your bath off. What's up?'

'My pills.'

'What about them?'

'They're gone.' I turn an accusing eye on her. 'I can't believe you let Sam in here.'

Her eyes widen. 'I didn't *let* him in. And anyway, your pills weren't in there. I would have seen them.'

I let out a frustrated yell and proceed to turn the rest of my drawers inside out and upside down. I know I put them in here. 'Shit!'

'Chill out, you can get some more. Are Tom and Victoria coming?'

I scoop up the contents of my underwear drawer and stuff them back in. 'I already did that. And no, they both have dates.'

'Your organisational skills are shocking,' she moans tiredly.

'Oh, is it Victoria and Drew's date tonight?' Kate looks at me with wide blue eyes.

'Yes!' I meet her wide eyes with my own.

'It'll never work. Hurry up in that bath; I need a shower.'

I grab my wine and head for the bathroom.

The water is glorious, and I wash my hair, shave everywhere, then reluctantly pull myself out before downing my wine and brushing my teeth.

An hour later, I've blow-dried and curled my hair, creamed up and got half a face of makeup on. My door opens and Kate's head pops around. 'How long?' she asks. Her fire red hair is in rollers and she looks at about the same stage of readiness as me.

'Half hour,' I confirm, opening my underwear drawer.

'Cool.' She shuts the door.

It opens again.

'What?' I ask without looking up from finding suitable underwear.

Within two seconds flat, I'm grabbed, my towel is yanked from my body and I'm on my back atop the bed with a hulking male looming over me.

WHOAH! I'm completely disoriented and still clinging to a pair of knickers that I was deliberating over. I don't even have a chance to focus on his face. His lips smash against mine, starting to work my mouth greedily. What the hell? There's no chance to fight him off or ask what he's doing here. He flips me onto my hands and knees, his fingers slide over my entrance – no doubt to check my readiness – before he undoes his fly and slams into me on a garbled yell.

I cry out, getting a hand clamped over my mouth for my trouble.

'Quiet,' he grates through merciless pounds.

Fucking hell! I'm completely helpless as he thrusts in and out with complete determination and purpose. The depth he's hitting soon has my vision blurry, my head spinning with desperation and pleasure. His hand leaves my mouth, returning to my hips, pulling me back against each of his hard advances.

'Jesse!' I yell desperately. He's merciless.

'I said, quiet!' he barks.

As my pleasure builds and builds, I find myself pushing back against him. He groans on each thrust, powering forward at a mind-blasting rate, colliding with my womb and sending me into a haze of shocked euphoria. I try to grab a pillow, but my disorientation has me grappling at nothing but sheets, and I can't find the strength to lift my head and use my eyes. I'm completely helpless.

I feel his grip on me tighten, the tense and swell of him pounding into me stretching me beyond comprehension. This is a possessive fuck. That's what this is. Not that I'm bothered. I might be helpless and at his mercy, but I'm still going to have a mind-bending orgasm.

His thrusts speed up and with one last pump and deep, slow grind, I splinter straight down the middle, and I'm charged with a mind-blowing orgasm that has me burying my face in the mattress to stifle my scream of release. His hoarse cry echoes around the room as he joins me in my crazy bliss, collapsing on top of me, panting loud in my ear. He's jerking and shuddering inside and all around me.

That really was shock and awe. I'm completely depleted and grabbing at valuable air to give my lungs some relief. They've really been through the mill today.

'Please tell me that it's you,' I pant, closing my eyes, soaking up the warmth of his body through his suit. He hasn't even taken his jacket off.

'It's me,' he breathes, moving my hair from my back and skimming my bare skin with his tongue.

I sigh happily, letting him nibble and lick me all over.

'Don't be having another shower,' he orders between tongue strokes.

'Why?' I frown into the sheets. I won't be, anyway – I haven't got time.

He withdraws, flipping me over and pinning my wrists on either side of my head. He gazes down at me, his styled hair of this morning now in disarray, but he looks no worse for it. 'Because I want *me* all over *you* when you're out.' He drops his lips to mine, taking a whole other tactic with my mouth, swirling his tongue, humming into me and nibbling my lips. It's a world away from the ferocious attack I've just sustained.

'Do men have an instinct for recently fucked women?' I ask around his lips.

'Mouth.' He pulls his face back, giving me a really disapproving look. 'You've had a drink.'

'No,' I blurt guiltily.

He looks at my wrists when he feels the tense of my natural reflex, then back at me with an arched brow. 'No more,' he demands softly, giving me another lavish kiss. 'I was hoping to find you in lace,' he hums through our joined mouths.

Releasing one of my wrists, he trails his finger down my side, over my sensitive hips and to the juncture of my thighs.

'You would have ruined it,' I gasp when he plunges two fingers into me. I've not even recovered from my last mind-numbing climax, and I'm set to go on another.

'Probably,' he confirms as he circles me deeply, pushing his fingers as far as he can get them.

'Hmmm.' I sigh in total satisfaction, tensing my legs underneath him.

'Don't be wearing anything ridiculous either.'

I throw my hand out to grab his shoulder and pull him down to my mouth, but he won't budge. He's looking at me expectantly and I realise ... he's waiting for a confirmation that I understand his command.

'I won't!' I cry desperately when he hits me with a delicious sweep of his thumb over my clitoris.

'Are you going to come, Ava?'

'Yes!' I yell at his face. Any moment now, I'm going to have an encore to my previous release, and it's going to be equally as satisfying and earth-shattering. 'Please!'

He moves in closer, his lips as close to mine as they can be without touching. 'Hmmm, that feel good, baby?' He pushes in deep and high, brushing my front wall.

'Oh God!' I cry. 'Jesse, please.' I lift my head to try and capture his lips, but he pulls back.

'You want me?'

I'm starting to burn, my legs tensing as he strokes between my swelling lips. 'Yes.'

'Do you want to please me, Ava?'

'Yes. Jesse, please!' I cry.

I'm completely stunned when he withdraws his fingers and rises from the bed.

What? No!

I'm on the cusp of falling over the edge, and just like that, my pending orgasm has disappeared, leaving me feeling like an unexploded bomb. 'What are you doing?' I ask in my stunned state.

'You want me to finish the job?' He cocks his head, tucking himself into his trousers.

'Yes!'

His eyes lock with mine. 'Don't go out.'

'No!'

He shrugs. 'My work here is done.' He kisses the air, staring at me through his hooded green pools, before he turns and walks out.

I'm flat on my back, naked, feeling like I've been marked, and I'm desperate for release. I can't believe he's just done that. I know what that was. That was a failed sense fuck followed up by a failed finger tease. It's a complete manipulation tactic.

'I'll sort myself out then!' I shout as the door slams behind him. I won't. It would be nowhere near as satisfying if I do it myself.

I huff, taking my naked body over to my underwear drawer to find my most racy set. Pink lace should do it. I slip it on and retrieve the posh boutique bag, smiling as I unfold the tissue paper that's protecting the five-hundred pound, ultimate taboo dress. *She who laughs last, Mr Ward!*

I battle with the zip again, sort out my half-finished makeup and present myself to the mirror. I'm very pleased with myself. The cream silk taboo dress looks damn good, my skin sun-kissed, my eyes dark and smoky and my hair a mass of chocolate waves. I slip my feet into my cream Carvella stilettos and spritz myself with Calvin Klein's Eternity.

'Fucking hell!' Kate screeches. I turn to face her, finding her looking up and down my tight, silk-clad body. 'He'll go mad!'

I scoff. 'The Lord of the Manor can fuck right off!'

Kate laughs. 'Oh, you are feeling brave. I love it!' She walks in looking her usual stunning self in a vivid green dress and navy heels. 'What did he do to deserve this?'

'He left me pre-orgasm after failing to fuck some sense into me.' I toss it out there casually and Kate falls onto the bed in a helpless heap of laughter. I can't help but laugh with her. I suppose it is quite funny.

'God love him,' she splutters through her hysteria. 'I'm glad I'm not the only one enjoying the best sex I've ever had.' She wipes the laughter tears from under her eyes.

I'm not at all surprised to hear that – not at all. Sam isn't walking around her apartment, semi-naked and with that dirty grin on his face because she's making him lots of cakes.

'He has me in knots.' I shake my head, returning to the mirror to apply my nude lipstick.

'Have we figured out how old he is yet?' Kate picks up my bronzer brush to give her pale cheeks an extra dusting.

'No idea. It's a no-go subject, just like the scar on his stomach.' She pinches her cheeks. 'Does it matter? And what scar?'

'No, it doesn't. And the scar is quite a nasty affair from here to here.' I run my finger from the middle of my lower stomach to my hipbone.

She looks at me in the reflection of the mirror. 'You're in love with him.'

'Crazily,' I finally admit out loud.

Chapter Twenty-seven

We bowl past the bouncers of Baroque in fits of giggles. We're not the least bit drunk, but the laughter is just rolling tonight.

'What are you having?' Kate asks as a barman approaches us at the bar.

'Wine,' I answer, smiling to myself. That was easy.

Kate gets served and we make our way through the Friday-night crowd to find the last available table at the back of the bar. I gingerly lift myself onto the barstool, keeping a good grip on the hem of my dress.

'So, tell me. Sam?' I ask off the cuff, knowing there's more to this than sex. I don't know Sam, but I know Kate very well, and for her to be dedicating so much time to a man, he must be pretty special. She hasn't spent so much time with a man since my brother. I smile at his impending arrival. I can't wait to see him, but I won't be talking about Dan tonight – not with Kate.

She shrugs. 'Fun.'

'Come on!' I exclaim. 'I've divulged far too much information on Jesse. Give me something!'

She sips her wine, placing it back down on the table casually. 'Ava, he's not the sort of man you settle down with. I'll take the fun while it lasts, but I won't be getting attached.'

I inwardly hiss as Kate reminds me of Sarah's words about building dreams. 'How do you know?' I ask, trying to rein in my drifting thoughts.

'I just do,' she says on a half laugh.

I'm a bit disappointed. Kate's lively, amazingly laid back and completely uninhibited – all of the things that Sam seems to be. What's the issue? 'I like him,' I admit. He might be an exhibitionist and a complete pest, but he's very endearing with it.

'Well, I like Jesse.'

I laugh. Yes, she would like him. He bought her a van. But then I recoil. 'You don't like him like *that*, do you?' Oh God, I'd never thought that Kate might be attracted to him. Well, everyone's attracted to him; I've been on the receiving end of numerous sneers from admiring women, but I never thought, not for a moment, that Kate might look at him like that.

'No!' She looks at me all offended. 'I like how much he clearly loves *you*.'

'What? He doesn't love me, Kate. He loves to fuck me.' I take a long glug of wine to dull the effect that Kate's statement's had on me. Or is it the effect of my alternative statement? Clearly loves me, or clearly loves to control me?

'Ava, again, you're the master of denial.'

'How old do you think he is?' I ask.

Kate shrugs. 'Mid-thirties.'

'You could ask Sam.' I don't know why I haven't thought of this before. Does Sam even know?

'Tried that.' She smiles and I sag. 'I'm going for a quick cigarette.' She slips down from the stool, retrieving her cigarettes from her bag. 'Wait here. We don't want to lose the table.'

She makes her way to the smoking area, leaving me pondering my diabolical situation. I'm in love with the trampling, unreasonable control freak and I don't even know how old he is. I knew I should have stayed away from him. I can't help but think that I could have easily rebuffed, denied and walked away from any other man, but Jesse is another story entirely. I'm addicted to him, and I'm not sure it's healthy.

'Ava?'

I'm dragged from my brief thoughts by a very familiar voice.

It's also a most unwelcome voice. I swivel on my tight, silk-clad butt.

'Matt.' I sound shocked, which is fine because I am.

'Shit, Ava. You look great.' He runs his smutty eyes up and down my body, making me feel uncomfortable and conspicuous. How does he make my skin crawl now? I loved him for four years. Or did I? What I felt for Matt seems to have paled into insignificance compared to how I'm feeling about Jesse.

'Thanks,' I say politely, taking in his shirt and black jeans. I hate those jeans. What does he want?

'What have you been up to?' He glances around nervously, and I know why.

Fucking. That's what I've been up to – lots of amazing fucking! 'Not a lot. Working heaps, looking for a new place.' Matt doesn't pick up on my hair being coiled around my finger. He never did pick up on my hair twiddling habit – a sign, maybe? But regardless of his ignorance to my habit, he knows there's another man in my life because he's had the pleasure of a trampling session.

'Not a lot,' he muses thoughtfully, looking at me accusingly. I've tensed up, but for what reason I don't know. I owe him nothing – no explanation, and certainly not my time *to* explain. 'It didn't take you long, did it?' he says.

His accusation pulls my eyes back to his in shock. 'Well, at least I waited until we were finished,' I spit, stunned by his cheek.

He rests his elbows on the edge of the table, getting way too close to my personal space. My back straightens, pulling me away. 'I was a twat.'

'Yes, you were. Is there a point to this?'

He smiles brightly – it's false. 'I just wanted to apologise again. I was out of line. I wouldn't blame you if you told me to fuck off.'

I smile sweetly. 'Fuck off.'

'There's no need to be like that. Can I buy you a drink for old times' sake?' he offers.

For old times' sake? What, like a celebration of how much of a knob he was? Please! I reposition myself on the stool with caution. This dress is ridiculous, and while I felt perfectly comfortable up until Matt found me, I now feel overexposed and vulnerable under the scrutinizing glare of my ex. 'No thanks.'

'Who was that man?'

'None of your business,' I retort harshly, looking around the bar nervously myself.

'He's a bit excitable, isn't he?' he laughs.

'Protective.' I'm defending Jesse's unreasonable behaviour now, but I'm not having my snide ex pass judgment, even if he's part right.

'What the fuck are you doing here?'

My shoulders tense. The sudden ice that emanates from Matt's body at the sound of Kate's voice is potent.

'I was just leaving,' Matt hisses.

'Fuck off then!'

He returns his eyes to me. 'It was nice to see you, Ava.'

Matt leaves me in peace, until Kate lets loose. 'What are you doing talking to that snake?' she blurts across the table as she lifts herself onto her stool.

'I was trying not to,' I defend myself.

'What did he want?'

'I don't know,' I reply. I do, of course, not that I'd dream of telling Kate. She huffs a little before swigging her wine, and I join her, finishing off my own glass. 'I'll get another,' I take some money from my clutch. 'Watch my bag.' I make my way to the bar to order another round of drinks and wait patiently for the barman to get my order.

This is my third glass of wine. I really am being a rebel, but after Jesse's performance at home, I'm on a private defiance mission to have the last say.

*

A few hours later, the bar crowd is thinning out and we're probably on our third bottle of wine. We're giggling like a pair of teenagers, and I'm getting pretty brave with my questioning.

'Were you really tied to the bed?' I ask cheekily. The grin that spreads across her face tells me I wasn't having my leg pulled. I'm not even that shocked. It must be the effect of the alcohol, or it could be all of the steamy sex that I've been getting myself lately. 'I knew it,' I laugh. 'You need to tell him to put some clothes on when he's wandering around the flat. I don't know where to look.'

'Are you mad?' Her eyes bug at me. 'What a waste of a fine physique!'

'What does he do, anyway?' I ask. He drives a Porsche and never seems to be at work.

She shrugs. 'Rich orphan.'

'Orphan?'

'Apparently,' she begins thoughtfully, 'his parents died in a car accident when he was nineteen. He has no siblings, no family, nothing. He lives off his inheritance and plays very hard.' She smirks again.

Sam's an orphan? I can't imagine losing my parents at that age – or any age, in fact. I suddenly see the cheeky chap in a very different light. You would never know something so dreadful had happened to him; he's always smiling and joking.

'How old is he?' I ask.

'Thirty,' she answers, almost reluctantly, like she feels guilty for knowing the age of the man she's screwing.

I let it pass. It's not Kate's fault that I'm clueless. 'What do you make of Drew?'

Her eyebrows jump up. 'He's a bit straight and aloof, isn't he?'

'Yes!' I exclaim. I'm glad I'm not the only one who finds him this way. 'Not Victoria's type at all.'

'Give it two dates, maximum,' Kate points her glass at me,

sloshing a bit on the table. 'She'll bore him to death with a run by run account of her latest visit to the tanning salon.' She nods and sips more wine. 'Hey, has Jesse mentioned anything about a party at The Manor?'

'Yes!' I blurt. 'Are you going?'

'Damn right I am! I can't wait to see the place.' Her eyes dance with excitement. 'I think a shopping trip is in order.'

'Oh, I'll probably make do with something I've got in my wardrobe.' I shrug. I've just spent five hundred quid on this stupid, miniscule dress. I go to lean back on my stool, swiftly remembering there's no back support, prompting me to grab the edge of the table. My wine flies up in the air. 'Shit!' I cry, just managing to save myself from falling arse first to the floor.

I join Kate in her helpless laughter, both our wine glasses swishing about as we titter and splutter. I need to stop drinking, right now. I'm on the cusp of falling over the edge of merriment and into the realms of slurring and staggering, and with my unreasonable Lord due at eight in the morning, I need to ensure I'm hangover free.

'I think we need to call it a night.' I hint in my most diplomatic tone.

Kate nods her agreement around the rim of her wine glass. 'Yep, I'm done.' She slips off the stool and staggers toward me. 'Oh, I love this track. Let's dance!' she screeches, pulling me toward the dance floor.

'Kate, there's no one on the dance floor!' I complain. There's almost no one in the bar either.

'Who cares?' she argues, stumbling toward the music, taking me with her. 'We'll go after thi… *Oh!*' She clatters to the ground, dragging me down with her on a yelp. 'Sorry!' she laughs.

We both lay sprawled on our backs across the floor, giggling and looking up at the dim lights of the bar. I would be embarrassed … if I wasn't so tipsy.

'Do you think the bouncers will come and help us up?' I splutter over my laughter.

Kate wipes a tear away. 'I don't know. Shall we yell?' She reaches over for my arm to support herself as she heaves her body up to a sitting position. 'Oh, shit.' she curses, her tone altering considerably from mischievous to serious.

'What?' I push myself up to find out what we are *oh shitting* about, only to discover Jesse looming over us, arms folded across his chest, with an extremely irked look on his handsome face.

Oh shit, indeed. I clamp my lips together for fear of laughing and pissing him off further.

'Oh no, that's me grounded for a month,' I titter in a low voice for only Kate to hear. She spits all over the place as she tries to suppress her laugh, and I lose the battle to restrain mine.

We both sit on the floor of the bar like a pair of drunken hyenas, whilst the colour in Jesse's face gets redder by the second. Kate laughs harder when Sam rocks up next to Jesse, rolling his eyes. Why can't my man give me an eye roll, instead of standing there looking like he's going to self-combust? I'm not even *that* drunk. My current location is only courtesy of my delinquent best friend leading me astray.

A burly skinhead bouncer approaches, and I nudge Kate with my elbow to signal our imminent ejection from the bar. 'Kate, if they don't allow us in for lunch any more, then I'll be really pissed off.' I love Baroque's BLT sandwich.

'You're already pissed,' she snorts, making another attempt to get up, using me as a prop.

'Jesse, sort your woman out,' the bouncer drawls, clasping Jesse's hand in greeting.

'Oh, don't worry.' He hits me with his most menacing glare. 'She'll be sorted out. Thanks for the call, Jay.'

What?

'Come on, you pest.' Sam jibes Kate, hoisting her up.

She throws her arms around his neck, giggling in his face. 'Take me to bed, Samuel. You can tie me up again.'

I watch as Sam restrains his laughter at Kate's performance, but he's not suppressing the chuckles because he's mad with Kate. Oh no, he's keeping a lid on it because of Jesse. He's trampling on my night again. I wasn't expecting to see him until eight in the morning, so he would never have known that I got myself a little pissed. And what's all this business with the bouncer calling him?

I return my tipsy gaze to Mr Unreasonable, pulling my best hacked-off face. His eyes are bulging, and I follow his glare down at my dress. Oh dear, I've contravened on two orders. I probably really will be grounded. I start giggling again.

'Up, now,' he snarls through a ticking jaw.

'Oh, lighten up, you bore!' I chide, more confidently than I'm feeling. I put my hand out to him for some help, knowing he won't leave me to struggle.

He sighs, shaking his head in a demonstration of his exasperation, before reaching down to pull me up. His eyes widen further when he gets the full frontal impact of the dress.

I start giggling again, but quickly calm myself down. 'Are you mad at me?' I look up at him in my tipsy state, batting my eyelashes as I grip the front of his grey suit.

'Crazy mad, Ava,' he says threateningly, grabbing my elbow and leading me out of the bar.

We find Sam helping Kate into the front seat of his Porsche, holding the top of her head as he lowers her in. She's still giggling. It sets me off again.

'Samuel, tonight is your lucky night!' she sings as Sam shuts her in.

Jesse and Sam exchange good-byes while Jesse keeps a firm grip on my elbow.

'See ya, chick.' Sam pecks my cheek, flashing me a quick private grin which I acknowledge with my own, while concentrating hard on not laughing and pissing off my unreasonable man any more than necessary.

I'm led to Jesse's car, placed in the front seat, gently but firmly, and all in complete silence. He looks really mad, but I'm drunk and defiant, so I don't care.

He reaches for my seatbelt, and I insolently bat him away. 'I can put a seatbelt on,' I grumble moodily, getting landed with a don't-push-me look, so, probably quite wisely, I place my hands in my lap, letting him lean across me to secure the belt. I steal an inhale of his scent. 'You smell delicious,' I inform him quietly.

He pulls back, his face still straight, his eyes still simmering with displeasure. But he doesn't say a word. He's giving me the silent treatment. He slams my door and slides in behind the wheel, pulling into the traffic haphazardly and with no consideration for other road users.

'Kate's house is that way.' I point out as he roars off in the wrong direction.

'And?' is the terse one-word answer I get spat at me.

'And … it's where I live,' I state firmly. He's not completely trampling my night. Kate and I have some of our best discussions over a post-alcohol cup of tea.

'You're staying at mine.' He doesn't even look at me.

'No, that wasn't part of the deal,' I remind him. 'I have until eight in the morning before you distract me again.'

'I've changed the deal.'

'You can't change the deal!'

He slowly turns his face to mine. 'You did.'

I recoil, giving him my most disgusted look, but I can't think of anything to say. He's right; I did break the rules of the deal, but that's only because his conditions are so fucking unreasonable. I sit back in the soft leather and give up. It's only eight-ish hours until eight o'clock, anyway.

*

We pull up at Lusso and I groan. The only time Clive ever sees me is when I'm drunk or being carried in from exhaustion. I open the door and take cautious steps, lifting myself to a standing position while Jesse watches me closely, no doubt waiting for me to stumble so he can scoop me up and give Clive the impression that I'm blotto again.

I shut the door softly and start walking toward the foyer. *I must not stagger, I must not stagger.* I reach the foyer, still in a vertical position, and give Clive a polite nod as I pass, but he doesn't say a word. He nods back at me, and then flicks his eyes to Jesse, and I know when he puts his head back down, without so much as a greeting, that he must have clocked Jesse's fierce face. I huff to myself, enter the lift, and wait courteously for Jesse to step inside.

'You need to get this code changed,' I mutter, punching in the developer code. He only has to notify Security and they'll see to it immediately.

He doesn't say a word. Oh, he's really working the silent treatment well. I look up, finding him staring at me, studying me closely, completely expressionless. I'm certain that he's about to pounce and give me some sort of Jesse-style fuck. Would he be fucking sense into me, or would it be a reminder fuck? Oh, it'll probably be an apology fuck! My tipsy brain relishes the thought, but then the lift doors open and he steps out before me, leaving me to follow behind. I'm shocked. I would have put my life on the certainty of being jumped.

He opens the door and strolls in without so much as looking at me, leaving me to shut it and follow him into the kitchen, where I find him grabbing a bottle of water from the fridge. He takes a few swigs before thrusting it at me.

I don't bother pushing it away, mainly because I'm thirsty, not because I'm behaving. I drink the water under his watchful eye, placing the empty bottle on the worktop when I'm finished.

'Turn around,' he orders.

I hold my breath as a million fireworks light up inside me and I follow through on his command, turning away from him, my libido screaming, my skin prickling. The feeling of his warm hands skating over my shoulders has me clenching my jaw and releasing my breath. He grasps the zip of my dress and slowly pulls it down, making a point of sliding his hands down my sides as he drags it down my body, kneeling as he goes. My ankle is tapped and I step out of the pooling material, turning back to look down at him knelt before me.

Gazing up at me, he slowly rises to his feet, dragging his nose up between my breasts until he reaches my throat. He breathes into my neck. I'm mentally begging for him.

My skin is burning for him to touch me; I want to grab him but I know this will be done on his terms.

'Do you want my mouth on you, Ava?' he asks softly.

My breath catches in my throat as his voice vibrates against my ear, and I sigh, long and breathy.

'You need to say the word.' He brushes his lips over my ear. My knees shake.

'Yes,' I gasp on an exhale.

'Do you want me to fuck you, baby?'

'Jesse.' I jerk as he strokes between my thighs.

'I know. You want me.' He bites down on my earlobe, the metal of my silver studs chinking against his teeth. I shudder, panting and desperate for him. But then he pulls away, leaving me standing a wanton mass of hormones in front of him. 'Stay there,' he orders firmly, walking away.

He's still fully dressed in his suit as he strides away from me and opens a cupboard, taking something out. Chocolate spread? My pulse accelerates.

Calmly, he makes his way back over to me while I run my eyes down his lean physique, delighting in the stiff bulge at his groin. I wait, undemanding and tolerant of his leisurely pace, and when he finally reaches me, he gets up close and personal, breathing his hot, minty breath all over me as his lips skim my cheeks, my eyes, my chin, finally resting gently on my lips.

I hum in pure pleasure, opening my mouth, but he breaks our kiss and starts lowering himself down my body. A barrage of heat floods me, my short, sharp breaths becoming suppressed and ragged. Looking up at me as he descends, his nose grazes my lace knickers, triggering my hands to fly out and grab his shoulders for support. He gives me that knowing smile and starts rising again, pressing his body against mine on his way.

'You're so affected by me,' he breathes in my ear.

I shiver, catching my breath. 'Yes, I am.'

'I know you are. It ... really ... fucking ... turns ... me ... on.' He steps away from me. What's he doing? His hands come up, and I register him holding my dress in one, and in the other ... a pair of scissors.

He wouldn't! He calmly opens the scissors and sets them at the hem of my dress. Then, very slowly, he snips up the centre as I watch agape. It seems he bloody would. A five-hundred pound dress? I can't even locate the ability to stop him or shout at him. I'm utterly stunned.

Not content with having my five-hundred pound dress in two pieces, he proceeds to calmly chop it up into a further few scraps before placing the mutilated material, calmly and precisely with zero emotion, on the island with the scissors. He turns back to face me.

I find my voice. 'I can't believe you just did that.'

'Don't play games with me, Ava,' he warns, all calm and controlled. He slips his hands in his trouser pockets and regards me closely as I stand in front of him, unequivocally staggered. All fuzzy tipsiness has completely gone. I'm sound-minded, steady and absolutely astounded by his demonstration of so-called power.

'You,' I point my finger in his face, 'are crazy!'

His lips form a straight line. 'I fucking feel it. Get your arse to bed!'

What? Get my arse to bed? The man is way past unreasonable – he's completely impossible! I feel my brow knit. If I spend any more time with this man, I'll be having Botox before I'm twenty-seven. 'I'm not getting in bed with you!' I kick my heels off and pivot, leaving the kitchen and my simmering control freak behind.

I take the stairs, slamming my feet down, huffing all the way. I could scream! He's a raving fucking nutjob!

I stomp across the open landing, letting myself into the farthest spare bedroom. I have a choice of others, but this one is my favourite and it's the farthest away from him! I slam the door behind me and crawl into the wonderfully dressed bed that still looks like it did on launch night. Flinging all the fancy cushions on the floor, I slam my frustrated head down into the pillow, immediately resenting that it doesn't smell of fresh water and mint. It's nowhere near as comfortable as Jesse's bed, but it will do for tonight. Tomorrow, I'm leaving. The man is deranged! There is just no bloody point even trying to have my own way, because even if he's gentlemanly enough to give it to me, he tramples all over it later anyway.

'Arse,' I mutter to myself.

The door opens wide, the light from the open landing gushing in, and I watch his silhouette grow larger as he closes in on me. What's he going to do now? Pump my stomach?

He bends down and scoops me into his arms without a word. If I thought it would get me anywhere, I would fight him off. But I don't. I let him carry me into his bedroom and place me in his bed.

I roll over onto my front, burying my face into a pillow, closing my eyes and pretending not to relish the comfort of his scent all over the sheets. I'm mentally exhausted and grateful it's the weekend. I might sleep for the whole of it.

I hear the shuffles and movements of Jesse getting undressed, and then the bed dips. I'm grasped around my waist and pulled with minimum effort into the hardness of his chest. I try to bat him away, ignoring the warning growl emanating from him.

'Get off!' I snap, peeling his fingers away from me.

'Ava.' His tone is seriously lacking patience. It just incenses me further.

'Tomorrow … I'm out of here,' I spit, heaving myself away from him.

'We'll see.' He almost laughs as he yanks me back into him, squeezing me to his body.

I stop fighting. It's a fruitless endeavour. Besides, I can't help the immense contentment I feel with his arms wrapped tightly around me, his hot breath in my hair.

I'm still boiling mad, though.

Chapter Twenty-eight

'Rise and shine, lady.' His nose is touching mine as I open my eyes.

I give my brain a few moments to kick into gear and my eyes time to adjust to the light, and when my focus eventually clears, I find he's looking down at me with bright green twinkling eyes. I, on the other hand, want to sleep some more. It's Saturday, and not even my need to tell him off will get me out of this bed any time soon.

I push him away, rolling over. 'I'm not talking to you,' I grumble, snuggling back down into my pillow. He gives my backside a swift slap before flipping me back over and pinning my arms down. 'That hurt!' I scowl at him and the corners of his lush lips twitch, but I'm in no mood for roguish Jesse this morning.

I'm swathed from head to toe in him as he gazes down at me, running his eyes all over my face. I should bring my knee up and catch him where it counts!

'Now, today can go one of two ways,' he informs me. 'You can stop being unreasonable and we'll have a lovely day together, or you can continue being a defiant little temptress, and I'll be forced to handcuff you to the bed and dig you in the tickle spot until you lose consciousness. What's it to be, baby?'

Me? Unreasonable? My jaw falls open as he watches me with interest. Does he seriously think I won't challenge him on that little proposal?

I lift my head so I'm right up close to his stubbled, irritatingly stunning face. 'Fuck … off,' I say, slowly and clearly, making him recoil and his eyes widen at my brashness. I'm pretty ashamed of myself, too, but he brings out the worst in me with his unreasonable ways.

'Watch your fucking mouth!'

'No! What the hell are you doing having doormen advise you of my movements?' That little memory has just landed in my waking brain. But if I'm right, and he's arranged for bouncers to monitor me, then I'll boil over.

'Ava, I just want to make sure you're safe.' He drops his head down, starting to chew his lip. 'I worry, that's all.'

He worries? He's known me for less than a month, and he's getting all protective and possessive? He tramples everywhere, derails me, cuts up my dresses and prohibits me from drinking.

'I'm twenty-six years old, Jesse.'

He returns his eyes to mine. They're dark again. 'Why did you wear that dress?'

'To piss you off,' I answer honestly, wriggling a little in complete vain. I'm not going anywhere.

'But you thought you weren't going to see me.' His brow furrows. Does he think I was wearing it for someone else?

'It's principle,' I mutter. I wanted the upper hand, even if he didn't know it. 'You owe me a dress.'

He smiles, nearly blinding me. 'We'll put it on our list of things to do today.'

What list would that be? Right now, I want to go back to sleep. Or he could wake me up another way. I squirm underneath him, and his eyebrows jump up in surprise.

'What's all that about?' he asks, blatantly trying to hide a grin.

Okay, now I know exactly what his game is. He's going to deny me, just like he did last night and just like he did before I went out. That's going to be his punishment for me defying him. He's cute. It's the worst thing he could do.

'You don't need to keep me safe,' I gripe, worming my way

free from under him. He can throw down the gauntlet all he likes.

'That's how much I care about you,' he calls to my back as I leave him lying on the bed.

Care? I want him to love me, not care. I walk across the bedroom to the bathroom, shutting the door behind me, feeling my heart slowly cracking.

I wash my face and make a grab for Jesse's toothbrush, only to find my own in the holder with it. *Huh?* I cake it in paste on a frown and set about brushing my teeth, glancing in the mirror to the shower and spotting my shampoo and conditioner on the shelf, along with my razor and body wash. Has he moved me in? I carry on brushing my teeth, opening the door back into the bedroom, finding Jesse sprawled on his front with his face buried in the pillow. I walk past him into the walk-in wardrobe, nearly choking on my toothpaste when I see a selection of my clothes hanging there.

He *has* moved me in! Did I not get a say? I might very well love him, but I've known him for a few weeks. Moving in? What does this mean? Does he want me here to take care of me? Well, if so, he can sod right off. Control me, more like.

'Problem?'

I swing around, my toothbrush hanging from my mouth, to find Jesse filling the doorway of the wardrobe, looking slightly apprehensive. It's a look that I've not seen on him before. My eyes drift down his torso, delighting in the flex of his muscles as he braces himself on the door frame with both hands. But I quickly refocus my attention away from his distracting chest, suddenly remembering why I'm in the wardrobe. I garble a load of inaudible words around my toothpaste and brush.

'I'm sorry; run that by me again.' His lips twitch at the corners as I yank my brush from my mouth.

He bloody well knows what's wrong with me. I garble again, my words a little more comprehensible with the absence of my brush, but the paste is still hindering proper speech.

He rolls his eyes and picks me up, taking me to the bathroom. 'Spit.' he commands as he places me on my feet.

I rid my mouth of all the paste and turn to face my unreasonable control freak. 'What's all this?' I wave my arm around in the general direction of everything.

He clamps his lips together to suppress a smile and leans forward, licking off the remnants of the paste from around my mouth, his hot tongue sweeping across my bottom lip slowly. 'There. What's what?' He flicks his tongue up to my temple, blowing a long, hot breath in my ear, and I tense when he reaches down to cup my sex, sending chills of pleasure flying through me.

'No!' I push him away from me. 'You're not manipulating me with your delicious godliness!'

He grins that roguish grin. 'You think I'm a god?'

I huff, turning back to the mirror. His head is expanding at a rate so fast I might be forced to jump out the bathroom window before I'm squashed against a wall.

Curving his arm around my waist, he pulls me against his front and leans down to rest his chin on my shoulder. He studies me in the reflection of the mirror, pushing his erection between my thighs and circling his hips, sending my hands flying down to catch the side of the vanity unit.

'I don't mind being your god,' he whispers on a husk.

'Why is my stuff here?' I ask his reflection, willing my body to behave and not get swallowed up by all his lovely godliness.

'I collected it from Kate's earlier. I thought you could stay here for a few days.'

'Do I get a say?'

He circles those damn hips again, milking a small cry from me. 'Do you ever?'

I shake my head at him in the mirror, and one corner of his mouth rises on a mischievous smile as he circles again. I'm not going to react to his damn hip swivels because I know he's going to leave me hanging again. And what's Kate playing at, letting all these men rummage through my belongings? There's more than two days' worth of clothes hanging in that wardrobe. What's his game?

'Get yourself ready, lady.' He kisses my neck and smacks my arse. 'I'm taking you out. Where would you like to go?'

I look at him, stunned. 'I get to choose?'

He shrugs. 'I have to let you have your way some of the time.' His face is deadpan. He's completely serious.

I should grab his offer of power with both hands while he's being so reasonable, but I'm suspicious. After his reaction last night, his massacre of the taboo dress and the silent treatment, I'm befuddled as to why he's woken up all balanced and stable.

'So, what would you like to do?' he asks.

'Let's go to Camden,' I suggest, bracing myself for his refusal. Men hate all that hustle and bustle and roaming around browsing at stuff.

'Okay.' He turns to get in the shower, leaving me at the sink wondering where my challenging control freak has gone.

At the bottom of the stairs I hear Jesse talking on his phone, and walking into the kitchen I instantly drool. He looks glorious in some worn jeans and a navy polo shirt, collar turned up – Jesse style. He's shaved and shoved some wax in his hair. He really is unreasonably handsome, as well as unreasonable everything else.

'I'll be in tomorrow. Is everything okay?' He turns on his stool, running an eye down my body. 'Thanks, John. Call me if you need me.' He places his phone down without looking away from me, folding his arms over his chest. 'I like your dress.' His voice is all low and husky.

I look down at my flowing floral tea dress. It sits on my knee so the length probably meets with his approval. I'm surprised

Kate packed it. It's a bit summery, with its cut-out back and lack of sleeves. I smile to myself. He hasn't seen the back yet, and I'm not showing him either. He'll make me change. I know it.

I pull on my thin knitted cream cardigan, then position my suede bag across my body. 'Ready?' I ask.

He pushes himself to his feet, approaching me all moodily. I expect a deep kiss, but I don't get one. Instead, he slips his Wayfarers on, takes my hand, and pulls me toward the door. I get to spend the whole day with him and he's not even going to kiss me?

'You're not going to touch me all day, are you?'

He looks down at our joined hands. 'I'm touching you.'

'You know what I mean. You're punishing me.'

'Why would I do that, Ava?' He pulls me into the lift. He knows damn well what my point is.

I look up at him. 'I want you to touch me.'

'I know you do.' He punches in the code.

'But you won't?'

'Give me what I want, and I will.' He doesn't look at me.

I don't believe this. 'An apology?'

'I don't know, Ava. Do you need to apologise?' He still keeps his focus straight ahead. Even in the reflection of the doors, he still won't meet my eyes.

'I'm sorry,' I practically spit. I can't believe he's doing this. And I can't believe I'm this desperate for the contact.

'Now, if you're going to apologise, at least *sound* sorry.'

'I'm sorry.'

His eyes meet mine in the mirror. 'Are you?'

'Yes, I'm sorry.'

'You want me to touch you?'

'Yes.'

He turns into me fast, pushing me up against the mirrored wall and completely blanketing me with his body. I feel instantly better. That wasn't too hard at all. 'You're beginning to understand, aren't you?' His lips hover over mine, his hips pushing into my lower stomach.

'I understand,' I pant.

He takes my mouth and my hands find his shoulders, my nails digging straight into his muscles. Yes, that's much better. I meet his tongue, melting into him completely.

'Happy?' he asks, breaking our kiss.

'Yes.'

'Me too. Let's go.'

We pull up in Camden for breakfast. It's a beautiful day and I'm already too warm in my cardigan, but I'll suffer for a little longer. There's still scope for him to take me home in disgrace and make me change.

Jesse collects me from the pavement, leading me across the road to a lovely little quaint café. 'You'll love it here. We'll sit outside.' He pulls out a large wicker chair for me.

'Why will I love it?' I ask as I sit on the polka dot cushion.

'They do the best Eggs Benedict.' He smiles brightly at me when he sees my eyes light up.

The waitress approaches on a dribble when she spots Jesse in all of his manly godliness, but he's completely oblivious.

'Can we have two of the Eggs Benedict' – he points at the menu – 'a strong black coffee and a cappuccino with an extra shot, no chocolate or sugar, please?' He turns his face up to the waitress, blasting her with one of his smiles, reserved only for women. 'Thank you.'

She appears to stagger slightly, and I laugh to myself. Yes, he had that exact same effect on me.

She eventually finds her voice. 'Would you like ham or salmon with your eggs?'

He hands her the menu, taking off his Wayfarers so she gets the full impact of his stunning face. 'Salmon, please.'

I shake my head in dismay and check my phone while the waitress makes a meal of writing out our basic order. 'White or granary?'

'Sorry?' I glance up from my phone and find the waitress still hovering.

'Would you like white or granary bread?' Jesse repeats on a small smile.

'Oh, granary, please.'

He returns his glorious greens to the wilting waitress. 'Both granary, thank you.'

She flashes her most willing smile before finally leaving us. 'How are your legs?' he asks, but I know that's not what's gotten him chomping on his bottom lip.

'Fine. Do you run often?' I already know the answer to this. No one gets up in the middle of the night to run fourteen miles unless they're serious about it.

'It distracts me.' He shrugs, sitting back in his chair, his expression thoughtful.

'Distracts you from what?'

He keeps his eyes on me. 'You.'

I scoff. He's obviously not running very much at the moment then, because he's spending most of his time trampling all over me. 'Why do you need distracting from me?'

'Because, Ava ...' He sighs. 'I can't seem to stay away from you and, even more of a worry, I don't want to.' His tone harbours frustration. Is he frustrated with me or with himself?

The waitress places our coffees on the table and lingers for a while, but she doesn't get blessed with another knock-out smile. He's focused on me alone. His statement is bittersweet. I'm delighted that he can't stay away from me, but slightly affronted that it seems to annoy him.

'Why would that be worrying?' I ask nonchalantly, while stirring my cappuccino and mentally pleading for some satisfactory answers. But after a few moments have passed and he still hasn't answered, I glance up, discovering the cogs whirling at a hundred miles an hour, his bottom lip getting a punishing chew.

He eventually exhales noisily, dropping his eyes. 'It's worrying because I feel out of control.' He returns his eyes to me, penetrating me with his fixed green stare. 'Feeling out of control is not something I do well, Ava. Not where you're concerned.'

Is he admitting that he's a completely unreasonable control freak? It's bloody obvious that he doesn't cope when he's defied – I've seen hard evidence of that.

'If you were more reasonable, you wouldn't feel out of control. Are you like this with all of your women?'

His eyes widen, then narrow. 'I've never cared enough about anyone else to feel like this.' He picks up his coffee. 'It's just fucking typical that I would go and find the most defiant woman on the planet to …'

'Try and control?' I raise my eyebrows at him, and he deepens his scowl on me. 'What about other relationships?'

'I don't have relationships. I'm not interested in getting involved. Anyway, I don't have time.'

'You've devoted enough time to trampling all over me!' I blurt over my coffee cup. If this isn't involved, then I don't know what is.

He shakes his head. 'You're different. I told you, Ava, I'll trample anyone who tries to get in my way. Even you.'

Our breakfast lands on the table, smelling divine. Tucking in, I ponder his words. 'Why am I so different?' I ask. My voice is small.

'I don't know, Ava,' he says quietly, slicing his way through his salmon.

'You don't know much, do you?' It's all he bloody says when I try and determine a reason for his controlling ways. I spark 'all sorts of feelings'. What am I supposed to make of all this?

'I know that I've never wanted to fuck a woman more than once. You, though, I really do.'

I recoil in horror, nearly choking on a piece of toast.

He has the decency to look apologetic. 'That came out wrong.' He puts his fork down, closing his eyes and rubbing his temples. 'What I'm trying to say is that ... well ... I've never cared about a woman enough to want more than sex. Not until I met you.' His temple rubs gets more aggressive. 'I can't explain it, but you felt it, didn't you?' He looks at me and I think I see desperation for confirmation. 'When we met, you felt it.'

I smile lightly. 'Yes, I felt it.' I'll never forget it.

His expression changes instantly – he's smiling again. 'Eat your breakfast.' He points his fork at my plate, and I resign myself to living without the knowledge I so desperately want. If he doesn't know, there's not much chance of me ever knowing. Would it make it easier to cope with him if I knew what made his complex mind tick? I might never know, but regardless, he's just – in not so many words – told me that he wants more than sex, hasn't he? So he cares about me. Does care equal control? And he's never had a relationship? I can't believe that for a second. Women throw themselves at this man. He can't just screw them all once. Christ, if he's never fucked a woman more than once, how many have there been? I'm just about to ask this question, but I halt mid-inhale. Do I want to know?

'We need to buy you a dress for The Manor's anniversary party,' he declares in an obvious tactic to distract me from my pressing questions and thoughts. I'm sure he knows what I'm thinking.

'I have plenty of dresses.' I sound really unenthusiastic, which is fine, because I am. I'm only half comforted by the fact that Kate will be there to help me through an evening of Sarah glaring at me and passing sly remarks. Has he fucked Sarah? I imagine it's possible if he only fucks women once. The thought makes me stab at my breakfast a little too harshly.

He frowns. 'You need a new one.' It's that tone that dares me to challenge him.

I sigh at the prospect of yet another wardrobe argument. I've more than enough options without buying a new dress. Besides, even if I didn't, I'd find something just to avoid a shopping trip with Jesse.

'Anyway, I owe you one.' He reaches over the table, pushing a loose tendril of hair behind my ear.

Yes, he does owe me one, but I don't want it because I doubt I'll have any say in what dress he buys me. 'Do I get to choose?'

'Of course.' He places his knife and fork on his plate. 'I'm not a complete control freak.'

I nearly drop my cutlery. 'Jesse, you're really very special.' I load my voice with all of the sweetness the statement deserves.

'Not as special as you.' He winks at me. 'Are you ready to hit Camden, baby?'

I nod, fishing my purse from my bag while he watches me with a bewildered look. I put a twenty under the salt shaker on the table and observe as he stands in an exaggerated huff, digs into his pocket and replaces my money with his, snatching my purse from my hand and stuffing my note back inside.

Control freak!

My phone starts dancing around the table, but before I can even instruct my brain to pick it up, Jesse has snatched it from under my nose. 'Hello?' he greets the mystery caller.

I look at him in disbelief. He really *doesn't* have any phone manners. Who is it, anyway?

'Mrs. O'Shea?' he says coolly.

My mouth falls open. No! Not my mother! I try to snatch my phone back from him, but he dances away from me with a wicked grin on his maddeningly handsome face.

'I have the pleasure of being with your beautiful daughter,' he informs my mother. I move around the table, and he shifts the other way, frowning at me.

I clench my teeth and wave my hand frantically at him, but he just raises his eyebrows and shakes his head slowly.

'Yes, Ava has told me lots about you. I'll look forward to meeting you.'

Oh, the irritating twat! I've not mentioned much at all to Jesse about my parents, and I certainly haven't mentioned him to them. Oh God, this is all I need. Glaring at him, I reach over but he jumps back.

'Yes, I'll put her on. It was lovely to talk to you.'

He hands me the phone, and I seize it from his hand with a vicious swipe. 'Mum?'

'Ava, who was that?' My mum sounds as mystified as I expected her to be. I'm supposed to be young, free and single in London, and now strange men are answering my phone. I narrow my eyes on Jesse, who's looking rather proud of himself.

'He's just a friend, Mum. What's up?'

Jesse clutches at his heart, pulling a wounded soldier impersonation, but his annoyed facial expression doesn't match his playful act – not in the slightest. I hear my mother hum in disapproval.

'Matt called me,' she states flatly.

I turn away from Jesse to try and hide my wide-eyed look. Why has Matt called my mother? Shit! I can't talk about this now, not in front of Jesse. 'Mum, can I call you back? I'm in Camden; it's loud.' My shoulders hit my earlobes at the feel of Jesse's eyes chiselling away at my back.

'Yes, I just wanted you to know. He was all friendly. It doesn't sit well.' She sounds furious.

'Okay, I'll call you later.'

'Fine, and remember, carefree fun.' She adds the last bit in a blatant reminder of my status – whatever that is.

I turn back to Jesse, finding the expression I knew I would: very unhappy. 'Why did you do that?' I yell.

'"He's just a friend"? Do you often let friends fuck your brains out?'

My shoulders sag in defeat. The man's constant change in reference to our relationship is burning my brain. He fucks me; he cares for me; he controls me ... 'Is it your mission objective to make my life as difficult as possible?'

His eyes soften. 'No,' he says quietly. 'I'm sorry.'

Good God, do we have a breakthrough? Has he just apologised for being an arse? I'm more stunned now than when he hijacked my phone and greeted my mother like she was an old friend. 'Forget about it,' I sigh, shoving my phone in my bag. I start walking down the street, toward the canal, and his arm is wrapped around my shoulder within seconds. My poor mother is probably giving my poor dad an earache right at this very moment. I know I'll be hit with twenty questions later. And as for Matt ... well, I know his game. He's trying to butter up the parents, the slimy little worm. He'll be sorely disappointed. My parents openly dislike him now, as opposed to putting up with him for my sake.

We spend the rest of the morning and well into the afternoon wandering around Camden. I love it here – the diversity is the best London has to offer. I could lose myself for hours in the cobbled back streets of the markets and stables. Jesse humours me while I poke about on the stalls, keeping close and constantly touching me. I'm so glad I apologised.

We walk through the food quarter, and I can't take the heat any more. It's not particularly hot, but with all the tourists and crowds, I'm feeling stifled. I remove my bag from across my body, taking my cardigan off to wrap it around my waist.

'Ava, your dress is missing a huge chunk!'

I turn around on a smile, finding him gaping at the cut-out section of my dress. What's he going to do? Undress me and cut it up?

'No, it's the design,' I inform him, tying my cardigan around my waist and replacing my bag over my body. He turns me around, pulling my cardigan further up my body in an attempt to conceal the revealed flesh. 'Will you stop?' I laugh, wriggling free.

'Do you do this on purpose?' he snaps, arranging his big palm in the centre of my back.

'If you want full-length skirts and polo neck jumpers, then I suggest you find someone your own age.' I mutter as he starts guiding me through the crowds with his hand firmly in place. I earn myself a dig in the ribs for my cheek. He'll have me in a burka next.

'How old do you think I am?' he asks incredulously.

'Well, I don't know, do I?' I toss back at him. 'Do you want to relieve me of my wondering?'

He scoffs. 'No.'

'No, I didn't think so,' I mutter, just as something catches my attention. I quickly detour to a stall full of scented candles and all things hippy, hearing Jesse curse behind me as he barges through the crowds to keep up with me.

I make it to the stall and I'm greeted by a new age type, with wild dreadlocks and plenty of piercings.

'Hi.' I smile, reaching up to grab the cloth bag from the shelf.

'Afternoon,' he says. 'Do you want some help with that?' He joins me by the shelf, helping me retrieve the cloth bag.

'Thanks.' I feel Jesse's warm palm on me again as I open the cloth bag and pull out the contents.

'What's that?' Jesse asks, looking over my shoulder.

'These,' I shake them out, 'are Thai fisherman pants.'

'I think you need a smaller size.' He frowns, running his eyes across the huge piece of black material that I'm holding up.

'They're one size.'

He laughs. 'Ava, you could get ten of you in those.'

'You wrap them around. One size fits all.' I've been meaning to replace my worn ones for months.

He moves to the side, keeping his hand exactly where it is, and looks at the pants dubiously. Admittedly, they do look like a pair of trousers for the world's most obese man, but once you figure them out, they're super comfy for knocking around the house on a lazy day.

'Here, let me show you.' The stall owner takes the trousers from my grasp and kneels in front of me.

I feel Jesse's palm tense on my back. 'We'll take them,' he spits out fast.

Oh, here comes a trample!

'You need a demo,' Dreads says cheerfully, jiggling the opening of the trousers at my feet.

I lift my foot to step into the trousers, only to have myself tugged back slightly. I glance up at him, flashing a warning look. He's being ridiculous.

'You have great legs, miss.' Dreads says happily.

I cringe. 'Thanks.'

'Give me those.' Jesse snatches the pants from Dreads before positioning me with my back to a shelf full of candles. Shaking his head and muttering under his breath, he kneels on one knee and opens the pants for me. I smile sweetly at Dreads, who seems to be oblivious to Jesse's trampling performance, probably too spaced out to notice, and I step into the pants, pulling them up while Jesse holds onto the two gaping sides, his frown line deep on his forehead. God love him!

I quickly take control of the wrapping for fear of Dreads trying to intercept. 'Like this, see?' I fold the pants over, tying them on the side.

'Wonderful,' Jesse mocks, looking at them in confusion. His eyes find mine, and I break out in a full smile. He shakes his head, his eyes twinkling. 'Do you want them?'

I start to unfasten and remove the trousers under Jesse's watchful eye. 'I'm paying,' I inform him.

He rolls his eyes on a disgusted snort, taking a wad of notes from his pocket. 'How much for the oversized trousers?' he asks Dreads.

'Just a tenner, my friend.'

I fold them up, shoving them in the bag. 'I'm paying for the trousers, Jesse.'

'Is that it?' Jesse shrugs as he shoves a note at Dreads.

'Cheers.' Dreads thrusts it in his bum-bag.

'Come on.'

'You didn't have to trample the poor man,' I moan. 'And I wanted to pay for the pants.'

He pulls me into his side, pressing his lips into my temple. 'Shut up.'

'You're impossible.'

'You're beautiful. Can I take you home now?'

I shake my head at my challenging man. 'Yes.' My feet are aching, and I have to commend him on his tolerance of my leisurely meander today. He's been pretty reasonable.

I let him lead me through the crowds until we emerge from the packed alley, where the sound of booming, heavy techno music assaults my ears. I look over, seeing neon lights creeping from the darkness of the factory building and crowds of people gathering at the entrance. I've never been in the place, but it's famed for its off the wall club wear and wild accessories.

'You want to see?'

I look up at Jesse and find he's followed my gaze to the entrance of the factory. 'I thought you wanted to go home.'

'We can have a quick look.' He redirects us to the entrance, leading me into the dimly lit space.

The music pounds my ear drums as we enter, and the first thing I notice is two club dancers, kitted out in hi-visibility underwear, performing some pretty jaw-dropping moves on a metal suspended balcony. I can't help but stare. You would think we were in a nightclub in the early hours. Jesse directs me to an escalator that takes us down to the bowels of the factory, and as we reach the bottom, my eyes are assaulted, attacked by florescent clothing in every colour and description.

'It's not lace, is it?' he muses, catching me gawking at a bright yellow miniskirt with metal spikes protruding from the hemline.

'Lace, it's not,' I agree. 'Do people wear this stuff?'

He laughs, nodding at a group of people who look like they might pass out with excitement. They must have a million piercings between them. I'm completely engrossed by my surroundings as we wander around the metal maze of steel corridors and down some more stairs, finding ourselves closed in on every angle by … sex toys. I cringe. The music is louder and absolutely vulgar, and I gape as I listen to some demented woman screaming about sucking cock on the dance floor, while a leather-clad dominatrix type grinds her crotch up and down a black metal pole. I'm not a prude, but this is way past my comprehension. Okay, we're in the adult department, and I'm feeling extremely uncomfortable. I look up nervously to Jesse.

His eyes are twinkling, his expression displaying an abundance of amusement. 'Shocked?' he asks.

'-ish,' I admit. It's not so much the merchandise – it's the pierced, tattooed, virtually naked bird in the corner, wearing eight-inch platforms and performing some highly illicit moves. That's what's got me scooping my tongue up from the floor.

Does Jesse go for all this stuff?

'It's a bit over the top, isn't it?' he muses, pulling me over to a glass cabinet. I exhale a sigh of relief at his statement.

'Wow!' I blurt, coming face to face with a huge, diamanté-embellished vibrator.

'Don't get excited,' Jesse whispers in my ear. 'You don't need one of those.'

I gasp, and he laughs lightly in my ear. 'I don't know. It looks like it could be fun,' I respond, thoughtfully.

It's him that lets out a shocked gasp this time. 'Ava, I'll die before you use one of those.' he flashes the offending object a disgusted look, 'I'm not sharing you with anyone or anything, even battery-operated devices.'

I laugh. He would trample a vibrator? His unreasonableness is off the scales. He looks down at me, giving me his roguish grin.

'I might stretch to some handcuffs, though,' he adds quietly.

'This doesn't turn you on, does it?' I gesture around the room before tilting my head up to him.

He looks at me with warm eyes, pulling me closer into his side to drop a tender kiss on my forehead. 'There's only one thing in this world that turns me on. And I love her in lace.'

I melt with relief and turn my eyes up to the man I love so much it hurts. 'Take me home.'

He gives me a half smile, landing a worshipful kiss on my lips. 'Are you making demands?' he asks against my lips.

'Yes. You've not been inside me for too long. It's not acceptable.'

He pulls back and watches me carefully, cogs flying, teeth chomping. 'You're right; it's not acceptable.' He resumes chomping and refocuses his attention ahead of us, leading me out of the dungeon and back to his car.

Chapter Twenty-nine

We burst through the door of the penthouse in a tangled embrace. I've waited all day for this. I'm about to explode with lust. I need him all over me, right now.

He grabs me around my waist so I straddle his hips and he walks us into the kitchen, flicking a few buttons on the remote control. My ears are instantly flooded with Placebo's 'Running up that Hill'. This only serves to spike my desperation for him more. He's a man of his word.

'I want you in bed,' he says urgently as he takes the stairs at an alarming rate.

The door to the master suite is kicked open, and I'm placed on my feet at the end of the bed.

'Turn around,' he says softly. I oblige, giving him access to the back of my dress. 'Please tell me you have lace on,' he pleads, unbuttoning my dress. 'I need you in lace.'

I hear him exhale a long, satisfied breath as he pulls my dress over my head and lets it fall to the floor.

I kick my shoes off and turn back around to face him, finding a lax mouth and hooded eyes. He's as desperate as I am. He reaches forward, slowly pulling down a lace cup on my bra, brushing his knuckles over my nipple. My heart starts a relentless sprint in my chest. He's in gentle mode – I love gentle Jesse.

I watch him reach over his back and grasp his t-shirt, pulling it forward over his head. His leanness will never cease to have me panting. There's not a scrap of fat on him.

'Have you had a nice day?' he asks softly, but he doesn't touch me. He just stands in front of me removing his shoes and socks, while I'm mentally begging for him to hurry up.

'I've had a lovely day,' I say, trying my hardest to ignore the passionate beats of the music surrounding us.

'Me too.' He's all serious and pensive. I don't know what to make of it. 'Shall we make it even better?'

Oh God. 'Yes,' I breathe.

'Come here.'

There will be no countdown necessary this time. I step forward, placing my hands on his solid chest, and tip my face up to meet his stare. We spend a few silent moments gazing at each other before his lips fall to mine, instantly catapulting me to Central Jesse Cloud Nine – my most favourite place in the universe.

I moan, moving my hands up in his hair to hold on to him as he lifts me and secures me against his body, our tongues lapping and circling slowly. He takes me to the bed, laying me beneath him, and places my hands above my head. He doesn't hold them there, although I know that's where they've got to stay.

He releases my mouth and sits up, leaving me hot, dazed and panting short, sharp breaths as he looks down at me, the cogs going into overdrive in that beautiful mind of his. I want to know what he's thinking. He's been slipping in and out of thoughtfulness for days now.

'I could sit and watch you writhe under my touch all day,' he murmurs as he plays with my breast, yanking down the other cup and lavishing that breast with equal attention.

My nipples twinge, being pulled and elongated by his fingers as he watches himself work me into a crazy wreck, his lips parted and moist. I want them on me now.

'Stay where you are.' He gets up from the bed pulling my knickers off as he goes, and I whimper slightly at the loss of his weight from me. I watch him slowly unbutton the fly on his jeans and drag them down his thighs, kicking them off calmly before drawing his boxer shorts down his legs. I clench my thighs together to control the dull pulse at my core that's just advanced into a steady throb at the sight of him bared naked and stunningly spectacular in front of me. Crawling back on the bed, he parts my thighs and runs his tongue straight up the centre of my sex.

'Oh God, God, God!' I cover my face with my palms, sinking my teeth into my own hand as he plunges his tongue into me, withdrawing and circling slowly before dipping back in. I might pass out.

My hips rotate in time to his tempo, seeking further friction, his palm spanning my stomach to keep me from bucking under him. Why did I ever run? Of all the stupid things I could do, running away from this man would get the gold.

He lifts his mouth and blows a cold stream of air across my flesh before returning to his inexorable pattern of torturous pleasure. When my head starts thrashing and I make a grab for his hair, he increases the power and I detonate around him, pushing my hips up on reflex and shouting out on a rush of desperate breath. He closes his mouth around my core, literally sucking the pulses out of me as I shake like a leaf and my back arches to breaking point.

Jesse moans. 'Hmmm, I can feel you throbbing against my tongue, baby.'

I can't even talk. The influence he has over my body is extraordinary. I don't think I'm weak; I think he's too powerful – he definitely holds the power.

My overworked heart starts to steady its beats as I weave my fingers through his hair, relishing in his attentive mouth dropping tender kisses down the insides of my thighs, nibbling and sucking as he goes. We're in tender lover mode, but for how long could be anyone's guess. I'm not going to try and kid myself that I've heard the last of my contraventions from last night, but I'm quite content to lie here with Jesse nuzzling between my legs for as long as he'll allow.

His teeth clamp lightly onto my clitoris and I shudder, hearing him laugh lightly as he kisses his way up my body until he finds my lips, sharing my release with me, brushing his soft mouth over mine as he gazes down at me. My arms find his shoulders and accept his weight as he buries his face in my neck and sighs, his raging arousal thumping lightly against my thigh. I shift my hips so it falls to my opening.

'You make me so crazy mad, lady.' He breathes into my neck, lifting himself and slowly driving into me on a stifled moan. I whimper, gripping every muscle around him. 'Please don't do that again.' He reaches down and snakes his arm under my knee, pulling it up to drape my leg over his shoulder before bracing his upper body on his forearms. Slowly, he withdraws and lazily works his way in again, his eyes fixed on me.

'I'm sorry,' I murmur, circling my hands in his hair.

He pulls back, driving forward on a groan. 'Ava, everything I do, I do to keep you safe and to keep my sanity. Please listen to me.'

I whimper on another deep, delightful plunge. 'I will.' I confirm, but I'm aware that I'm raging with pleasure and, once again, he can make me say anything he wants. I don't need keeping safe – except, perhaps, from him.

'I need you.' He looks despondent, throwing me off completely. 'I really need you, baby.'

I'm mindless on pleasure, totally swallowed up by him, but he can't keep saying things like that – at least not without elabourating. He's making my brain a knotted mess of coded statements. Is he getting confused with needing and wanting? I'm past the wanting stage and only mildly afraid that I've let myself fall into the realms of really needing this man.

'Why do you need me?' My voice is broken and husky.

'I just do. Please, don't ever leave me.' He plunges forward again, enticing a collective moan.

'Tell me,' I all but groan, clenching at his shoulders but ensuring I keep my eyes fixed on his. I need more than his confounding brainteasers. These shallow waters are becoming muddy as well.

'Just accept that I need you and kiss me.'

I look up at him, torn by my body's need for him and my brain's need for information. He's leisurely working his way in and out of me at the most dreamy pace, gradually encouraging another build-up of pressure to begin. I can't control it.

'Ava, kiss me.'

My body wins. I pull his face down to mine, worshipping his wonderful mouth as he sinks in and out, rolling his narrow hips each time. The mechanical tense of my body sets in as my pleasure peaks and I start to wobble on the edge of release, short sharp breaths escaping as I try and rein in my impending climax.

'Not yet, baby,' He warns softly, grinding hard on another drive forward.

How does he know? I concentrate hard, but with this music and Jesse working my mouth so delicately, I'm really struggling. I claw my fingers into his shoulders, a wordless signal that I'm tipping the edge, and he moans, biting my lip and jerking forward.

'Together,' he mumbles against my mouth.

I nod my acceptance as he increases his strokes and carries us both closer to ultimate ecstasy, all the time maintaining his controlled, accurate drives.

'Nearly there, baby.'

'Jesse!'

'Hold on, just hold on,' he says calmly, plunging forward again, executing a painfully deep, delicious rotation of his hips, pushing himself forward as far as he can.

We both cry out.

'Now, Ava.' He withdraws, driving forward again, harder.

I let it go, feeling him throb and jerk inside me as we swallow each other's moans and both roll over, descending into a calm, unhurried fall into nothing. My flesh trembles around his beating cock and my heart is hammering in my chest.

I kiss him adoringly as he relaxes on me, holding my leg over his shoulder and pushing his body further into me, releasing everything he has, moaning in pure, raw pleasure.

The unwelcome invasion of moisture creeps into my eyes, and I fight real hard to prevent the tears from falling and ruining the moment as he continues to accept my reverent kiss, meeting my slow, sweeping tongue stroke for stroke. I'm trying to tell him something with this kiss. I'm desperate for him to recognise it.

I love you!

He pulls back, breaking our kiss, and frowns at me. 'What's the matter?' he asks softly, his voice full of concern.

'Nothing,' I reply too quickly, mentally cursing my wretched hand for shifting on the back of his head. He searches my eyes, and I relent on a sigh. 'What is this?' I ask as he moves slowly inside me.

'What's what?' The confusion in his voice is quite clear. I kick myself for opening my big mouth.

'I mean me and you.' I feel stupid all of a sudden, wanting to retreat under the covers.

His eyes soften and he swivels his hips slowly. 'This is just you and me,' he says simply, like it really is that simple. He kisses me gently, releasing my leg. 'Are you okay?'

'Fine,' I reply, more harshly than I intended. Is this man so thick-skinned he can't see a woman in love when she's lying underneath him?

You and me, me and you. That much is bloody obvious. I don't see anyone else in bed with us. I wriggle a little underneath him, and he narrows his sludgy eyes on me.

'I need a wee.' I say in my most convincing I'm-not-upset tone. I fail miserably.

He latches onto his bottom lip, eyeing me suspiciously, but he pulls out, reluctantly freeing me from beneath him. I reach around to unclasp my bra before I make my way to the bathroom, shutting the door behind me.

Why can't I just say it? I need to rid my mouth of the words that are causing me so much bloody agony. He must know how I feel. I drop to the feet of this man like a slave, giving my mind and body up to him at the drop of a hat. I don't believe, not for a moment, that he doesn't recognise all these signs.

I brace my hands on the vanity unit, letting out a long sigh. This is not where I planned to be but I'm here, skirting precariously close to a broken heart. The thought of my life without him in it ... I reach up and rub my chest. The very thought has my heart constricting in pain.

I jump when the door opens and he strolls in, all naked and stunningly glorious. He positions himself behind me, resting his hands on my waist, his chin on my shoulder. Our eyes lock together for the longest time.

'I thought we made friends?' he questions on a slight pucker of his beautiful brow.

'We did,' I shrug. I had expected far more retribution than what I just received. Yes, he shredded the taboo dress, but all things considered, he's been quite reasonable today.

'Then why are you sulking?'

'I'm not sulking,' I say, oversensitive. It's bloody obvious that I am.

He shakes his head on a long, tired sigh and circles his hips against my lower back. He's hard again. He's going to distract me from my sulks with his unreasonable sexual manipulation.

'Ava, you're the most frustrating woman I've ever met.'

My eyes widen at his cheek. He thinks I'm frustrating? His mouth clamps onto my neck, penetrating me with heat.

'Are you holding out on me for a reason, lady?'

'No,' I breathe. I never hold out on him. I give myself up to him, unreservedly and willing, every time. A little gentle persuasion is sometimes required, but he gets what he wants in the end.

He reaches down and slowly starts rubbing his palm up and down between my thighs. It's the perfect amount of friction at the perfect tempo. I hold his eyes in the mirror. Fucking hell, I'm gagging for him again. I drop my head back, giving him perfect access to my neck, his tongue working a firm, heavy trail up the column of my throat, circling at the sensitive hollow under my ear.

'You want it again?' he teases in my ear as he works my core.

'I need you.'

'Baby, those words make me so happy. Always?'

'Always,' I confirm.

He growls his approval. 'Fuck, I need to be inside you.' He yanks my hips forward and positions himself at my entrance before hammering into me on an ear-piercing yell that echoes around the vast bathroom.

'Oh, shit, Jesse!' I support myself on the vanity unit, bracing myself for the onslaught.

He crashes forward. 'Watch ... your ... mouth!'

I'm subjected to a relentless, desperate round of punishing blows as he yells like a man possessed, yanking me back, impaling me to the most excruciating depths. My head is spinning, my body abused, and I'm out of my mind on the most intense, painful and pleasurable drug that is Mr Challenging himself.

I drop my limp head, and his hands move to my shoulders. 'Look at me!' he yells, pounding me with a purposeful blow at his demand. I draw in a sharp breath, drag my heavy head up and find him in the mirror, but it's hard to focus. I'm being thundered forward, my arms struggling to hold me as he slaps against my backside on continuous groans. His frown line is so deep, his neck muscles strained. The demanding, brutal sex Lord has returned.

'You'll never hold out on me, will you, Ava?' he barks through laboured grunts.

'No!'

'Because you're never leaving me, are you?'

Oh, here we go again. All the coded sex talk scrambles my brain more than the formidable assault my body is under. 'Where the fuck am I going?' I scream in frustration on another merciless blow.

'Mouth!' he roars urgently. 'Say it, Ava!'

'Oh God!' I cry. My knees buckle and his hands move quickly to my waist, capturing me, my world going completely silent as I ride out the vibration of waves that piston through me so harshly, I think my heart might have ceased from shock.

'Jesus!' He falls to the floor, rolling onto his back so I'm laying across him, my back to his front, his arms sprawled out at his sides. I'm being heaved up and down on top of him, my mind is a foggy, churned-up mess, and my poor body is wondering what the hell just happened. That was a sense fuck if ever there was one. But for what purpose?

'I'm fu ...' I snap my mouth shut before I earn myself another scorn, but he still lifts an arm and finds my hip to have a little dig. 'Hey!' I complain. I suppressed the urge. It's an improvement.

He engulfs me in his arms and inhales into my neck. 'You didn't say it.'

'What? That I won't leave you? I won't leave you. Happy?'

'Yes, I am, but that's not what I meant.'

'What did you mean?'

He exhales deeply into my ear. 'Never mind, want to go again?'

I splutter on a laboured breath. I know I won't be able to say no – for a start, he won't let me. I feel the slight jerk of a hushed chuckle under me.

'Absolutely. I can't get enough of you.' I keep my voice steady and serious.

He freezes under me, but then increases his vice-like hold. 'I'm glad. I feel exactly the same. But my heart has been through enough in the last twenty-four hours, what with your defiance and lack of obedience. I don't know how much more it can take.'

'It must be your age.'

'Hey, lady.' He rolls us over so I'm face down on the bathroom floor and he's blanketing me. He bites my ear, blowing hot breath into it. 'My age has nothing to do with it.' He chomps at my lobe a bit more as I writhe under him. 'It's you!' he says accusingly, grabbing my hip.

'No!' I scream, making a futile attempt to free myself. 'Okay, I give in!'

'I wish you fucking would,' he grumbles, releasing me.

'Old man,' I mutter on a grin.

I'm pulled to my feet in lightning speed and pushed up the wall, my arms pinned above my head. I purse my lips to suppress my laugh. 'I prefer God,' he notifies me, hitting me with a heart-stopping kiss, thrusting his body against mine and pushing me up the wall. 'I really can't get enough of you, lady.'

I smile.

'You're my ultimate temptress.' He sweeps over my face with his lips, and I sigh against him. 'Are you hungry?' he asks.

'Yes.' I'm famished, actually.

'Good.' He matches my smile. 'I've fucked you, and now I'm going to feed you.' He tucks me under his arm and walks us into the bedroom. 'Put lace on,' he says softly, making his way into the wardrobe and appearing a few minutes later in some green, striped lounge pants. I smile. I love him in sludgy green. 'I'll meet you in the kitchen. Deal?'

'Deal,' I confirm quietly. He winks before striding out of the bedroom, leaving me to find my lace.

I look around the room for any signs of my bag, seeing nothing, so I wander into the wardrobe but only find my dresses and shoes. He said a few days. There's more than a few days' worth of clothes in here, all hanging neatly in their own little space. I smile at the thought of Jesse making a little gap for me in his vast wardrobe.

With my towel still wrapped around me, I make my way downstairs to the kitchen, finding Jesse with his head in the fridge.

'I can't find my stuff,' I inform the fridge door.

His head pops up from behind the fridge, his eyes running up and down my towel-clad body. 'I'll take naked,' he says, shutting the door and sauntering over to me with a jar of peanut butter. 'Cathy's off and the fridge is empty. I'll order in. What do you fancy?'

'You,' I grin.

He smiles, reaches forward and whips the towel off, throwing it to the side and running his appreciative gaze down my naked body. 'Your god needs to feed his temptress.' He flashes his dancing eyes to mine. 'The rest of your stuff is in that dirty great big wooden truck that you had dumped in my bedroom. What do you want to eat?'

I ignore him and shrug. I could eat anything. 'I'm easy.'

'I know, but what do you want to eat?'

'I'm only easy with you.'

'You fucking better be. Now, tell me, what do you want to eat?'

'I like anything. You choose. What time is it, anyway?' I've lost all concept of time. In fact, I lose all concept of everything when I'm with him.

'Seven. Go and take a shower before I abandon dinner and take you again.' He turns me around, smacking my backside to send me on my way.

I take my naked body back up the stairs to fulfill his instructions, and when I reach the top, I glance down and see Jesse standing by the archway to the kitchen, quietly watching me. I blow him a kiss as I disappear into the bedroom, just catching a glimpse of his knee-trembling smile as he vanishes from view.

'I was just coming to find you.' He pauses from forking various dishes onto two plates. 'I like your shirt.'

I look down at the white shirt I snatched from his wardrobe. 'Kate didn't pack me any slobby clothes.'

'She didn't?' He raises an eyebrow, and I know instantly, Kate did pack me some slobby clothes. That or she didn't pack at all – I suspect it's the latter. 'Where do you want to eat?'

'I'm e—' I snap my mouth shut on a shrug.

'Only for me, yes?' He grins, shoving a bottle of water under his arm and picking up the plates. 'We'll slum it on the sofa.' He leads me into the colossal open space and nods at the gigantic sofa, so I sit in the corner section, accepting the plate he hands me. It smells delicious and it's Chinese. Perfect.

The doors on the massive television cabinet start sliding across, revealing the biggest frameless flat-screen TV I've ever laid my eyes on.

'Do you want to watch television or would you prefer music and conversation?' He looks at me on a small smile as my fork hangs out of my mouth. I didn't realise how hungry I was.

I chew and swallow as soon as I can. 'I'll take music and conversation, please.' That was an easy choice. He nods, like he knew that would be my answer, and the next thing I know, the room is swamped in the calming tones of Mumford and Sons.

'Good?'

I glance over and find him facing me, one knee up and his

arm resting on the back of the sofa holding his plate. 'Very. You don't cook?'

'I don't.'

I smile around my fork. 'Why, Mr Ward, is that something you *don't* do well?'

'I can't be amazing at everything,' he says, completely straight-faced, studying me closely. He really is an overconfident arse.

'Your housekeeper cooks for you?'

'If I ask her to, but most of the time I eat at The Manor.'

I suppose it makes sense that he'd take advantage of the lovely food at his disposal. I know I would. 'How old are you?'

He pauses with his fork midway to his mouth. 'Thirty-ish.' He takes his forkful of food, watching me as he chews.

'-ish,' I mouth.

'Yes, -ish,' he counters, a smile playing on the corners of his lips.

I return to my food, not in the least bit bothered by his vague answer. I'll keep asking, and he'll keep evading. Maybe I should try with my own versions of persuasion – maybe a truth fuck or a countdown? What would I do to him on zero? I drift into musing over exactly what I could do on zero, between mouthfuls of my Chinese dinner. I can think of plenty, but nothing I could carry out with ease. He'd overpower me, very easily. The countdown is off the menu, so it's a truth fuck then. I need to invent the truth fuck. What could I do?

'Ava?'

I look up, finding Jesse and his frown line studying me. 'Yes?'

'Dreaming?' he asks, his voice laced with concern.

'Sorry.' I put my fork down. 'I was miles away.'

'You were.' He takes my plate and slides it onto the coffee table. 'Where were you?' He reaches over to pull me into his lap.

I snuggle happily. 'Nowhere.'

He shifts up the sofa, taking my place in the corner, and

positions me under his arm. I rest my cheek on his bare chest, throw my leg over his groin and inhale him in his entire fresh water splendor, letting the soft music and the feel of Jesse ease me into a peaceful rest.

'I love having you here,' he says quietly, playing with a lock of my hair.

I really love being here too, but not as a puppet. Would it always be like this? I could do exactly this, day in, day out – it's been a lovely day. But could I live with the controlling, unreasonable side of him?

I run my finger along the line of his scar. 'I love being here too,' I whisper.

'Good. So you'll stay?'

'Yes. Tell me how you got this.'

He reaches down, clasping my hand to prevent any further touching of the area. 'Ava, I really don't like talking about it.'

Oh? 'I'm sorry.' I feel bad. That was a plea. Something terrible happened to him, and it makes me feel sick to know that he was hurt in some way.

He pulls my hand up to his face and kisses my palm. 'Please, don't be. It's not something that's important to the here and now. Dragging up my past serves no purpose other than to remind me of it.'

His past? So he has a past? Well, everyone has a past, but the way he said it and the fact that we're talking about a vicious scar here makes me really nervous. I look up at him. 'What did you mean when you said that things are easier to bear when I'm here?'

He looks down and places his hand on the back of my head, pushing my cheek back down to his chest. 'It means I like having you around.' His tone is dismissive. I don't believe him for a minute, but I leave it anyway. Does it matter?

I push my lips into the void between his pecs, nuzzling into him while giving myself a mental ticking off. I'm basking in the sun on Central Jesse Cloud Nine, and I'm loving every minute of it, until the need for another countdown or a sense fuck.

And it will come – I have no doubt.

Chapter Thirty

I wake abruptly and sit up in bed. I feel refreshed, revitalised and rested. The only thing that's missing is Jesse.

I peek under the covers, finding I'm still in my underwear, but the shirt has been removed. I don't remember coming to bed. I sit quietly for a few moments, listening to a constant whirring sound, accompanied by a consistent *thud thud thud* in the distance.

What is that?

I make the long journey to the edge of the bed and out onto the landing, where the sounds are slightly louder but still muffled. Scanning the space below, I see no sign of Jesse, so deciding he must be in the kitchen I make my way down the stairs.

As I approach the archway into the kitchen, I stop and back track, looking through the glass door to the gym, set on an angle just before the kitchen. Jesse is there, in a pair of running shorts, going hell for leather on the treadmill. I watch him running with his back to me, his solid expanse of skin shimmering with sweat beads as he watches the sports news on the suspended TV in front of him.

I leave him be. I've already disturbed one run, so I make my way into the kitchen to fill the kettle and go about making myself a coffee.

The familiar sound of my phone's ring tone fills the room, and I look across the kitchen to see it charging on the worktop. I scoop it up and disconnect it from the charger. It's my mother, and I'm promptly reminded of her call to me yesterday – the one that I've not yet returned and really, *really* don't want to. My wide awake, good mood is instantly drowned out.

'Hi, Mum,' I greet cheerfully, screwing my face up in apprehension. Here come the twenty questions.

'Oh, you're alive. Joseph, cancel the search party. I've found her!'

I roll my eyes at my mum's idea of funny. 'Point taken. What did Matt want?'

'I have no idea. The man never called us once when you were together. He asked how we were, made small talk, you know. Why is he calling us, Ava?'

'I don't know, Mum,' I moan tiredly.

'He mentioned another man.'

'He did?' My tone is high-pitched, a complete giveaway to my surprise and probably my guilt, too. Damn you, Jesse Ward, for intercepting my phone. It would have been easier to brush off Matt's tales if I didn't have to explain about the mystery man who answered my phone yesterday.

'Yes, he said you were seeing someone else. So soon, Ava. Really?'

'Mum, I'm not seeing someone else.' I do a quick check over my shoulder to make sure I'm still alone. I'm doing more than seeing someone. I'm in love with someone.

'Who was that man who answered your phone?'

'I told you, just a friend.'

'Good. You're in your mid-twenties, in London Town and fresh out of a shitty relationship. Don't be falling into the arms of the first man who shows you a bit of attention.'

I blush scarlet on the spot, even though she can't see me. I don't think you could describe what this man gives me as 'a bit of attention'. At only forty-seven herself and having had Dan at just eighteen and me at twenty-one, she missed out on all the benefits of being young in London. I know she won't be pleased if she finds out I'm being swallowed up in lust.

'I won't, Mum. I'm just having lots of fun,' I assure her. I'm having fun all right. Just not the sort of fun that she has in mind. 'How's Dad?'

'Oh, you know. Golf mad, badminton mad, cricket mad. He has to keep on the go or *he'll* go mad.'

'It's better than sitting on his backside all day, though,' I say, collecting a mug from the cupboard and making my way to the fridge.

'He made such a fuss about leaving the city, but I knew he would be dead in a few years if I didn't get him out. Now I can't tie him down for anything. He's always got something happening.'

I open the fridge – no milk. 'That's good, isn't it? Keeping him active?' I sit myself on the barstool without my needed coffee.

'Oh, I'm not complaining. He's lost a few pounds too.'

'How much?' This is good. Everyone always said that Dad was a walking heart attack candidate, with his weight, love of a few too many pints and a stressful job. As it turns out, everyone was right.

'Just over a stone.'

'Wow, I'm impressed.'

'No more than me, Ava. So, what have you got to report?'

Loads! 'Nothing much. I've been stacked out at work. I se-cured the next project from the developer of Lusso.' I need to talk work. I'll have no hair left if she starts prying into my social life.

'Brilliant! I was showing Sue the photos on the Internet. The penthouse!' she sings.

'Yeah.' Forget coffee. I need some wine.

'Can you imagine living in such luxury? Your dad and I are not short of a few, but that's a whole other level of wealth.'

'It is,' I agree. Okay, the subject of work hasn't gone as I planned. 'What time does Dan land tomorrow?' I blurt out to divert the conversation.

'Nine in the morning. Are you coming down with him?'

I flop forward onto the worktop. I've hardly given Dan's impending arrival a second thought, what with all the crazy shit going on.

'I don't think so, Mum. I'm just so busy,' I whine, mentally pleading for her to understand.

'That's disappointing, but I understand. Maybe Dad and I could come up to see you when you've sorted a place of your own?' She's hinting that I need to pull my finger out. I've done nothing in that area of my life.

'That would be really good.' I don't fake my enthusiasm. I would love for Mum and Dad to come back to London for a visit.

'Wonderful. I'll speak to your dad. I'd better go. Send my love to Kate.'

'I will. I'll ring next week when Dan's there,' I add quickly before she hangs up.

'Lovely. Take care, darling.'

'Bye, Mum.' I slide my phone across the counter and drop my head in my hands.

If only she knew. My dad would probably have another heart attack if he found out about my current state of affairs, and my mum would be moving me down to Newquay. The only reason my dad didn't drive up after Matt and I split up was because Mum called Kate to find out if I really was okay. What would they think if they knew I was caught up with a neurotic, self-assured control freak, who is – in his own words – fucking me into oblivion? The fact that he's super-wealthy and owns the penthouse would not soften the blow. Christ, Jesse is probably closer to my mum in age than I am.

I swing round on my stool when I hear a commotion coming from outside of the kitchen. Getting up to go and investigate, I'm nearly taken off my feet when Jesse's naked chest comes flying at me.

WHOAH-!

'Fucking hell, there you are.' He grabs me, lifting me up to his sweat-riddled body. 'You weren't in bed.'

'I'm in the kitchen,' I splutter in my dazed state. He's squeezing me so tight I'm struggling to breathe. 'I saw you running. I didn't want to disturb you.' I wriggle a little to indicate that I'm being constricted to death and he releases me, setting me back on my feet, his glistening, stubbled face giving me the once over. His panicked features ease a bit as he holds me steady by my forearms in front of him. 'I was just in the kitchen,' I repeat. He looks like he could keel over at any moment. What's wrong with him?

He shakes his head slightly, as if ridding himself of a nasty thought, picks me up and walks me to the worktop, sitting me on the cold marble. He pushes his way between my thighs.

'Sleep well?'

'Great.' Why does he look like someone's broken some really crappy news? 'Are you okay?'

He blesses me with a heart-stopping smile. I feel instantly at ease. 'I woke up with you in my bed wearing lace. It's ten-thirty on a Sunday morning and you're in my kitchen …' he runs his eyes down my front, 'wearing lace. I'm amazing.'

'You are?'

'Oh, I am.' He tips my face up, planting a light kiss on my lips. Oh, I could wake up to this every morning. 'You're too beautiful, lady.'

'So are you.'

He brushes the hair away from my face, looking at me affectionately. 'Kiss me.'

I fulfill his request immediately, taking his lips calmly and following the slow, gentle strokes of his tongue. We both hum in harmony, but our intimate moment is broken by the loud shrill of Jesse's phone.

He grumbles and reaches past me, still maintaining our kiss, and glances up at the screen as he holds it over my head. 'Oh, go away,' he gripes against my lips. 'Baby, I've got to take this.' He pulls away and answers, keeping himself firmly between my thighs, his free hand around my waist. 'What's up, John?' He starts chewing his lip. 'What's he doing there?' he asks, dropping a chaste kiss on my lips. 'No, I'll be there … yes … see you in a bit.' He hangs up and studies me thoughtfully for a few seconds. 'I need to go to The Manor. You'll come.'

I recoil. 'No!' I blurt. I'm not being yanked off Central Jesse Cloud Nine by *her*!

He frowns. 'But I want you to come.'

Absolutely not! It's Sunday, I'm not working, and I'm not going to The Manor. 'You'll be working.' I search my brain for a feasible excuse for me *not* to go. 'You do what you need to do, and I'll see you afterward,' I reason instead.

'No, you'll come,' he presses forcefully.

'I'm not coming.' I try to wriggle myself free of his grasp, but I'm going nowhere.

'Why?'

'Just because,' I snap, earning myself a mighty scowl. I'm not about to start whining about Sarah and offloading trivial jealousies on him.

He searches my eyes. 'Please, Ava. Will you just do what you're told?'

'No!' I shout.

I watch as he closes his eyes, clearly trying to gather some patience, but I don't care. He can force me to do many things, but I'm not going to The Manor. I sit on the worktop, waiting for him to disintegrate under my disobedience.

'Ava, why do you insist on making things more difficult?'

'I make things more difficult?' I gape at him. It's him who needs some sense fucking into him.

'Yes, you do. I'm trying really hard here.'

'Trying hard to do what? Send me crazy? It's working!' I beat him away from me and storm out of the kitchen, hearing him curse as he follows me up the stairs.

'Okay!' he yells from behind me. 'You will wait here. I'll be as quick as I can.'

'I'll go home,' I shout over my shoulder, continuing on my way and shutting myself in the bathroom when I get there. I'm not waiting around for him to come back. His being reasonable and relenting to my refusal to go with him has just been trampled by the follow-up of 'you *will* wait here'. I WILL do no such thing! I splash my face with cold water to try and cool down my raging temper. Why has he not given me the countdown? That's what he usually does when I don't conform.

I hear him in the bedroom on his phone, and wondering who he's talking to, I open the door.

'See you in a while.' He hangs up, throwing his phone on the bed. Who is he seeing in a while? He stands with his back to me for a long time, his head dropped. He's thinking, and I feel like an impostor all of a sudden.

Eventually, he exhales heavily and turns toward me. He watches me for a short time before heading into the bathroom to take a shower, leaving me standing in the middle of the room wondering what to do. He's acting strange. No countdown; no manhandling. What's going on? Yesterday was so perfect, and now I'm back to mind meltdown. It looks like I didn't need Sarah to yank me off Central Jesse Cloud Nine after all. I've managed to do that all by myself.

Ten minutes later, I'm still standing twiddling my thumbs, trying to work out what to do with myself. I hear the shower shut off, and he comes out of the bathroom, heading straight into the wardrobe without a word. I'm troubled by his defeated expression that also harbours a bit of sorrow. I think I actually want him to explode or give me the countdown. I have no idea what he's thinking, and it's the most frustrating feeling in the world.

He appears at the wardrobe door. 'I need to go,' he utters regretfully. He looks completely tormented. 'Kate's on her way over.'

I frown. 'Why?'

'So you don't leave.' He goes back into the wardrobe, me following swiftly behind.

Pulling some jeans on, he looks up at me briefly but gives nothing away. He grabs a black t-shirt from a hanger, pulling it on over his head quickly before he sets about getting his Converse on.

'I'm going home,' I assert, but he still doesn't look at me. What's wrong with him? I can feel my temper flaring at his lack of receptiveness, and not knowing what else to do, I start pulling down my clothes from the hangers, draping them over my arms as I do.

'What are you doing?' He takes them from my hands, hanging them back up. 'You're not leaving,' he growls.

'Yes I am,' I shout, yanking them back down.

'Put the fucking clothes back, Ava!'

I hear a rip of material as I fight him, and within a few seconds, my arms are free of clothes and I'm being hauled from the wardrobe. I'm pinned to the bed, struggling against him in complete defiance, but I go nowhere. If he tries to fuck me, I'll scream!

'Calm the fuck down!' he yells, grabbing my jaw and pulling it to the centre so I have to look at him. I slam my eyes shut, puffing and panting like an exhausted greyhound. I'm not going to let him manipulate me with sex. 'Open your eyes, Ava.'

'No!' I sound so childish, but I know if I do I'll be swallowed up in lust.

'Open!' He shakes my jaw slightly.

'No!'

'Fine,' he shouts, while I continue to struggle. 'Listen to me, lady. You're not going anywhere. I've told you repeatedly, so start fucking dealing with it!' He shifts his body so he has a firmer grip on me. 'I'm going to The Manor, and when I get back we're going to sit down to talk about us.'

I stop struggling. Talk about us? What? Like a proper discussion about what the hell is going on here? Because I'm desperate to know this.

'Cards on the table, Ava. No more fucking about, no more drunken confessions and no more holding out on me. Do you understand?' His breathing is heavy, his tone determined.

This is what I've wanted all along – clarity and understanding of our relationship. I'm so bloody confused. I need to know what all this is and then, maybe, I can work out whether I need to break away. And what's this about drunken confessions and holding out?

I open my eyes to sludgy green gazing down at me. He relaxes his grip on my jaw. 'Come with me, I need you with me.' He's almost pleading.

'Why?'

'I just do. Why won't you come?'

I take a deep breath. 'I don't feel comfortable.'

'Why don't you feel comfortable?'

'I just don't,' I snap.

His brow knits and he commences lip chomping. 'Please, Ava.'

I shake my head. 'I'm not coming.'

He sighs. 'Promise me that you'll be here when I get home then. We need to sort this shit out.'

'I'll be here,' I assure him. I'm desperate to sort this shit out, too. I'm not going anywhere.

'Thank you,' he whispers, resting his forehead on mine and clenching his eyes shut. I feel immense hope blossoming inside me at his determination to *sort this shit out*.

He lifts himself, without so much as kissing me, grabs his phone and leaves the room.

I stay on the bed, recovering from my pointless physical battle, wondering what's going to be established from the laying of cards and sorting of shit. I'm torn between admitting to him how I feel, or waiting to hear what he has to say first. What will he say? So much needs clarifying. What is *us*? An intense, hot affair or more? I need it to be more, but I can't cope with his trampling and unreasonableness. It's exhausting.

There was no denying the look of pure torment on his handsome face. What's running through that complex mind of his? Why does he need me? So many questions …

I close my eyes, trying to re-establish some steady breaths, and find myself drifting into a semi-exhausted coma, but the phone next to the bed starts ringing, snapping my eyes open.

Kate! I scramble up the bed and answer. 'Send her up, Clive.' I fling a t-shirt on and run down the stairs, throwing the door open as Kate exits the lift. I'm so glad to see her, but why he thinks I need babysitting is beyond me. I run at her, flinging my arms around her desperately.

'Whoah! Is someone happy to see me?' She returns my violent hug, my face buried in her red locks. I didn't realise how much I needed to see her. 'Are you going to invite me into the tower, or are we staying put?'

I pull away. 'Sorry.' I blow my hair out of my face. 'I'm a mess, Kate. And you've been letting men rummage through my things again.' I add on a scowl.

'Ava, he turned up at six in the morning, banging until Sam answered. I just let him do his thing. It's not like anyone can stop him. The man's a rhinoceros.'

'He's more than that.'

She looks at me all sorrowful, taking my hand and leading me back into the penthouse. 'I can't believe he lives here,' she mutters, directing me into the kitchen. 'Sit.' She points to a stool.

I rest my backside on the seat, watching as Kate refreshes her memory of the impressive kitchen. 'I can't make you tea because he has no milk. The housekeeper is on holiday.'

'He has a housekeeper,' she says to herself. 'Of course he does.' She shakes her head and goes to the fridge, collecting two bottles of water before coming to sit next to me. 'What's going on?'

'What am I going to do, Kate?' I rest my head in my hands. 'I can't believe he called you here, just so I don't leave.'

'Doesn't that tell you something?'

'Yes, that he's a control freak. He's so intense,' I look up to Kate, who's smiling faintly. What's there to smile about? I'm in turmoil here. 'I don't know where I am with him.'

'Have you told him?' she asks, with a perfectly plucked brow arched at me.

'No. I can't.'

'Why?' she blurts.

'Kate, I don't know what I am to him. He can be so gentle and loving, saying things I can't get my head around, and the next minute, he's brutally fierce, unreasonable and controlling. He tries to control me!' I open my water, taking a swig to moisten my dry mouth. 'He manipulates me with sex when I don't jump at his command, tramples anyone, including me, if they get in his way. He's bordering on impossible.'

Kate looks at me with compassion in her bright blues. 'Sam told me he's never seen Jesse like this before. Apparently, he's famed for his easygoing nature.'

I laugh. I could describe Jesse with many words. *Easygoing* would not feature anywhere on my list. 'Kate, he's not easygoing, trust me.'

'You obviously bring out the worst in him.' She smiles.

'Obviously,' I agree. 'He brings out the worst in me too. He hates me swearing, so I do it more. He has an issue with exposing my flesh to anyone other than him, so I wear shorter dresses. He tells me not to get drunk, so I do. It's not healthy, Kate. One second he tells me that he loves having me around, the next I'm his current fuck. What am I supposed to think?'

'But you're still here,' she says thoughtfully. 'And you're not going to get any answers if you don't ask the damn questions.'

'I do ask questions.'

'The right ones?'

What are the right questions? I look at my best friend and wonder why she's not kidnapping me from the tower and hiding me away from Jesse. She's seen him in action – surely that would be enough for any best friend to intervene. 'Why are you not telling me to leg it?' I ask suspiciously. 'Is it because he bought you a van?'

'Don't be stupid, Ava. I would toss that van right back at him if you wanted me to. You're more important. I'm not telling you to leg it because I know you don't want to. What you need to be doing is telling him how you feel, negotiating acceptable levels of intensity.' She grins. 'In the bedroom is fine, yes?'

I smile. 'He said he'd make sure I'll always need him. He has. I really need him, Kate.'

'Talk to him, Ava.' She gives me a little nudge on the shoulder. 'You can't go on like this.' She shakes her head.

I definitely can't go on like this; I'll be in an asylum within a month. My heart and brain are being yanked from one side to the other by the hour. If it means slapping my heart down on the table for him to trample all over, then so be it. At least I'll know where I am. I'll recover … eventually … I think.

I stand up. 'Will you take me to The Manor?' I ask. I need to do this now before I bottle it. I need to tell him how I feel.

Kate springs up from the stool. 'Yes!' she sings enthusiastically. 'I've been dying to see this place.'

'It's a hotel, Kate.' I roll my eyes, but let her have her

excitement. My car's at hers, so I'm kind of stuck without her. 'Give me five.' I run upstairs to change into my jeans and ballet pumps, meeting Kate at the front door in record time. I send Jesse a quick text to tell him I'm on my way.

It's time to lay my cards on the table.

Chapter Thirty-one

We walk into the Sunday evening sunshine, but I don't see Margo Junior. I scan the car park for the big, pink van, but it's not like you can miss the giant heap of metal.

'Oh, I hope you don't mind.' Kate laughs nervously, just as I spot my Mini, roof down and parked in one of Jesse's spaces.

'You're a cheeky cow!'

She waves off my insult. 'Don't you narrow those big browns on me, Ava O'Shea. If I didn't drive her, then she would be sitting outside the house for eternity. It's a waste.' The indicators flash, and I put my hand out for the keys, which she reluctantly hands over on a huff.

We drive out toward the Surrey Hills discussing the merits of domineering men. We both reach the same conclusion: yes to sex and no to all other aspects of a relationship.

The problem is, Jesse manages to drag sex into all aspects of our relationship, using it, mostly, to get his way. This could all be over within an hour, and even though his overbearing ways are difficult to deal with, the thought sends an unbearable ache to my stomach. But I have to be sensible here. I'm already in way over my head.

I pull off the main road, up to the gates, and they open immediately, letting me through.

'Holy shit!' Kate exclaims as we drive up the long gravel driveway, flanked by trees.

She's in awe already and she hasn't even seen the house yet. We eventually emerge into the courtyard. It's busy.

'Holy fucking shit!' She gapes at the imposing property, leaning forward in her seat. 'Jesse owns this?'

'He does. There's Sam's car.' I pull into a space next to the Porsche.

'I can't believe he comes here to have lunch,' she grumbles, joining me on my side of the car. 'Holy fucking shit!'

I laugh at Kate's amazement – she doesn't shock easily. I lead her toward the steps, expecting to find John greeting us, but he doesn't appear. Instead, I find the double doors ajar, so I push my way through, looking back at Kate. She's gazing around, openmouthed and wide-eyed.

'Kate, shut your mouth,' I scorn her lightly.

'Sorry.' She snaps her mouth shut. 'This is one fancy place.'

'I know.'

'I want a tour,' she says, craning her neck to look up the stairs.

'Get Sam to give you a tour,' I say. 'I need to see Jesse.' I head past the restaurant and toward the bar, spotting Sam and Drew immediately.

Sam gives me a huge, cheeky grin as he swigs his beer, but spits it out when Kate follows in behind me. 'Fuck! What are you doing here?' he splutters.

Drew turns, clocks Kate and breaks out in uncontrollable laughter. I frown, and Kate looks less than delighted.

'I'm pleased to see you, too, dick!' she spits indignantly at a stunned Sam.

He quickly shoves his beer on the bar, pulling a stool up close to him. 'Sit!' He bashes the top of the stool, giving Drew a worried look.

'Don't order me about, Samuel!' The look of disgust on her face is fierce. I've never seen Sam so twitchy before.

He pats the stool again, smiling nervously at her. 'Please.'

Kate makes her way over, resting her bum on the stool, and Sam pulls her even closer. She'll be on his lap soon.

'Buy me a drink,' she demands on a half-smile.

'Just one,' he affirms, signaling to Mario. Jesus, he's breaking out in a sweat. 'Ava?'

'No, I'm good. I'm going to find Jesse.' I start walking backward.

'Does he know you're here?' Sam asks, all wide-eyed.

What's the matter with him? 'I sent him a text.' I glance around the bar, seeing plenty of familiar faces from my previous few visits to The Manor. I'm pleased to note there's no Sarah, but this means nothing, of course. She could be anywhere in this huge house. 'But he didn't reply,' I add. It's only now I realise how strange that is.

Sam gives Drew a nervous look, prompting Drew to laugh harder. 'Wait here. I'll go and get him.'

'I know where his office is,' I say on a frown.

'Ava, will you just wait here?' Sam's face is pure panic. It makes me suspicious. He fixes Kate with a stern glare as he gets up. 'Don't move.'

'How much have you had to drink?' Kate asks, eyeing his bottle of beer. Has Kate picked up on his unease too?

'This is my first and last, trust me. I'm going to get Jesse, then we're leaving.' He looks around the bar nervously. I'm convinced he's hiding someone or something. I'm beginning to wish Sarah *was* in here because then I would know for sure that she isn't with Jesse.

He jogs off, leaving Kate and I exchanging puzzled faces.

'Excuse me, ladies,' Drew gets up. 'Nature calls.' He leaves us at the bar like a couple of spare parts.

'Oh, fuck this,' Kate exclaims, taking my hand. 'Give me the tour.' She pulls me back toward the entrance hall.

'A quick one,' I agree, taking over the lead and guiding her up the massive staircase. 'I'll show you the rooms I'm working on.'

We reach the balcony landing and Kate's gasps increase as she takes in the opulent splendor of The Manor. 'This is some serious special,' she mumbles, gazing around in awe.

'I know. He inherited the place from his uncle when he was twenty-one.'

'Twenty-one?'

'Hmmm.'

'Wow!' Kate blurts. I look behind me, finding her gawking at the huge stained-glass window at the foot of the second staircase.

'This way,' I call behind me, walking through the archway that leads to the extension rooms, leaving Kate to scuttle after me. 'There are ten altogether.'

She follows me into the middle of the last room, gazing around. I can't deny, they are mighty impressive, even as empty shells. Once completed, though, they'll be royal worthy. But will I get through to completion? After our little *sorting of shit* I might not see this place again. I can't say that would disappoint me. I don't like coming here.

I wander farther into the room and follow Kate's gaze to the wall behind the door. 'What's that?' Kate asks the question that's batting around in my own head.

'I don't know. It wasn't here before.' I run my eyes over the huge, wooden, crucifix-style cross propped up against the wall. With giant, black, wrought-iron screw eyes bolted to the corners, it looks imposing, but it's still a fine piece of art. 'It must be one of the big wall hangings that Jesse was talking about.' I approach the piece, running my hand over the highly polished wood. It's spectacular – if a little intimidating.

'Oh. Sorry, ladies.' We both swing around, finding a middle-aged man in overalls holding a sander in one hand and a coffee in the other. 'Looks good, huh?' He points up at the frame with his sander as he takes a slurp of his coffee. 'I'm just checking the size before I make the others.'

'You made this?' I ask in disbelief.

'I certainly did.' He laughs, joining me by the cross.

'It's stunning,' I muse. It'll fit in perfectly with the bed I designed that Jesse loved so much.

'Thank you, miss,' he says proudly. I turn around and see Kate observing the piece of art on a frown.

'We'll leave you to it.' I give Kate the let's-be-going nod, and she smiles at the workman before following me out of the room.

We walk back through to the gallery landing. 'I didn't get it,' she grumbles.

'It's art, Kate.' I laugh.

'What's up there?'

I follow her gaze up the staircase to the top floor, stopping to look with her. Those intimidating doors are slightly ajar. 'I don't know. I think it might be a function room.'

Kate takes the stairs. 'Let's have a look.'

'Kate!' I start after her. 'Kate, come on.'

'Just a peek,' she says, pushing against the doors. 'Fuck!' she screeches. 'Ava, look at this.'

Okay, my curiosity has been well and truly teased. I run the rest of the way up the stairs and into the function room, skidding to an abrupt halt next to Kate.

Fucking hell!

'Excuse me!'

We both look in the direction of the foreign-accented voice, and a dumpy lady holding cleaning cloths and anti-bacterial spray comes wobbling toward us. 'No, no, no. I clean. The communal room is closed for cleaning.' She shoos us back toward the door.

'Chill out, Señorita,' Kate says with a laugh. 'Her boyfriend owns the place.'

The poor woman recoils at Kate's harshness, giving me the once over before bowing. 'I'm so sorry.' She shoves the spray in her apron and clasps my hands in her tanned wrinkled fingers. 'Mr. Ward, he not say you come.'

I fidget uncomfortably on the spot at the woman's panic, throwing Kate a disgusted look, but she doesn't notice. She's too busy looking around at the colossal room we're standing in. I smile reassuringly at the Spanish cleaner, who's got herself in a bit of a pickle over my presence.

'It's fine, really,' I assure her. She bows again, moving off to the side, leaving Kate and I to try and comprehend our surroundings.

I gaze around, and the first thing that strikes me is how beautiful the room is. Just like the rest of the house, this room has been lavished with beautiful materials and furniture. The space is huge, easily spanning half of the entire building's floor area, and as I look around I realise that it backs onto itself, circling around the stairwell. We've entered the centre of the room. The ceiling is high and vaulted, and wooden beams stretch from end to end with over-elabourate, gold chandeliers hanging between them offering a hazy glow of light. The room is dominated by three arched, Georgian sash windows, dressed in crimson, with blinds edged in gold jute braid. Miles and miles of gold silk, piped in crimson braid, is softly gathered and held in place at the sides by simple gold ombres, and the deep red walls provide a dramatic backdrop for elabourately dressed beds that are positioned around the room.

Beds?

'Ava, something tells me this isn't a function room,' Kate whispers.

She starts to wander off to the right, while I remain frozen, trying to grasp what I'm looking at. It's an immense, super-luxurious, communal bedroom – The Communal Room.

The walls are free of paintings, allowing space for various gold metal frames, hooks and hoists, which all look innocent enough, like extravagant wall hangings, but as my mind starts to recover from its shocked state, the significance of the room and its contents starts to filter into my brain. A million reasons try to distract me from the conclusion that I'm slowly drawing, but there is no other explanation for the devices and contraptions surrounding me.

The delayed reaction finally crashes down. 'Fucking hell,' I whisper to myself.

'Watch your mouth.' His soft voice rolls over me, and I fly around to find him standing behind me, watching quietly, his hands in his jeans pockets, his face completely expressionless. My tongue is like lead in my mouth as I search my brain for something to say. What can I say? My head is invaded with a million memories of the last few weeks – all of the times that I've brushed things off, ignored things or, more to the point, been distracted from things. Things he's said, things other people have said – things I thought odd but didn't pursue because I was distracted by him. He's been distracting me this whole time. He's been going out of his way to keep all of this from me. What else is he keeping from me?

Kate appears in my peripheral vision. I don't have to look at her to know she's probably displaying a similar facial expression to mine, but I can't drag my eyes away from Jesse to be sure.

He flicks his gaze in Kate's direction, smiling at her nervously, just as Sam barges into the room.

'Oh, fucking hell! I thought I told you to stay put!' he shouts, fixing Kate with a furious glare. 'Damn you, woman!'

'I think we need to go,' Kate says quietly, walking toward Sam and taking his hand to lead him out of the room.

'Thank you.' Jesse nods at them before returning his eyes to me. His shoulders are slightly raised, signalling his tension. He looks really worried. He should be.

I hear Kate and Sam's hushed, angry whispers as they take the stairs, leaving us alone in the communal room.

The communal room. It all makes sense now. That crucifix downstairs is no wall art. The strange gridlike contraption in the suite was no antique. The women sauntering around the place like they live here are not businesswomen. Well, they might be, but not while they're here.

Oh God help me.

I watch as Jesse's teeth start a vicious workout on his bottom lip. My strained heartbeats are quickening by the second. This certainly explains the thoughtful moments he's been drifting in and out of over the last few days. He must have known I would find out. Was he ever going to tell me?

He drops his eyes to the floor. 'Ava, why didn't you wait at home for me?'

My shock starts to simmer into anger as everything starts clicking into place. 'You wanted me to come,' I remind him.

'Not like this.'

'I sent you a text. I told you I was on my way.'

He frowns. 'Ava, I haven't received a text from you.'

'Where's your phone?'

'It's in my office.'

I go to retrieve my mobile, but then his words from this morning seep back into my brain. 'Is this what you wanted to talk about?'

He lifts his eyes back up to mine, and there's no mistaking the regret in them. He didn't want to talk about us at all. He wanted to talk about all this shit.

'It was time you knew.'

My eyes widen. 'No, it was time for me to know a long time ago, Jesse. Fuck!'

'Watch your mouth, Ava,' he scolds me gently.

'Don't you dare!' I cry, slapping the heel of my hand against my forehead. 'Fuck fuck fuck!'

'Watch …'

'Don't!' I pin him with a fierce glare. 'Jesse, don't you dare tell me to watch my mouth!' I gesture around the room. 'Look!'

'I see it, Ava.' His voice is soft and placating, but it's not going to calm me down.

'Why didn't you tell me?' Oh my God, he's a glorified pimp.

'I thought you would have grasped The Manor's operations on our first meeting, Ava. When it became obvious that you hadn't, it just got harder and harder to tell you.'

My head hurts. This is like the thousand pieces of a jigsaw puzzle slowly clicking into place. He must think I'm something else. He dropped enough hints with his specifications and requirements, but because I was so distracted by him, I missed them all. He owns a sex club? This is fucking awful. And the sex? Oh God, the bloody sex. He really is a sexpert extraordinaire, and it's not because of previous relationships. He said himself that he didn't have time for relationships. Now I know why.

'I'm going to leave now, and you're going to let me go.' I say it with all of the determination I feel. I really have been a play-toy to him. I'm way past dense – I'm completely brainless. He's still frantically chewing his lip as I sidestep him, taking the stairs in a complete daze.

'Ava, wait,' he pleads, following me.

I'm swiftly reminded of the last time I fled here. I should have kept running. I block out his voice, concentrating on getting myself to the entrance hall without breaking my leg in a fall. I pass the first-floor bedrooms and mentally slap myself again.

'Ava, baby, please.'

I reach the bottom of the stairs and fly around to face him. 'Don't even think about it!' I shout at him. He recoils in shock. 'You'll let me leave.'

'You've not even given me the chance to explain.' His eyes are wide and full of fear. It's not an expression I'm familiar with from Jesse. 'Please, let me explain.'

'Explain what? I've seen everything I need to see.' I shout. 'No explanation required!'

He steps toward me with his hands out. 'You weren't supposed to find out like this.'

I'm suddenly aware of an audience watching our little altercation. Sam, Drew and Kate are all standing at the bar entrance looking uncomfortable … pitiful, even, and John looks grave as he assesses Jesse. And then there's Sarah. She looks as smug as can be. I know now that she must have picked up my message on Jesse's phone. She opened the gates and she opened the door. She's got her way. She can have him.

I don't recognise the snide, cocky-looking man standing next to her, but he's looking at me with an unfriendly glare. I watch him turn his eyes on Jesse with a sneer. 'What a fuckup you really are,' he spits at Jesse's back, his tone full of hatred. Who the hell is he?

I watch as John grabs him by the scruff of the neck, shaking him a little. 'You're no longer a member, motherfucker. I'll be escorting you from the grounds.'

The cocky creature laughs a cold, sinister laugh. 'Be my guest. Looks like your tart has seen the light, Ward,' he hisses.

Jesse's eyes turn black in a nanosecond.

'Shut the fuck up,' John growls.

'Revoked membership,' I whisper. 'He got too excited.'

The man directs his cold eyes back at me. 'He takes what he wants and leaves a trail of shit behind him,' he snarls, his words punching all the air from my lungs. I notice Jesse stiffen from head to toe. 'He fucks them all and fucks them off.'

Turning my gaze back on Jesse, I find his eyes are still black, his frown line a burden on his forehead. 'Why?' I ask. I don't know why I'm asking this. It's not going to make a jot of difference. But I feel I deserve some sort of explanation. He fucks them all – once – and fucks them off.

'Don't listen to him, Ava.' Jesse steps forward, his jaw tense to snapping point.

'Ask him how my wife is,' the nasty piece of work spits. 'He did the same to her as he did to all the others. Husbands and conscience don't get in his way.'

And that's all it takes to tip Jesse over the edge. He turns and flies at the man like a bullet, taking him clean from John's grasp and to the parquet floor on a loud crash. Sam yanks Kate back and there are a few gasps as everyone watches Jesse kick ten tons of shit out of the man.

I'm not compelled to scream at him to stop, even though he looks like he could possibly kill him. I walk out of The Manor, get in my car and wait when I see Kate fly down the steps. She jumps in but doesn't say a word.

When we reach the gates, they open without me stopping. I'm surprised – I was preparing to ram them down.

'Sam,' Kate says when I look at her. 'He said we're better off out of here.'

I hadn't considered until now that all of this is news to Kate as well. She seems ever the laid back, take-it-in-her-stride Kate.

I, however, feel like I'm freefalling into Hell.

Chapter Thirty-two

I walk through Kate's front door and straight upstairs to the flat like a zombie.

Kate makes no attempt to try and extract more information from me, instead letting me fall onto the sofa in a tear-stained heap.

My eyes widen when the front door slams, and Kate runs out to the banister. 'It's just Sam,' she reassures me as she comes back into the lounge.

'He has a key?' I ask. Kate shrugs it off, but this small snippet of news has me smiling to myself. Will she take it back in light of this newfound knowledge?

My phone rings again and I reject the call ... again.

Sam steams into the lounge, looking as nervous as he did at The Manor. We both look up at him as he does a little tennis spectator impression, flicking his eyes from me to Kate and back again a few times before stalking over to Kate and all but hauling her out of the lounge by her elbow. 'We need to talk,' he says urgently. I crane my neck around, watching as he practically throws her into her bedroom, slamming the door behind him.

I lie on the sofa, my tea resting on my stomach, and close my eyes. They don't stay shut for long. Mental images of Jesse are imprinted on my brain. I'm never going to be able to sleep again.

My phone starts again and reaching down, I stab the reject button, staring up at the swirly artex ceiling of the lounge.

I've never felt pain like this before. It's excruciating and way beyond fixable. He owns a fucking sex club? Why couldn't he be a banker or a financial advisor? Or ... a hotel owner.

I knew there was something wrong, something dangerous. Why didn't I take a few moments to try and gather my senses? I know exactly why – because I wasn't allowed to, I wasn't given a chance to.

I sit up when I hear Kate's high shrill voice travel across the landing, followed by Sam's placating tones trying to calm her down. She flies out of her room with Sam in tow, struggling to pull her back.

'Get your fucking hands off me, Samuel. She needs to know.'

'Wait a minute ... Kate ... arhhhhhh! What the fuck did you do that for?' Kate retrieves her knee from Sam's groin, leaving him in a folded, groaning mess on the landing, before barging into the lounge and punching me with her blue stare.

'What?' I ask apprehensively. 'What do I need to know now?'

She throws Sam a filthy look when he appears at the lounge door grasping his groin, and then points at a chair aggressively, silently demanding he sit. He limps over, lowering himself on a painful hiss.

'Ava, he's on his way over,' she tells me calmly. I don't know why she chooses this tone. It's not going to calm me – not at all.

I gasp, looking at Sam in the chair, who's refusing to meet my eyes. He wasn't going to tell me? I was stupid to think Jesse would make this easy. 'I need to leave,' I wail as my damn phone starts again. 'Fuck off!' I shout at the stupid thing.

'Take her.' Kate swings around to Sam. 'She's in no state to drive.'

'Oh no, not me.' He holds his hands up, shaking his head. 'It's more than my life's worth. Anyway, I need to talk to you.' He jerks his head toward Kate.

We all jump at the sound of an almighty crash at the door, my heart promptly leaping into my throat as I look at Kate.

Sam groans, and it's not because of the pain Kate's inflicted on him.

'You dirty little turncoat,' she mutters angrily, piercing Sam with her sharp blue eyes.

'Hey, I didn't say a fucking word!' He's on the major defensive. 'It wouldn't take a fucking rocket scientist to work out where she is.'

'Don't answer it, Kate.' I plead.

A combination of more bangs play out on the front door. God, I don't want to see him. My defences are not strong enough right now. I jump at a succession of more bangs, followed by a chorus of car horns.

'For fuck's sake,' Kate yells, running across the room to look out of the window. 'Shit.' She pulls the blind up, getting up close and personal with the glass.

'What?' I join her at the window. I know it's him, but what's with the racket?

'Look!' she yells, pointing down below. I force my eyes to follow her hand and see Jesse's car abandoned in the middle of the street, his driver's door wide open and a line of traffic starting to build up behind it. He's not left enough room for cars to pass, causing tempers to flare and car horns to honk. It's all clearly audible from up here.

'Ava!' I hear him bellow, proceeding to thump the door a few more times.

'Oh, fucking hell, Ava,' Kate moans. 'That man's a walking, talking detonate button and you've just pressed it!' She starts stalking out of the lounge.

I rush after her. 'I pressed nothing, Kate. Don't answer the door!' I lean over the banister, watching Kate fly down the stairs to the front door.

'I can't just leave him out there causing anarchy on the street.'

I panic and run back into the lounge, passing Sam, who's still in the chair rubbing his sore spot, mumbling inaudible words.

'Why didn't you tell Kate?' I ask him sharply on my way back to the window.

'I'm sorry, Ava.'

'You need to apologise to Kate, not me.' I turn back, finding no trace of the fun-loving, cheeky chap whom I've become so fond of. Instead, there's a tense, uneasy, timid man.

'I have apologised. And I couldn't very well tell her until Jesse told you. You should know, this has been eating away at him since he met you.'

I laugh at Sam's attempt to defend his friend and look out of the window again. Jesse is still pacing outside, clearly desperate, smashing the buttons of his mobile. I know who he's calling and, like I knew it would, my phone starts shouting in my hand. I stare down onto the street, panic flooding me when a driver from one of the held-up cars gets out.

Kate walks out, waving her arms at Jesse. He ignores the driver who's approached, turning to Kate instead. His hand gestures are urgent as they speak, and after a few minutes, Jesse gets in his car. Relief washes over my entire being, but he only moves it slightly so it's parked in a more considerate fashion, allowing the other motorists to pass.

'Oh God, Kate! What have you done?' I yell at the window.

'What's going on?' Sam asks from his chair. I don't answer him.

I stand, unable to move, watching as Jesse leans up against my car, his head dropped in defeat, his arms hanging by his sides. He looks up at Kate, and even from here I can see the anguish riddling his face. She reaches over to him, rubbing her palm up and down his arm. It's a gesture of comfort. It's killing me.

After an eternity of watching them on the street, Kate finally turns, making her way back to the flat, but to my utter horror, Jesse starts to follow, and Kate makes no attempt to stop him.

'Shit, no!' I exclaim, throwing my hands to my head in dread.

'What?' Sam shouts anxiously. 'Ava, what?'

I quickly consider my options, but it doesn't take long because there are none, except to stand here and await the confrontation. There is only one way in and one way out of this flat, and with Jesse on his way in, any plans to escape the inevitable altercation are totally floored.

Kate walks into the lounge, looking rather sheepish. I'm furious with her, and she knows it. I pin her with my most filthy stare as she smiles at me nervously.

'Just hear him out, Ava. The man's a mess.' She shakes her head sorrowfully, then looks at Sam, her expression changing instantly. 'You, get in the kitchen!'

Sam scowls. 'I can't fucking move, you evil cow!' He rubs himself again, rolling his head back on the chair. Kate huffs and pulls him up as he groans, closing his eyes and gingerly limping from the room.

I can't believe her. She backs out of the room, giving me eyes full of sympathy. She wouldn't have to act so fucking sorry if she hadn't let him in – the stupid, stupid woman. I turn to face the window before he walks in. I can't look at him. I'll dissolve into tears if I do, and I don't want him to have any excuse to comfort me or wrap his big, warm arms around me. I brace myself for his voice to wash over me, every frazzled nerve ending buzzing and every muscle tense.

For a while, I hear nothing, but as every hair on the back of my neck tingles, standing upright, I know he's near. My body's response to his potent presence has me closing my eyes, taking a deep breath and praying for strength.

'Please, look at me, Ava.' His voice is quivering, full of emotion, and I swallow the tennis ball-sized lump in my throat, fighting back a barrage of tears that are pooling in my eyes. 'Ava, please.' I feel his hand brush down the back of my arm.

I flinch. 'Please, don't touch me.' I find the courage I need to turn around and face him.

His head is dropped, his shoulders sagged. He looks pitiful, but I mustn't be swayed by his sorrowful state. I've been influenced too many times by manipulation, and this ... this is just another form of manipulation ... Jesse style. I've been so blinded with lust I haven't been seeing straight.

His glazed eyes pull themselves from the floor to meet mine. 'Why did you even take me there?' I ask.

'Because I want you with me all of the time. I can't be away from you.'

'Well, you'd better get used to it because I don't want to see you again.' My voice is calm and controlled, but the pain that slices through my heart in response to my own words is enough to floor me on the spot.

His eyes swim, searching mine. 'You don't mean that. I know you don't mean that.'

'I mean it.'

His chest is expanding on each deep inhale, his hair is in disarray and his frown line a crater across his forehead. The distress splashed across his face is like an ice spear through my heart. 'I never meant to hurt you,' he murmurs.

'Well, you have. You've trampled into my life and trampled all over my heart. I tried to walk away. I knew there was more than meets the eye. Why didn't you let me walk away?' My voice starts to trail off as the gravel in my throat starts to win the battle and tears start to pinch at my eyes. Damn me, I should have listened to my instincts.

He starts chewing his bottom lip. 'You never really wanted to walk away.' His voice is barely audible.

'Yes I did!' I blurt on a sniffle. 'I fought you off. I knew I was heading for trouble, but you were relentless. What happened? Did you run out of married women to fuck?'

He shakes his head. 'No, I found you.' He steps forward, and I remove myself from his reach.

'Get out,' I say calmly, my body shaking, my breathing

hitching – all evidence that I'm far from calm. I barge past him, knocking his shoulder.

'I can't. I need you, Ava.' His pleading voice is going to haunt me for the rest of my days.

I swing around violently. 'You don't need me!' I fight to keep my voice solid. 'You want me. Oh God, you *are* a dominant, aren't you?' Flashes of all our sexual encounters pass through my mind at a hundred miles an hour. He's truly fierce in the bedroom and pretty fierce outside it too.

'No!'

'Why the control issue then? And the commands?'

'The sex is just sex. I can't get close enough to you. The control is because I'm frightened to death that something will happen to you … that you'll be taken away from me. I've waited too long for you, Ava. I'll do anything to keep you safe. I've lived a life with little control or care. Believe me, I need you … please … please don't leave me.' He walks toward me, but I step back, fighting the instinct to let him swathe me. He stops. 'I'll never recover.'

No! I can't believe he's being so cruel as to use emotional blackmail. 'Do you think this is going to be any easier for me?!' I scream, the tears starting to flow rapidly.

The little colour that was left in his face drains out before my eyes, and he drops his head. He has no comeback to that. What can he say? He knows what he's done to me. He's made me need him.

'If I could change how I've handled things, I would,' he whispers.

'But you can't. The damage is done.' My tone oozes contempt.

He looks up at me. 'The damage will be worse if you leave me.'

Oh God. 'Get out!'

'No,' He shakes his head frantically, taking a step toward me. 'Ava, please, I'm begging you.'

I move away from him, mustering up my most determined expression, swallowing constantly to keep the lump in my throat at bay. This is so incredibly painful. This is exactly why I couldn't see him. I'm so angry with him, but seeing him so whitewashed is heartbreaking. I have to keep reminding myself that he's let me down in the cruelest way. He's misled me, deceived me and, essentially, bullied me into bed with him.

You let me fall in love with you!

He stares at me, the pain in his sludgy eyes immeasurable. I'll cave if I don't look away – so I do. I drop my gaze to the floor and silently beg him to leave before I fall apart and welcome the comfort he always gives me.

'Ava, look at me.'

I take a deep breath, turning my eyes to his. 'Good-bye, Jesse.'

'Please,' he mouths.

'I said, good-bye.' The words carry an air of finality that I really do not mean.

He searches my face for such a long time, but he eventually abandons trying to find any scrap of hope in my eyes. He turns, and he silently leaves.

I provide my lungs with the desperate rush of breath they need, walking on my unstable legs to the window. The front door slams, vibrating through the house, and Jesse appears, dragging himself to his semi-abandoned car. I flinch, letting out a sob as he smashes his fist through the window of his car, sending shards of glass spraying all over the road before he throws himself in and repeatedly punches the steering wheel. After what seems like years of watching him pound on his car, he roars off, tyres screeching, car horns blaring.

I get out of the shower and dry my hair before resuming the foetal position on my bed. I'm completely numb. I feel like my heart has been ripped out, trampled on and shoved back into my chest a battered mess. I'm somewhere between grief and devastation, and it's the most painful thing I've ever experienced. My life has fallen apart. I feel empty, betrayed, lonely and lost. The only person who can make any of this better is the person who's made it all happen. I don't feel like I'm ever going to recover from this.

'Ava?' I lift my pounding head from my pillow and find Kate standing in my doorway. The sympathy on her face enflames the hurt a little bit more. She perches on the edge of the bed, stroking my cheek. 'It doesn't have to be like this,' she says softly.

How so? How can it be any other way? I just have to ride out this pain and see if I have the strength to deal with any of it – start all over again. But at the moment I'm content to just lie here feeling sorry for myself.

'Yes, it does,' I reply on a whisper.

'No, it doesn't.' She's firmer this time. 'You still love him. Admit you still love him. Did you tell him?'

I can't deny it. I do. I love him – so much it hurts. But I shouldn't love him. I know I shouldn't. 'I can't.' I turn my face into my pillow.

'Why?'

'He owns a sex club, Kate.'

'He didn't know how to tell you. He was worried you would walk away.'

I look at Kate. 'Well, he didn't tell me, and I've still walked away.' I settle back down into my tear-drenched pillow. 'You heard that man. He destroys marriages. He screws women for fun. Why are you not shocked?' I mutter into my pillow. I know she's laid back, but this is shocking stuff.

'I am … a bit.'

'You could've fooled me.'

'Ava, Jesse is crazy about you. Sam never thought he'd see the day.'

'Sam can say what he likes, Kate. It doesn't change the fact that he owns a place where people go to have sex and he sometimes joins in.' I shudder, feeling sick at the thought.

'You can't punish him because of his past.'

'It's not his past though, is it? He still owns the place.'

'It's his business.'

'Leave me alone, Kate.' I beg. Her defending all of this is just pissing me off. She should be supporting me, not trying to justify Jesse's misdemeanours.

I feel her weight lift from the bed on a sigh. 'He's still Jesse,' she says as she leaves my bedroom, and me alone to mourn my loss.

I lie in silence trying to rid my head of all the inevitable thoughts. It's no good. My brain is assaulted by flashbacks of the last few weeks – of our first meeting when he floored me, the texts and the calls and then the stalking ... and the sex. I flip myself onto my stomach, sinking my face into my pillow.

Kate's words keep pinballing around in my mind: *He's still Jesse.* Do I even know who Jesse is? All I know is a man who swept me up in his intensity and blindsided me with his physical being.

Another piece of the puzzle falls into place when I recall him telling me that he has no contact with his parents. They disowned him when his uncle died and Jesse refused to sell The Manor. It makes sense now. It had nothing to do with the inheritance or sharing the estate, and all to do with their twenty-one-year-old son being left to run a super-posh sex club. Of course they would be concerned. Their disapproval of Jesse's relationship with Carmichael is absolutely warranted. Jesse said he was having the time of his life. What young man wouldn't be in a house where anything goes? He really has had lots of practice, and there's a distinct possibility that he really has never fucked a woman more than once – apart from me.

It doesn't take much intelligence to figure out why I was being scrutinised by all of those women when I was at The Manor. They all want him. No, they all want him *again*.

He played it risky by taking me there, but when I think carefully, no one ever approached me – I was never alone, never free to roam. Did everyone know I was oblivious? Were they under instruction to keep quiet, to stay away? He really did go out of his way to keep me in the dark. How did he think he could get away with it? Sarah's comment on leathers ... I push my face into the pillow in complete despair.

'Ava?'

I look up and see Sam standing in the doorway, looking as deflated as he was earlier. 'He beat himself up on a daily basis trying to think of how he could tell you. I've never seen him like this before.'

'You mean rejected?' I say sarcastically. 'No, I can't imagine Jesse Ward did get many knockbacks.'

'No, I mean crazy about a woman.'

'He's just crazy, Sam.'

He frowns, shaking his head. 'Yes, about you. Do you mind?' he asks, standing at the edge of my bed.

'Help yourself,' I grumble uncharitably.

He perches on the edge of the bed. I've never seen him so serious. 'Ava, I've known Jesse for eight years. Not once have I seen him behave like this over a woman. He's never had a relationship beyond sex, but you came along and it's like he found purpose. He's a different man, and while you might have been frustrated over his protectiveness, as a friend, I was happy to see him finally care so much to behave like that. Please, give him a chance.'

'He wasn't just protective, Sam.' Protectiveness is just the start of a long list of unreasonable ways.

'He's still Jesse.' Sam repeats Kate's words, looking at me pleadingly. 'The Manor is a business. Yes, he mixed business with pleasure, but he had nothing else.' He smiles, picking my hand up in his. 'If you can tell me that you can walk away from him, no second thoughts or regrets, then I'll shut up now and leave. If you can tell me that you don't love him, I'll walk away. But I don't think you can. You're shocked, I realise that. And yes, he has a history, but you can't ignore the fact that he adores you, Ava. It's written all over his face, expressed in everything he does. Please, give him a chance. He deserves a chance.'

I'm trying to deal with something I just don't understand and probably never will. He owns a sex club. This drama doesn't feature into my idea of a normal, happily ever after. He cares enough to behave like this? He adores me? Does adore equal love? I ignored all of Jesse's pillow talk in the beginning – all the 'you're mine' talk and rubbish about never letting me leave. He said the word *love* a lot, but not in the context I so desperately wanted to hear. 'I love you in lace', 'I love sleepy sex with you', 'I love having you here.' Should I have looked further into all of it? Was he telling me what I wanted to hear but in a backward way? He persistently sought reassurance from me that I would stay. If all he needed was comfort that I was staying put, then I did that plenty of times, didn't I? I always told him I would stay. But I didn't know about The Manor then. And now I do, and I've left.

He always wanted me in lace, not leather. He claimed me as his. He was possessive to the absolute maximum – unreasonably so. He always wanted to keep me covered, never wanting me to be exposed to anyone but him. Leather, sharing and the exposure of female flesh must be a regular occurrence at The Manor. Was he was trying to make me the complete opposite of everything he knows? Everything he's used to?

I sit up. I need to talk to him. I can get over The Manor, I think, but I know for absolutely sure that I'll never get over Jesse. Seeing him so fraught and desperate must at least mean he's hurting. He wouldn't behave like that if I didn't mean something to him, would he? So many questions. And there's only one place I'll find the answers. I *owe* myself those answers.

I look at Sam, and a small smile spreads across his cheeky

face. 'My work here is done,' he mimics Jesse's words as he gets up on a little wince. 'That evil cow.'

I smile on the inside. This bombshell obviously hasn't affected Kate in the same way it has me. I throw on the nearest clothes I can find and grab my car keys. Tears flood my eyes and guilt punches a great hole in my stomach. He was the one who wanted the cards on the table. He was going to tell me about The Manor, but was there something else he wanted to tell me? I hope so, because I'm on my way to find out. Sarah's warning about building dreams on Jesse comes crashing back into my mind as I race down to my car. Maybe she's right, but I can't live not knowing.

Chapter Thirty-three

I drive to Lusso in a stupid fashion, overtaking, banging my car horn impatiently and running a few red lights. When I pull up at the docks, I see Jesse's car parked on an angle, spanning two of his allocated spaces. I abandon my Mini on the road, let myself in the pedestrian gate – thanking all things holy that I remember the code – and rush into the foyer, finding Clive at the concierge desk, looking more cheerful than usual.

'Ava! I've finally got the hang of all this ruddy equipment,' he declares delightedly.

I brace myself on the high, marble counter to catch my breath. 'Great, Clive. I told you it would come.'

'Are you okay?'

'I'm fine. I'm just going up to Jesse.'

The phone on the desk starts ringing, and Clive holds his finger up in a signal for me to excuse him for a second. 'Mr. Holland? Yes sir, of course, sir.' He hangs up, scribbling a few notes on his pad. 'Sorry about that.'

'That's okay. I'll make my way up.'

'Ah, Ava, Mr Ward hasn't notified me of your visit.' He scans his screen, and I gape at him. Is he having me on? He's seen Jesse carry me in and out of this place on numerous occasions. What's he playing at?

I smile sweetly. 'How are you finding the job, Clive?'

He immediately becomes willing and animated. 'Well, I'm basically a personal assistant to thirteen filthy rich residents, but I love it. You should hear some of the requests I get. Yesterday,

Mr Daniels asked me to organise a chopper ride over the city for his daughter and three friends and ...' he leans over the counter, lowering his voice. 'Mr. Gomez up on fifth has a different woman every day of the week. And Mr Holland seems to have a thing for the Thai birds. But keep that to yourself. It's all confidential.' He winks.

'Wow, it sounds very interesting. I'm glad you're enjoying it, Clive.' I broaden my smile at him. 'Do you mind if I head up?'

'I need to call first, Ava.'

'Call then!' I huff impatiently, standing and shifting irritably while Clive rings up to the penthouse.

He hangs up and dials again. 'I'm sure I saw him pass through,' he mutters on a frown. 'Maybe I didn't.'

'His car's outside, he must be here,' I push frantically. 'Try again.' I point to the telephone and Clive presses a few buttons again as I look on.

He hangs up again, shaking his head. 'No, he's definitely not there. And he hasn't put a DND on his system, so he's not asleep or busy. He must have gone out.'

I frown. 'DND?'

'Do not disturb.'

'Oh. Clive, I know he's home. Please, can I go up?' I plead. I can't believe he's being so difficult.

He leans over his desk, narrows his eyes on me and looks to either side, checking the coast is clear. 'I can get in serious trouble for not following protocol, but as it's you, Ava,' he winks, 'go on.' He thumbs over his shoulder and straightens his green hat.

'Thanks, Clive.'

I jump in the lift, punch in the code, praying he hasn't got around to re-programming it in the short time I've been gone, and let out a relieved breath of air when the doors close and I start my journey to the penthouse. He's got to answer the door yet – I don't have a key.

My stomach does a few three-sixties as the lift door slides open and I'm faced with the double doors into Jesse's apartment, but I frown to myself when I see the door is already open. And there's music – very loud music.

I walk to the door, gently push it open, and my ears are bombarded from every direction by 'Angel'. The words hit me like a thunderbolt, immediately putting me on guard. Right now, it sounds so loud and depressing, not soft and ardent like it was when we made love. I need to turn it down, or off. It's so affecting. And with it coming from all of the integrated speakers, there's no escaping it. Maybe he's not here. Maybe the system has malfunctioned because he couldn't possibly sustain this noise level for long. I clamp my hands over my ears as I glance around the huge space, trying to locate a remote control before running into the kitchen, where I spot one on the island. I quickly find the volume button to turn the music down – a lot.

Once I've taken care of the noise levels, I go in search of him. As I reach the stairs, I kick something and watch as it clatters across the floor, but quickly pick up the bottle and place it on the console unit at the bottom of the stairs before taking them two at a time.

I go straight to the master suite, but he's not in there, so I proceed to frantically search every other room on the floor. He's in none of them. I get halfway down the stairs, stopping abruptly when my eyes land on the empty bottle that I scooped up.

It's vodka, or it was. It's been drained dry.

A wave of uneasiness rolls over me as a million thoughts invade my head. I've never seen Jesse drink – not ever. Every time alcohol has been on offer, he's refused, ordering water instead. It never occurred to me to wonder why. But now, thinking about how carelessly the empty bottle was tossed on the floor, I realise something isn't right.

His insistence on me not drinking on Friday comes rushing

back into my mind like a tidal wave, and the time in The Blue Bar, when he was so keen to feed me water, suddenly doesn't seem so unusual or unreasonable.

I hear a crash, and my eyes snap from the empty bottle of vodka to the outside terrace. 'Oh, please no,' I whisper to myself.

The huge glass doors are open. I sprint the rest of the way down the stairs, across the living space, skidding to a halt at the doors when I see Jesse struggling to get himself up from one of the sun loungers. Have I had my eyes closed for the past few weeks? I've missed so much.

He has a towel wrapped around his waist and a bottle of vodka in his hand, which he's keeping a tight hold of as he fights to push himself up on his free arm. He's swearing profusely.

I'm frozen on the spot as I watch this man I've fallen in love with, a physically powerful, passionate and captivating man, reduced to a drunken wreck. How did this slip past me? I've not even wrapped my head around all of the other shit that's been landed on me today. And now this on top of everything else?

Once he's hauled himself up, he turns to face me. His eyes are hollow, his face washed out. It doesn't look like him.

'You're too late, lady,' he slurs viciously, glaring at me. He's never looked at me like this before. He's never spoken to me like this before, not even when he's been crazy mad with me.

'You're drunk,' I blurt, knowing it's a stupid thing to say, but all other words have run, screaming loudly, from my brain. My eyes have been tortured way past repair today.

'That's very observant of you.' He lifts the bottle and swigs the rest of the vodka before wiping his mouth with the back of his hand. 'Not drunk enough, though.' He walks forward purposely, and I instinctively move out of his way, knowing he would cause me damage if he crashed into me.

'Where are you going?' I ask as he passes me.

'What's it to you?' he spits, without so much as looking at me. I follow him into the kitchen, watching as he drags another bottle of vodka from the freezer and tosses his empty into the sink. He starts unscrewing the cap. 'Bastard!' he hisses, shaking his hand, and it's then I notice the mass of swelling and cuts marring it. He perseveres with the screw cap, eventually removing it before knocking back a huge swig.

'Jesse, your hand needs looking at.'

He throws his hand up in front of him, taking another mouthful from the bottle. 'Look then. Yet more damage you've caused,' he snarls. *I've caused?* 'Yeah, you can stand there ... stand there looking all bewildered ... and ... and ... confused. I fucking told you!' he shouts. 'Didn't I warn you? I ... I warned you!' He's hysterical.

'Warned me about what?' I ask quietly while trying to mentally calculate how much he's had. This is the third bottle I've seen. Can anyone drink that much?

'Fucking typical,' he shouts at the ceiling.

'I didn't know,' I whisper.

He laughs. 'You didn't know?' He points the bottle at me. 'I said you would cause more damage if you left me, but you still left anyway. Now look at the fucking state of me.'

I flinch at his words. I feel like crying, but shock is controlling the tears. This is not the Jesse I know. This man is a stranger – a hurtful, cruel and merciless man who I don't love at all. I don't need *this* man.

He starts pacing toward me, and I back away. I don't want to be anywhere near him. 'That's it, run away.' He continues stalking forward, gaining on me with every step. 'You're a fucking prick tease, Ava. I can have you, then I can't, then I can again. Make your fucking mind up!'

'Why didn't you tell me you're an alcoholic?' I ask as my back hits the wall. There's no more retreating space. *Why didn't you tell me everything?*

'And give you another reason not to want me?' he spits. He then seems to consider something. 'I'm not an alcoholic!'

He's on top of me, looking down at me. This close up, his eyes are even more hollow and dark.

'You need help,' I say on a cracking voice. I'm going to need help, too.

'I needed you and ... you ... you left me.' His breath is hot, but it's not his usual minty smell. All I can smell are alcohol fumes, so whoever claims you can't smell vodka is lying.

I plant my palms on his bare chest to push him away, applying only a little pressure for fear I might push him over. It's laughable. This tall, lean, strapping man, but he's so unstable on his feet. His chest feels like him – *that* I recognise, but it's the only part of him that I do at the moment.

He takes a step back, tipping the bottle to his lips again. I want to grab it and smash it on the floor. 'Sorry, am I invading your space?' He laughs. 'It's never bothered you before.'

'You weren't drunk before,' I retort.

'No ... I wasn't. I was too busy fucking you to think about having a drink.' He looks at me with disgust, leaning forward. 'I was too busy fucking you to think about anything. And you loved it.' He smirks. 'You were good. In fact, you were the best I've had. And I've had a lot.'

Rage flies through me like a rocket. So fast I don't even notice that my hand has flown out and slapped him clean across his face – not until the sting sets in and it starts throbbing.

He holds his face to the side, where my vicious hand has put it, before slowly turning it back to me. He laughs mildly. 'Fun, wasn't it?'

I look at him in complete contempt, shaking my head. I feel like I'm being dragged through a madcap movie. This sort of shit just doesn't happen, especially not to me. Sex houses, crazy madness and alcoholic arseholes. How did I get caught up in all of this freakiness?

'You're one fucked-up, sorry state.'

'Watch your mouth,' he slurs.

'You don't get to tell me what I can say!' I shout. 'You don't get to tell me how to do anything any more!'

'I'm.A.Fucked.Up.Sorry.State.And.It's.All.Because.Of.*You*.' He punctuates each and every word on a slur, jabbing his finger in my face. I fear I might actually punch him in his drunken face if I don't leave now. But all of my stuff is here, and I need to get it. I don't want to ever come back.

I brush past him, hurrying for the stairs. With any luck, he's too drunk to climb them and I can snatch my things up without any further vicious exchanges.

I take the stairs fast, barrelling into the bedroom and standing for a few moments wondering where he would've put my bag.

Finding my overnight case tucked neatly behind some shoe boxes in the wardrobe, I yank it free, pulling down my clothes from the hangers and scooping up my things from the floor at the same time. I rush back into the bedroom, finding Jesse standing in the doorway. It's taken him a lot longer than usual, but he's made it up the stairs. I ignore him and run into the bathroom, all but flinging my toiletries into my bag.

'Does this bring back memories, Ava?'

I look up, finding him stroking the top of the vanity unit, his face straight as he caresses the marble counter. I try to blank out our launch night encounter. In this very suite was where I finally surrendered to this man. In this bathroom was where we made love for the first time. No, we fucked for the first time. And now it all ends here, too.

He's blocking my path with his tall, swaying body, and I notice the bottle of vodka has been abandoned, his towel working its way loose. I try to sidestep him, but he moves with me, hampering my attempts to pass.

'You're really going?' he slurs softly.

'You think I would stay?' I ask, exasperated. I'd thought I could overcome The Manor and all the crap that accompanies it, but this on top of all that has just catapulted my already crumbled world into complete obliteration. No amount of love or feelings could ever fix this mess. He's led me on a merry dance. He's purposely deceived me and manipulated me.

'So, that's it? You've turned my life upside down, caused all this damage, and now you're leaving without fixing it?'

I look up at him in shock. Does he think that he's the only one affected by all of this? I've turned *his* world upside down? Even inebriated, the man is delusional.

'Good-bye, Jesse.' I push past him, heading straight for the stairs, fighting the urge to look back. The devastating man I fell in love with, the man who I thought would be engraved on my mind's eye for the rest of my life, has been cruelly replaced by that nasty, drunken creature.

'I wanted to tell you, but you had to be your usual difficult self!' he roars at my back. 'How can you walk away?' I flinch at his harshness but keep going. 'Ava, baby, please!'

Halfway down the stairs, I hear a loud clatter and a collection of bangs and crashes. This just makes me run faster. Any dream of falling into his strong, loving arms has been sensationally dashed. My happy ever after with my lovable rogue has been chewed up and spat out. I could have tumbled into a relationship with Jesse without a clue about his dark secrets. When would I have eventually found out?

I should be thankful. At least I know now, before it's too late.

Before it's too late?

It's way past too late.

I approach Kate's door in a numb haze and it swings open before I have a chance to put my key in the lock.

'What's happened?' she asks, her eyes wide and concerned as Sam appears behind her. One look at his face tells me he knows exactly what's just happened.

Every aching muscle gives way, including my heart, and

I collapse to the floor in a heap, sobbing uncontrollably. I'm vaguely aware of arms wrapped around me, rocking me back and forth. But they don't comfort me.

They're not Jesse's.

Bonus Chapter for THIS MAN

Launch night at Lusso – Jesse's POV

What the fuck is this prick rambling on about? He must see that I'm not interested, but it doesn't shut him up. There's no need to kiss my arse any more because I've bought the fucking place. He's earned his commission. Leave me the fuck alone!

I nod my head every now and then to the estate agent, even though I can't hear a word he's saying. All I'm hearing is an unconvincing, sweet voice telling me she's not interested. I study her red-covered back closely. I should never have left her place last night, not until she relented and admitted she's feeling something, too. I know she feels it. I have a newfound determination after spending all day locked in my office achieving fuck all, except mental torture. And now I'm standing in my new home, surrounded by snotty society, resisting the urge to set off the fire alarm to clear the place so I can have her alone.

I smile to myself when I see Ava's redheaded friend look past her, her eyes widening when she clocks me. She remembers me, and just when I'm about to sack this irritating knob off, Ava turns and clocks me, too. Her eyes do more than widen – they nearly fall out of her head. I don't have a chance to flash her my smile. She swings back around, clearly shocked by my presence. This only boosts my determination. She wouldn't act so stunned if she didn't care.

Turning my eyes back onto the estate agent, I see his mouth moving, but nothing he's saying is filtering through. 'Yeah, thanks.' I slap his upper arm, a completely inappropriate farewell, but I've got somewhere I need to be.

I make my way over to her, lip-reading her friend's words. She's telling her I'm coming. Oh yes, lady. I'm coming.

I arrive by the two girls, Ava refusing to turn, her friend clearly amused, which means this beautiful girl has been talking about me. My already high confidence shoots through the roof.

'Nice to see you again, Kate.' I say smoothly. 'Ava?'

She doesn't acknowledge me, and her friend's eyes are shooting between us in amusement. 'Jesse,' Kate nods at me. 'Excuse me. I need to powder my nose.' Placing her glass on the counter, she leaves us alone. I'm grateful.

After a few seconds of waiting, I soon realise she isn't going to budge, the stubborn woman, so I slowly circle her until I'm confronted with her exquisite face. My cock instantly starts to throb. 'You look stunning,' I say quietly, running my eyes over every perfect square inch of her features. I've tasted those lips. I don't know what I'll do if I don't get to taste them again.

'You said I wouldn't have to see you again.' She's in instant defence mode. It doesn't bode well.

'I didn't know you would be here.' I'm all defensive, too, but I have no right to be.

'You sent me flowers.'

I fight to keep the smile from my face. 'So I did.'

'Please, excuse me.' She goes to pass me, and I panic, quickly moving to stop her.

'I was hoping for a tour,' I blurt, laughing privately at my own audacity. I know this place inside out.

'I'll get Victoria. She'll be happy to show you around.'

'I would prefer you.'

'You don't get a fuck with a tour,' she retorts harshly, making me recoil. She's standing in front of me, looking like she's just literally fallen from the heavens, and she's using vulgar language like that?

'Will you watch your mouth?'

I expect her to tell me where to go, but she doesn't. 'Sorry,' she mutters, 'and put my seat back when you drive my car.'

Now I really can't help my smile, and I'm filled with immense satisfaction when she starts shifting uncomfortably. I bet she loved my little joke.

'And leave my music alone!'

'I'm sorry,' I whisper. 'Are you okay? You look a little shaky.' I can't help it. I lift my arm, desperate to feel that smooth skin again. 'Is something affecting you?'

She pulls away. 'Not at all.' She's lying. I can see her hand twitching by her side as she fights not to reach for her hair. That's her tell. 'Did you want a tour?'

My smile broadens further. 'I would *love* a tour.'

She virtually stomps out of the kitchen and starts waving her hand around. 'Lounge,' I've seen the lounge. I've seen everything a million times, so I keep my eyes on the gentle sway of her hips as she leads me around my new home. 'You've seen the kitchen,' she calls over her shoulder, giving me a little peek of her luscious lips. 'View.' She points across London before trekking back into the penthouse and stalking across the open space toward the gym.

People try to stop me as I pick up my pace to keep up with her, but I brush them off with a quick handshake or a polite nod of my head.

'Gym,' she mutters as she enters, before leaving as soon as my Grensons cross the threshold. I laugh to myself as I follow her up the stairs. It takes every single piece of willpower not to grab her and haul her into a bedroom. Fuck me, I want to sink my teeth into her tight arse as it sashays up the stairs.

After opening and closing every door on the first floor and

shortly spitting what rooms they are, she paces into the master suite. My bedroom. Oh fuck, does she realise she's just entered the lion's lair? This does not assist in cooling down my raging hard-on. 'You're an expert tour guide, Ava.' I muse as I land in front of quite a boring piece of art. But there's something about the shabby old rowing boots – something charming. 'Care to enlighten me on the photographer?'

'Giuseppe Cavalli.'

'It's good. Is there any particular reason why you chose this photographer?'

She's silent for a while, and I know it's because she's studying me. She likes what she sees, and she likes what she felt when I had her in my arms. I'm not going to let her deny it, so she'd better not even try and insult my intelligence with another rejection.

'He was known as the master of light.' She's joined me in front of the piece, and I look down at her, almost encouragingly. 'He didn't think that the subject was of any importance. It didn't matter what he photographed. To him, the subject was always the light. He concentrated on controlling it. See?' She lifts her hand and points out the reflections across the rippling water.

I nod thoughtfully to myself, impressed and quite intrigued, but the woman standing next to me is what I'm more intrigued by, so I turn my stare back down to her as she continues.

'These rowing boats, as lovely as they are, are just boats, but see how he manipulates the light? He didn't care for the boats. He cared for the light surrounding the boats. He makes inanimate objects interesting, makes you look at the photograph in a different ... well, a different light, I suppose.' She cocks her head thoughtfully, lengthening the column on her neck, revealing perfect, smooth, taut skin. Jesus, the woman is like nothing else I've seen.

I let her finish her observations, quite happy to just watch her, but then she looks up at me, and I can see she's mentally battling the urge to fold on me.

'Please don't,' she whispers.

'Don't what?' I know damn well what.

'You know what. You said I wouldn't have to see you again.'

'I lied. I can't stay away from you, so you do have to see me again … and again … and again.' I say it slowly, making clear my intention, and she inhales as she starts stepping back away from me.

I'm not letting her get away this time. 'You persistently fighting this is only making me more determined to prove that you want me.' I keep my eyes on hers. 'I'm making it my mission objective. I'll do *anything*.' I really will.

The bed halts her retreat and she throws her hands up. 'Stop,' she blurts, and I do, but only because she's clearly upset. 'You don't even know me.' She's desperately trying to convince herself that this is crazy. It is, and it scares me, but I can't walk away again.

'I know you're impossibly beautiful.' I walk forward, thinking I can make her feel so much better if I can just hold her. 'I know what I feel, and I know you're feeling it, too.' I stop as the fronts of our bodies brush. I can feel her heartbeat through her dress and my suit. 'So, tell me, Ava. What have I missed?'

She drops her face, but I waste no time pulling it back up to mine, feeling like a total bastard when I see tears in her eyes. 'I'm sorry.' I slide my hand around to cup her cheek and gently wipe her tears away.

'You said you would leave me alone.' She flicks me a questioning look.

'I lied. I'm sorry. I can't stay away, Ava.'

'You've already said that you're sorry, yet here you are again. Am I to expect flowers tomorrow?'

My strokes of her cheeks pause, and it's *my* face that hides now. I really am a bastard, but I wouldn't be doing this if I didn't know for certain that she wants me. Why is she being so stubborn? There's nothing left for it. I need to remind her – remind her of how it felt. I lift my eyes and slowly start lowering my lips to hers. I need to be gentle.

She doesn't stop me, and when our lips skim just a tiny bit, she's the one who takes the lead, grabbing my jacket and breathing heavily in my face. I'm shaking like a fucking leaf, relieved and pent-up on days' worth of lust.

'Have you ever felt like this?' I ask, pulling her closer and working my mouth across to her ear.

'Never.'

I sag in relief and nip at her lobe. 'Are you ready to stop fighting it now?' I ask softly, licking my way up her ear and back down until I'm at the smooth flesh that meets her neck. She smells and tastes divine.

'Oh God,' she gasps, and I swallow her words of submittal by tenderly plunging my tongue into her mouth, silently grateful when she accepts it.

'Hmmm,' I hum, breaking our kiss reluctantly to get a solid confirmation from this beautiful woman. 'Is that a yes?'

'Yes.'

A million sparks light up inside of me; hope that I just don't understand bombarding my entire form. I nod and proceed to show my appreciation by scattering light kisses all over her face. 'I need to have all of you, Ava. Say I can have all of you.'

She hesitates, but only briefly. 'Take me.'

I don't waste any more time. I curl my arm around her tiny waist and lift her slight frame from her feet, carrying her to the wall and gently pushing her up against it as our lips become more frantic, more desperate now we're both on the same page. My hands are everywhere. I can't help it.

I refuse to release her lips when she starts pushing my jacket away from my shoulders, stepping back just a fraction to help her. Nothing will stop this. When I'm free from my suit jacket, I thrust her back into the wall, a bit harder than I intended, but she doesn't seem bothered by my eagerness. She's meeting my franticness perfectly.

'Fucking hell, Ava,' I breathe, 'you make me crazy.' I circle my hips to try and alleviate the throb in my cock, pulling a quiet cry from her lips. Her hands are clenching at my hair, the feeling out of this world, and it prompts me to yank her dress up to her waist and roll into her once more. Nipping at her bottom lip, I pull away, breathing uncontrolled bursts of air in her face as I deliver another grind of my groin, delighting in her moans of pleasure. She breaks our eye contact and lets her head fall back, the temptation of her exposed throat way too much to resist. I'm lost.

'Jesse …'

I'm only mildly aware of her panting my name as I bite my way across her skin. 'Jesse, people are coming, you have to stop.' She starts squirming in my embrace, rubbing up against my solidness.

Fuck!

'I'm not letting you go, not now.' I groan the words out, silently begging her not to stop this.

'We need to stop.'

'No.' I sound demanding, but I can't help it. Fuck, I know there are people wandering around, and I fucking hate them for it.

'We'll do this later.'

'That leaves you too much time to change your mind.' I carry on biting at her neck, unwilling to release her from my grasp for fear of never getting my hands on her again. But then my jaw is grabbed and she pulls me from my happy nuzzling.

'I won't change my mind.' Our noses are touching. 'I will not change my mind.'

She means it; I can see it in her determined eyes ... but I'm not risking it. I push my lips hard on hers and tell her so. 'Sorry, I can't risk it.' I pick her up and carry her to the bathroom.

'What? They'll want to see in there, too!'

'I'll lock the door. No screaming.' I grin down at her. She remembers my crassness, and I'm glad she's smiling about it. The delivery of such a tactless line to such an exquisite woman should've earned me a slap.

'You have no shame.'

Her grin, followed up by a cheeky laugh, makes my cock nearly explode ... so I tell her that, too. 'No. My cock has been aching since last Friday, I finally have you in my arms, and you've seen sense. I'm going nowhere and neither are you.'

I kick the lovely wooden door of my lovely new bathroom shut and place her gently down between the double sink unit before hastily returning to lock the door. *Nothing* is interrupting this.

When I turn to face her, she's looking at me, her dreamy chocolate eyes shimmering with lust. Fucking hell, this woman can't be real. Reaching up to my shirt, I slowly start unbuttoning it as I walk slowly over to her. I'm not rushing because I can see clearly that she's completely given in. This is happening.

I leave my shirt hanging open and hold my breath as I watch when she places her finger in the centre of my chest, dragging it lightly down the middle. My hands instinctively find her waist and my body moves between her thighs.

I glance up and find her watching me closely, and my lips twitch in ... happiness. For the first time in forever, I feel happy. 'You can't escape now.'

'I don't want to.'

'Good,' I mouth, dropping my gaze to her lips as she continues with her drifting finger, back up my chest, my throat, until it rests lightly on my bottom lip. I bite down, my happiness intensifying tenfold when she smiles at me and works her hand into my hair.

'I like your dress,' I say, skating my eyes down the gathered material at her waist until I'm focused on her lovely thighs.

'Thank you.'

'It's a bit restrictive.' I pull at a piece of the red material playfully, smiling to myself when I sense her breathing quicken.

'It is.'

'Shall we remove it?' I tilt my head thoughtfully as she smiles.

'If you like.'

'Or maybe we leave it on?' I pull away and hold my hands up – a stupid thing to do. I already miss the feel of her, so I immediately run my palms around her back to find the zip. 'But then again,' I whisper in her ear, 'I have firsthand knowledge of what's under this lovely dress.' *And it's fucking incredible*, I think to myself as I breathe in her ear and slowly draw down the fastening. I don't know why I'm thinking it. I should tell her, so I do. 'And it's far superior to the dress. I think we'll get rid of it.' She needs to know that I'm seriously pussy whipped.

I pick her up and set her on her feet, pushing the lovely dress away, revealing a sight that has been carved on my mind since Tuesday. I kick the redundant dress to the side and absorb her for a few moments, before I lift her back onto the counter, the feel of her in my arms as satisfying as looking at her. I want to carry her everywhere, have her glued to me.

'I like that dress,' she argues.

'I'll buy you a new one.' I brush off her concern. I know she doesn't really give a damn about the dress. I take up my position between her legs and take hold of her petite bum, tugging her closer and rolling my hips while we study each other. My cock isn't going to hold out much longer, but I'm enjoying savouring her at the moment.

Feeling around her back, I unclasp and remove her bra, sighing when my eyes are blessed again by her pert, perfectly formed breasts. And then the little temptress only leans back on her hands, accentuating the subtle push of her chest toward me.

I raise my eyes to hers and lift my hand, covering her entire throat with my palm. 'I can feel your heart hammering.' I sound enthralled. I *am* enthralled. She completely captivates me. Slowly, I glide my hand down her front until it's resting softly on her flat tummy. I find her eyes again, just to check she's real, even though I can feel her perfectly. 'You're too fucking beautiful, lady,' I say firmly. 'I think I'll keep you.'

When she bows her back, I smile, and then let my mouth drop to her nipple, taking her other breast in my spare palm, massaging gently as I suck her into my mouth. She's moaning, her body turning lax, and my aching cock rubs delicious circles into her. I'm fighting to keep control, but I want to worship her first, make the most of this time. She's unpredictable, with her constant fighting and relenting. It worries me.

She's getting a little frenzied, her breathing erratic and rushed, so I find my way to her knickers and slip my finger into the side, resisting the temptation to rip them off now. Fuck, she feels perfect everywhere.

'Shit,' she yelps, her body flying up and clenching my shoulders.

I don't back down. 'Language, lady,' I warn, taking her mouth and thrusting my fingers deeply into her, gasping at the rightness of her internal, heated muscles grabbing onto me. She's moaning relentlessly, pushing her body into mine and greedily contracting around me. I can sense her desperation. I know her already – a stupid thought, given my limited time with her, but the perfection of this convinces me that I need to lengthen this time – make it for ever.

'Come,' I demand, pushing deeper and higher, pressing my thumb onto her pulsing clitoris, my heart hammering wildly as I watch her disintegrate into a mass of twitching nerves.

When she yells, I quickly tackle her mouth, soaking up her pleasure-filled moans as she shakes in my arms. Her eyes are closed while I devote my time to easing her down, kissing her face everywhere until she finally opens her eyes and gazes at me on a little sigh.

Fuck ... me.

I lean in and kiss her again, her whole form like a magnet to me. I can't get enough of her. 'Better?' I slip my fingers out and smile when she hums, running my damp finger across her full bottom lip as we watch each other.

And when her palms lift and smooth down my cheeks, I'm powerless to stop myself from turning into one, kissing it lovingly before letting my eyes find her again.

Her shocked gasp throws me for a moment, until I realise someone is trying to get into my bathroom. I slap my palm over her mouth and smile at her shock.

'I can't hear anything,' someone says. Ava's eyes widen further, so I release her mouth and replace my palm with my lips, hushing her quietly.

'Oh God, I feel cheap,' she cries, her head falling to my shoulder.

Cheap? She's the furthest you could get from cheap. 'You're not cheap. Talk crap like that, I'll be forced to kick your delicious backside all over my bathroom.' I immediately realise my error. Fuck, did I really just say that? Her confused face tells me I did. I don't know why I'm concerned. She already knows that I own The Manor, even if she thinks it's a fucking hotel. Whatever made her think that? And how the hell will I tell her what really goes down there? I don't want to tarnish this with my dirty history.

'Your bathroom?' Her question distracts me from my dilemma, her puzzled face making me smile.

'Yes, my bathroom. I wish they would stop strangers roaming around my home.'

'You live here?'

'Well, I will as of tomorrow. Tell me. Is all this Italian shit worth the outrageously expensive price tag they attached to this place?' I didn't mean to say that at all. I love the Italian shit she's loaded it with.

'Italian shit?' she coughs, and I can't help laughing at her shock. 'You shouldn't have bought the place if you don't like the *shit* that's in it.'

'I can get rid of the shit.' I'm winding her up now, her irritation actually turning me on ... even more.

Her eyebrows lift in shock, but soon lower into a scowl.

'Unravel your knickers, lady. I wouldn't *get rid* of anything in this apartment,' I land her with a forceful kiss. 'And you're in this apartment.'

She's mine again. She's meeting my hard tongue lashes stroke for stroke, her hand shooting to my shoulders and clinging on harshly.

That's it. I can't wait any longer. I need to have the ultimate with this woman. I've never wanted anything so much in my life. Lifting her from the counter, I yank her knickers down her legs, my gentle approach fast disappearing. I cast them aside and ease her back down, making quick work of removing her shoes and mentally thanking her for taking the initiative to start on my clothes. Her awestruck face doesn't escape my notice, and neither does her recoil when she spots my scar. I don't need her prying into the whys and wherefores of that, but before I can distract her from it, she screws my shirt up and tosses it to the side.

'I'll buy you a new one,' she says casually, making me smirk.

Leaning forward, I home in on her lips again and moan when I feel her hands working my trousers, but soon pull away on a surprised furrow of my brow when she yanks my belt free and the bathroom is filled with a sharp thrash of leather.

I'm trying to hide the shock. 'Are you going to whip me?'

'No,' she replies slowly, before discarding the belt, her uncertainty reassuring. But then I'm seized by the waistband of my trousers and hauled forward. 'Of course, if you want me to ...'

I fight a smile onto my face. She's playing with me. 'I'll bear that in mind.'

Her eyes burn through mine as she unfastens me, and my eyes clench shut when I feel her small palm skim across my throbbing cock. Oh sweet Jesus, I'm twitching uncontrollably, sending a silent prayer to the ceiling to maintain my control, struggling further when I feel the unmistakable heat of her tongue licking up the centre of my chest.

'Ava, you should know that once I've had you, you're mine.' I don't know where the fuck that statement came from.

'Hmmm,' she hums, licking my nipple and pushing my boxers down my thighs, finally freeing my painfully stiff cock.

She gasps, and I smile. Oh yes, lady. And it's soon going to be claiming you all to itself ... For ever.

I waste no time removing my remaining clothes, as equally rapt by the nakedness before me as she is. I didn't think my pulse could race any faster ... until she reaches forward and rolls her thumb over the head of my arousal.

'Shit, Ava.' I take her hips, and she gasps. 'Ticklish?'

'Just there.' she blurts, tensing in my hold.

'I'll remember that.' I smash my lips back to hers, my body tingling, my hips thrusting when she starts stroking me. It's becoming urgent, and when she inhales sharply, I clamp down on her lip. 'You ready?' I blurt, wondering what I'll do if she says no, but her quick nod fires me into action and I bat her hand away from me, grab her under her arse and pull her up and forward, straight onto my waiting cock.

She cries out. Shit, I've hurt her, but damn, she feels incredible – like nothing that's come before.

'Okay?' I wheeze. 'Are you okay?'

'Two seconds. I need a few seconds.' Her legs wrap around

my waist, and I swing her around, pushing her up against the wall and letting my forehead drop to hers as I give her the time she needs to adjust. Fucking hell, I'm sweating, panting like a dog as I ease out of her gently, desperate not to put her off. Then I plunge forward, controlled and carefully.

'Can you take more?' I fight the words through my regulated breathing, hoping to God she accepts me. Her breasts push into my chest, a silent message, but I need the words. 'Ava, tell me you're ready.'

'I'm ready,' she breathes, and with that, I rear back and drive forward purposefully. And I don't stop. I'm growling in appreciation as I pump into her time and time again.

'You're mine now, Ava.' There I go again. What the hell has gotten into me? She doesn't object, filling me with contentment – something that I've never felt. 'All mine,' I reinforce, meeting her forehead with my own and retreating before I really let rip, pounding forward repeatedly, like a crazy man, desperate and sweating.

She screams. It's music to my ears. I'm claiming her.

And she's letting me.

I relish in her repeated cries of pleasure, feeling her muscles tightening around me as I take her mouth again, our sweaty bodies slipping and sliding, feeling amazing.

'You're going to come?' I can feel it. She pulsing and squirming.

'Yes!' She bites me.

Fucking hell! 'Wait for me.' I order, more harshly than I intended, increasing my pace.

She screams. Shit, she's going.

And so am I.

'Now, Ava!'

I push into her, holding myself there, heaving into her neck. My fucking legs feel unstable. I'm a wreck. 'Oh, fuccccckkkkk,' I groan, releasing into her as I lazily circle my hips, wheedling every lazy modicum of pleasure as she moans into my shoulder. We're doing this again *very* soon. Shit, I'm dizzy.

'Look at me,' I demand gently. I need to check she's real, and when her heavy head lifts and her face finds mine, I look straight into those eyes and accept something really special has happened here, and I don't know whether to be delighted by it, or frightened to fucking death.

Softly circling my hips, I kiss her. 'Beautiful.' I push her back into the warmth of my chest and transport her back to the counter, resting her down gently and reluctantly slipping out of her.

I take her face between my palms and kiss her. 'I didn't hurt you, did I?'

She answers by pulling me into her arms and squeezing me tightly, my face naturally finding its place in the crook of her neck and my palms feeling her back. I feel an overwhelming sense of belonging, like after years of stumbling random-ly, doing things without thought or consideration, I've finally found where I need to be. But will she accept me?

I'm not getting off to the best start – I didn't use a fucking condom. Pulling back, I stroke her heated face with my knuckles. 'I didn't use a condom,' I feel like a complete tosser. 'I'm sorry, I got so carried away. You're on birth control, right?'

'Yes, but the pill doesn't protect me from STDs.'

I smile, not in the least bit insulted. I have no right to be. 'Ava, I've *always* used a condom,' I peck her forehead, 'except with you.'

'Why?' she asks, puzzled. I don't blame her. I'm quite befud-dled by it all myself.

'I don't think straight when I'm near you.' I start dressing myself, wondering why that is. She knocks all rationality right out of me, has me thinking stupid thoughts and behaving like a total nut job.

Taking one of the fancy facecloths from the shelf by the sink,

I run it under the tap, hating the idea of wiping myself away from her. When I turn, I find her legs are closed tightly. She's feeling awkward, and on a small frown, I separate them again. I never want her to feel uncomfortable with me, which is a ridiculous claim, given my recent behaviour around this woman. She's still here, though.

'Better,' I mutter, placing her palms on my shoulders while I reluctantly sweep the cloth across her skin, cleaning her up and flicking a little glance up. I know she's watching me. 'I want to toss you in that shower and worship every inch of you, but this will have to do. For now, anyway.' I give her a quick kiss, resenting having to dress her. 'Come on, lady. Let's get you dressed.' I love that she lets me do it all, and I love the fact that she tenses and spasm when I can't resist another taste of her neck. She'd better get used to my lips all over her, because I don't plan on putting them anywhere else ever again.

My shirt is handed to me, and I shake out the creases as best I can. 'There really wasn't any need to screw it up, was there?' I grin as I dress myself and she watches closely.

'Your jacket will cov—' she stops, her eyes widening. 'Oh.'

'Yes. Oh.' I snap my belt, and grin further when she flinches, only because she seems alarmed by it. 'Okay. You ready to face the music, lady?' I signal for her hand, and she wastes no time giving it to me. Smart girl. 'I'd say quite loud, wouldn't you?'

I break out in a full-on, blast her back smile as she shakes her head. I can't believe I said that to her, either.

Her face displays an abundance of alarm when she catches herself in the mirror. I don't know why; she looks just flawless. 'You're perfect.' I unlock the bathroom and pull her out, scooping up my jacket as we pass. As we take the stairs, I don't like the tensing I sense travelling from her into me through our joined hands – not one little bit, even less when I feel her physically trying to remove her hand from mine. Instinct tells me to keep hold of her ... so I do.

Welcome to the sensual world of…

This Man

Young interior designer Ava O'Shea has
no idea what awaits her at The Manor.
A run-of-the-mill consultation with a stodgy
country gent seems likely, but what Ava finds
instead is Jesse Ward – a devastatingly
handsome, utterly confident, pleasure-
seeking playboy who knows no boundaries.
Ava doesn't want to be attracted to this man,
and yet she can't control the overwhelming
desire he stirs in her. She knows that her heart
will never survive him, and her instinct is telling
her to run, but Jesse is not willing to let her go.
He wants her and is determined to have her.

Includes a brand-new bonus scene
from Jesse's perspective

Look for the other *This Man* novels

www.jodiellenmalpas.co.uk

www.orionbooks.co.uk

ORION
FICTION

UK £8.99

ISBN 978-1-4091-5148-7

0 0 8 9 9

9 781409 151487

Also available in
ebook and audio